Hilary Norman is the author of fourteen internationally bestselling novels written under her own name and translated into seventeen languages, including *The Pact* and *Susanna*, and of *If I Should Die*, a thriller published under the pseudonym Alexandra Henry. Her previous novels, *Too Close, Mind Games, Blind Fear, Deadly Games, Twisted Minds* and *No Escape* are also published by Piatkus.

Also by Hilary Norman

Guilt

Hilary Norman

PIATKUS

Visit the Piatkus website!

Piatkus publishes a wide range of best-selling fiction and non-fiction, including books on health, mind, body & spirit, sex, self-help, cookery, biography and the paranormal.

If you want to:

- read descriptions of our popular titles
- buy our books over the Internet
- take advantage of our special offers
- enter our monthly competition
- learn more about your favourite Piatkus authors

VISIT OUR WEBSITE AT: www.piatkus.co.uk

Copyright © Hilary Norman 2004

First published in Great Britain in 2004 by
Piatkus Books Ltd of
5 Windmill Street, London W1T 2JA
email: info@piatkus.co.uk

The moral right of the author has been asserted

A catalogue record for this book is available from the British Library

ISBN 0 7499 3500 6

Set in Times by
Phoenix Photosetting, Chatham, Kent

Printed and bound in Great Britain by
Bookmarque, Croydon, Surrey

My gratitude to the following for their kind help:

Sarah Abel; Howard Barmad; Peter Beal; Jennifer Bloch; Howard Green; Sara Fisher; Foote's of Golden Square; John Gibson; Gillian Green; Ann Hogan; Peter Johnston; Jonathan Kern; Dr Norman Litvin, FCS(SA)Ophth FRCSEd; Moorfields Eye Hospital; Joanne and Des Moran; Herta Norman; Judy Piatkus; David Risley and Folly Rescue; Helen Rose; Dr Jonathan Tarlow; Sue Watkins.

And most especially: Mr Rhodri D. Daniel, BSc(Hons) FRCS FRCOphth DO; Rhiannon Jones; and Josephine Knight, Principal Cello, English Chamber Orchestra and Professor at the Royal Academy of Music. All experts in their fields, all generous enough to give precious time and to share a little of their knowledge – in all cases with remarkable patience.

As always, all characters and situations are entirely fictitious.

For David,
with love and pride

Chapter One

'Tell me,' Silas Graves said to Abigail Allen during their first dinner together, 'your deepest, darkest secret.'

It was a beautiful spring evening, and he had brought her to the San Carlo in Highgate High Street in north London, had chosen one of his favourite restaurants, wanting to please her, wanting her to feel relaxed.

'If I tell you that,' Abigail answered, 'you'll never want to see me again.'

'I doubt that very much,' Silas said.

'Don't doubt it,' Abigail said.

Silas shrugged. 'Tell me anyway.'

She laid down her fork, rested it beside the *carpaccio* on her plate, and gave a small sigh.

'Please,' Silas said.

A sunburned young man two tables away gave a raucous laugh.

Abigail shuddered, then said, quietly, rapidly:

'When I was thirteen, I killed my parents and a boy named Eddie Gibson.'

She glanced to her left, then her right, then forced her eyes back to his face.

Waited to be left alone again.

Silas's eyes were intently, avidly, on hers.

'How on earth,' he asked, 'did you manage that?'

Chapter Two

When Silas was five years old, he had become a brother.

'Look,' his father, Paul Graves, had told him outside the hospital nursery, holding him up so that he could see the new infant in her cot on the other side of the window. 'That's your little sister. Isn't she just the most beautiful baby you've ever seen?'

Silas had looked down.

Ugly, he thought, his stomach clenching.

Wrinkly and blotchy and squirmy, with tufts of dark hair, wholly unlike himself, with his pale skin and hay-coloured mop.

He looked up at his father. 'Mummy says I was the most beautiful baby.'

Paul Graves smiled. 'So you were,' he said. 'And now your sister is.'

Silas looked back down at the cot.

'Feel sick,' he told his father.

And was.

'You must tell us, darling,' Patricia Graves, his mother, had said next day, cradling the new baby in her arms, 'if there's anything you want to know, or don't understand.'

Silas had looked into the gentle brown eyes in which he had, until yesterday, had perfect faith, and asked the question now crowding his mind, gobbling up and spitting out all other thoughts.

'Who do you love more, Mummy?' he asked. 'Me or her?'

'We love you both equally, Silas,' Patricia said, placidly, oblivious to the tumult in her son.

Silas frowned. 'You used to say you loved me more than anything in the whole world.'

'And it was true.' Still tranquil. 'I did love you – and your daddy – more than anything or anyone else.'

Silas felt his world shift. His mother had never qualified that declara-

3

tion before, had never so much as hinted that her love was like a cake, to be cut into slices.

'And now,' Patricia went on, 'I – we – love you *and* Julia that way.'

Julia.

Ugly Julia.

His mother must have seen something in his face, for the calm – the smugness – wobbled just a little in her eyes.

'It doesn't mean I love you any less, Silas, darling,' she said.

But it did. He knew it meant exactly that.

Three slices now.

He looked at his baby sister's sleeping face, and wanted to rip her apart.

'Do you understand, Silas, my darling?' Patricia asked, anxiously.

Silas blinked, then turned his sea green eyes back to her face.

'Yes, Mummy,' he said.

He understood very well.

Chapter Three

When Silas was ten years old and Julia was five, Paul Graves had left their big old red-brick house near the foot of Muswell Hill one November morning – ostensibly to go to his law office in High Holborn – and had not returned.

'Is Daddy dead?' Silas had asked his mother after several weeks.

'No, darling,' Patricia had answered. 'I'm sure he isn't.'

Silas supposed that was true, since they had neither buried nor burned him.

'Is he in prison?' he asked.

'Why on earth would you ask that?' His mother was wide-eyed.

'One of the boys at school's father's in the Scrubs,' Silas replied.

'Well, your father is not.' Patricia paused. 'And please don't say things like that in front of Julia.'

'I wouldn't,' he said. 'I know better than that.'

'Yes,' his mother said. 'I know you do.'

For the first fortnight after Paul Graves had gone, Patricia had wept a good deal of every day, but then she had, with a great effort, brought herself under control, and had taken to weeping only at night in her bedroom.

Lying sleepless in his own room, Silas had heard her, night after night, and had felt both desolate for, and angry with her. Angry because he knew that, given the opportunity, he could have comforted her, could have more than made up for the absence of the man who had – so far as Silas could see – done little more for his wife than leave early each morning and come home for dinner before going to bed.

Let me in, Mummy, he yearned to say to her, listening to her quiet sobbing through the wall. *Let me help you.* But he did not dare say those things because he was afraid that she might laugh at him, push him away.

Reject him.

She did not. On the night when Silas had finally summoned the courage to leave his room and go to hers, to turn the handle and actually go inside, Patricia, lying in the dark, a handkerchief pressed against her mouth, had turned on her bedside light and asked, in a semi-strangled voice, if something was wrong with either him or Julia.

'Nothing's wrong with us,' he had said. 'Except I can't bear it.'

'What can't you bear, Silas, darling?'

'You crying in here, all alone, when . . .'

'When what?'

Silas had taken a deep breath.

'When I could help you,' he said.

Let me in.

Patricia had pushed back the bedcovers and had let him in.

'You're cold, darling,' she said.

He *was* cold, freezing, so she let him wrap himself around her, and he was tall for his age, almost as long as she was, and she was warm and soft and smelled of flowers, and Silas laid his head on her shoulder and breathed her in, and felt her body relax, just a little, against him.

'You won't need him anymore now,' he told her.

Patricia sighed.

'You won't need anyone but me,' Silas said.

When Silas had been sleeping in her bed for about two weeks, Patricia woke up in the middle of the night to a curious sound.

She lay quite still for a moment before realizing it was coming from her son.

He was humming softly under his breath.

Breathing strangely, too.

Rhythmically.

Patricia sat up suddenly.

'Silas, stop that this instant.'

She reached for the light switch, threw back the covers.

'For God's sake,' she said sharply. 'Don't be so disgusting.'

Silas smiled up at her, a lazy, rather proud smile.

'Stop it *now*,' Patricia told him again.

The smile vanished, his hand fell away from his erect, not quite grown – *quite grown enough*, she thought, despite herself – penis, and he frowned at her sulkily.

'Cover yourself up,' his mother told him.

Silas moved hastily, put it back in his pyjama trousers, his cheeks flushing.

Patricia laughed. 'All the same.'

He was still frowning. 'What's the same?'

'Males,' she said, her tone disparaging. 'If you only knew.'

'Knew what?' Silas asked.

'How ridiculous you look.'

His green eyes narrowed, and the pink in his hot cheeks became a flush of humiliation and anger. 'Don't laugh at me, Mother.'

He had never called her that before.

Patricia supposed that laughing at a prepubescent boy might have been the wrong approach, but then again, she had expected him to jump guiltily, rush to cover himself up, and instead he'd looked pleased with himself, which had shocked her more than a little.

'I'm sorry, my darling,' she said. 'But you must understand that if you're going to do disgusting things like that—'

'I thought,' Silas said, 'that's what all men do.'

Now Patricia's face was hot. She wondered if she should get up or tell him to go back to his room; was, once again, rather surprised that he had not got out of bed of his own accord.

'Firstly,' she said, 'you're not a man.'

Her son's eyes grew colder.

'Secondly, don't answer me back.'

'Sorry,' Silas said.

'As I was saying—'

'You don't want me to do disgusting things like that.'

Patricia glared at him, trying to gauge how cheeky he was being.

'If you find that you absolutely must—' she managed to speak coolly '—from time to time, then kindly do it in private, in your own bedroom.'

'Don't you like me sleeping with you, Mother?'

She thought, but was not quite certain, that he might be feeling hurt.

'It's nice,' she answered, carefully, 'to have the company. But you're not a little boy any more, so maybe—'

'No,' he broke in, firmly, clearly, 'I'm not.'

'Silas, I'm trying—'

'It's all right,' he said. 'I understand.'

'Do you?'

His expression was suddenly full of sympathy. 'You look very tired, Mummy.'

'I am,' Patricia agreed.

'Why don't you lie down again?'

She hesitated, briefly, then lay back against her pillows.

'Now close your eyes,' Silas said.

'Silas, maybe you should—'

'Close your eyes, Mummy—' he was gently insistent '—and let me stroke your hair, the way you like, till you fall asleep again.'

Patricia knew she was too tempted, too weary, to resist.

'No more of that,' she said.

'Of course not, Mummy,' he said.

It only took about a minute before he felt her relax again, felt her actually letting go, falling asleep. For a moment or so, continuing to stroke her hair, he felt good about that, about himself, about the power of his gentle hands, of his love for her, and hers for him.

But then her words sprang back into his mind.

Ridiculous. Disgusting.

Silas took his hand away.

Chapter Four

They were perfect together.

Silas had known they would be from the very beginning.

It had been a mild April afternoon and he had been sitting in a taxi in heavy traffic on his way to a bread-and-butter rag trade shoot when she had caught his eye. Not because of her clothes – very undesigner T-shirt and jeans – or even her looks, but because of the way she was carrying her cello. Big and cumbersome as it was in its ancient looking case, the young woman was conveying the instrument out of the Wigmore Hall with the kind of tenderness a mother might have shown an overgrown and clumsy, but greatly loved, child.

Silas, sitting in the back of the stationary taxi, had watched her set her burden down on the pavement and push her hair out of her face, and, without taking his eyes off her, had felt on the seat for his camera, opened its case, raised it and zoomed in.

Long, blond, heavy, almost butter-coloured hair, just a shade or two darker than his own. Oval, pale face. Nose not quite straight, all the finer for it. Wide, grey eyes. Sad, intriguing eyes.

Silas *loved* intriguing.

He took a few shots, then, grateful for once for the gridlock, examined the rest of her. Nice breasts, good shoulders and strong, but feminine arms, slim waist. Pretty skinny all over, he thought; not model-skinny but almost underfed.

He thought she looked tired.

'Shat upon,' he murmured, and took another photograph.

She began to lift the cello again.

'Pull over, driver, please,' Silas said sharply. 'Just for a moment.'

He opened the door.

'That looks very heavy,' he called.

She looked up, startled, saw the taxi, the young man getting out, realized he was talking to her, set down the instrument case again.

'It's fine,' she said, warily.

Silas kept distance between them. 'I thought you might like to take my taxi.' He saw her brow crease. 'Don't worry,' he added quickly. 'I'm not expecting to share it.'

'I couldn't possibly steal your taxi,' she said.

Her voice was accented. Scottish. Low, husky, *sexy*.

'I'm offering it to you, so it wouldn't be stealing, especially not—' he was suddenly desperate not to lose her, '—if you do something for me in return.' He saw doubt on her face, found a visiting card in his jacket, held it out to her like an offering. 'Like get in touch sometime, if you wanted to.'

She wrapped her arms around the cello, her eyes darting down at the card, then up again into his face.

'Just take it,' Silas said, urgently. 'And the taxi. Please.'

'All right.' She took the card, slid it quickly into her jeans.

'Good.' He felt intense relief. 'Thank you.'

She smiled, began to lift the cello into the taxi, and Silas suppressed the urge to help her, waited till she was in, then stooped to talk through the window to the driver.

'I'd like to pay for—'

'No,' she said, swiftly, from the back. 'Please don't.'

Silas smiled at her. 'Just my own fare,' he said. 'Don't worry.'

The driver took his money, waited to be told where to drive to.

'Chalk Farm, please,' she said.

Silas shut the door. The driver indicated, checked his wing mirror.

Quickly, impulsively, she leaned forward and dragged down the window.

'My name,' she told Silas, 'is Abigail Allen.'

He had only just managed, three work-jammed days later, to locate her manager – a man named Charlie Nagy who had, entirely properly, refused to give out information, but said he'd be glad to pass on any message – when she telephoned him.

'Is that Silas Graves?'

'It is.' He knew, instantly, that it was her.

'This is Abigail Allen,' she said. 'You might not remember me.'

He smiled, looking up at his photographs of her, enlarged to poster size and mounted on every wall of his Crouch End studio.

'I remember,' Silas had told her.

They had spoken for several minutes. He had asked her what she had been doing at the Wigmore Hall, and she had explained that she had been filling in for a cellist who'd come down with flu, and then Silas said he'd only been there once, but had greatly admired the mural over the stage.

'Something to do with the Soul of Music, isn't it?' he asked, though he knew precisely what the work symbolized, having looked it up that morning.

'And Psyche,' Abigail said, 'transcribing music.'

'And Love,' Silas said, 'with roses in her hand.'

And the rest had followed just – almost – as sweetly.

Chapter Five

Every day of every week, unless she was in rehearsal or playing or working at her other job, Abigail practised the cello in her room in Chalk Farm.

It was a small, claustrophobic, unprepossessing room on the top floor of an old, narrow, off-white, dingy house near the station, and the floor vibrated each time a tube train on the Northern Line passed beneath the building. But her window was blessed with a view of a lovely old chestnut tree which, in all seasons, helped, together with her music, to blot out the ugliness of her immediate surroundings.

Helped, too, to blot out other things.

Things.

Abigail managed the business of living well enough. Waiting on tables part-time in a Finsbury Park café in between going to auditions and rehearsals and engagements – anything that she and Charlie Nagy (whose small artists' management company looked after a number of far more accomplished and successful soloists, but who still found time to manage Abigail's insignificant diary commitments) could secure for her. And she'd certainly played a hotchpotch of engagements since coming down to London from Glasgow; over the past several months she'd played at two weddings, a funeral, as background music for the afternoon tea customers at a Thames-side hotel, and once even in the window of a newly-opened furniture store in South Kensington.

To an outsider, it might have seemed that a talented young woman with such a hectic life must have any number of friends, but despite outward appearances, Abigail lived her life, for the most part, alone.

Alone, she knew, was what she deserved.

The music infinitely *more* than she deserved.

She was like a lover with her cello. She surrounded it with herself, gripped it with her knees, let the back of it rest against her breasts, curving the fingers of her left hand over its four strings, bowing with her right, her hair sweeping down and across her face with each motion. Her guilt aside, the cello – her mother's, made more than fifty years before some-where in Bavaria – was the only true constant in her life. Alone with it, Abigail felt able to release her innermost emotions into her music; and physically, too, the beautiful smoothness of the spruce and maple woods of which it was made so comforted her that on warm summer days and evenings, she played wearing just a slip or even less.

There was no one to see her; there had been no one close to Abigail for many years. There were acquaintances, naturally: musicians and her col-leagues and regulars in the café; and of course there was Charlie, who might, Abigail realized, have liked to become more to her than friend and manager, but who had long since accepted in his kind, easy way, that she was not interested in anything more.

Not with Charlie, nor with anyone else.

Alone was what she deserved.

She thought, from time to time, that she ought perhaps to have killed herself years ago. Drunk bleach, or tied a sack of rocks around her waist and drowned herself in some dirty, cold canal. A painful, ugly end.

The end she deserved.

She had no right even to her music, to its riches and companionship. No right to the sounds and sensations and glory of it. No right to the instrument that enabled her to achieve those things.

No right to anything.

They had all said it was an accident, and that she was a victim.

Not her fault.

The Sheriff's determination.

'All my fault,' Abigail had told her mother as she lay dying.

'You mustn't say that,' Francesca Allen, passionate at the last, had told her. 'Never say that, not to anyone . . . Swear it.'

Her mother's last words.

Setting her daughter free.

14

Chapter Six

When Silas was fifteen, on a Wednesday night in May, Patricia Graves had brought home a stranger named Graham Francis, had made a special dinner (something, Silas remembered years later, to do with veal and mushrooms and rice that he'd hated) for their guest and her two children, and had then announced that she was going to be married again.

Silas and Julia – who was ten now, and tall, skinny and dark, like their mother, and who was no longer (had, Silas had long since realized, never *been*) even remotely ugly – had stared at each other helplessly while Patricia had held tightly to Graham Francis's hand.

Silas had waited, his jaw growing painful from clenching, to see if Francis would leave or stay. And then, after the stranger *had* finally left, having bestowed a discreet, but tender kiss on his fiancée's cheek at the front door, he went on waiting until after Julia had gone to bed.

'What about our father?' Silas asked his mother, as she loaded the noisy old dishwasher in the large, comfortable kitchen of which he was very fond.

'Your father's been gone more than five years, darling.'

'He's still your husband, though, surely?'

'Not after the divorce goes through.' Patricia poured powder into the dispenser, and glanced at him sideways. 'We've talked about this, Silas.'

He was silent for a moment.

'What about us?' he said, tightly. 'If you marry him, what about you and me?'

'It won't change anything about us, darling,' Patricia said.

Silas had enough experience to know that if that wasn't exactly a lie, it was certainly his mother's way of not facing up to reality. Any remotely significant change led to turmoil and upheaval, sometimes short-term, sometimes with greater ramifications, like having to give up the place he'd been promised at Highgate School because his father's desertion had left his wife a whole lot worse off, and if they were to be able to stay in the house they all loved – Patricia had told her children at the time – other economies would have to be considered. Which was why both Silas and Jules (as she was now known to most people) were at local authority schools, Jules happy enough, Silas not exactly *un*happy, but resentful nonetheless.

'Won't *he* want to sleep with you?' he asked his mother now.

'Of course he will.' She closed the door of the dishwasher.

'We sleep together,' Silas said.

His mother straightened up, put out her hand, touched his arm. 'Obviously that will have to change, darling,' she said, kindly. 'But nothing else will.'

'But that,' Silas said, 'is everything.'

Chapter Seven

When Silas was eighteen and Jules was just thirteen, Patricia and Graham, on a January holiday in Andorra, had gone skiing off-piste and been killed by a comparatively minor, but locally lethal, avalanche.

'That's it now,' Silas said to Jules. 'We're on our own.'

There was no one else. No uncles or aunts, and the only living grandparent – Paul Graves's mother (who had, like Patricia and the children, never discovered what had happened to her son after his disappearance eight years earlier) – now had some kind of dementia and lived in a nursing home, and Graham's parents were (thankfully, Silas felt, and said, to Jules) both dead.

Which made him the head of the family.

'You'll be all right,' he comforted his sister. 'I'll look after you.'

'I know you will,' Jules said, and wept in his arms.

Silas made the arrangements, had the bodies flown home, instructed the undertaker that his mother was to be buried, in accordance with her own wishes, and his stepfather (who had left no such directions) cremated, and that if anyone objected to that on Graham's behalf, then they were welcome to make their own alternative arrangements.

'Shouldn't they be together?' Jules, shocked, had asked him.

'I don't think so,' Silas had replied with finality.

'But it seems so . . .' She wavered, her eyes miserable.

'What does it seem?' Silas asked coldly.

'Unkind,' Jules said. 'Not right.'

He refused to speak to her after that for more than a week. Silas was good at making his soft-hearted sister suffer, knew how to punish her by simply freezing her out, knew it would invariably not be long till she begged him to forgive her. Which, of course, he would, because he loved her and because she was, after all, all he had left now.

The pardon came, on that occasion, the following Sunday, after she'd cooked him his favourite roast pork and fresh apple sauce lunch, and even if her crackling hadn't been a patch on Patricia's, it hadn't been too bad either, and Silas recognized what a great effort she'd made, considering her grief.

'You won't ever let me down again, will you, Jules?' he asked, after lunch.

'Again?' She looked distressed.

'You questioned my decision about Graham,' Silas said.

'Only because I thought Mummy would have been unhappy about it.'

'Mummy isn't here any more,' Silas said, gentle now. 'Just you and me now, Jules, and I need to know you're on my side.'

'Always,' Jules told him fervently.

She gave him a big hug, almost crying with relief at being forgiven, and for a moment or two, holding her, Silas felt it was almost like having their mother back again. Their *real* mother, pre-Graham-the-stranger.

'Would you mind—' he felt choked with sudden emotion '—if we slept in the same bed tonight?'

He had taken over Patricia's and Graham's bedroom within a week of their deaths, had boxed his stepfather's belongings and dumped them in one of the two spare bedrooms, and brought his own clothes and personal paraphernalia in from his old single room. It felt right to him, returning to the bed where he and his mother had been perfectly content until Graham's arrival in their lives, but he had still felt lonely, had not slept really well lying in the big bed all on his own.

'Of course I wouldn't mind,' Jules said, 'if it'll make you feel better.'

'Good,' Silas said, and drew away.

Jules saw tears in his eyes, reached out and stroked his cheek tenderly.

'Poor Silas,' she said.

He woke, one night, lying inches from his sister in his mother's bed, with an erection.

Disgusting.

Patricia's voice was so clear she might have been standing beside the bed.

Silas took a breath, edged carefully from beneath the duvet, grabbed his dressing gown, and made it into the bathroom.

Still hard.

Ridiculous.

He told himself, even while he was in the bathroom, masturbating under a towel, wishing he'd remembered to get the lock on the door fixed, that his mother was gone, and that even if she were not, he was a grown man now, a *man*, for fuck's sake, and all men wanked now and then, and there was nothing wrong with it. But still he felt angry with himself, for his inability to control the impulse, felt ashamed, afraid in case Jules woke up and heard him or, worse, came into the bathroom and saw what he was doing, in case she was disgusted, the way their mother had been, or worst of all, in case she *laughed* at him.

Even that wasn't his greatest fear, he realized. His greatest fear was that if she knew what he was doing, Jules might not want to sleep with him any more, and he didn't want to sleep alone again.

He finished jerking off into the towel, his free hand jammed against his mouth to muffle his involuntary cry.

No more, he told himself, getting over it, folding the towel back over the rail, confident at least that Jules seldom used this bathroom, so that he would be able to get back to it in the morning, toss it in the washing machine without her knowing.

It wasn't right, anyway, getting a hard-on in that bed, certainly not next to his little sister. That bed, that bedroom – whatever Patricia and Graham had got up to in the three years they'd spent together – was meant for perfect love, the kind he'd shared with his mother until *he* had come along. The kind he shared with Jules now.

Not for sex. Not now, anyway. Maybe, some day, in years to come, with the right woman, a wife maybe, someone who loved, *really* loved him.

In the meantime, there was no shortage of girlfriends, many of them coming Silas's way via John Bromley, a guy from school who was a bit of a legend where women were concerned, and while Silas liked to think he didn't actually need anyone else's leftovers, he also accepted that he was somewhat lazy when it came to pulling. If it weren't for John, Silas sometimes thought he might not bother at all. As it was, he was certainly only interested in seriously good-looking girls, or at least girls interesting looking enough for him to want to photograph.

Some of them liked having their pictures taken, some found it a bit odd, because though there was no burning passion in him to take ground-breaking or even simply very beautiful photographs, he did tend, when he was in the mood, to get a bit obsessive about getting shots exactly the way he wanted them, playing about with backgrounds, or making backgrounds vanish altogether, so that the women looked like they were flying or floating, stuff like that, cool stuff, all good practice for when he got to college and studied photography full-time.

As for sex itself, Silas thought he might enjoy it more if he were better at it. He had always preferred, wherever possible, to be good at whatever he did and not to bother too much about the rest, and he wasn't sure that he *was* outstandingly gifted on the sexual front. Bromley claimed (not that Silas exactly believed him) that he could make it go on and on till his women were screaming with pleasure. In Silas's case, it all tended to be a bit speedier and more urgent than that. Not that he'd any real complaints. Except that redhead, Sonia Something-or-other who he'd met when he and John had gone to the Spaniard's one Sunday, and Silas hadn't madly fancied her, but it was obvious John had his eye on her, and he was in the mood that day for competition.

Anyway, Sonia-the-redhead had been a good five or so years older than him, and she'd also had a great body and been decidedly up for it, and when Silas had gone back to her place off Parliament Hill he'd suddenly felt incredibly horny, and photographing Sonia undressing (she hadn't minded that one bit) had made him harder than he could ever remember having been before. But then they'd done it, and he hadn't been able to wait for her, hadn't really been all that fussed about even *trying* to wait, if he was candid, because the best part had been the build-up and he generally liked the preliminaries more than the main event.

'Selfish bastard,' Sonia had called him, because he'd come before her, and Silas had considered walking out straightaway, but then he'd relented and given her a hand-job instead, partly because he figured if he didn't make the effort she might bad-mouth him to Bromley or some of her girlfriends.

Not that he cared that much. Sex served a definite purpose, he'd decided a long while back, but it was strictly physical, nothing more. Messy and – unlike the fakery in most movies – not especially beautiful.

Masturbation, at least, he thought now, creeping out of the bathroom and going back to the bed in which Jules was still thankfully sleeping peacefully, got it over and done with without fuss.

Disgusting. His mother's voice in his head again. *Ridiculous.*

'Piss off, Mother,' Silas said, also in his head.

Chapter Eight

When Patricia's will was read to Silas and Jules by her solicitor Stephen Wetherall in his office in Lincoln's Inn, it transpired that their mother had left legacies of five thousand pounds to Silas and ten thousand pounds to Jules. More cash to his sister, Patricia had written in a side letter, because Silas was handsome, clever, charming, and a man to boot, and would therefore, she was sure, find life easier than Jules might. Patricia had bequeathed the house on Muswell Hill and the remainder of her estate to Graham who, she wrote, had made her very happy; but in the event of his failing to survive her, the house was to go to Jules, the residue to Silas.

Silas did not wait for any pleasantries after the reading, picked up his grey winter coat, stalked out of the office, jumped into Patricia's Ford Escort and gunned away. By the time Jules got home in the taxi summoned for her by the kindly solicitor, her brother was upstairs in the big double bedroom, packing.

'What are you *doing*?' She was distraught.

'I'd have thought that was obvious.' He picked up a tumbler of malt whisky from his bedside table, held it up. 'Decided the Glenlivet was probably *his*, so I figured you wouldn't mind too much.' He tipped the pale liquid down his throat.

'Silas, stop it!' Jules, who had wept for a good part of the drive home, now began again. 'I know you're upset, but you don't—'

'Upset's a bit of an understatement, sis.' He put down the glass, tossed two cellophane-packed shirts and a black sweater into the open case on his bed.

'You don't understand.' Jules darted forward, pulled out the sweater, clutched it to her. 'I've already asked Stephen about changing the will. I think it's awful of Mummy to have done that to you, and in a way it was quite insulting to me, too, saying I need it all more because I'm a girl and not very pretty and always reading.'

'She didn't say any of that,' Silas said.

'You know it's what she meant,' Jules said, which was true, because Patricia had always been nagging at her daughter to make more of her looks and to get her head out of the books she loved so much. 'But anyway, she only wrote what she did about the two bequests, didn't she? The house wouldn't have come to me if Graham hadn't died, too, and at least she left you all the rest, and Stephen says it's quite a lot.'

'I don't care about the money,' Silas said, though he was not quite certain that was true. 'But let me guess what Stephen said about you changing the will.' He turned to one of the open wardrobes. 'Big fat *no*, right?'

'He said no to that.' Jules still clung to the sweater. 'But apparently I could write over half the house to you if I wanted.'

Silas turned around. 'I wouldn't ask you to do that,' he said. 'Anyway, you're too young, surely?'

'Now I am,' Jules admitted. 'But when I'm older—'

'When you're older—' Silas cut her off '—I could be long gone.'

'Silas, *don't*!' She threw down the sweater on the nearest chair. 'Please don't talk that way!'

He shrugged. 'I'm sorry, but it's hardly my fault.'

'Not mine either.' Jules came closer, put out a tentative hand, touched his arm. 'Silas, you can't leave me, I couldn't bear it.'

Silas stepped away, took two pairs of jeans out of the wardrobe.

'And I'm only thirteen—' Jules fought on desperately '- so if you went, someone else, some *outsider*, would have to come and live here with me, and surely you'd hate that too, and it doesn't matter what it says in Mummy's will, this is still *our* house, isn't it? Yours and mine.'

Silas folded the jeans, laid them on top of the shirts, picked up the sweater Jules had dropped on the chair.

'I could write a letter now,' Jules said, desperately, 'promising you the house when I'm eighteen or whatever age I have to be.'

'Half of it, you mean.' Silas picked a bit of fluff off the sweater.

'Half, or *all* of it,' Jules said. 'I don't *care* about the house. All I care about is you not leaving me, Silas, darling.'

He watched her scrub away tears with the back of one hand.

'What if we had half each,' he said, slowly, 'and you wanted to sell your half?'

'Same if you wanted to,' Jules said.

'No,' Silas said. 'If this was my house, I would never sell it.'

'Nor would I,' his sister said.

'You might if you fell in love with some stranger and he wanted you to.'

'I wouldn't,' she said, passionately.

Silas sat on the bed beside his case. 'You might, Jules. You're not as tough as me. You might be persuaded.'

Jules looked at him for a moment, then came and sat beside him.

'You're right,' she said. 'I'm not as tough as you.'

Silas chewed his bottom lip, then smiled. 'All right, sis, you win. All to me, then, so we can be sure of keeping it in the family.'

'And you'll stop packing?'

He nodded, smiled again.

'Thank you.' Jules was eager. 'Help me write the letter.'

'I'll help you draft it,' Silas said. 'But you'll have to make sure Wetherall knows it's your idea, and he'll have to word it properly.' He paused. 'And I'll write a letter too—' he was easy now, confident again '—promising to always look after you.'

Jules moved closer to him. 'We'll always look after each other.'

Silas looked at her.

'You say that now,' he said.

It wasn't just hurt or wounded pride, or even especially the need to own the house that had got to Silas so badly. Their house was genuinely far more important to him than it was to Jules, who was still pretty much a kid, for God's sake, a girl who was, at heart, a romantic, and who would in time, he was absolutely certain, think about moving to some other home.

Silas would never do that. This was his family home. No big fancy pile, no estate, just a good, solid, handsome and rather valuable house. One that had already stood the test of many years, that might throw up the odd crack or problem now and then, but would not easily crumble.

Their house. That was what mattered to Silas. It was 'the Graves house', in the same way that the house next door was 'the Brook house'. Continuity and constancy mattered to Silas. The house having belonged to his parents and then to his mother, and continuing to belong to him and Jules.

To Jules alone now, if Patricia had her way. Though that, he was fairly confident after his chat with his sister, would change in time.

What would not change, would never now change, was that he hated his mother for doing this to him. He had known, of course, since the stranger, that she was not a person to be depended upon, that she had no real loyalty, but her *will* . . .

He clenched his jaw at the mere thought of it.

Her will had finished Patricia for him forever.

Once Jules had written her letter – once that side of things was settled, morally if not yet strictly legally – Silas was certain that they would rub along very nicely. His sister was not a fussy child, very clean, thank Christ, but not obsessively hygienic or tidy or wanting to alter things for no good reason. Jules was, all things considered, a practical and sensitive person.

Which was what their house was suited to, Silas felt: practical, sensitive people who would take care of it and not change things unnecessarily. Its overall size and shape, and the construction of its rooms were in need of no alteration; the house had cool, shady rooms for summertime and warm, cosier spots for winter. It was a bit dark in places, but that was a small price to pay for being shielded from a busy road by beautiful old trees; and anyway, most big old houses had dark nooks and crannies, and their house had lovely bay windows in the living room and master bedroom and an elegant staircase.

Silas had never realized until his mother had tried to rob him of it how *much* he cared about the house. Had never been aware, as he now was, of it being an almost living thing, a kind of organism in its own right, like an outer, protective skin.

Just an overcoat, he'd tried telling himself when he'd walked out of Stephen Wetherall's office. *A shelter at most.* But he hadn't really believed it. It was much more than that, would always be more, so long as it remained their house. The Graves family's house.

His house.

Chapter Nine

Until she met Silas, the best times of Abigail's life had taken place back on Allen's Farm, her parents' home in the Pentland Hills, south of Edinburgh. From first awareness to around age twelve, she had, she believed, been almost completely happy.

School in the village. Regular drives with Francesca – born in Glasgow to a passionately musical Italian mother and Scottish father – to West Linton to buy provisions and treats. Lambing, the hardest working time of year for her parents and the farmhands, but the sweetest for Abigail because Douglas, her daddy, let her help in the pens when homework and music practice permitted, and even her mother, on rare occasions, had been known to let her help bottle feed the more helpless, weest ones. And that had been followed, all too soon after they were weaned, by trips to Lanark with her father, and that had been sad, of course, even horrible – sort of, though not *exactly*, knowing what was going to happen to the lambs – but even at an early age, Abigail had been told by Dougie that market was a vital part of farming and what put food on the table, and she'd never seen her daddy lay rough hands on any of their creatures, and she trusted him and understood what had to be.

Twice each year – once for a Festival concert, once for the Christmas lights – the Allens went on a day trip to Edinburgh. Abigail liked the lights well enough, but a boy at school named Jamie Cochrane had warned her once that the rocks beneath the castle were crumbling away, and that it was only a matter of time till the whole pile came crashing down onto Princes Street.

'Right onto your head,' he'd said.

Her parents had both laughed when she'd shared that fear with them, had told her not to fret, that the castle was and would remain perfectly solid and exactly where it was, but still, after what Jamie Cochrane had told her, Abigail had done her best to try to persuade them to stay on the shopping side of the street.

Allen's Farm was where she had felt safest. Just them and the labourers and the sheep and the gorgeous colours and smells of the land and the grasses and wildflowers, and the snug freedom of the timeless landscape wrapping around them. Allen's Farm was where Abigail had wanted to, had felt sure she would be *able* to, stay forever. When some of her school-friends talked about their longing to be in bigger, more exciting cities like Edinburgh or Glasgow or even London, Abigail found she could picture no place or lifestyle more perfect than her own.

'When I grow up,' she told Jeannie McEwan at school, 'I'm going to be a farmer, just like my daddy.'

'But your Ma wants you to do music,' Jeannie pointed out.

'That's just silliness,' Abigail dismissed. 'If I go round the world play-ing her cello, who'll take care of the farm?'

'Maybe you'll get a brother,' Jeannie suggested.

'They can't have any more babies,' Abigail said, frankly, for that was something else that her father had explained to her a long while back, that there was something the matter with her mother's womb, and that they had been lucky to have her. She'd found it easy enough to understand because her daddy had said it was just like what had happened to one of the ewes the previous spring – except, of course, that the ewe had gone to the abattoir after that, which, to Abigail's mind, made her mother's predicament rather less sad by comparison.

'There's so much more to life than Allen's Farm.'

If her mother had said that to Abigail once, she'd said it at least a dozen times. Important and necessary as it was, farming, Francesca Allen said, not untruthfully, was poorly paid, frequently virtually *un*paid, drudgery.

'There are wonders in the world away from the hills, away even from Scotland,' she told her daughter. 'Things you'll be able to see for yourself, *live* for yourself, if you listen to me.'

'But I love the farm, Ma.' Abigail always responded simply, stead-fastly. 'I love it more than anything.'

'Now you do,' Francesca said. 'But when you're older—'

'I'll be the same,' Abigail insisted.

Usually at such times her mother smiled wearily but knowingly and let the subject rest, though there was no capitulation in that, for there was a strand of cast-iron resolve inside Francesca. She might have stamped on her own mother's dreams for her; might have given up the place that could have been hers at the Glasgow Conservatoire for love of Douglas Allen; might have made the decision to become a farmer's wife rather than a concert cellist; might have learned to regret that as she had lurched with Dougie from one farming crisis to the next. But Abigail, by age eight, had already shown more musical potential (in Francesca's opinion as her teacher, not just as her mother) than she ever had, and so she would be damned if she'd see that squandered.

Dougie, for his part, said as little as possible about it. Thrilled by his daughter's love of the land, it saddened him considerably to contemplate the farm passing, ultimately, into the hands of strangers, but he knew how deep his wife's passions ran, how much she'd given up for his sake, how fervently she believed in Abigail's musical talent, and, being a peaceable man, found it frankly easier, as a general rule in their everyday lives, not to antagonize his wife.

'What if she refuses to go on playing?' he had once asked.

'She will not refuse,' Francesca had replied.

And Abigail had not, for, like Dougie, she disliked confrontation and loved her mother. And playing the cello ('violoncello', her mother called it sometimes, in her most serious moods) had been a pleasure from the age of six, when Francesca had first sat her down with the beautiful old instrument, reducing the length of the extendable spike at its base to make it a little less formidably tall, and allowing her to get used to its shape and construction, and its feel too – smooth wood first, then the strings – watching her daughter's expression as she created her own first sounds with her fingers – and then with the bow . . .

'Touch it,' she had told Abigail. 'It's horsehair. All bows for stringed instruments are made of hair from the tails of male horses.'

'Does it hurt them?' Abigail had promptly wanted to know.

'No more than it hurts you when I cut your hair,' her mother had answered.

'Why male horses, Ma?'

Given that her daughter had already observed on the farm, with interest and plentiful questions, a few years of ewes in season being covered by rams, Francesca saw no reason not to explain that mares' tails tended to become wee-soaked, whereas a stallion's, for obvious reasons, did not.

'Now—' Francesca had moved smartly along '—sit nice and straight, Abigail, and see if you can hold the cello firmly with your knees.' She paused, watched for a moment. 'If we had more money,' she said, 'we might have been able to find you a smaller instrument, but—'

'No,' Abigail had jumped in swiftly, struggling to find a position where she might be able to feel some degree of control over the body of the instrument and its long neck. 'I like this one, Ma, really.'

Her mother had watched, smiling, satisfied with the beginning.

'When you're ready,' she said, 'take the bow again – with your left hand, not your right, sweetheart – and hold it here—' she showed her '—almost at the end, just below what they call the frog—'

'Frog?' Abigail's grey eyes were round.

'I've no idea why it's called that,' Francesca said, 'but it is.'

She showed Abigail how to prepare to use the bow, placed her right thumb against the stick, curved the middle finger around the first joint, then arranged her other fingers, and waited for the child to either fidget or drop the bow or grow bored with the fussiness of it.

It was a tribute, Abigail realized a long while later, to her mother's teaching and to Francesca's own talent as a cellist, that she had not, for the most part, grown bored with her lessons. She found the music that her mother played very beautiful, felt a great desire to emulate her, experienced, almost from the very beginning, a true thrill when she managed to produce warm, sometimes rich sounds from the precious instrument. And even if she might, quite often, rather have been out in the fields or sheep pens with her daddy, if practising regularly was what it took to keep her ma in a good mood, then, certainly for the time being, Abigail was happy to comply.

Much later on, looking back on the latter part of that early life, Abigail found it hard to identify exactly when she had begun to change from that contented, amenable child into the increasingly stroppy, often sullen creature who had, finally, destroyed everything that had been wonderful in her life. Puberty, perhaps, teasing so-called maturity into her body and mind.

No excuse.

'A terrible accident,' they all said.

Her fault, whatever they said.

But Ma had told her never to say that, so she had not.

And so, instead of being shut away from decent people, Abigail had been free. To go and live with her Auntie Betty, Dougie's sister, and her husband, Bill Innis, in their poky terraced house near Ravenscraig, with no garden to speak of, and no real air to breathe, and no animals to play with, which was all, of course, the very *least* of what Abigail deserved. And for a while, after she went to them, her aunt and uncle had done what they could to love their depressed and depressing niece, but Abigail had not been able to endure anyone being nice to her, so in the end the best Betty and Bill had found themselves able to do had been to put up with her until she was old enough to leave.

Francesca's cello was what had saved Abigail from total self-destruction. It was the only solace she had permitted herself in the months and years after the tragedy, the only item of value she had asked to take away from the farm. Because keeping the cello, and taking care of it, and practising on it every moment she could, was all she could do for her mother now.

28

She wasn't allowed to play at home any more because of the neighbours, and Auntie Betty had never really understood her sister-in-law, had thought Francesca's love of classical music a symptom of what she called her 'foreignness'. So Abigail had asked Miss Howe, the music teacher at her new school, if she might keep the instrument and practise there, and Gwen Howe, who had a special love of the cello, and who had found herself moved in equal parts by her pupil's great tragedy and by her dedication, had volunteered to take over where Francesca had left off, teaching her privately, after school hours, for no payment, and had managed, in time, to encourage Abigail all the way into a place at the Glasgow Conservatoire.

The place that ought, by rights, to have been her mother's. The place that she felt ashamed to accept, but knew she had to, for Francesca's sake.

Sometimes, in the three years that followed, surrounded by so much life and prodigious talent and by the noisy, busy city, and by the music itself, Abigail found that for just a little while she almost forgot Allen's Farm and her parents and past contentment, even, very seldom and fleetingly, succeeded in pushing *that* day to the back of her mind. But then, almost immediately, she would drag it back to the forefront, slap it back across her mind's eye, where it belonged in all its agony.

The agony was all she had a right to.

It served a purpose sometimes, gave her playing an edge and depth that others noticed and were a little impressed by. No one ever felt, when Abigail played, that they were in the presence of any kind of greatness, but her tireless commitment and that dark edge lifted her above some of her contemporaries, led her first into a professional string quartet in Glasgow and then (after a long period of introspection, during which she made her decision to abandon Scotland for the vaster anonymity of London) onto the books of Nagy Artists.

Where, despite Charlie Nagy's enthusiasm and kindness, Abigail came to see the harsh truth of what she had regularly been warned about: that the greatest problem faced by the vast majority of cellists was lack of work.

Harsh truths suited Abigail. What few engagements did come her way were more than she deserved. She played, still, for Francesca, had intended it, at the outset, merely as a kind of penance, but then the music had brought her a measure of contentment which, in turn, had heaped yet more guilt on her. And Abigail, not knowing what else to do, had accepted both the music and the guilt, and rejected everything and everyone else.

Had kept herself isolated. A secret leper.

Until Silas.

29

Chapter Ten

When Silas was twenty and nearing the end of a photographic course at City of Westminster College, his father had come home.

Almost a decade had passed since he had walked out on his wife and children without a word, but Paul Graves looked more like twenty than ten years older. What hair he had left was grey, his skin was pasty and lined, his chin appeared, his son observed, almost to have caved in, and, though it was only September and quite warm, he looked very cold.

'Bit of a shock for you,' Graves had said to Silas on the doorstep.

Even in those first moments of pure, hard shock, Silas had found himself hoping that when it came to his own ageing process his mother's genes would be stronger than this man's; Patricia had of course been comparatively young when the avalanche had killed her, but had she lived, Silas could not picture her ever having grown as gracelessly old as the first of her husbands.

'What do you want?' he asked, at last.

'Not going to ask me in?' Paul Graves said.

Silas shrugged, opened the door and let his father in.

'You're lucky to find me here,' he said. 'I'd normally be at college.'

'Studying to be the new Bailey or whatever,' Graves said.

'Whatever,' Silas said, anger already quietly rising.

He wished, he thought, walking ahead of Graves into the living room, that he could have gone to find Jules, warn her, perhaps try to stop her coming home, but she'd have left school by now, and anyway, he'd be damned if he was going to leave this man alone in the house.

'Julia on her way home?' Graves asked.

Silas turned, glanced at him with distaste, said nothing.

'Want to go and meet her? Make it a bit less of a shock for her?'

Silas sat down in the armchair that, even now, he remembered had been his father's. *Armchair, cigarette, scotch, newspaper or telly or both, every evening.*

Until he'd fucked off.

'You can leave me for a bit,' his father said. 'I won't steal anything.'

'You might,' Silas said. 'How should I know?'

'If you prefer, I'll wait out in the street.'

They both heard the key in the lock.

Silas got swiftly to his feet. 'Wait here.'

He shut the living room door behind him just as Jules was coming in.

'What's up?' she asked, seeing his expression.

'You won't believe it,' Silas said, and told her.

'God.' Jules had turned very pale.

'You okay?' Silas took her arm, ready to support her. 'Sis?'

She nodded. 'What about him? Is he all right?'

'He looks like shit,' Silas said. 'Down and out in Muswell Hill.'

'God,' Jules said again.

She tried to start towards the sitting room, but Silas kept hold of her arm, held her back for another moment.

'Don't put out the welcome mat, Jules. He's a bastard, remember.'

'But we don't know,' she said, 'what he's been through.'

'He's not dead, is he,' Silas said.

Graves appeared sorry, in a mournful, self-pitying fashion, for deserting his family, but circumstances, he told them, had been difficult.

'What circumstances?' Silas asked.

His father had sat down wearily, heavily, on the sofa, when bidden, and Jules – having seen how cold he looked, and having gone, without telling Silas, to switch on the central heating – was sitting stiffly in one of the armchairs, while Silas was now up on his feet, choosing physical superiority.

Graves answered his son with a vague, helpless shake of his head. 'Pointless going over it all now.'

Silas looked away from him with disgust, looked at Jules, saw, with dismay, that patently she was feeling sorry for the man who was, he supposed, still their father in the biological sense, but who seemed, at least to him, as much a stranger as Graham Francis had been when their mother had first brought him home.

'I heard what happened to your mother,' Graves said. 'I was very sorry.'

'Not sorry enough to come back for her funeral,' Silas said.

Jules had still not spoken. She was tall for fifteen, still slim but strong-limbed from netball and swimming, though sitting there now looking back and forth between her brother and father, she looked, Silas felt, a little smaller, diminished by shock, he supposed.

Bastard, he thought again, violently, for doing that to her. *Stinking bastard.*

'I can imagine,' Paul Graves ventured, 'how bitter you must be.'

Jules opened her mouth to speak.

'Can you?' Silas got in first, cuttingly.

'I think so,' Graves said quietly. 'You both look marvellous.'

'No thanks to you,' Silas said.

'No,' his father agreed. 'But still, it makes me feel proud to see you like this.' He went on quickly. 'You have your mother's bone structure, Julia.'

'She's called Jules,' Silas said.

'Sorry.' Paul Graves smiled at his daughter. 'I didn't know.'

'You knew about my photography course,' Silas said.

'I've tried to keep an eye on you both.' Graves flushed. 'From afar.'

'Where have—?'

'You haven't said what it is you want.' Silas cut in on Jules's question.

'Silas,' she said, reproachfully.

Her father darted her a look of gratitude.

'So?' Silas said. 'What do you want?'

Paul Graves swallowed hard. 'I was wondering,' he said, 'if you could see your way to putting me up for a day or two.'

Silas stared down at him, then turned on his heel and left the room.

'I'm sorry,' Jules said to her father, then got up and followed her brother out into the hall. 'Silas, don't be too hard—'

'He's kidding, right?' Silas said.

'Of course he's not kidding,' his sister said. 'Just look at him.'

'He looks like a tramp,' Silas said. 'He's a bloody disgrace.'

Jules reached behind her, shut the living room door. 'We have to help him.'

'For God's sake, Jules, you have to be the softest touch in the world. We do *not* have to help that man.'

'He's our father.'

'Ten years, Jules.'

'I know,' she said, softly. 'I know, but—'

'You were only five.' When Silas was angry, his sea green eyes seemed darker, pupils dilating dramatically, spreading pools of black into the colour.

'I know,' Jules said again. 'And I understand it's partly for my sake you feel so angry with him—' she touched his arm '—but I still don't see that we can just kick our own dad out into the street.'

'Don't call him that.'

Jules said nothing.

'I'm aware—' Silas withdrew his arm '—that this is still, technically, your house, Jules, but I would like to point out—'

'Please don't start all that again, Silas.'

'But I would like to point out, if I *may*, that I am still the adult here, the one who's been taking care of you and running this household for the last two years.'

'Yes, of course you have, but—'

'The one you've made certain promises to.'

'Yes,' Jules said, 'I have, and I'm not forgetting any of that.' She stood her ground. 'But I don't really see what it's got to do with putting our father up for the night, letting him get cleaned up, giving him a decent meal.' She paused for breath. 'He looks *ill*, Silas.'

'You'll have to cook it,' Silas said, after a moment. 'I won't.'

'I cook most of our meals, don't I?' Jules asked.

'And I won't have him using my bath.' Though Jules still shared the master bedroom most nights, she still maintained her own bedroom and bathroom. 'And you can turn off the heating again. It's only September, for God's sake.'

Jules glared at him. 'At least we should find out what he's come for.'

'Money, I expect,' Silas said.

'We've got plenty, haven't we?' Jules said.

Silas gave her one of the cold looks he knew made her wretched, saw, with satisfaction, the bolshie glare dwindle away.

'Please,' she said. 'At least let's tell him he can stay tonight.'

'He'll want to stay longer.'

'He might not,' she said.

'The more we do for him,' Silas said, 'the more he'll want.'

'I'm not saying we have to do more,' Jules said. 'Just please let him stay here with us this one night.'

'So long as you accept,' Silas said, 'that's all.'

'I do,' Jules said.

He knew she was lying.

The next morning, when Jules went upstairs to the spare room with a cup of tea, there was no answer to her knocking.

Tentatively, she opened the door.

The cup and saucer trembled in her hand.

Paul Graves was in bed, his face a strange, ugly colour, his eyes open and staring. Unseeing.

Jules bent down, put the teacup and saucer on the carpet, backed out of the room and went to find Silas, still sound sleep in the bed that Graves had once shared with their mother.

'He's dead,' she told him, shaking him awake. 'Silas, he's *dead*.'

'Huh?' He was bleary.

'Silas, wake up. Our father's *dead*.'

He got out of bed, pulled on a T-shirt over his shorts, came with her to see.

'He's dead, all right,' he agreed.

Jules had begun to cry. 'He looks so . . . *odd*.'

'Dead looks odd sometimes, I suppose.' Silas put his arm around her. 'Don't upset yourself, Jules.'

'He's our father,' his sister said.

'Not any more,' Silas said.

Jules gave a strangled sob and turned to leave.

'Where are you going?' Silas asked.

'To phone,' she answered, 'for help.'

'What for?' he said. 'Too late for an ambulance. Or Doc Isaacs.'

Peter Isaacs had been their family doctor since they were small.

'We've still got to call someone.' Jules scrubbed at her eyes. 'We have to have a thingie.' She scrambled for the words. 'Death certificate.'

'I don't think so,' Silas said.

'We have to do *something*.'

Silas held out his hand, and she came to him. He drew her close, pulled her gently back to the bed. 'Look at him, sis,' he said. 'You said yourself he looks odd, and you're right.'

She took one more look and closed her eyes, tears spilling down her cheeks.

'I'm sorry, darling—' Silas persisted '—but what do you suppose the ambulance men or even Doc Isaacs would say? Think they'd just say: oh, right, he's dead, here's the certificate, go bury him?'

'Even if they don't—' Jules's eyes were open again '—what does that matter? They'll still come and take him away and examine him or whatever, and then—'

'Jules,' Silas said sharply. 'Shut up.'

He led her from the room, closed the door, fetched a sweater for her to pull over her nightie because she was shivering, then brought her down to the kitchen, boiled the kettle, made her a cup of strong, sweet tea and waited till she'd had a few sips.

'Right,' he said. 'I need you to listen to me carefully, Jules, okay?'

She nodded, still shivering.

'Drink your tea.'

'I am.'

'What we are *not* going to do here—' Silas sat down, pulled his chair close to hers '—is phone anyone for any kind of help.'

'Why not?' Jules asked.

'Because it would stir up all kinds of complications.'

'What do you mean?' She paused. 'Tell me you don't mean the house.'

'I hadn't thought about the house, though that's a good point.'

'Silas, please.' Jules was disgusted.

'What I was thinking is that there's every chance that whoever we call might feel that because he looks the way he does – odd – maybe his death might have been a bit *odd* too.'

'What do you mean?' she asked again, bewildered.

'Don't be naive,' Silas said. 'Our father disappears a decade ago, comes home, spends one night in the spare room in his old house – now our house – sorry, still *your* house – and you find him dead, looking *odd*, next morning.'

'But that's what happened,' Jules said.

'Maybe so.' Silas paused. 'But that might not stop them thinking one of us might have done something to him.'

Jules looked aghast. 'That's mad. No one would think that.'

'They might.' He watched her face. 'There's only one way to be sure that doesn't happen.'

'How?'

'No one else knows he came back,' he said, simply. 'Or even, necessarily, that he was still alive. We're his own children and *we* didn't know, did we?'

A frown was forming between Jules's arched eyebrows. Silas put out a finger, tried to stroke it away.

'So all we really need to do,' he said, slowly, 'is bury him.'

Jules didn't speak.

'In the garden.' He saw her expression change, grow appalled. 'We can't risk taking him out, sis – I don't think I'm up to coping with the body-in-plastic-bag-in-car-boot routine, and I'm sure you're not.'

Jules stared at her brother for a long moment.

'This is a joke, Silas. Please tell me it's a joke?'

'Our father just died,' he said. 'Would I joke at a time like this?'

He steered her through his plan, told her, with steadily-increasing conviction, that it was the right – the only remotely *sensible* – thing to do in the circumstances, and though Jules did not think, at any point, that she truly believed him, she did not know what else *to* do.

Silas had been, for the last two years, *everything* to her, as she had, she realized, been to him. He had been her protector, had nursed her through illness, had comforted her through her first, startlingly painful, period. He'd paid the bills, seen to repairs, bunked off from school to cheer her on

36

in netball competitions, helped her with prep, read her essays, regularly brought her home books he thought she might enjoy. He drove her to friends' homes or to the cinema or wherever she wanted to go after dark or when the weather was bad, collected her again to bring her home rather than letting her take the tube or risk travelling with a bad driver.

He was, had always been, the strongest influence in her life.

And so now, as she had so often in the past, she gave in.

They waited until nine, when it was dark, before Silas commenced work on a patch near the back of the large garden where, each spring, daffodils sprang up; a rough, grassy area which was, in daylight hours, well-shaded by a large oak tree and which ought therefore, Silas had calculated, to be reasonably obscured from the Brook family next door.

'Surely we should wait till much later?' Jules had panicked at the early start, realizing even as she said it that she'd feel similarly whatever time they – *he* – chose to begin. 'Till they're definitely fast asleep.'

'Better earlier,' Silas had said, 'while they're watching TV.'

'What if they're *not*?' she asked. 'What if they're reading or just quiet?'

'If they hear us,' Silas said, 'they'll come to their windows, and we'll see them and stop for a bit.' He had stroked her hair, tried to soothe her. 'It'll be okay, Jules.'

'Let's not do this,' she had said, for at least the fifth or sixth time. 'Please, Silas, let's just not do it. Let's phone someone instead.'

'Too late now,' he told her. 'We found him this morning.'

'We might not have,' Jules reasoned. 'We might have just come home.'

'We haven't just come home,' Silas said. 'And that's something the Brooks or any number of other people might know.' He'd given her one of his gentle, reassuring smiles. 'All you need to do is keep watch, darling. I'll do all the work.'

Finding the ground much too hard to dig with the spade he'd found in the garden shed, he began with a tool he thought their former gardener (a man named Archie, who'd quit several months back, for which Silas was now grateful) had called a pick. It had a curved steel head, pointed at both ends, and Silas found, after a few practice mishits, that if he swung it the way one might swing an axe for wood-chopping, it drove quite deeply into the hard earth, breaking it up well enough for him to begin properly digging, soon after, with the spade.

He was already painfully aware, by the time he'd dug about two feet of raggedy-shaped grave, that he'd be unlikely to be capable of getting out of bed next day, let alone going to college. His back, shoulders, arms and hands seemed ablaze with pain, and yet he found that he was, simultane-ously, almost relishing an unfamiliar sense of strength; for Silas had never been a natural sportsman, was slenderly built, a young man attractive to women for his graceful, lazy movements rather than muscle-power, and there was something about digging his father's grave that was bizarrely invigorating.

Jules stopped him, once, with a soft, strangled sound and a frantic gloved hand around his wrist to halt the digging, because an upstairs light had been switched on next door, and the silhouette of a man – presumably Max Brook – was clearly visible behind the net curtains.

'Don't worry.' Silas was gasping, breathless and sweat-drenched, but calm. 'He'll probably draw the heavy curtains any minute now.'

A few seconds later, they were drawn, blacking out the house.

'We'll have to wait now,' Jules said, 'till they're asleep.'

'They're probably watching TV up there,' Silas said.

'You can't be sure,' Jules said, anguished.

Silas eased her grip from his wrist. 'I need to carry on, sis.'

'You can't,' she said. 'Please, not yet.'

'If I wait,' he told her, 'my back's going to seize up, and then I'll *have* to stop digging, and we'll have a bloody great hole to explain tomorrow.'

The more surreal the night grew, the more grisly the burial became, the more Jules retreated to somewhere deep inside herself and the easier it became, for the most part, for Silas to control her, guide her through the process.

He would have liked, truly, to have spared her certain things – every bit of it, if he'd been able – but though he did manage the wrapping of the body (sheets first, then black plastic bin liners, stapled *and* taped together for extra strength) by himself, and might even have found the strength to drag it single-handedly along the corridor, down the staircase and out into the garden, he knew that Jules would have been even more appalled had they not carried their father's body bag with at least some small measure of dignity, trying not to bump him on the way.

'Careful,' he said as they heaved Paul Graves through the kitchen towards the back door. 'I don't want you hurting your back.'

'I don't care—' Jules's voice was desperately strained '—about my back.'

'I do,' Silas said, panting. 'I love you, Jules.'

They paused for breath, and she bit her lip, said nothing.

'What?'

She shook her head.

'What did that look mean, sis?'

'You say you love me.'

'You know I do,' he said. 'You *know* that.'

'But I hate what we're doing.' Jules's eyes were swimming with tears again. 'I hate it so *much*, Silas, and you're *making* me ...' Her voice choked up.

'Because I have to,' Silas said. 'It has to be done, you know that.'

'Does it?' She shook her head violently, looked down at what they were carrying, gave another short, furious sob, took a breath. 'Come on then.' She began to lift her end again, the feet end, her *father's* feet.

'Jules, wait a—'

'If it has to be done,' she said, 'let's get *on* with it.'

Chapter Eleven

He had tried, afterwards, when it was all finished, to make it up with her, to find a path back to the way it had been before, but it was impossible. Nothing, he knew, would or could ever be the same again after that night.

His fault. Their so-called father's.

Coming back like that. *Wanting* things.

If he'd lived, Silas knew, too, Graves would have been a vicious thorn in their flesh for ever, would have gone on wanting, demanding, expecting, and Jules would have gone on wanting Silas to give in. Their father would have come between them then for certain, *really* spoiled their relationship, their pure brother-sister love.

'How will we ever forget it?' Jules asked him a few weeks after the burial, looking out of the kitchen window at the oak tree, shedding leaves, like great golden toasted tears, over and around the grave. 'How will we ever be able to forget what we've done?'

'All we've done,' Silas said, 'is lay our father to rest.'

Jules was silent for a while.

'What if someone comes looking for him?' she asked.

Silas looked through the window, then back at her.

'They won't,' he said.

'You can't be sure.'

'I think I can,' Silas said. 'He had no one, did he? Not at the end. Or else he wouldn't have come back to us.'

'He might.'

He lay awake all that night, his sister sleeping huddled beside him, thinking.

'I've decided,' he said next morning, in the kitchen, 'we should have a pond.'

She looked up from her cornflakes. 'What do you mean?'

'A fishpond,' Silas said, waiting for his toast to pop up. 'Something

41

vaguely ornamental and attractive, something distracting, with a paved surround.'

Jules stared at him.

'Near the oak,' he said.

He took her into the garden to show her where.

Not that she hadn't already understood.

'It's because,' Silas explained, 'of what you said last night, about people coming to look for him. It was you that made me think of this.'

She wished she'd said nothing. 'You said there wasn't anyone *to* come back.'

'And I don't think there is,' he reiterated, 'but better safe.'

Jules looked down at the place. It did not look much like a grave now, even to her, muddied by rain, littered by leaves. Yet still it made her feel sick, both physically and, deeply, vilely, emotionally.

'We'll do it together,' Silas told her. 'It'll be almost fun, and then we can stock it with fish and you can take care of them.'

She thought, abruptly, that he had gone quite mad. Her nausea was not dissipating. A pond meant *digging* again, and she felt certain that just hearing the sound of a pick or spade striking, sliding, scraping through dirt and soil would make her want to scream, would drive *her* mad.

'I'll get a manual,' he went on. 'A DIY thing: how to dig your own pond. Or just go to a garden centre, ask them – or you could find the right thing, if you like, since you spend half your life in bookshops. It's not all that hard, apparently – I read about it in one of the Sundays. You dig a hole, put some kind of liner in it, line that with something else, like carpet, then fill it with water.'

'I don't understand,' Jules said.

She felt suddenly peculiar, muzzy-headed, as if this were not real, as if she were not actually standing out in the garden at breakfast time in her school clothes in autumn drizzle with her brother talking about . . .

She shook her head in an effort to clear it. 'How can you talk about digging?' she said. 'Digging anything at all, *ever*, after what we've done, let alone saying it could be almost *fun*?'

'Calm down, sis,' Silas said.

'And anyway, surely—' she spoke more slowly, as if that might help make him see sense '—the very last thing in the world we should think of doing is to dig here, of *all* places?'

Silas shook his head. 'Not right here.' He looked at the grave, then raised his right arm, pointing. 'The pond would go over there, okay?'

Jules didn't answer. Nothing was okay, and her brother was still mad.

42

'We'd dig the pond – just a small, pretty thing – and around it we'd lay this paving or whatever – that's what would be covering *it*.'

Our father, Jules thought. *It.*

'And apart from knowing all about building ponds,' she said, 'do you know about paving, too?' The muzzy sensation was going, though she wasn't sure she hadn't preferred it to clarity. 'Do they teach you that between photography lectures?'

Silas was not accustomed to his little sister using sarcasm with him, and he didn't care for it.

'I'm not a complete fool, Jules.' He waited for her to say that of course he wasn't, but she didn't say anything, just stood waiting. 'I know enough to find out how to do things, to work it all out properly. I know we'll have to dig down a little way to make the paving even.' He saw her face change. 'Don't start freaking out.'

'Too late,' she said. 'I've freaked, and I think you have, too.'

'Shut up, Jules,' Silas said, 'and listen.'

'Can't I listen inside?' Jules spread out her hands, palms up. 'Out of the rain?'

'In a minute.' He returned to his plan. 'We dig a little way, no more than a couple of feet, and then we pour concrete, enough to make sure things are nice and even, as I said, and don't crack up later.'

In her mind, Jules could already see a zigzag crack. 'Wouldn't it be better just to leave it alone?' She forced herself to look down at the grave. 'It looks okay now, doesn't it?'

'The leaves have helped,' Silas said. 'It won't always be autumn.' He shook his head, deciding to forgive her, understanding her anxieties. 'I've decided it's not quite safe enough, sis. You never know who might come poking around sometime in the future. We might even want to sell up one day, who knows?'

'We couldn't,' Jules said. 'Not now.'

'Because our father's buried here,' Silas asked, 'or because you're scared someone might find out?'

'Both, I suppose.'

'I'm trying not to think about the first thing,' Silas said. 'But practically speaking, if we do this, we could leave some day. The pond, and somewhere nice to sit nearby, could be a selling point. Not to anyone with little kids, obviously, because they'd want to fill it in or dig it up.'

'Who's going to buy a big house unless they want children?' Jules asked.

'Not many young couples could afford a place like this,' Silas said easily. 'This would go to a family with older kids, I'd imagine.'

'You've really thought this through, haven't you?'

Silas saw the way she was staring at him.

Didn't much like it.

'Right through,' he said, coldly.

They had done it, actually made their pond, and it had been back-breaking work for both of them, and Silas asked for Jules's help all the way through this time. This was daylight work, after all, in full view of the neighbours, nothing illicit about it, according to Silas, something to be proud of.

Max and Tina Brook came to call one Sunday afternoon in mid-December to say how impressed they were with what they'd done.

'Are you going to keep carp?' Max Brook asked.

'Koi,' Tina Brook said. 'Lovely things.'

'Bit pricey,' Silas said.

'So brave,' Tina Brook said, in the living room, drinking the coffee that Jules had made them, 'doing it yourselves.'

'Most people employ builders,' her husband said. 'Landscape firms.'

'Or whoever's supposed to build ponds,' Tina said.

'Anyone can do it,' Silas said.

'Helps if you're young,' Max Brook said, smiling at Jules. 'And strong.'

Jules flushed, a deep, hot red.

'Are you all right?' Tina asked.

'She's fine,' Silas said.

It was, when it was finished, a lovely pond. Silas, driving to every garden centre he could find between Muswell Hill and points north, all the way to Welwyn Garden City, had found, for the centre of the pond, a grey carved stone Cupid that looked just sturdy enough not to be *too* kitsch, and a ruggedly handsome stone bench seat, which they had concreted to the crazy paving they'd laid all round the pond and right over the top of their father's grave. There were plants in the water, which Silas had read were essential for oxygenation, and half a dozen fat goldfish, though he had been warned that predators – cats or foxes or even herons – were likely to steal them unless precautions were taken. Silas had taken the view that if the fish went, frogs would probably take over, and so long as the pond was kept looking reasonably attractive, it didn't really matter.

'It's actually quite a nice memorial, don't you think?' he said, looking at the finished project. 'If it makes you feel better thinking of it that way.'

Jules looked at the bench, thought about what lay beneath it.

'Memorial to what?' she said, quietly, and then shuddered.

'In a way,' Silas said, gently, 'it's really not all that sad, sis.'

'I don't know,' Jules said, 'how you can say things like that.'

'He wanted to come back, didn't he? Come back to his old house, to us.'

'We don't really know what he wanted,' Jules said. 'Do we?'

Silas saw her brown eyes searching his face for a moment.

'I suppose we don't,' he answered evenly. 'But *if* staying here was what he wanted,' he went on, 'then he's got his wish, hasn't he?'

Chapter Twelve

When Silas was twenty-five and Jules was twenty, she fell in love with Ralph Weston, a zoologist at the Natural History Museum. Sufficiently in love, for the first time in her life, to want, passionately and unhesitatingly, to live with a man other than her brother.

More significantly, to face up to the inevitably unenviable task of telling Silas she wanted to leave home.

Leave him.

It was remarkable, Jules sometimes thought, what one could get over. Not forget, but at least put away. For love. For peace of mind. For fear of losing the person closest to you.

For fear itself.

She had to remind herself, periodically, when she was feeling angry or frustrated with Silas, of all he still did for her, was to her. The plentiful ways in which he had gone on, for all these years, encouraging her, praising her cleverness, wanting good things for her. The things from which he *dis*couraged her – like going to university, as she had, for a while, hoped to do until he had finally convinced her that it was not right for her, that she was not the adventurous kind, that she thrived on consistency, on home and familiarity, and, of course, books.

'Why not consider skipping a degree,' he had suggested to her, 'and go straight into what you'd probably end up doing if you did bother with university?'

It was two years now since he had stood as guarantor for Jules so that she might open a bookshop in Crouch End – in the main road between Shanklin Road and the clock tower, just a small distance from the photographic studio he had created in the basement of a terraced house in Edison Road off Crouch End Hill. Two years since Jules had kept her word to him and written over their home to Silas – 'in natural love and friendship', as directed by his own solicitor, to emphasize that no money had changed hands. Jules had been grateful to him for making Jules's

Books more easily possible, even if she was perfectly aware that the shop, like the dampening of her university ambitions, had sprung from his wish to stop her going farther afield. Away from home. From him.

Not going away to study was a small disappointment to her, but an extension of the bargain they'd struck after the unpleasantness about their mother's will. Jules knew what damage Patricia had done back then, how deeply wounded Silas had been.

Had been wounded, too, by Paul Graves, eight years earlier.

About whom Jules tried not to think.

Tried.

The bargain had been that they would take care of each other, never betray each other, would remain loyal to each other. Jules thought, was almost sure, that if called upon to do so, Silas would probably have laid down his life for her. He had said as much, once.

'I would die for you, Jules,' he had told her.

She had believed him. He was, when all was said and done, her beloved big brother. No less so because he was flawed.

She recognized the flaws more readily now that she was older and just a little wiser. But those flaws – the neediness, the demands, the tendency to freeze her out as punishment when he did feel let down by her – were, because they demonstrated his vulnerability, in some ways what made her love him even more.

'So where,' Silas enquired after she had told him about her plans to live with Ralph Weston, 'were you thinking of doing that?' He paused. 'In my house?'

Hurt and irritation flared inside her.

Stay calm, she told herself.

'No.' Her reply was steady. 'As I've told you, Ralph has a flat in Camden Town, so we'll be living there.'

'Leaving me then,' Silas said.

Jules heard the flatness. 'Not leaving you, Silas, not really.'

'You'll be moving out,' he said.

'Yes, but—'

'You'll be sleeping with him instead of me,' Silas said.

He remembered having much the same conversation with Patricia, after she had broken the news about her plans to marry the stranger.

'Of course I will,' his sister said.

'Just like her,' Silas said.

There were still no special women in his life. His eye for beauty and the nature of some of his photographic business – freelancing for advertising agencies and catalogue work, which slotted in comfortably with the actors' portraits and the bread-and-butter weddings and baby commissions – meant there was no shortage of good-looking women, a fair proportion of whom were attracted to him.

Still no great love affairs, however. There had been one spell of something a little special with a model from Stuttgart named Kate, that might, he supposed, have come close to love, in that the relationship had combined decent sex with affection on both sides. But Kate had fallen harder than Silas, had wanted more than he had been willing to give, and so it had ended, and that had been fine too. The fact was, he could get sex almost any time he pleased. And for affection, he had always had Jules.

Till now.

Ralph Weston was a tall, untidy-looking man with curly, slightly receding brown hair and dark eyes, who wore round spectacles, quite ancient-looking corduroy trousers and an assortment – all almost identical – of blue shirts and V-necked pullovers. He had met Jules at a book launch party at the Africa Centre and had fallen wildly in love with her, finding her strikingly attractive, intelligent, sensitive and – with the exception of what seemed a rather complex and private relationship with her brother – very open.

'It's unusual,' Ralph had remarked during an early date in a small fish restaurant in Kentish Town where, as he'd already briefly explained, they knew about a food allergy of his that made random restaurant dining a dangerous lottery, 'to find a brother and sister still as close as you and Silas at your age.'

Jules had agreed that it probably was unusual and had changed the subject, asked about his allergy.

'Nuts,' Ralph had replied. 'Quite common, but a hell of a nuisance.'

'I knew a girl at school who was so sensitive she had to carry adrenalin.'

Ralph had patted his jacket pocket, smiled.

'Scary,' Jules said.

'Not too often, thank God,' he said. 'So long as I'm careful.'

He waited until their waiter had poured their wine.

'So you've never moved out?' He sipped from his glass. 'No travel bug?'

'Bit of a homebody, I suppose,' Jules said. 'Pretty dull, really.'

'Hardly,' Ralph said.

She noticed how warm, almost velvety, his eyes were.

'Compared to you,' she said. 'Zoology. Exotic travel.'

'Not that often,' he said.

'And didn't you say you keep snakes?' Jules asked.

'Just a handful,' Ralph said, and grinned.

Jules tried to remember what he'd said at the party.

'Some kind of python, wasn't it?' she said, and shuddered.

'A burrowing python.' Ralph elaborated. '*Calabaria reinhardti*.' He saw the expression on her face and grinned again. 'Nice, harmless little chaps, stay hidden most of the time, or actually all the time if they're left in peace.'

'Sounds sensible,' Jules said wryly.

'I suspect,' Ralph said, 'that you might prefer Asali.'

'Asali?'

'It's Swahili for Honey,' he explained. 'She's my dog.'

'Aren't you allergic to fur?' Jules asked.

'Thankfully not to Asali,' Ralph said.

She had thought, when he'd first mentioned the snakes and his fondness for them, that perhaps it might be wise to keep her distance, but then she'd found that, pythons aside, Ralph really did appear to be a perfectly rational, sane man. His flat (if she overlooked the room in which the tank, with its accompanying timers for lights, micro-climate heating and humidity controls, was housed – and he was right, the snakes were not visible beneath the deep litter – not that Jules had looked for long) was cosy, simply furnished, the only exotic touches coming from African paintings and sculptures he'd collected over the years.

'I certainly like Asali,' Jules had said on her first visit to Ralph's flat, fondling the ears of his honey-coloured wire-haired dachshund. 'But I don't think I could ever warm to your other flatmates.'

'I don't expect you to,' he had assured her.

'Sounds like a weirdo,' Silas had said when he first heard about the snakes.

'Not at all.' Jules remembered her own reaction, and tried not to overreact. 'He's perfectly normal and extremely nice. He just loves his work and animals.'

'Reptiles,' Silas said.

'He has a dog, too,' Jules pointed out.

'Still,' he'd said, 'I think you ought to be careful.'

'About what? His snakes are perfectly harmless.'

'So he says.' Silas paused. 'And there's this allergy, too.'

'It's *his* allergy,' she said. 'It's not contagious.' She looked at his face, saw real anxiety in his eyes. 'We're only dating, darling.'

'But you haven't exactly been around, have you, sis?'

'Not as much as you,' Jules said, 'but more than enough to know my own mind.'

However extensive his experience with women might be, Silas still never brought any of them to the house on Muswell Hill. He went to their homes, took them, sometimes, to hotel rooms or back to the studio, but though Jules had told him several times that she would gladly keep out of their way if he did want to bring someone home, Silas had steadfastly refrained from doing so.

'This is our house,' he had said. 'I share it with you, no one else.'

Which was, as Jules realized, neither normal nor healthy. There was no more to their bed-sharing than there had ever been, nothing more, of course – of *course* – than comfort, but it was decidedly more Silas's comfort than her own. On the whole, Jules slept quite peacefully in the big bed, but there were nights when she lay there sleepless, craving privacy – though when she did creep out and go to her own room, she was all too often woken by Silas tapping on her door, seeking company.

'I understand,' he had said on one of those nights, 'if you need space, sis, but I wish you'd warn me, and then I wouldn't bother going to bed till I'm exhausted, and at least I'd stand a chance of getting a bit of sleep.'

'I know you say you don't sleep without me.' Jules felt exasperated. 'But what you don't seem to understand is that I can't always sleep *with* you.'

'You're still awake now,' Silas said.

'Because you're talking to me,' Jules replied testily.

After which he'd gone off in a huff and neither of them had slept.

Now, thanks to Ralph, the habit was finally going to be broken.

'Does he know we sleep together?' Silas asked on the last Saturday afternoon of March, the day before Ralph was due to come to the house for Sunday lunch – two Sundays after he and Jules had made their decision to live together.

'No.' Jules was already dreading the first meeting between the two men.

'Because you think he might not understand,' Silas said.

'I'm not sure that anyone would really understand,' Jules said.

'Dirty minds,' Silas said.

'Ralph doesn't have a dirty mind,' Jules said.

'Ralph sounds perfect,' Silas said coldly.

'No one is perfect, Silas,' Jules said.

The roast having slipped pleasantly down, the washing up having been quite companionably shared by all three of them and conversation having been easier than Jules had feared, Ralph carried Asali – who didn't care much for walking – outside into the garden and put her down on the lawn.

'Mind the pond,' Silas said.

And watched his sister's face grow strained as the dachshund trotted over the crazy paving towards the oak tree.

Jules still hated it, went out there as seldom as possible, had long ago developed a technique, when working near the kitchen window, of turning her body at an angle to the worktop so that she no longer needed to look out in that direction.

For the most part, Silas took care of the pond. The fish had, as predicted, only survived a few months, thanks to a local black and white tomcat who could regularly be seen sitting at the edge, gazing intently into the water. For a while, after the fish had gone and frogs and toads had arrived to take their place, Silas had become interested from the photographic viewpoint, experimenting with different lenses and techniques. Then, growing bored with frogs, he had restocked the pond and connected Patricia's old sprinkler for when the cat came back.

'I know you don't much like going near it,' he had said to Jules when the pond was a year old and in need of cleaning. 'But I am going to need your help with this job, sis. We have to get the fish out first, then drain it and get all the muck out. Bit much for one person.'

'Can't we get someone else to do it?' Jules had felt ill at the notion.

'Getting strangers involved?' Silas had shaken his head. 'Not the best idea.'

And now, there was Asali sniffing around the pond, and Ralph sitting down on the stone bench, holding out his hand to Jules.

'Come and sit with me,' he said.

'It's too cold,' Jules said, wretchedly.

'I'll give you my jacket,' Ralph said, taking it off.

It was the first time she had ever sat on the bench.

First and last, she swore to herself.

Saw Silas watching her face.

'You do know, don't you,' he said later, when they were alone, 'that you can never, ever tell him what we did?'

Ralph and Asali had gone back to Camden Town, because Ralph had an urgent paper to write, and Jules had said that she might start packing up some of her things for her move.

'But we didn't actually do anything,' Jules said, slowly, thoughtfully. 'Nothing terrible, anyway. That's what you said back then, Silas.'

When he was in one of his particularly cold moods, Silas's eyes seemed to become flatter, more opaque, like pebbles. They were, in general, to

Jules, who knew him so very well, like a temper-barometer: the spreading blackness of anger, the stony, less readable, quality of chilliness.

They were very cool now.

'Whatever I said back then,' he said, 'someone else might not understand.'

'Ralph isn't just someone else,' his sister said.

'I know you've never been the brightest, Jules,' Silas said, 'but you're not stupid, so don't pretend to be now.' He saw her hurt. 'And don't look wounded, not when I'm the one here who's being betrayed.'

'How am I betraying you?' Jules asked, though she did, of course, know.

'You know how,' Silas said.

'Maybe . . .' She hesitated, then pushed on. 'Maybe it's all for the best, my going to live with Ralph.'

'I daresay you think it is, for you.'

'I meant for you,' Jules said quietly.

'How could you possibly work that out?'

'Maybe it's time,' she ventured, 'you found someone for yourself, Silas.'

The eyes were pebble-flat again.

'You said,' he reminded her, 'that we'd always be together.'

'And we will be.'

Jules reached for his hand, but he pulled it away.

Distancing now, rather than merely cold.

'So like her,' Silas said.

Chapter Thirteen

Abigail was a virgin when Silas made love to her for the first time.

'An anachronism,' she told him, readying herself for mortification. Twenty-six years old and still intact.

'A miracle,' Silas said.

'A freak,' she said.

'Never,' he told her, fiercely, 'say that again.'

Her mother's adjuration on her deathbed came back to Abigail. *Never say that.* Francesca loving her enough, even then, to want her to have a future.

And now, all those years later, here was Silas, with his remarkable eyes that looked right into her soul, who had already plucked the pain out of her heart and flung it away and taken her over.

She fancied, that first night, in his house, less than two weeks after their chance meeting in Wigmore Street, as he undressed her, ran his hands over her, possessing her, that he was more than just a man, something more exotic and transforming.

Like an eagle, she thought, as he wrapped himself around her, or maybe a phoenix that had swooped down and was now folding her in its wonderful wings, and Abigail had never been especially fanciful before, her music the only escape she had ever allowed herself.

No longer.

'You know,' Silas told her softly, 'that you're the first woman I've ever brought here, to my bed. The first woman I've ever truly wanted to make love to.'

Even in the midst of her rapture, she found both those statements hard to believe.

'Don't doubt me, Abigail,' Silas said, urgently.

He knew she couldn't begin to understand the importance of what he had told her. The importance of the lovemaking itself – he had never,

never, experienced this before, the extraordinary sense of confidence and strength that real love had given him. And of the second thing, of his bringing her here, to *this* bed. He had almost changed his mind at the last minute, had found himself suddenly hearing his mother's words again – *ridiculous* – *disgusting* – had fleetingly considered taking Abigail to another bedroom, but then he'd realized not only how pathetic he was being, but how strange that would have seemed to her, perhaps even tawdry, and that was the last thing he wanted now, and he had managed to thrust Patricia's words away into the void, to focus on Abigail alone.

'Please don't doubt me,' he said again to her now. 'Not ever.'

Abigail shook her head, stared up at him. 'I won't.'

She felt such power in him – and in herself, too, as her body made its new discoveries – and for a few moments, as he made love to her, she felt almost as if a boulder had crashed onto her, was constricting her breathing, obliterating her thought processes, halting everything, and was then lifted away, leaving her brand new, remade, all burdens removed.

Silas's now.

She had made her confession to him, had told him everything, and he had not rejected her, had embraced it as part of her.

She felt born again.

'Tell Jules what you did,' he said, the first time he introduced her to his sister.

It was the end of May, and they were in the house, in the kitchen, sitting at the table drinking the Colombian coffee he'd had fresh ground at W. Martyn earlier in the day because Abigail had said she liked it last time.

'No,' Abigail said, startled, and a little wounded.

'It's perfectly all right,' Silas reassured her. 'Jules knows how to keep secrets.'

Abigail noticed Jules flush slightly. She had experienced a sense of instant liking for the tall, strong-featured, dark-haired young woman who was such a physical contrast to her brother, but at that moment she saw that Silas had a degree of power over Jules too, and Abigail realized, with another of those thrills, that there had to be something very special about a young man who could exert that kind of loving power.

'Tell her, Abigail-Abeguile,' Silas said.

It was the first time he had called her that, and oh, God, she *loved* it.

'I'll tell it for you then,' Silas said, not waiting for her.

It had happened – Silas began telling her tale with such confidence and accuracy that Abigail, half-appalled, half-bemused, thought it might almost have been a story he'd heard many times over, perhaps even invented himself – on August the fifteenth, her mother's thirty-fifth birth-day.

Her parents had been ready to leave for Edinburgh in time for lunch at the George Hotel before the afternoon concert at the Usher Hall to which Francesca Allen had been looking forward for many weeks. Francesca, wearing the primrose silk suit that Douglas Allen had bought for her thir-tieth birthday at Jenners, her long, butter-coloured hair (the same colour as Abigail's, almost the same as his own, Silas told Jules, as if he had seen Francesca Allen's hair for himself) up in a French pleat; Dougie hand-some in his best suit and tie, already yearning for the moment, several long hours away, when he could hang it all away again in his wardrobe.

Both checking their watches, waiting for Abigail.

Always waiting for Abigail these days, it seemed to them.

Abigail, now thirteen and in the grip of her recently acquired, hormone-driven rebellion, sick of being acquiescent, fed up with being a goody-goody, letting her parents know that at every available opportunity, and thinking, almost all the time, about Eddie Gibson.

Eddie Gibson, sixteen, slim-hipped, with a shiny cowlick of dark hair and strong, sunburned arms from working on the forecourt of his dad's garage four miles from Allen's Farm. Filling Abigail's mind ever since she had met him, confusing her body, pushing out most of the content-ment that had been hers until lately.

Eddie had a lot of opinions to share.

Eddie said that farming was crap. Eddie said that taking care of lambs, when they were just going to be turned into chops, was hypocrisy. Eddie said that he'd heard a cello once, and that it had sounded to him like a cow in labour, so Abigail practising, just to keep her mother happy, was a waste of time.

'Living's what counts,' Eddie said.

Francesca and Dougie had only seen Abigail and Eddie together once, had both been struck by the same foreboding and had promptly told their daughter that under no circumstances was she to see him again.

'It's the bike,' Eddie told Abigail. 'They're prejudiced because of my bike.'

The bike was an old black Triumph that he and his dad had rescued from a breaker's yard and restored till it gleamed.

'My beastie,' he called it, and kissed Abigail.

The kiss melted her.

He melted her.

And the bike too, its power, the sheer violence of its roar.

Eddie kissed her again.

Only kisses, never anything more, not yet, at least.

'You're too young, Abby,' he told her, 'for more.'

'I'm not,' she told him back, tossing her hair.

'You're gorgeous,' Eddie said, 'and you're a grand kisser, but you're thirteen.'

'Why should that matter?' Abigail asked.

He laughed. 'Ask your ma and dad.' He ruffled her hair, grinned again, wickedly. 'Or maybe better not.'

The birthday outing had been planned months ago, and even Dougie – stiff collar and tie notwithstanding – was looking forward to it.

Not Abigail, who had other plans.

A once-only invitation from Eddie to ride the Beastie.

'Does it have to be that day?' Abigail had asked him.

It did, Eddie had told her, because his father would be at a meeting with his bank and if Abigail wanted this as much as she had said she did, then if she got out of going to Edinburgh, this would be her big chance to catch the bus to their place early and hang around the house with his ma till she went shopping.

'Of course,' he had said, 'if you don't really want to . . .'

'You know I do,' Abigail had said. 'More than anything.'

'Or if you're scared,' Eddie had said.

That was something else that had come along with periods and melting kisses and bloody-mindedness. Courage, or at least, bravado.

'Not me,' Abigail had told him.

'Where *is* she?' Dougie asked at five to eleven, after they'd both called Abigail's name several times without reply.

'I'll go up and chivy her along,' Francesca offered.

She came back down a moment later.

'She's not there, and her dress is still hanging.'

Dougie frowned. 'So where is the girl?'

Francesca's mouth was taut with anger. She was warm from waiting around, could feel a line of perspiration on her forehead, her day already spoiled.

'One guess,' she said.

When Eddie Gibson's mother put down the phone, she, too, was angry at having been made to listen to a jumped-up spaghetti-eater reading her the riot act because she didn't know how to control her own daughter.

'Take her home,' she ordered her son. 'Now, or there'll be hell to catch.'

'I don't want to go home,' Abigail said.

Mrs Gibson ignored her.

'And this is the last time you see her, Eddie,' she said.

Abigail wept most of the way home, sitting on the pillion of the Triumph, arms clasping Eddie's hard body for what might, if the parents had their way, be the last time, and by the time they reached the broad gate at the end of the long lane that led to the farmhouse, and she saw her mother's distant, rigid figure waiting outside the front door, Abigail was so upset and so furious that she rapped Eddie smartly on his shoulder and shouted at him to stop.

'What?' He stopped the bike, twisted around to see her.

'Let me,' she said, and began to dismount.

'More than my life's worth,' Eddie told her.

'Who's the scaredy cat now?' Abigail, her face flushed from heat and anger, put her hands on her hips, glared towards the farmhouse and her mother, then back at Eddie, still sitting astride the bike. 'I have to show her, Eddie – she has to see she can't control every second of my life!'

Eddie grinned at her. 'You sure?'

'Of course I'm sure.'

He kissed her then, with real admiration. 'You're quite something, you know, Abigail Allen,' he said, and dismounted too, changed places with her.

Abigail twisted the throttle, revved up the Beastie, then suddenly reached up, pulled off her helmet and threw it away, sent it spinning into the long grass, and Eddie gave a whoop and did the same with his, and Abigail twisted the throttle again, and the Beastie roared and shot off through a cloud of midges and on down the lane.

'Dougie!' Francesca cried out in alarm.

Douglas came running out of the house with Nell, one of the border collies, at his heels, and Sammy, the other collie, Nell's brother, who'd been lazing in a puddle of sunlight over by the barn, stood up and trotted over to join them at the front door.

Abigail, her hair whipping around her face, saw them gawping, her mother irate but scared at the same time, shouting something at her, and her daddy, all done up in his suit and tie, and he was looking afraid, too . . .

Eddie spotted the mud slick on the cobbles first, smacked her on the shoulder.

'What?' Abigail twisted her head and shoulders.

'Slow *down*!' Eddie yelled.

Too late.

The Beastie began to skid, tilting as it went, and starting out it might have looked, to a spectator, like a bike at a motocross rally, shooting away through the mud to gain position, but Abigail had lost control, had never really *had* control to begin with, and they were moving so fast, moving towards the farmhouse, and even before the bike began to flip, it felt as if they were flying.

The Beastie looked almost graceful as it left the ground.

Abigail began to scream.

Behind her, Eddie was yelling, and either side of them the collies were barking, and the Beastie's motor was screeching, grinding, and right in front of them, seeming to come closer, *closer*, Francesca stood, both hands clapped over her mouth, and then Dougie was running towards them, his arms outstretched.

'*No!*' Abigail screamed. 'Daddy, *no!*'

They landed.

Eddie's yell cut out at exactly the same time as the motor.

Ceased to be.

As the hem of the left leg of Abigail's jeans caught on a jagged dagger of broken chrome, and the Beastie went on sliding, skating, sparking, over the ground. Francesca, seeing it was going to hit Douglas, threw herself suddenly forward to try to save him, and the bike slammed into them both, rammed them hard into the wall to the left of the front door, spraying blood over Francesca's primrose silk suit and Dougie's white shirt, and over the doorstep and the lemons on the little tree in the terracotta tub that Francesca had bought three years earlier because it made her think of Italy.

'Oh, my God!' Abigail, on her back on the cobblestones, face up to the blue sky, screamed.

Nell and Sammy stopped barking, backed away from the scene, whining.

'Oh, my God, oh, my God,' Abigail went on screaming to the sky.

The only other person left living to make any sound at all was her mother.

Still just alive, an endless half-hour later, as they put her in the ambulance, reaching for her daughter's hand.

'All my fault,' Abigail sobbed, her tears diluting her mother's blood, turning it pinker. 'Oh, God, Ma, it's all my fault.'

'You mustn't *say* that,' Francesca, dying, pulled her close, hissed into her ear. 'Never say that, not to anyone. It was Eddie riding the bike, not you.' She struggled for breath. 'Promise me that's what you'll tell them, Abigail. Swear it on all the saints.'

'But Ma—'

'*Swear* it,' Francesca whispered.

So Abigail did.

'Her mother died in the ambulance,' Silas told Jules, finishing the story. 'Her father was already gone, and Eddie – dead, too, broken neck – took the rap posthumously, thanks to Abigail's mum.' He lifted his wine glass. 'Praise God for Francesca Allen.'

'My God,' Jules said. 'What a tragedy.' She got up and put her arms around Abigail, tears in her brown eyes. 'You poor, poor girl.'

Abigail stared at her. 'Don't you think I'm a terrible person?'

'For a few moments' rebelliousness?' Jules said. 'You were only thirteen, and my God, all the pain you must have suffered.'

'But what about Eddie?' Abigail asked. 'Putting the blame on him.'

'I've told you,' Silas said. 'It made no difference to Eddie.'

'But to his parents,' Abigail said.

'No real difference to them either,' Silas said.

They were all silent for a moment.

'At least, thank God,' Jules said then, 'you've got Silas now.'

Abigail looked at him, at Jules's brother, her slender lover with his hair the colour of hay, that regularly flopped over his forehead and had to be pushed back off his lean face, out of his beautiful eyes.

'I know,' she said.

She turned the niggle over in her mind for a while before she said, after Jules had gone home: 'My story was for you, Silas.' Soft reproach. 'Not to share.'

'But telling Jules,' he said, 'is like telling me.'

'Not really,' Abigail said.

'Of course it is. Jules is part of me.' Silas paused. 'As you are now.'

'Am I?' she asked him. 'Am I really?'

'For ever,' Silas said.

Chapter Fourteen

For a long, long time after they had all died, after the Procurator Fiscal's investigation and the funerals and the Sheriff's inquiry, after the selling of the farm and the livestock and the endless horrors of sympathy and comfort, Abigail had prayed, alone in her room in her Auntie Betty's house and on Sundays in church:

'If you bring them back, I'll be good and play the cello and not see Eddie and not want to be a farmer and do whatever they want me to do.'

And then, years later, long after she had given up on that childish prayer, after she had moved out of her aunt's and uncle's home, and only at those times when her loneliness had become temporarily more overwhelming than her guilt – and then, never in church, for she had only continued to go there for as long as Betty and Bill Innis had taken her with them – she had prayed:

'If you send me someone to love again, I'll be good to them, and I'll do whatever they want me to do.'

She had never really believed that anyone would be sent.

She had known, with absolute certainty, that she did not deserve it.

And then, there he was. Her phoenix.

She had looked up the word, to be quite sure it was fitting. She disliked the first definition, because it referred to the legendary bird that set fire to itself every five hundred years and then rose from the ashes, and fire meant pain, and she didn't want to associate Silas with anything painful.

The second definition was, as she had thought, perfect: *A person or thing of surpassing beauty or quality.*

That, without a shadow of doubt, was Silas.

So the next time he called her Abigail-Abeguile, when they were lying naked in bed after making love, she responded by calling him Phoenix.

'I love it,' he said, and thanked her, as if she had given him a gift.

'How can you thank me?' she asked.

He looked at her then with more love than she had ever seen in her life.

'You have no idea,' he told her.

'Of what?' Abigail asked.

'Of what it means to me to have you,' Silas said.

'I know,' she said, 'what you mean to me.'

'What's that?' he asked.

'Everything,' Abigail said.

The green eyes grew even more intense, seemed almost luminous.

'Tell me,' he said, 'that I'll always be able to trust you.'

'Always,' she told him.

'I've been terribly betrayed,' he said, 'in the past.'

'I'll never betray you,' she told him.

'I love you, Abeguile,' Silas said.

'I love you, Phoenix,' Abigail said.

Chapter Fifteen

She came to live with Silas that July, less than three months after their meeting, in the house that had belonged first to his parents, then to his mother alone, then to his sister, then entirely to him. They slept in the big bedroom, in the double bed in which Silas had slept first with Patricia, then with Jules – though he never told Abigail that, nor did he tell her about the grave in the back garden, because he felt that she might not understand those things, that even if she could understand, they might still diminish her adoration of him, and he didn't want anything ever to do that.

He spent as much time with her as he could, introduced her to his favourite shops and cafés and restaurants around Muswell Hill and Highgate and Crouch End. He took her with him to work at the studio in Edison Road, encouraged her to assist him during portrait sittings, saw from the outset that there was no need to *dis*courage her from messing with equipment because she was patently afraid of damaging anything, had learned young from Francesca about protecting precious possessions – namely the cello. And for that side of Abigail's life, Silas had a local builder convert one of the spare upstairs rooms into a music room, encouraging her to play, loving to sit and listen to her, sometimes for hours at a time.

'Don't you get bored listening to me grind on?' Abigail asked one September afternoon when she'd been concentrating on scales and studies.

'No more than you get bored watching me work at the studio,' Silas said. 'And you don't grind.'

The partially soundproofed room he'd commissioned had three biscuit-coloured walls and one that had been handpainted as a tangle of dark green and russet foliage out of which peeped a pair of gleaming golden eyes.

'I think they belong to a fox,' Silas had suggested whimsically, the first time Abigail had seen the room, locked till then so that he could surprise her. 'Escaped from a hunt and now living in the sanctuary of your very own private forest.' He had broken off. 'What's the matter?'

'It's so beautiful.' She took in the straight-backed chair and music stand in the centre, the Regency style chaise longue, two more chairs and two small tables, one near her chair, all in pale wood. 'I don't deserve it.'

'Nonsense,' Silas said. 'Is there anything more you need? I thought maybe one of those metronome things?'

'Nothing,' Abigail said. 'It's perfect.'

'Don't you think it's time', Silas asked, 'you stopped being so hard on yourself?'

'I don't know if I can,' she had said.

'Even if you'd told the truth,' he said, gently, 'and taken the blame – even if they'd charged you with something, even manslaughter, you'd have served your time long ago, been free and clear.'

'I'd still have done it though,' Abigail had said. 'Still have killed them.'

'I hope you're not over-practising,' Silas said at the end of October, 'just because of the room. After all, there's no real need to go overboard now, is there? Since you're not professional any more.'

'Aren't I?' Abigail asked.

Silas smiled. 'You don't need to play for money now. I have enough.'

Which was true, with much of Patricia's estate still tucked away in tax-efficient places, and with no mortgage, thanks to her life insurance.

'Money isn't everything,' Abigail said.

Silas frowned. 'I thought you said you had no great ambition. That you only really played for your mother's sake.'

'At the beginning,' Abigail said. 'But in a lot of ways, after a while, it was playing that saved me.'

'I thought you said that I saved you,' Silas said.

'You did,' she said. 'You have.'

'Charlie Nagy phoned me today,' she told Silas less than a week later over dinner at the big old oak table in the kitchen. 'Remember him?'

Silas remembered Nagy's refusal to pass on Abigail's contact details, remembered accepting that it had been correct behaviour by the artists' manager, but recalled too a brief flaring of anger because Nagy had been an obstacle, a trip-wire to be jumped in order to reach the woman he'd known he wanted at first sight.

'Of course I remember.' He put down his fork. 'What did he want?'

'He said he's hardly heard from me.'

November had brought rain and wind, and so Abigail had cooked Irish stew, which she had never much liked, but which Silas had told her he adored. His tastes in food, she had discovered, were eclectic but erratic. He liked Japanese food almost any time, Chinese only occasionally, Indian never. He'd seemed to enjoy Hungarian goulash at a restaurant in Hornsey one week, but when Abigail had tried cooking it a month later, he'd said she was mistaken, that he hated anything with paprika, and then, having told her that the only fish he liked were what he termed 'elegant' – dover sole or monkfish or turbot – he'd contradicted himself by stopping his black VW outside Toffs on Muswell Hill Broadway and going in to buy cod and chips.

Abigail didn't care if he was capricious about food or occasionally difficult to cook for. She loved cooking for him, loved making him happy, remembered, often, her old prayer asking God to send someone for her to love, and was immeasurably grateful.

'Why should Charlie Nagy be expecting to hear from you?' Silas asked now.

'He said there might be some work, if I'd like it.'

Silas said nothing, picked up his fork again, but did not eat.

'What's the matter?' Abigail asked.

He thought about it for a moment. 'Jealousy, I think.'

'Why?' She was amazed. 'Why on earth should you feel jealous of Charlie?'

'Not of him.'

'I don't understand,' Abigail said.

'Orchestras,' Silas said, 'are filled with attractive men.'

Abigail laughed.

'Audiences too,' Silas added. 'All looking at you.'

'I'd never look at them,' she said. 'Not when I have you.'

'I'm not joking,' Silas said.

Abigail telephoned Nagy Artists next day to tell Charlie she'd decided not to work for a little while longer.

'That's a pity,' Nagy said.

She told him she was sorry, and he told her that, work or not, if she was ever anywhere near his office in Bayswater, he'd love it if she dropped in for a cup of something, and she told him she certainly would.

One week later, he telephoned again.

'Your other half was here,' he said.

'What do you mean?' Abigail asked.

'Silas came to my office today to see me,' Nagy said.

Abigail was silent, confused, Silas having told her that morning he was going to spend most of the day at a photo shoot in Berners Street in the

West End.

'He told me that I'm not to take any notice of what you said last week,' Nagy went on, 'and that if any suitable engagements come up, you are available, after all.'

'Goodness,' Abigail said.

'So which is it?'

She told him she'd get back to him.

'Why did you do that?' Abigail asked Silas that night, snuggling beside him under the snowy white duvet cover he'd taken her to Harrods to buy the day after she'd agreed to move into the house.

'Because I felt I'd disappointed you,' he replied. 'And I couldn't bear that.'

'If I was a bit disappointed,' she said, thoughtfully, 'it was only because I thought you didn't trust me, and I thought you knew you could.'

'I do,' Silas told her. 'I'm just a very jealous man.'

'I know that now, Phoenix,' she said.

'So you'll beware, Abeguile?'

She half closed her eyes in a sleepy smile, pushed away the duvet, reached for his hand, laid it on her left breast.

'You didn't tell me,' Silas said, 'how good-looking Charlie is.'

'I never thought about it.'

'So you do agree he is good-looking?'

'Nice looking,' Abigail allowed.

'He isn't married, is he?' Silas asked. 'Or with anyone special?'

'Not so far as I know.'

'Gay?'

Abigail smiled. 'No.'

'Why does that make you smile?' Silas wanted to know. 'Do you have some particular reason for knowing that Charlie isn't gay?'

'You really are jealous, aren't you?' Abigail said.

'Don't ever try finding out,' Silas said.

Chapter Sixteen

'What's Ralph really like?' Abigail asked one day at the studio late the following March, after a session with two-year-old twin boys that had drained everyone present except for the children themselves.

'You've met him often enough,' Silas said, slumped on the couch.

'Not that often, and never properly,' she said. 'The longest I've spent with Ralph was at our wedding.' She thought. 'And once at that dinner party, and once when I was in Jules's shop and he dropped in.' She had, on several occasions since she and Jules had found out how well they got along, spent a few hours at a time helping out at Jules's Books as well as at the studio. 'Other than that, he always seems to be working.'

They had married, at Marylebone Register Office, shortly before Christmas, had honeymooned in Venice, which had been cold and wet and grey, though Silas had said that made it less like a corny backdrop and had taken countless rolls of film, and Abigail had found every moment thrilling. Jules had asked her, when they'd been planning, if perhaps she might not rather have gone somewhere warm, but Abigail had told her not in the least, for she had never much liked heat, and tended, in any case, to associate it with the hot August day of her mother's last birthday.

'Ralph doesn't like me,' Silas said now.

'You've never said that before.' Abigail was surprised. 'Why shouldn't he like you?'

Silas shrugged. 'You'll have to ask him at the party.'

Jules was throwing a surprise bash for Ralph's thirtieth birthday, had told Abigail that if it were left up to Ralph to consider a real celebration for himself, they'd have to wait forever.

'I wouldn't dream of asking him,' Abigail said. 'If Ralph's stupid enough not to like you, then he doesn't interest me.' She paused. 'Except, doesn't it make Jules sad?'

'I expect it does,' Silas said.

The party was good fun, though Abigail could see, now that she was taking time to actually look, that whatever Ralph Weston's feelings might be about his brother-in-law, Silas unquestionably disliked Ralph a good deal. Jules, on the other hand, seemed quite blissfully content whenever she was around her husband – to whom she had now been married for almost three years – and the gentle-looking zoologist, keeper of snakes (though the tank room was strictly out of bounds at the party), patently adored his wife.

Three days after the party, having just closed the bookshop for the evening, Jules parked Patricia's old Escort on a yellow line in Edison Road and ran down the steps into the basement studio.

Silas was in the room that doubled as reception and office, sitting at his desk, going over contact sheets with a magnifier.

'Nice surprise,' he said, looking up.

'No Abigail today?' Jules asked.

He shook his head. 'She's been in town, rehearsing for the Berlioz at All Souls.'

Jules took a moment, looking around at the walls covered, as always, with photographic prints. For some time after Silas had first fallen in love with Abigail, he had taken to plastering every wall in the place with enormous enlargements of her pictures – until Abigail herself had seen them and begged him to take them down. Now, at least, one had to actually *look* to realize what a disproportionate number of photographs of his wife still hung among those of his clients.

'What did you want her for?' Silas went on looking over the contacts.

'I didn't,' Jules said. 'It's you I've come to see.'

'My,' he said, dryly. 'Something wrong?'

'On the contrary.' Jules hoped she was appearing calmer than she was feeling. 'It's been a very long time since I've felt this good.' She paused. 'Though you may not agree with the reason when I tell you.'

Silas put down his magnifier and waited.

'I've told Ralph,' Jules said, 'about our father.'

Silas didn't move.

'He's off to Johannesburg soon—' Jules felt unnerved by her brother's absolute lack of reaction '—for the symposium he told you about the other night, and we were talking about how much we were going to miss each other—' still not a flicker on his face '—and I don't remember exactly why, but we got onto the subject of secrets, and I've felt for so long that it was wrong of me to be keeping something so important from him, and . . .'

'And?' There was the chill. No mistaking it.

'And he was fine about it.' Jules went straight on, regardless.

70

'Was he?' Silas's eyes were pebble-flat.

'He was very shocked, of course,' Jules said. 'But after a bit, he told me he felt almost relieved.' She paused. 'He said he'd often thought you and I had some big secret, that wondering about it was sometimes worse than knowing.' She took a breath. 'He says he's glad I love him enough to have shared it with him.'

'Yes,' Silas said. 'I think I can understand that.'

'Can you, Silas?' Jules felt a flare of hope. 'Really?'

'I'm married myself now, sis,' he said. 'Of course I understand.'

'Yet Abigail doesn't know, does she? About our father.'

'No.' He was definite. 'Nor do I want her to. Ever.'

'Don't you think she'd feel the same as Ralph if she did?' Jules asked, gently. 'She's shared her own past with you, after all, and she loves you so much.'

'I know she does,' Silas said. 'But Ralph doesn't have to live in our house. Abigail does.'

Jules forced herself to think about the fishpond.

'Yes,' she said. 'I suppose I can see how that's different.'

'Very different,' Silas said.

'So you really don't mind?' Jules asked. 'That I've told Ralph?'

'Not really,' Silas said. 'So long as he doesn't start discussing it with anyone else, or with me, come to that.'

'He won't tell anyone,' she said swiftly. 'He wouldn't do that to me.'

'Good,' Silas said.

Two days later, when Charlie Nagy telephoned with a last-minute offer to take one of the cellists' places playing Beethoven's *Pastoral Symphony* on the Western Symphony Orchestra's guest engagement at the annual Easter Festival in Deauville, Abigail, excited as she was by the prospect, told Charlie that Silas was out taking wedding photographs and that she needed to speak to him before agreeing to anything.

'Silas has been fine with your working, hasn't he?' Charlie said.

'I know,' she agreed. 'But this is ten days abroad.'

'Only the other side of the Channel,' Charlie said.

'I'll phone you back.'

'Twenty minutes, or it's gone,' Charlie told her.

Silas responded promptly to her urgent message on his mobile.

'If you want it, my love, you take it,' he told her.

'I do want it,' Abigail said. 'So long as you don't mind.'

'Not one bit,' Silas said, 'so long as you don't mind my coming too.'

'I can't think of anything I'd love more,' she said.

*

Silas made the plans in consultation with Charlie, arranging for the two of them to spend a fortnight in Deauville. For the duration of the engagement at Salle Elie de Brignac, they were to stay with the other WSO musicians, after which, Silas told Abigail, he'd reserved the last four nights at the Royal Hotel.

'It's near the Casino,' Silas said, 'very luxurious, overlooking the sea.'

'I don't need luxury,' Abigail told him, 'so long as we're together.'

'I like luxury,' Silas told her, 'so you'll just have to put up with it.'

Abigail usually enjoyed rehearsal sessions, but having Silas with her, she found, made it especially pleasurable. Given permission to observe as the orchestra worked, he remained in the background, silent and well-mannered; then, back at the hotel, he helped with her own practice, turning sheets for her, humming her sections with her in the bath, telling her, as she washed her hair, that he thought her the finest musician in the orchestra.

'Don't be silly,' Abigail said.

'I only hear you,' Silas said. 'Even when you play with a hundred others, I only hear you.' He paused, bent and kissed her mouth. 'Your mother would be very proud of you.'

Afterwards, when the music was done with, the applause a memory, new colleagues bade farewell to, Abigail and Silas had barely changed hotels and enjoyed just a day and a half of private time when Silas – in the midst of ordering a lavish dinner at *Le Yearling* – received an urgent call from Lily Tree, a contact of his at *Sleek* magazine, telling him she had a fashion shoot that three big names had turned down and which was now Silas's for the taking, so long as he could get back to London by morning.

'I told her no, of course,' Silas said, back at the elegant table with its small red-shaded lamp, overlooked by equestrian prints.

'But it sounds so great,' Abigail said, dismayed for him.

'Lily said it could be quite a boost for me.' He picked up the menu again. 'But it's out of the question. I'm not walking out on our holiday.'

'You have to,' Abigail told him.

'I don't have to do anything, especially not leave you.'

'It's just a holiday,' she pointed out. '*Sleek*'s really important, surely.'

'Sure,' Silas said.

'Call her back,' Abigail told him.

'She may already have passed it on,' he said.

'All the more reason to call her *now*,' she said.

He returned again after more than fifteen minutes, apologized to Abigail and their waiter, went back to the matter of ordering dinner.

'Well?' Abigail searched his face. 'Have you got it?'

'I have,' Silas said, 'and I'm very pleased with myself.'

'Good,' she said. 'That's great.'

'I'm especially pleased with myself because I've organized things so that you don't miss out on the rest of your holiday.'

Abigail was dismayed. 'I'm not staying without you.'

'You won't be alone, darling.' Silas's hair flopped over his forehead and he pushed it quickly back. 'That's what's so lovely. Jules is coming to join you.' He grinned at her startled expression. 'She's lonely with Ralph still in South Africa, and she said she'd love to take my place. If you don't mind, that is.'

'I'd rather be with you.' Abigail felt uncertain.

'Want me to call her back, tell her it's off? She said she was going to make arrangements with a neighbour to take Asali.'

'Then you can't stop her – it would be horrible.'

He lowered the menu again, reached for her hand. 'I shouldn't have spoken to her without asking you first,' he said.

'Don't be silly,' Abigail said. 'You only did it for me.'

'I hope you know that's true,' Silas said, seriously.

'Of course I do,' Abigail said.

'That's settled then.' He picked up the menu again. 'Better order before they boot us out. All this planning's made me absolutely ravenous.'

The warmth that already existed between Abigail and Jules grew as they explored Deauville itself and the Normandy coast and countryside, with plenty of time to chat more freely, though Abigail couldn't help noticing that at some point during almost every conversation, Jules seemed compelled to reaffirm her loyalty to Silas.

'Without Silas,' she said in their rented Peugeot on the road to Honfleur the first morning, 'I'd never have been able to open Jules's Books.'

'Silas and I were close before our mum died,' she said, drinking *café au lait* in a small bar near the harbour, 'but afterwards, he became mother and father as well as my big brother.'

'I know he was hurt when I moved out to be with Ralph—' over brioches and melon next morning, bundled up in sweaters in early sunshine on Abigail's balcony '—but once he got used to the idea, he was very supportive.'

'I think Ralph occasionally finds our closeness a bit much—' later the same day, strolling back to the car after buying Calvados at a farm near Pont-l'Evêque '—but he doesn't have any family now except me, so it's hard for him to understand that Silas and I were everything to each other for so long.'

'I think I can understand that,' Abigail said.

She had been hesitant, till then, to mention what Silas had said about Ralph not liking him, but now, tentatively, she did so.

'He's quite wrong,' Jules said.

'I couldn't help noticing,' Abigail went on, 'that they did seem quite strained with each other at the party.'

'Ralph has nothing against Silas,' Jules said, firmly, as they reached the Peugeot, and she unlocked the doors.

'I suppose,' Abigail said, not wishing to upset her, 'they're just so different.'

'Worlds apart,' Jules agreed, getting into the car. 'Nothing at all in common.'

'Except you,' Abigail said.

Chapter Seventeen

'Something wrong?' Abigail asked Jules the next afternoon – the last of their holiday – while they were sheltering from a sharp downpour in the doorway of an antique shop on the quai de la Touques in Deauville.

Jules shook her head and smiled. 'Just thinking about Ralph, trying to imagine where his plane might be now.' She checked her watch. 'Maybe somewhere over the Pyrenees, maybe a little closer to home.'

'And you won't be there to greet him when he arrives.' Abigail was suddenly ashamed. 'Because of me.'

'We'll be back tomorrow,' Jules said, easily.

'Silas should never have made you come.'

'He didn't. I wanted to come, and Silas only did it because he adores you.' Jules linked arms with Abigail. 'And I'm very grateful to him for giving us this time together.'

As evening approached, Abigail suggested they eat in the hotel so that Jules would be on hand if Ralph happened to phone – and as they were finishing their first course, there was a call for Jules, and when she returned to the table her eyes were brighter because Ralph had landed safely, had assured her that he didn't mind too much her not being at home because he was exhausted from his long journey, but was very much looking forward to meeting their train when it got in from Portsmouth Harbour next afternoon.

Arriving at Waterloo, however, it was not Ralph, but Silas waiting for them on the platform.

'I didn't realize,' he said, embracing both women, then taking the cello and Abigail's suitcase, 'that he was meant to be coming.'

They looked around.

'I'm going to wait,' Jules said. 'You two go on if you like.'

'Don't be silly,' Abigail told her. 'We'll all wait. He's probably stuck in traffic somewhere.'

They walked slowly to the barrier, Jules repeatedly checking back over her shoulder to be sure they hadn't missed Ralph in the crush of passengers, but there was no sign of him.

'Here,' Silas said after several minutes, fishing his mobile phone out of his jacket pocket and handing it to his sister. 'May as well try the flat, just in case.'

Jules keyed in the number, frowned. 'Engaged.'

'Might be the lines,' Silas said.

Jules tried again, shook her head.

'Maybe he's trying to leave word for you,' Abigail suggested. 'Maybe there's a message desk here.'

They all looked up and down the concourse.

'There's an information sign,' Silas said. 'I'll go and ask.'

He was back minutes later, shaking his head. 'Nothing.' He looked at his sister. 'Phone still busy?'

Jules nodded, handed the mobile back to him.

'There could be a fault on your phone line at home,' Abigail said.

'Even if there is,' Jules said, 'that doesn't explain why Ralph isn't here.'

'So what do you want to do, sis? Wait a bit longer or go home?'

'I suppose—' Jules wavered '—assuming he's actually *using* the phone . . .'

She waited tensely while Silas tried the number one more time. It was a mild enough afternoon, but she felt very cold.

Silas shook his head.

'You two go home,' Jules said. 'I'll take a taxi.'

'Don't be ridiculous,' Silas told her.

'I wish you'd sat in the front.' Abigail, in the passenger seat of the VW, twisted around to look at Jules. 'Your legs are much longer than mine.'

'I'm fine.'

Abigail heard the tension in her voice. 'Don't fret too much,' she said. 'I'm sure something urgent must have come up.'

'Zoologists don't have urgent things come up,' Jules said.

'They must do sometimes,' Abigail said lamely, glanced at Silas, saw that his sister's mounting anxiety was starting to make him nervier too.

'This isn't like him,' Jules said.

Ralph's old blue Mini was parked in a resident's bay near the flat, two cars away from Jules's Escort.

'Doesn't mean anything,' Jules said shortly, getting out of the car. 'He takes tubes and buses most of the time.'

She unlocked the street door, then stopped, standing still on the threshold.

'Jules?' Abigail said, gently.

'Something's wrong,' Jules said.

'Let's go up.' Silas took control. 'Want me to go ahead?'

Jules shook her head, took a step onto the doormat, looked towards the stairs, made a small, strange sound, like a tiny, constricted moan, then went upstairs quickly, jerkily, looking, Abigail thought, almost like a marionette.

Her hands shook as she unlocked their front door, pushed it open.

It was dark inside, all the inner doors closed.

'Ralph?' Jules's voice, unanswered, hung in the silence.

Silas reached past her, found the light switch, flicked it.

The small rectangular hall looked normal, everything in place: a painting of an elephant that Jules had bought Ralph for a previous birthday; the carved mirror they'd found together a year ago in a market in Ravenna, a yellow Post-it note with shopping reminders – *notepads, pencils, pasta* – written on it stuck to the glass; the pine hatstand in one corner, a raincoat and hooded jacket hanging on two of its hooks.

Jules glanced automatically down, saw a litter of envelopes on the floor.

'Oh, dear God,' she said, very softly, and then swiftly, suddenly, she moved to the bedroom door and thrust it open.

The curtains were not drawn, and in the late afternoon light it was apparent that the bed had not been slept in, though Ralph's steel suitcase lay open on the floor in the middle of the room, a blue shirt sleeve hanging untidily out, a plastic laundry bag on the top, books and a notepad beside it and, next to that, half-hidden by a white T-shirt, a leather-framed photograph of Jules.

Standing behind his sister, observing the room, Silas turned, looked at Abigail, saw that she was looking intently at the closed kitchen door.

Their eyes met, and then, without a word, he went to that door.

Opened it.

'Jesus,' he said, softly.

Behind him, Abigail gave a small, constricted gasp.

'What?' Jules's voice was harsh, sharp, as she pushed past her sister-in-law and brother, and then halted, briefly frozen, just inside the kitchen.

'Jules,' Silas said.

She took another step forward and sank onto her knees.

Beside her husband's body.

Nothing to be done, that much was instantly clear.

Ralph was wearing a blue T-shirt and jeans, his feet bare. His face was slightly mottled, looked puffy, slightly swollen, his round spectacles askew, his eyes behind them staring, bloodshot; his mouth was open, as if he had been gasping for air, perhaps choking, and his lips were bluish with traces of something that looked like foam in the corners. He was wearing his MedicAlert bracelet, his left hand was at his throat, the right, its fingers splayed, looked as if he might have been reaching for something.

Jules touched his face, the quivering oval tiger's-eye ring that Ralph had bought her from a previous trip to Africa accentuating the trembling of her hand. Her breathing, which had seemed virtually to cease, began again, harshly, rapidly, and the trembling spread from her hand along her arm to the whole of her body. She touched his cheek again, stroked it with her open palm, then, abruptly, bent lower over him, slid her arms around his body and raised him a little off the floor, holding him to her.

'Sis,' Silas said.

Jules's lips were moving, though no words were audible.

'Darling,' Silas said.

He felt Abigail's hand, icy cold, clutching his own, stopping him, looked at her, saw the shake of her head, knew she was telling him to leave Jules, and for an instant he resisted, but then he knew his wife was right, drew her close instead, let her lean against him.

They stood that way for several moments before Silas noticed the small black cordless telephone on the floor a few feet away.

'Look,' he said, very softly.

Abigail reacted first, drew away from him, went to pick it up.

'That's why it was engaged,' she said, very softly, and handed it to Silas.

He pressed a key. 'Must have been trying to call for help, and dropped it.'

Jules made a choking sound.

'Darling.' Silas put the phone on the small pine kitchen table, turned, bent down again, laid a hand on his sister's shoulder. 'Let me—'

'No.' She shook off his hand, shrank lower, still cradling Ralph.

Abigail was staring at the table.

A foil carton sat close to the phone, full of food. Something with rice – chicken, perhaps, or mushroom, all too congealed to identify.

A fork lay at the edge of the table, rice grains still clinging to its prongs.

Abigail remembered Jules once telling her about the dangers of anaphylactic shock, the speed with which it could strike people with severe allergies.

Like Ralph.

*

'It makes no sense,' Jules said in her new, harsh voice.

'Try and sip that, sis.'

Silas had called the doctor, poured brandy for all three of them, found two blankets, one to wrap around Jules's shoulders, the other to cover the body, though she had snatched that from Silas, laid it gently over Ralph herself, refusing to cover his face.

They were all on the floor, waiting, sitting vigil.

'I wonder,' Jules said, abruptly, 'if he fed the snakes.'

'I shouldn't worry about them,' Silas said.

'Ralph cared about them,' she said sharply.

'I know, sis,' Silas said.

'We can check on them later,' Abigail said.

Jules looked up at the table, at the foil carton of food. 'Whatever *that* is, Ralph wouldn't have bought anything suspect.'

'Try not to think about it now,' Abigail said gently.

'He never went anywhere he wasn't well known.' Jules was still trembling, her face ashen, though she had not yet wept. 'He understood his allergy much too well for that.'

'Perhaps,' Silas said, 'if he was very tired.'

'Even so,' Jules said.

Abigail recalled the previous evening in Deauville. Jules coming back after her phone call from Ralph – their last conversation – saying how exhausted he'd told her he was after his flight.

She looked at Jules again, saw in her eyes that she, too, remembered.

'When the doc's been,' Silas said, 'I think you should come home with us.'

'I won't leave Ralph,' she said.

'I know, darling,' he said. 'But afterwards.'

Jules stared at him. 'They'll want to take him, won't they?'

'I expect so,' Silas said.

Abigail bit her lip, waited for the other woman to protest, maybe refuse.

Jules stroked Ralph's hair, bent her head, kissed his forehead.

'Where *is* that bloody man?' Silas said, suddenly, angrily.

'There's no hurry,' Jules said.

The tears came then, silently at first, and then her mouth opened in a great, ugly, gasping sob, and Silas put his brandy glass down on the floor, moved closer, put his arms gently around her, and Jules, still clinging to Ralph, let her brother hold her as she wept, howled against his shoulder. And Abigail, watching, remembering the way her eyes had glowed less than twenty-four hours before, after she'd talked to Ralph for the last time, began to cry too, quietly, for Jules.

And then another feeling came back to her, an old, sick, horribly familiar feeling. Because if Jules had not been with her last night in France, if she had been here with Ralph, then this would not have . . .

Stop it, she told herself.

She stopped crying, blanked out her guilt, and that was familiar, too, Abigail knew, almost a reflex. And then she grew angry with herself again, for this was about Jules and Ralph, not about *her*.

More guilt.

Her greatest talent.

Chapter Eighteen

Everyone who knew Ralph agreed with Jules that it was inexplicable, that he had been far too aware of the dangers of his allergy to make such a fatal error of judgment. And yet the pathologist's postmortem report was irrefutable. Ralph had eaten a small amount of rice, chicken and mushroom cooked with peanut oil, and his death had resulted from cardiopulmonary arrest resulting from hypotension and hypoxia caused by anaphylactic shock.

Natural causes.

Ralph's mistake stemming from fatigue.

'I don't believe it,' Jules kept on saying to everyone who would listen. 'It makes no *sense*, not if you knew how careful he was.'

Denial, they said – she knew they must be saying – behind her back.

She supposed, in the end, that they were right.

Finding the flat unbearable to live in – even more so, strangely, she thought, once Ralph's snakes had been removed – Jules had come, with Asali, to stay with Silas and Abigail.

'Just till after the funeral,' she'd insisted at first, but then, with them both encouraging her to stay on – and since she had decided by then, in any case, to sell the flat – she remained with them until late July, when she moved again into a top floor flat in an old terraced house between Highgate and Crouch End. The rooms were reasonably spacious and bright, there was a Yorkstone fireplace in the sitting room, the kitchen was modern and well-fitted and – all that really mattered – it was not the kitchen in which they had found poor Ralph.

'Will Asali be all right,' Abigail had asked when Jules had first told them about it, 'on the top floor?'

'We'll have access to the back garden,' Jules explained, 'and I'm buying a share of the freehold, and no one in the house minds dogs.'

'It's too far from us,' Silas had said.

'Much closer than Camden Town,' Jules had pointed out. 'And now we're *all* going to be driving, it's no problem.' She'd smiled at Abigail, to whom she had given Ralph's old Mini (Silas having had his garage check it over), and who was now having driving lessons.

'You do know, don't you—' Abigail took her aside the day before Jules exchanged contracts on the purchase '—that we both really love you being here? That we'd love nothing more than for you to stay.'

'I do know,' Jules replied, 'and I thank you for it, but I do really need my own place again.' She paused, looked intently at Abigail. 'You do understand that, don't you, darling?'

'Of course we do,' Abigail answered.

'Not we,' Jules persisted. 'Do *you* understand?'

'Of course I understand,' Abigail said.

Her answer seemed wholehearted, but Jules knew, with a sense of sadness, that it was not entirely truthful, because Abigail still partly blamed herself for Ralph's death. Jules had told her that it was pointless to think that way, that if anyone was going to take that line of thought it should be her, as his wife, but it had been clear to Jules that Abigail had remained unconvinced. Which meant that her sister-in-law, still so permanently immured in older guilt, probably believed that Jules was moving out because she did, privately, blame her for the tragedy.

While the truth, in fact, was very different.

The truth was that since Jules had returned to the house in Muswell Hill, Silas had asked her, a number of times, to come into their room and share their bed.

'It'd be like old times,' he had said.

'You weren't married in the old times,' Jules, startled, had pointed out.

'Abigail won't mind,' he had told her.

'I think Abigail would mind very much.' Jules, more shocked now than startled, had tried to force a light note into her response. 'God, Silas, what a weird notion to come up with.'

'I'm sorry,' he had said.

Jules had heard the cool tone and shaken her head, because Silas's hurt feelings were not, these days, her uppermost consideration. Existing without Ralph, getting through each successive day and night without going mad thinking about the lonely, frightening way he had died – not that remembering all the goodness that had gone before, all the warmth and fun and companionship and sexiness and tenderness, was any better, not yet at least. Those things were what she was struggling with for the time being, not her brother's rather perverse whims.

'I'm only offering you love,' Silas had said, 'and warmth.'

'But it's not a normal thing to offer,' Jules had told him. 'Can't you see that?'

'No, I can't,' he had answered. 'Having the two most important women in my life sharing my bed, cuddling up for comfort, strikes me as the most normal, natural thing in the world.' He had paused. 'It's everything I could wish for, Jules.'

That was when Jules had known that she had to go.

She thought, in fact, at that point, that if it had not been for her shop – and she thought she did need Jules's Books quite badly now, both for occupation and for hanging onto one thing that was solid and familiar – she might have gone much further away.

But she did not.

She waited until the end of August, when she was altogether settled in her new flat – she and Asali, who waited on the rug by the side of her bed each night for Jules to pick her up and place her on her duvet, where the dachshund would snuggle down and watch with her warm, sharp little eyes until Jules turned out the light – before she invited Silas and Abigail around for a light supper of cold salmon, and broke her news to them.

'That's wonderful.' Abigail, thrilled, jumped up and came to put her arms around her. 'I can't believe it.'

'Why didn't you tell me?' Silas had not moved from his chair.

'I am telling you,' Jules said.

'Before,' Silas said.

Abigail looked at him, startled by his coldness.

'You must be at least four months' gone,' Silas said.

'Spot on,' Jules said, calmly, though her cheeks were flushed. 'I didn't say anything because I wasn't certain exactly how I felt about it. And because, I suppose, I wanted a little time alone with it.' Her flush grew, and she smiled. 'With him.'

'A boy?' Abigail forgot Silas's strangeness. 'Oh, Jules, I'm so happy for you.'

'Silas?' Jules looked at her brother. 'Aren't you happy for me?'

He waited another moment, then got to his feet and held out his arms in answer, and his sister stood up too, came to him, into his arms, and began to cry.

'I'm sorry,' Silas said. 'I love you, Jules.'

'I love you, too,' she said, her voice muffled against his shoulder.

Abigail stood, a little apart, relieved and joyful for them both.

'You'll make a wonderful uncle,' she said softly after a minute or two.

And father, came into her head.

'What will you do about the shop?' Silas asked, drawing away from Jules.

'Do?' she said. 'Nothing.'

'But you can't run a business and be a mother.' He took his sister's hand and led her to the couch, where Asali was lying on a soft cushion.

'Of course I can,' Jules said. 'Especially now I have Drew.'

Though Abigail still came to help in the bookshop now and again, Jules had decided, during the period of her greatest need, to take on a full-time assistant, and Drew Martin, a kind-hearted young gay man who had not long since been dumped by his lover and who tended to care for Jules like a mother hen, had proven a godsend.

Silas, not especially keen on Drew, lifted an eyebrow. 'You'll at least come back to the house, live with us again.'

Jules drew away from him, smiled. 'No, darling.'

'But you'll have to,' he said. 'You can't be alone.'

'I won't be,' Jules said, and put a hand on her belly.

Something in Silas's expression cooled again. 'No,' he said. 'I suppose not.'

Abigail frowned.

Silas noticed. 'What?' His tone was short.

'Nothing,' she said.

He made love to her with extra passion that night.

'You'll never betray me, will you, Abeguile?'

He hadn't called her that for a long while, she realized. Had not asked her that question for even longer. She had almost forgotten how vulnerable he could be.

'Never,' she told him with a rush of love.

'Swear it,' he said.

'On our unborn children,' Abigail said.

Silas pulled away, looked hard into her face. 'You're not pregnant, too?'

'No,' she said, smiling. 'Of course not.' She was on the Pill; they had talked about it after the first time, and had agreed to wait, to enjoy what they had.

'Good,' he said.

Something in Abigail went cold. 'Why good?' she asked.

'Because if you were,' Silas said, 'I'd have to share you.'

Abigail, having a sandwich lunch in the shop with Jules the following Wednesday, the first in September (Drew took Wednesday afternoons and alternate Sundays off), told her what Silas had said.

'That doesn't really surprise me,' Jules said.

'I thought he liked babies.' Abigail had seen him on various occasions smiling at infants and at toddlers with such warmth that her heart had turned over just thinking of the future.

'He does,' Jules said. 'But he is, as you know, a very jealous man.'

'But he wouldn't, surely, be jealous of his own child?'

'I think he might.' Jules saw the naked disappointment on Abigail's face and felt pity for her. 'You must have realized how possessive he is. It's because he loves you so very much, darling, that he might not be in a rush to share you, not even with a baby.'

'But in time?' Abigail said. 'He hasn't ever told you that he doesn't ever want to have children, has he?'

The door opened and a woman, shaking and closing her umbrella, came in.

Jules stood up to greet the customer, glanced quickly back at Abigail, saw her concern and longing.

'Of course he's never said that,' she said.

Chapter Nineteen

As Jules's pregnancy developed, Abigail found herself thinking increasingly about having babies of her own. The thoughts came with an urgency that surprised her, for if, in the past – before Silas – she had thought about having children, she had always pushed the idea away, had instantly condemned herself for allowing herself such desires, told herself she did not deserve children, that they did not deserve such a mother.

Now, though, surrounded by love, observing her sister-in-law at every stage, hope became very real, turning into a kind of hunger. Having a child – children – with Silas seemed suddenly to Abigail the zenith of everything; the potential perfecting of the second chance he had given her. Except that *he* still did not want to know, became irritated, even annoyed, when she pressed him on the subject.

Patience, she told herself.

Yet sometimes, she couldn't resist pushing a little further.

'You are looking forward to being an uncle, aren't you?' she asked one mid-October afternoon in Edison Road, while they were in the midst of sorting out the studio's third-quarter VAT return.

'Of course I am,' Silas answered.

'You don't see your nephew being any kind of threat, do you?'

'Who put that in your head?' he asked sharply.

'It was you,' she said. 'When you said you didn't want to share me.'

'You used the word "threat",' he said.

'Wrong word, maybe.' Abigail paused. 'But Jules thinks you may feel my having a baby might somehow take me away from you.'

'You don't want to listen to Jules,' Silas said. 'She's always had odd ideas.'

'You adore Jules.'

'Do I?' Silas said oddly.

Abigail frowned. 'Don't you?'

'Jules let me down,' Silas said. 'You're the only one I trust now.'

*

That exchange left Abigail feeling unsettled.

It was not the first time she had felt that, were such a thing possible, her husband might not have minded isolating her from the rest of the world. Having encouraged her to take the engagement with the WSO, Silas had since become discouragingly negative about the jobs Charlie had steered her way, saying the work was beneath her, not challenging enough, leading nowhere.

Being still far more content in her marriage than she had ever dreamed of being, Abigail had no great urge to spend much time with other people, but she *had* hoped, now of all times, to see as much of Jules as possible, and though she had taken and passed her driving test and was, therefore, freer than ever to go where she pleased in the Mini, Silas was being a bit petty even about her seeing his sister.

'Jules and Drew are stocktaking one night next week—' she had mentioned a few weeks earlier, as they were driving home after dinner at Benihana in Swiss Cottage '—and I said I'd go and lend a hand.'

'Bad idea,' Silas had said.

'I'd enjoy it,' Abigail had said, gazing out of the window into the dark.

'I've been thinking, in fact,' he'd gone on as if she hadn't spoken, 'that now that Jules has Martin—' he seldom used Drew's first name '—you should give up working at the shop altogether.'

'Why would I want to do that?' She'd turned to face him, startled.

'Working for relatives is never a good idea,' Silas had told her.

'I work for you at the studio.'

'That's very different.'

'I don't think it's at all different.'

'I'd have thought,' Silas said, a little coolly, 'that working with me while you wait for the right kind of engagements would be enough for you, but if it isn't, why don't you start teaching music?'

'I'm not qualified to teach.' Surprised again, she thought of the jobs he'd discouraged her from accepting. 'Anyway, according to you, there are no "right" engagements.'

'Of course you're qualified. You went to the Conservatoire.'

'I didn't study to be a teacher.'

'I'll bet the average parent round here wouldn't care about that.' Silas had flashed his lights at the car in front. 'You have the music room – it would be perfect.'

'I don't want to teach.' Abigail had felt suddenly irritated. 'I *do* want to go on working at Jules's Books.'

'Then you must do—' Silas was frosty '—as you please.'

'I shall,' Abigail had told him.

*

88

When Jules telephoned Abigail one morning at the end of October to ask if she would consider coming along to her weekly natural childbirth classes at the hospital, with a view to acting as her birthing partner, Abigail, deeply touched, answered immediately and unreservedly that she would be honoured.

'How could you say yes—' Silas was at his desk in the studio when she came in to give him the news '—without asking me?'

Abigail, still taking off her rain jacket to hang on the hatstand in the corner, glanced at him in surprise. 'I didn't imagine you'd need asking. I thought you'd be as thrilled as I was.'

'You're not,' Silas said, 'always as sensitive as you claim, are you?'

Realization struck. 'You thought Jules would ask you.' Instantly she was filled with shame. 'Oh, God, I'm sorry, I should have thought.'

'No, you shouldn't,' he said coldly. 'Jules wouldn't have asked me because she knows I'd refuse.'

'Then what—?' Abigail sat down on the couch, perplexed. 'I don't get this. How can you possibly be objecting to your sister asking your wife to help her with something so wonderful, especially after Ralph?'

'For God's sake,' Silas said, 'be her damned birthing partner if it's that much of a big deal to you.'

'Why are you being so nasty?' Abigail felt bewildered.

'You know why,' Silas said.

Abigail stared at him. 'You can't possibly still be angry with Jules for wanting to stay in her own home.'

'Angry's not the word I'd use,' Silas said.

'Don't be so pompous.' She was incredulous. 'Jules is your sister, and we're all she has now.'

'She'll have her child,' Silas said.

'Oh, for God's sake.' Abigail got up, pulled her jacket from the stand and went to the door. 'Grow up, Silas.'

The intensity of her disappointment with him, the pain of arguing with him when she loved him so much, the fear that her standing up to him might damage their marriage, began to prey on her mind, destroying the peace that had been so hard-won.

She began to practise more regularly in the music room, the old memories haunting her again: flashbacks to the yard at Allen's Farm, the roar of the Beastie, the mud and blood and the screaming.

She drew her bow back and forth across the cello's strings too violently, her hair falling wildly about her face; making noise rather than music, fancying she heard her mother's reproach for doing so, and instantly, despising herself, ceasing her raucous abuse of the instrument and holding it closer, cradling it, reminding herself that she loved it, *had* to love it, for Francesca's sake.

Abigail was frequently aware, had always been aware through the years, that her focus at such times was all on her mother, all her atonement revolving around Francesca, though she had killed her daddy, too, and Eddie – and then *blamed* poor Eddie. But almost always she would thrust such thoughts away, thrust *them* away, her victims, slamming them back again into the stone wall, into the ground, into the space deeper inside her head, because she could not cope with them too.

Her mother was more than enough to bear.

She was shopping with Jules for baby things at Peter Jones on the afternoon of the third week of November when Jules – aware that Abigail's sporadic work hours at the bookshop and studio were leaving her deeply unfulfilled – suggested that she get in a taxi and go to see Charlie Nagy in Bayswater.

'He may not be there,' Abigail said.

'Phone him,' Jules said.

'I can't just leave you high and dry.'

'You won't be,' Jules assured. 'I'll go home – I've had more than enough.'

'There you are then,' Abigail said, mindful that Jules was now seven months' gone. 'You're too tired to manage all these bags.'

'You take the bags then.' Jules grinned. 'And I'll snooze on the tube.' She patted her large bump. 'One more good thing about this little chap,' she said. 'At least he usually gets me a seat.'

The offices of Nagy Artists, just off Queensway, consisted of one large room on the top floor of an old building with a slightly sloping floor, timber ceiling beams, two desks – one for Nagy, the other for his part-time assistant, Toby Fry – and an aged, cracking brown leather couch. Framed photographs, posters and programmes covered the walls, and the air smelled of coffee and the small panatella type cigars that the thirty-two-year-old enjoyed.

Nagy, alone in the office, not troubling to conceal his pleasure at Abigail's visit, had welcomed her with a hug and set to brewing fresh coffee.

'I know I've turned down a few things lately,' she said now, sitting on the couch facing a photograph, among various others, of herself on the platform at the Wigmore Hall.

'More than a few,' Charlie said, hovering over the coffee maker.

Abigail flushed, fingered a split in the leather. 'I know,' she said. 'Sorry.'

'Doesn't matter,' he said.

He poured into two mugs, added milk, handed her one and sat down at the far end of the couch.

'So,' he said. 'What's up?'

Abigail regarded him for a moment. He had a roundish face, a small, neat beard, rather less dark curly hair than when they'd first met, twinkly brown eyes that turned down at the outer corners, and he was wearing the kind of clothes he often favoured, crisp white shirt, colourful embroidered waistcoat and jeans.

'Thing is,' Nagy said, 'are you still sure, about wanting work?'

'Very sure,' Abigail answered positively.

'I just thought—' He stopped.

'Thought what?' she asked.

He fiddled with the cuff of his left shirt sleeve. 'Nothing.' He smiled. 'I must have got the wrong idea. I'll be glad to go on keeping my ear to the ground for you.'

'Thank you.' Abigail paused. 'Wrong idea about what?'

He shook his head. 'Nothing at all,' he said. 'How's Silas?'

'He's fine.' She felt the awkwardness lingering in the air, frowned. 'Has he been to see you again?'

'No.' He leaned over the coffee table, withdrew a panatella from a tin.

'Are you sure?' Abigail asked.

Nagy took a dented silver cigarette lighter from his trouser pocket.

'Why wouldn't I be?' he said.

She raised the subject that evening, while she was checking the bolognese sauce for their spaghetti and Silas was preparing a salad.

'Have you seen Charlie lately?' she asked as casually as she could manage.

'Charlie Nagy?' He had already rinsed the iceberg lettuce, but now he was inspecting each leaf in the colander. 'Why do you ask?'

'I just wondered,' Abigail said, tasting the sauce.

'Do I take it you've seen him?'

He often answered questions with questions, putting her on the defensive, though she supposed it was silly for her to feel that way. Still, she found herself now explaining to him about being in Peter Jones, and Jules urging her to take the opportunity to drop in on Charlie, and then waited for him to ask why she hadn't simply told him that she'd seen him.

'Hardly round the corner,' was all Silas said.

'Closer than here or Crouch End,' Abigail said, and added black pepper.

'Any work going?' Silas asked.

'Not at the moment.' She stirred the sauce again, then laid the wooden spoon over the top of the pan. 'He seemed a bit odd about my asking about it.'

'How so?' His eyes flicked in her direction, before he turned back to the sink, shook the colander and tipped the lettuce into a big ceramic bowl. 'The sauce smells good.'

'Almost done,' she said.

Silas took olive oil, balsamic vinegar and mustard from a shelf and began making dressing. 'I wish you hadn't gone to see Nagy.'

'Why not?'

'Because—' he whisked with a fork '—as a matter of fact, he and I have had a few chats lately, and because – though I'd much rather not be telling you this now – we've been collaborating on something for you.'

'What sort of something?'

'A bit of a plan.' Silas tasted his dressing. 'Too early to talk about.'

'But if it concerns my work,' Abigail said.

'It's a surprise, my darling,' he said. 'And there's no point trying to wheedle it out of me or Nagy. You just keep up your practice.'

'What—' her jaw felt tight '—am I supposed to be practising?'

'Just your usual stuff for now,' Silas said.

'This is silly,' she said.

'Humour me, darling,' he said.

He began to spend even more time than usual with her in the music room, listening, observing and frequently – a little compulsively, Abigail thought – photographing her as she played. When she said, lightly, that he'd surely taken enough pictures of her, Silas replied, good-naturedly, that he could never have enough. When she said, more emphatically, that the clicking and flashes were putting her off the music, he said it was a good exercise in concentration, though he did stop for a while after that, urged her to go on practising harder.

'What *for*?' she asked regularly, still to no avail, until finally, one evening in the second week of December, she grew exasperated enough to throw down her bow and say she wasn't going to play another note until he'd explained himself.

'I'm fed up,' she said, 'with being treated like a child.'

'What was that—' Silas got up from the chaise longue, picked up the bow '—if not a tantrum?' He gave it back to her.

She took it, glared at him, stood up.

'What are you doing?' he asked.

'Nothing,' she said. 'As I told you.'

92

Silas watched her start the process of loosening the bow hair in readiness for putting it and the cello away.

'I suppose you leave me no choice, but to tell you,' he said.

'About time,' Abigail said.

'It's my anniversary gift to you,' Silas said.

She said nothing, guilt already rising, cheeks growing warm.

'A one-woman recital,' he went on, 'at the Jerome Hall. Post-anniversary, actually – I had to wait till the end of January to get a booking.'

Now she was incapable of speech.

'It's in aid of three children's charities.' Silas smiled at her expression. 'When I say one-woman, Nagy's found you an accompanist.'

'You are joking,' Abigail said. 'About this whole thing?'

'I would never joke about something so important.' The smile had faded. 'You know I've wanted something more worthy of you. This is it.'

She sat down again on her chair. 'Silas.'

'What, my darling?'

'Silas, there's no way I'm good enough for this.'

'Of course you're good enough. Or you will be, if you start working harder.' He smiled again. 'If I didn't believe you were good enough, do you imagine I'd have spent a small fortune putting down the deposit for the hall?'

She went, after a sleepless night, to see Charlie again.

'You have to stop this,' she told him as soon as Toby Fry, Charlie's assistant, had observed her distress and taken himself discreetly off on some outside chore.

'You, of all people—' Charlie was smoking one of his little cigars and wearing a blue waistcoat with racing cars woven into the pattern '—must know it's not exactly easy to stop Silas Graves from embarking on something he's set his heart on.' He paused. 'It must be nice having a husband with such great faith in you.'

'But you don't, do you?' Abigail had heard the wryness in his tone.

'I have considerable faith in you,' Charlie answered.

'But you know – honestly – that I'm just not up to this terrible idea.'

'I think—' he strove for kindness '- it's going to be tough on you.'

Abigail, sitting on the couch, dropped her face into her hands, then raised it again. 'He says it's too late to cancel, but surely it can't be?'

'I'm afraid it can,' Charlie confirmed, 'insofar as the charities would lose out and the insurers wouldn't stump up unless you were seriously ill or worse.'

'Great,' Abigail said flatly. 'Just great.'

Charlie leaned back in his chair and blew smoke into the air.

Abigail's panic rose again. 'What'll I play?' Her pause was frantic. 'Couldn't I at least share the platform?'

'You will be,' Charlie reminded her.

'I'm not talking about an accompanist.' She was scrabbling for ideas. 'A quartet – I could cope with that – I might even enjoy it.'

'Too late.' He looked sympathetic. 'Tickets and programmes under-way, charities already advertising.'

'But they'd have a much better deal with more musicians.'

'Except that Silas,' Charlie told her gently, 'has got people believing you're the most exciting thing since du Pré.'

The sound Abigail let out was half-snort, half-wail. 'He *can't* have.'

'Okay then,' Charlie said, 'try Hai-Ye Ni.'

'Silas hasn't even *heard* of Hai-Ye Ni, and if you're trying to make this better, Charlie, you're not succeeding.' Her horror was magnifying. 'He doesn't have a clue about what makes a *good* cellist, let alone a genius.' She leaned forward in a gesture of pure appeal. 'Please tell me no one really believes such nonsense.'

'I've exaggerated,' Charlie said.

'Have you really?'

'A bit,' he said.

'Oh, God,' Abigail said.

Nagy got up from behind his desk, came over to the couch, sat down beside her and put one arm around her.

'Do the Bach Adagio,' he said, pushing her hair out of her still-appalled eyes. 'And maybe the Mendelssohn – *Lieder ohne Worte.*'

'God,' Abigail said. '*God.*'

'I know,' Charlie said.

'No, really,' she said. 'This is a nightmare.'

Chapter Twenty

'You'll be wonderful,' Jules said a week later in the shop.

'I will not be wonderful.' Abigail was up on a ladder, dusting the Christmas decorations which had already been up for a month. 'I will be, at my absolute best, adequate.' She stopped dusting, her face morose. 'More likely, the way I'm feeling, I'll be crap.'

'Silas thinks you're wonderful.' Jules stretched, rubbed her back.

'Silas,' Abigail said bitterly, 'is turning into Mrs Worthington.' She looked down at Jules. 'You okay?'

'Fine.' Jules paused. 'If you really believe what you've just said – if this is really going to be so hellish for you – maybe you should cancel.'

'How can I,' Abigail said, 'with starving, abused children involved?' She reached for a tinselly garland, flicked the duster at it. 'I suppose at least it won't matter to them if I'm a lousy cellist so long as they get something to eat.'

'You're not lousy,' Jules assured her. 'You're very good.'

'I'm not too bad,' Abigail allowed, 'playing as part of a group, but I'm no soloist.'

'I thought there was going to be a pianist.'

'To accompany me.' She grimaced. 'Her name's Sara Ellis, and she's very good and very kind, and she's done nothing to deserve this.'

'I think,' Jules said, 'you're starting to over-dramatize.'

'I don't,' Abigail said bluntly and began her descent. 'They may not actually lynch me,' she said, 'but if you ask me, we'll be lucky if the audience and charities don't sue under trades descriptions.'

By the evening itself, after a Christmas and New Year entirely spoiled, from her point of view, she was a sick, trembling wreck.

'I can't go on,' she told Silas, resplendent in black tie.

'Don't be silly,' he said.

'Tell them I'm ill,' she begged. 'Tell them I'm dead.'

'Abigail Allen Graves—' he gripped her shoulders '—you're not only alive and well, but you're going to go onto that platform in—' he glanced at the clock on the dressing room wall '—twenty-three minutes, and you're going to play like a dream.'

'What I'm going to do—' Abigail took a step back, out of his grip '—in less than *one* minute, is throw up again.'

The audience – a diverse crowd, Silas, Charlie, Jules (now heavily pregnant) and the charities having flogged tickets with every tactic they could come up with – settled themselves into the Jerome Hall's rather uncomfortable red seats and applauded with generous enthusiasm when Abigail and Sara Ellis took to the platform and readied themselves to begin with Saint-Saën's *The Swan*. But though Abigail made no monumental errors and though, on the three occasions when she did falter, the accompanist managed to cover for her, she felt, by the end, a palpable and acutely embarrassing sense of relief flowing up to the platform.

'Thank you,' she said, struggling against tears as she embraced Sara before making her escape. 'You saved me.'

'Nonsense,' the kindly younger woman said. 'You were very good.'

'I was dreadful,' Abigail said. 'I warned them I would be, and I was.'

'You were brilliant.'

Silas swept into her dressing room with a bouquet of roses and lilies and a bottle of champagne.

'Never—' Abigail took the flowers and dumped them on the dressing table '—do *anything* like that to me again.'

She was standing in her slip, having ripped off the gorgeous dove-grey silk long dress he'd insisted on buying for her the week before. Now, seeing the startled pain in his eyes, she thought for one second about stopping, but knew that she could no more, at that instant, have stopped wind from blowing.

'Maybe you really did mean well—' her cheeks were still burning with humiliation '—and it's very nice you think I'm talented, and maybe I am the most ungrateful cow on earth, but do you have any *idea* what I felt like on that platform?' She shook her head, stormed straight on. 'Like some wretched child shoved on stage by a ghastly, pushy parent from hell.'

She saw the pain turn to anger, thought, for a brief moment, that he might be about to hit her, or maybe smash the bottle. But then, suddenly, the heat was gone and distaste took its place.

'Ungrateful,' he said, 'just about covers it.'

And without another word, he turned and walked out.

Abigail let out an ugly, strangled sob, took a step towards the door, then remembered she was undressed.

'Silas,' she said.

She stood staring at the door, willing it to open again, and shame had already doused her own anger, and what did any of it *matter*, for Christ's sake, if she ended up hurting the man who loved her enough to have done this for her – *for* her, not *to* her.

'Oh, God.' She turned, found the jeans and sweater she'd arrived in hours earlier, tugged on the jeans, realized she was still wearing the long slip, dragged it up over her head and pulled on the sweater, her hair flying with static.

The door opened.

'Silas, I—'

It was Charlie, looking uncomfortable because he had just seen Silas grabbing Jules by her arm and all but dragging her with him towards one of the exits.

'Only me,' he said. 'Sorry, darling.'

Abigail turned to the mirror, brushed violently at her hair, tried not to cry.

'I think Silas has gone,' Charlie said. 'Taking his sister with him.'

Abigail burst into tears.

'Darling.' Appalled, Charlie put his arms around her. 'I'm so sorry, I didn't mean to upset you. Maybe they're coming back.'

'No,' she sobbed against his jacket.

'That's right,' Charlie said, helplessly. 'Let it out.'

Abigail pulled away, wiped her eyes with the back of her hand. 'No.' She shook her head. 'I'm sorry.'

'What for?'

'For being so *pathetic*.' She dragged some tissues from a box on the dressing table, wiped her eyes again, then blew her nose and found, suddenly, that she was still furious. 'You know what I'd like to do, Charlie?'

'Go home,' he supposed. 'I'll take you.'

'No.' Abigail threw the tissues in the bin. 'He puts me through this whole terrible *farce*, and then, because I finally tell him how I feel, he walks out on me.' She took a breath. 'I do not want to go home.'

'It wasn't a farce,' Charlie said. 'You were fine.'

'I was not fine,' she said. 'But it's done with, thank God, and at least the charities have made some money, and hopefully all those poor people in the audience will soon have forgotten how awful I was.'

'You were far from awful,' Charlie maintained, 'and you looked wonderful.'

Abigail smiled at him, turned to the mirror, picked up another tissue and wiped away the mascara smudges beneath her eyes. 'I'm still not ready to go home yet,' she said. 'What I'd really like to do, if you're up for it, is go out to dinner with you.'

Charlie looked dubious.

'You're worrying about what Silas will think,' she said.

'I am,' Charlie said ruefully. 'A bit.'

'Which is exactly what he'd like you to do,' Abigail said, 'and I'm a bit fed up right now with him always getting his own way.'

'He does seem very good at that,' Charlie admitted.

'Not tonight,' she said.

The beautiful grey dress caught her eye, gave her a swift pang of regret, but quickly and determinedly she picked it up and folded it into the large carrier she'd brought it in.

'Please, Charlie,' she said. 'Let's go out for dinner.'

'There are very few things in the world I'd like more,' he said, 'than to take you out to dinner right now.' He sighed. 'But no one knows better than I how much effort Silas put into organizing this evening.' He reached for her hand, squeezed it. 'Not to mention time and money. The man adores you, Abigail, and I can't blame him for that.'

All the anger left her, another, far more familiar emotion taking its place. 'Oh, God,' she said. 'I was so *horrible* to him.'

'Just emotional,' Charlie defended. 'Every right to be.'

'No.' She shook her head. 'I was vile, Charlie.'

'Can't imagine that.'

'Can't you?' She paused, grimly. 'You should.'

The drive in Charlie's ancient MG back to Muswell Hill seemed endless; more like rush-hour, he said – for want of anything better to talk about, with Abigail silent and miserable beside him – than late evening.

'I'm sorry, Charlie' she said, when they were almost home.

'What for?' he asked.

'It's only just occurred to me that Silas isn't the only person to have spent a lot of time and trouble organizing this evening.' Her face was flushed, her eyes agitated. 'I've behaved badly to you, too, for weeks and weeks, so ungratefully. I don't deserve you any more than I do Silas.'

Charlie braked at the traffic lights more sharply than he'd intended. 'You stop that,' he told her.

'No, Charlie, I mean it.'

'So do I,' he said forcefully. 'You're a valued client who performed well tonight, under difficult conditions, and you're also, so far as I'm concerned, a friend.'

'That doesn't mean—'

'Yes, it does.' The lights changed to green, and the MG growled back into motion. 'I know Silas meant this as a huge compliment, but he should have consulted with you first, and since he didn't, maybe I should have done it instead, but it's certainly not your fault that neither of us did.'

'Thank you.' She paused. 'Do you think he'll forgive me?'

'The man's not a complete prat, is he?'

'Anything but,' Abigail said.

'Well, then,' Charlie said.

Though Silas's VW was parked in the drive, the house was in darkness, but no sooner had Charlie drawn up at the kerb beyond the trees and got out to open Abigail's door than the front door opened and light spilled out onto the pathway, framing Silas.

'Thank you, Charlie.' Abigail gave him a swift kiss on the cheek.

'Good luck,' he said and watched her walk up the path.

Silas, still in his tuxedo, bow tie dishevelled, hair rumpled, did not move.

'I'm so sorry,' Abigail said, stopping a foot away from him, uncertainly.

'I should have listened to you,' he said, 'instead of bulldozing you into something you didn't want to do.'

'But you were doing it for me,' she said, 'and I acted like a spoiled brat.'

'You were very upset,' Silas said. 'I shouldn't have walked out on you.'

'I can't really blame you,' Abigail said.

He held out his arms, and she came into them, felt nothing but relief as he held her close, let her lean against him. He smelled of whisky, and his body was tense and very warm, and she thought she had never loved him more.

'Goodnight, Charlie,' she heard him call, over her shoulder.

'Night, all—' Charlie's voice called back from the road '—God bless.'

Abigail attempted to turn around so that she could wave, but Silas's arms tightened around her, and she gave in, relaxed against him.

'I love you so much,' she said.

'I love you too.' He held her even tighter, closer.

Too close for her to see that his eyes had turned pebble flat, and that the look he was giving Charlie, as he got back into the MG, was ice cold.

Chapter Twenty-One

One week after the recital at the Jerome, on the fourth of February, Jules's son was born.

She had begun having contractions two days earlier and had phoned Abigail, who had shot over to Highgate in the Mini and whisked her straight into the Whittington Hospital, before skulking foolishly back home with her to the flat two hours later.

'I blame Braxton Hicks,' Jules had said, sinking heavily onto the sofa beside Asali, while Abigail was in the kitchen making tea.

'He only named the contractions,' Abigail called. 'He didn't invent them.'

'I'd better phone Drew.' The dachshund rolled onto her back, offering her soft stomach to be caressed. 'Tell him he doesn't have to pick up Asali.'

'I'm still not sure why she isn't coming to us.' Abigail brought two mugs into the sitting room. 'So much easier with the garden.'

'Drew's really looking forward to having her,' Jules had said.

The fishpond, which had, for a long time, first because of her great happiness with Ralph and then in the face of his loss, almost ceased to burden Jules, now came regularly back into her mind.

Her child, their son, would soon be in the world.

A mother ought not to keep ugly secrets from her child.

A child ought not to be exposed to ugliness.

Jules remembered, suddenly, that first time with Ralph in the garden at Muswell Hill, Asali sniffing around the pond, Ralph sitting on the stone bench holding out his hand to her.

'It's all right.' Abigail's voice broke into the memory. 'Don't worry about it.'

Jules looked up at her, startled.

'If Asali's happy at Drew's—' Abigail sat down in an armchair '—that's fine, isn't it. No need to look so troubled.'

'I'm not troubled,' Jules lied.

Abigail lived in that house, had helped Silas clean the pond, had sat in that garden, probably on that bench, many times, and was in total ignorance of what lay beneath. Abigail, who, for all the dark sadness of her own history, was, Jules thought, the most trusting person she had ever known.

That was very wrong, too. A deep, abiding wrong that Jules could not imagine ever being able to put right. Certainly not while Silas had no wish to do so.

'Sure you're okay?' Abigail had asked Jules.

Jules had nodded, mustered a smile.

'No more pains?'

'Not yet,' Jules had said.

Plenty more pain two nights later, when the real thing got underway.

Jules had taken herself by taxi to the Whittington at eight in the evening, had waited to be certain before calling her brother's house again.

'Drive safely,' she told Abigail. 'No need to rush.'

'You sound very calm,' Abigail said.

'Before the storm, I expect,' Jules said.

Silas came to the phone to wish her luck.

Abigail waited till he'd finished.

'Are you sure you won't come too?' she asked him.

'What for? Jules asked you to be her partner, not me.'

'You told me that was because she knew you'd refuse,' Abigail reminded him.

Silas raised an eyebrow.

'Phone me when it's all over,' he said.

He did come then, at around noon next day, bearing blue and white flowers from Moyses Stevens, and bunches of fat blue-black grapes, and an exquisite silk and lace christening gown which had to have cost the earth and about which Abigail had known nothing.

The baby was beside Jules's bed, but Silas made straight for his sister, looked at her long and hard, as if seeing her in an entirely fresh light, and then stroked her bedraggled hair with great tenderness before, finally, turning to his nephew.

'He looks,' he said, 'like our mother.'

'I think he looks like Ralph,' Jules said.

'No.' Silas was decisive. 'Just like Mother.'

Jules and Abigail both looked closely at him, trying to judge whether or not that was, in his heart and mind, a good or a bad thing, saw tears swimming in the sea green eyes, and were more than a little relieved.

'What's his name?' he asked.

'Oliver,' Jules said. 'Ollie.' She smiled. 'Ralph liked it.'

'Is that it?' Silas asked.

Jules knew what he meant. 'Oliver Ralph Silas Weston,' she said.

'Just scraped in then,' Silas said.

Chapter Twenty-Two

Just over a fortnight after Ollie's birth, three weeks and two days after the recital, Silas turned to Abigail immediately after hitting the button to turn off his alarm clock's buzzer, and told her that he wanted her to drop Charlie Nagy as her manager.

'Why on earth—' she felt as if she'd been shaken roughly out of sleep '—would I do a thing like that?'

'For one thing,' Silas replied, pushing away their duvet, 'I don't think he's ever been much of a manager.'

'He's been a very good manager and friend.' Abigail sat up, rubbed her eyes, pushed the hair out of her face, forced herself to wake up.

'Be that as it may—' Silas got out of bed '—it seems he's been lining his pockets.' He picked up the glass of water from his bedside table, drank what was left of it, saw the confusion on her face. 'Syphoning off some of the charities' proceeds, to be exact.'

'Don't be ridiculous.' Abigail was stunned. 'Charlie would never do anything like that.'

'I hope you don't think I'd invent such a thing?'

'No, of course not, but . . .' She shook her head, stared up at him. 'It's a mistake, Silas. Who's told you this?'

'The accountants.'

'Let me talk to them,' Abigail said. 'I'll tell them they have it wrong.'

'I doubt, somehow, that they'll believe you.'

'But I've known Charlie for years.'

'Not that well, surely?'

'Well enough,' she said, stoutly.

'Your loyalty becomes you.'

'It's nothing to do with loyalty,' Abigail said. 'I just believe in him.'

Silas smiled, stooped and kissed the top of her head.

'Fire him,' he said.

*

She waited, in painful suspense, for three days, until a morning when Silas was fully occupied at a shoot, then went to Bayswater.

'I take it he's told you,' Charlie said, 'what he's accusing me of?'

'He says it's the accountants,' Abigail said. 'Not exactly him.'

'I've spoken to the accountants.' Charlie's face was drawn, his hands, as he lit one of his little cigars, not entirely steady. 'They don't appear to be all that sure about it. They said if I want any more information, I should speak to your husband.'

'It's all a stupid, dreadful mistake.' Abigail sank down onto the couch, then wondered if she was still welcome. 'Do you mind my being here, Charlie?'

'Why should I?'

'Like you said, he's my husband.'

'But you don't appear to agree with him on this.'

'Of course I don't.' Abigail, too restless to sit, got up again. 'I know you'd never do such a thing. It has to be a simple misunderstanding.'

'Hardly simple,' Charlie said dryly.

'No,' she admitted.

She accepted his offer of coffee, stayed a while longer, did her best to assure him that her faith in him was rock-solid, thought she succeeded. But even as she was chatting, reassuring, reaching out to him in friendship, Abigail was also registering the fact – to her very great dismay – that if she really believed Charlie, then that meant she did *not* believe Silas.

That was something she didn't want even to think about. Not just her own lack of belief in her husband, but the fact that she thought he might possibly have invented something so *nasty* about someone.

Yet that fact – or at least, the possibility of that fact – she realized as she left the agency and made her way to the tube station, did have to be examined.

Why would Silas do such a thing?

Jealousy, perhaps, she considered, waiting for the Central Line train?

The train pounded in and she got on, found a seat facing a man eating a cheeseburger, closed her eyes to blot out the sight, wished she'd brought the Mini into town. Her mind returned to the night of the recital, to the scene in the dressing room at the Jerome, to Silas's storming out. Could it be, perhaps, that he had expected her to chase after him? Had he seen Charlie going into the dressing room, and might it have bothered him that Charlie had brought her home?

Daft.

Except that Abigail knew, from the way he'd been about Jules not telling him immediately about her pregnancy, then refusing to move back home, that Silas had an unforgiving streak in his nature.

Still, giving a friend – a client – a simple lift home was hardly something that merited forgiveness. And Silas couldn't have known that Abigail had wanted to have dinner with Charlie that night, that she would have done just that had Charlie not insisted on driving her straight home.

The thoughts went on nagging at her while she walked towards the Northern Line at Tottenham Court Road, waited for a train to Highgate. That other, older conversation came back to her again, the one in which Silas had wanted to know if Charlie might be gay, and she'd said, light-heartedly, something about him really being a jealous man, and he'd said: 'Don't ever try finding out.'

So maybe jealousy could be behind this, after all. Perhaps Silas's mood had been darker than she'd realized after the dreadful way she'd behaved after the recital, the way she'd let her humiliation, her *temper*, get the better of her, the way she'd berated him instead of thanking him.

Though she'd thought he'd been as relieved to see her as she had been to see him when Charlie had dropped her off – though she'd kissed Charlie first – just a kiss on the *cheek*, for goodness sake . . .

Maybe it wasn't sexual jealousy, she thought, getting on the High Barnet-bound train. Maybe it was more of a loyalty issue – maybe Silas had been stewing over the possibility that she'd been talking about him to Charlie – and that *was* true, after all, wasn't it? If Silas believed she'd actually criticized him to the other man, then perhaps this accusation, the demand that she fire Charlie, was all down to that unforgiving streak.

If it was jealousy, though, Abigail supposed she ought, up to a point, to be flattered. It was, after all, an ongoing symptom of his love for her. And love, in her very limited experience, was often linked with control. Her mother had wanted to control her, hadn't she?

Not like this.

Nevertheless, she thought as the train drew into Euston, it *was* love, and Silas had saved her from a life of loneliness, and she did love him too, desperately, and there were things you had to do for the people you loved.

Play the cello.

Fire your manager.

Beware of your own anger.

Especially when you knew – better and more agonizingly than anyone – that you had a knack for destruction.

Chapter Twenty-Three

Things might have been all right at the christening, early in April, if Jules had not asked Abigail if she would consider playing, unaccompanied, in the church.

'This is something,' she said, 'that I really, badly want.'

'Are you sure?' Abigail asked.

'Never more so,' Jules said.

After that – Jules told Abigail later – it seemed only right and proper to invite Charlie Nagy, who she liked and who, she realized – even if Silas did not appear to – had been a good friend to Abigail; and in Jules's opinion, Abigail had far too few friends, which was at least partly due to Silas, so she had determined to seek neither Abigail's nor Silas's opinion about extending the invitation.

Arriving alone at St Barnabas Church on Highgate Hill on the day in question (Abigail having arrived early so that she could be sitting, ready and waiting with her cello, near the font), and catching sight of Charlie in a pew three rows from the front, Silas strode straight over to where Jules stood waiting with Oliver in her arms.

'You'll have to tell Nagy to leave,' he told her.

'Forget it,' Jules said.

'I won't have him at my nephew's christening.'

'God.' Jules reddened slightly, smiled at the vicar. 'Stop being so pompous, Silas, and kiss Ollie instead.'

'As soon as that man leaves,' Silas said.

'Darling—' Abigail's left arm cradled her cello, her right hand was clenched around the bow '—*please*. Not now.'

'I think maybe we might begin,' the vicar asked.

Silas ignored him.

'I suppose you knew about this,' Silas said to Abigail.

'Abigail did not know,' Jules told him. 'For heaven's sake, Silas, get a grip, for Ollie's sake, if no one else's.'

In the third row, Charlie stood up.

'No.' Jules threw a look of abject apology in the vicar's direction and walked swiftly down the aisle to the third row. 'I'm so sorry about this, Charlie.'

'Best if I go,' he said quietly.

'Absolutely not.' Jules stroked her son's dark hair. 'Please, Charlie.'

Charlie nodded, sat down again.

'Right,' Silas said to Abigail. 'That's it. We're leaving.'

'Don't be silly.' Abigail stood up, hampered by the cello. 'Silas, forget Charlie and focus on Ollie.' Jules was coming back to the font. 'See how gorgeous he looks in your lovely gown.'

'Yes, Mr Graves,' the vicar said. 'He really is a beautiful baby.'

'Abigail.' Silas ignored the other man again. 'Come on.'

'I don't believe you, Silas,' Jules said angrily, and Ollie began to cry. 'Now see what you've done, acting like some tyrant.'

'That really is it.' Silas turned to Abigail again. 'Are you coming or not?'

'Not.' Abigail sat down again, clung to her cello, and determined not to cry.

As Silas stalked out of the church.

She played the *Prelude* from Bach's Cello Suite No. 1, playing, curiously, she thought, more beautifully than she ever had in her life, her misery, she supposed, flowing out of her into the music.

'You made the whole thing,' Jules told her afterwards, back at the flat, while her guests ate and drank and chattered. 'You cut right through the bad atmosphere, made it so moving.'

'It must have been very hard for you,' Charlie said, then turned to Jules. 'You should have let me leave. I wouldn't have minded – at least, I would have understood.'

'I wouldn't,' Jules said.

Charlie watched her move away to talk to some of her other guests. 'She really is very nice, isn't she?' he said to Abigail.

'Jules is the nicest person I know.' Abigail shook her head. 'I just don't understand what got into Silas.'

'Want me to drive you home?' Charlie asked gently.

Abigail remembered the last time he'd done that.

'No, thank you,' she said. 'I'm not leaving yet.'

'Have you spoken to him since church?'

She shook her head again, clenched her jaw.

'Maybe you should phone,' Charlie said. 'Make sure he's all right.'

'I expect he is,' she said, tightly.

'Phone anyway,' he said. 'For Jules's sake, if not his.'

'You're a very nice person too, aren't you?' Abigail said.

'Not according to Silas,' Charlie said, and grinned.

She phoned from Jules's bedroom, where Asali had burrowed her way into the pile of coats on the bed, found Silas not at home, but at the studio.

'Are you okay?' She almost hoped he would say that he was not, that he was unwell, anything to at least slightly mitigate his behaviour.

'As well as can be expected,' Silas replied.

Abigail took a breath. 'Will you come to Jules's?'

'I'm not sure that would be a very good idea.'

'It would be the best possible idea,' Abigail said. 'Jules would certainly enjoy the party far more.' She paused. 'And you'd be making me happy.'

There was a pause.

'Is he there?' Silas asked.

'Yes,' Abigail answered.

He hung up.

'If you'd like to stay here tonight,' Jules said almost two hours later, 'Ollie and I would be more than happy to have you.'

'I don't know about Ollie,' Abigail said, 'but you look absolutely shattered. And I think I'd probably be a bit of a downer.' She paused. 'One downer per family's enough for any christening.'

'You made it perfect,' Jules reminded her. 'And my brother's a perfect fool.'

'I still can't believe he did that to you.'

'You, too,' Jules pointed out.

'I don't matter, not today. This was your day, and Ollie's.'

'All the same to Ollie,' Jules said. 'But I have wanted to think of this as Ralph's day, too, in a way, and Silas did his best to ruin it.'

'I'm so sorry,' Abigail said.

'Not your apology to make,' Jules said.

In Edison Road, Silas was sitting at his desk browsing over the most recent shots he'd taken of Abigail during a stroll they'd taken on the Heath last Sunday. She was laughing in some of the pictures, but in others she was calm-faced, her features in repose.

He examined those, trying to see if the young woman he had first seen outside the Wigmore Hall – the skinny, tired girl who'd lifted her cello as if it had been a huge child – was still visible.

The fragility was still there, the vulnerability in the beautiful grey eyes.

Not there earlier that day, in church.

111

Disappointment, embarrassment. Even anger.

Abigail, the stroppy wife.

Something well and truly missing, and here in these photographs too, he suddenly saw. The wonder, the gratitude with which she had so often gazed at him, because she loved him so much and because he loved *her*, and because he didn't mind the terrible thing she had done.

It was a long time since she had called him Phoenix.

In Jules's sitting room, Abigail sat on the sofa beside Charlie, who was gently scratching the dachshund's ears.

'Jules says she seems to like the baby,' he said.

'Asali is a wise dog,' Abigail said.

'Whenever you're ready,' Charlie said, 'if you like, I'll give you a lift.'

'Thank you,' Abigail said. 'But I'm still not ready to go home.'

The doubts she'd felt earlier when he'd offered to drive her had gone. The call and Silas's bloody-mindedness had seen to that.

'Would you like—' Charlie was tentative '—to go to a restaurant?'

She shook her head. 'I'm not very hungry.'

Too upset to eat. Too fed up to go home and even *think* of forgiving Silas.

'You'd be very welcome, if you wanted, to come to my place for a cup of something,' he said.

'Make it a glass of something strong,' Abigail said, 'and you've got a deal.'

Silas, just arrived and looking for a parking place outside his sister's flat, saw them emerge together, saw that Abigail was not carrying her cello, was unencumbered, stepping lightly.

He stopped, turned off his lights, reversed into a resident's bay.

Watched them get into Nagy's MG.

Waited till the old sports car growled into life.

Waited till it had moved off to the end of the road, then turned his lights back on and followed the other car as it turned left into Hornsey Lane.

If Nagy turned left at the next main junction, Silas realized, that probably meant they would be going to Muswell Hill.

The MG turned right into Hornsey Rise.

South.

Silas waited a moment, and followed.

All the same.

All so easily influenced by other men. Graham Francis first, robbing him and Jules of Patricia; then Ralph, luring Jules away from him.

Now Nagy was trying to steal Abigail, he knew it, *knew* it.

Silas's jaw clenched so hard he could hear his back teeth grind.

Don't let him.

Easier said.

She's your wife.

But if Abigail was tiring of him, doubting him. If Nagy tempted her . . .

Let no man put asunder.

The MG was three cars ahead, speeding on.

Silas's head ached.

He thought of Nagy touching her, taking advantage of her, and Christ knew Abigail was vulnerable, more than most . . .

No man.

In the kitchen of his garden flat in Notting Hill, Charlie Nagy opened a bottle of red wine and emptied a pack of dried *fusilli* into a pan of boiling water, and told Abigail, sitting at his counter, that even if she thought she had no appetite, something warming and simple might make her feel a little better.

She drank the wine, played with some pasta, drank some more wine.

Not being, ordinarily, a big drinker, the alcohol went to her head, suddenly, while Charlie was answering the telephone.

'Know what I need, Charlie?' she said when he'd finished.

'Tell me,' he said.

'A cuddle,' Abigail said. 'That's what I need.'

'Perhaps,' Charlie suggested, 'you need to go home.'

'Not yet,' she said. 'Cuddle first.'

Charlie thought about Silas's seriously nasty side, and hesitated. And then he looked at Abigail, swaying slightly on one of the stools at his breakfast counter, and found it impossible not to give in and put his arms around her.

'Oh, God, Charlie,' she said.

Her hair, its wonderful pale gold, tickled his chin, smelled of shampoo. He wanted to bury his face in that hair.

'Oh, *God*, Charlie—'

She pulled away, got clumsily off the stool, ran from the kitchen.

'Abigail?'

He went into the hall, saw that she'd vanished into the bathroom, heard, from the sounds behind the closed door, that she was being sick.

He winced in sympathy, thought of following her, holding her head, helping.

'Not a great idea, Charlie,' he murmured to himself.

He waited, instead, in the hall, for her to emerge.

'I'm so sorry,' she said when she did, plainly embarrassed.

'Don't be silly.' He took her arm, circumspectly, helped her into the sitting room. 'Poor you,' he said. 'What a bugger of a day.'

'It's not,' she agreed, weakly, 'been too great.' She sank into an armchair. 'I shouldn't really say that. The christening was beautiful, and the party, and you making supper for—' She stopped abruptly at the thought of food.

'Here.' Charlie handed her a glass of water. 'Sip it.'

'I should never have drunk so much.'

'I shouldn't have let you.'

'I'm not a child,' she pointed out. 'I ought to have known better.'

They sat for a little while longer, and then Abigail, feeling stronger, told Charlie she was ready now to go home.

'High time anyway,' she said, 'for you to get a bit of peace and quiet.'

'I'm in no rush for you to go,' Charlie said. 'But I suppose you ought to.'

'Silas will probably be worrying.' She shook her head. 'I daresay I shouldn't be letting that trouble me, but I'm afraid I can't help it.'

'Of course you can't,' Charlie said. 'You love him.'

She nodded.

'Let me get my keys,' he said.

'No,' she said quickly. 'You're not driving.'

'I haven't had that much—'

'I'll get a cab.' She smiled. 'If you don't mind calling for one.'

'It's not necessary,' Charlie said.

'It's totally necessary,' Abigail insisted. 'I won't let you drive all that way.'

They emerged into Jasper Gardens fifteen minutes later, arms linked as they walked down the short pathway and just along the road to the Vauxhall parked by Garden Walk in which a man, presumably her driver, sat reading by the car's small interior light.

'You going to be okay?' Charlie asked Abigail at the kerb.

'Course,' she said. 'Quite sober now.'

The driver leaned back to open the rear door, checked she was his fare.

'Thank you, Charlie,' Abigail said.

'Nothing to thank me for,' he said.

'You're a very good friend,' she told him. 'Means such a lot.'

'To me, too,' he said.

Standing behind a white van parked on the opposite side of Jasper Gardens, the VW parked out of sight in the next road, Silas raised his

Nikon and took a series of photographs of his wife and her former manager embracing.

The pain in his head was intense now.

Observing them through the viewfinder, he found, did nothing to lessen it.

Chapter Twenty-Four

Getting home, finding the house empty, Abigail phoned the studio and heard the answering machine pick up.

She waited for the tone.

'Silas?' She paused. 'Silas, are you there?'

Nothing.

'Silas, I'm home, and I'm hoping you're on your way home too.'

She waited another moment, then sighed, hung up.

She wondered if she should try Jules in case she'd heard from him, but that seemed unlikely, and Jules was almost certainly fast asleep by now, and either way, this wasn't the kind of call Jules ought to be troubled by on the night after her son's christening, and then, irrelevantly, she remembered that she had left her cello at Jules's flat, and would have to phone her tomorrow, and it was strange, after so many years, but even now she felt bad not having the instrument with her, as if she were still, somehow, letting Francesca down . . .

It was another two hours before Silas came home.

Abigail heard him closing and locking the front door, then coming up the staircase, and she considered for a moment pretending to be asleep, but if he didn't wake her up, that would just mean putting off the inevitable unpleasantness till morning, and there was still, she supposed, enough of the practical farmer's daughter left in her to see no purpose in that.

She sat up in bed and turned on her bedside light.

He was still wearing the suit he'd come to church in, though it was creased now, the jacket grimy-looking, the tie gone. He looked worn out.

'Are you all right?' she asked.

'Do you care?' He stayed near the door.

'That's a foolish question.'

'As a matter of fact,' Silas said, 'I'm very far from all right.'

Guilt overcame her, pushed her swiftly out of bed and across the room to his side. She put out her hand, afraid of being rebuffed but needing to touch him, touch his cheek. His skin was cold, yet his body was giving out waves of heat, and he smelled – or perhaps it was just his clothes that smelled – of something that she couldn't place, something sour.

'Silas?' She withdrew her hand, chilled by something in his eyes. 'What's happened? Where have you been?'

He gave no answer, just mirrored what she had done, put out his right hand and touched her cheek with his fingertips.

'Silas?' she said, uncertainly.

He took a breath, dropped his hand back to his side. 'A drink,' he said, 'before we talk. A brandy, I think.'

'I'll get you one,' Abigail said. 'You get ready for bed.'

'Nice thought,' he said, 'but I'll come down with you.' His smile was fleeting and very strained. 'Not bedroom talk, I'm afraid.'

The sense of chill in Abigail lingered as she watched him sit down in an armchair, as she found the bottle of cognac, poured him his drink – nothing for herself, God knew she'd had more than enough to last her – and handed it to him.

'You'd better sit down too,' he told her.

'I will,' she said, 'in a minute.'

'Yes,' Silas said. 'I rather expect you will.'

He took a swallow of brandy, shut his eyes briefly, then opened them again.

'You appear,' he said, 'to have an aptitude, Abigail, my beloved, for luring men to unfortunate ends.' He paused. 'First, Eddie Gibson.'

Abigail gazed at him, horror beginning to creep.

'And now—' Silas drank more cognac '—poor Charlie Nagy.'

She felt her legs going, sat quickly down.

'Told you,' Silas said.

'I don't understand.'

'Abigail-Abeguile,' he said. 'I don't think I ever realized before how apt a name that is for you.'

'What,' Abigail asked, 'have you done?'

'You might as well ask what *you* have done.'

'Silas—' harsher now '—what's happened to Charlie?'

'Gone,' he replied.

'What do you mean?'

'Joined the ranks of those who've loved Abigail Allen.' His mouth twisted as he smiled. 'Suppose I should beware.'

'Silas, what have you *done*?'

'Take it easy, sweetheart.'

118

Sweetheart.

She stared at him, felt her heart pounding, her palms sweating.

'I saw you together,' Silas told her. 'Saw Nagy with his arms around you – my wife – his mouth all over you.'

'There was nothing like that,' Abigail protested. 'All we did was say—'

'So I waited till your cab was gone—' he cut her off '—and then I gave Nagy the kicking he deserved.'

She was wordless again, staring again.

'Left him in the alley just along from his flat,' Silas said. 'Garden Walk, it's called, but it's really no more than a jumped-up alley. You probably haven't noticed it unless you know Jasper Gardens quite well.' He paused. 'Do you know it?'

She thought her heart might be about to burst.

'No?' He shrugged. 'Makes no difference. All that matters now is that Charlie Nagy's dead, and that it looks exactly like a mugging – *exactly* – and if anyone asks – not that they will, but just in case – you're going to say that I was home, that at the time of the attack – around the time you were getting into your cab, you'd only recently talked to me here. Here, at home, waiting for you.'

Abigail was having trouble breathing, and that word – *the* word – was jangling in her ears like manic tinnitus. *Dead. Dead.*

She closed her eyes, and the darkness spun around her.

She remembered Charlie, so kind and gentle, bringing her water in his sitting room after she'd been sick.

'He'd come out with his wallet in his back pocket, so I took it,' Silas was continuing, 'pulled out the cash – no cards, just thirty or so quid – and dumped it – the way they do – muggers, I mean – in a wheelie.'

Abigail opened her eyes again. 'You're making it up.'

Hope sprang up like a small creature bounding up through her chest.

'And now—' he went straight on like a well-drilled soldier on a mission '—you and I are going to burn my clothes and shoes, because I think there's a bit of blood and maybe worse on them, and we're not going to take any chances.'

'No.' Her voice sounded thick, unfamiliar in her ears, and hope was already dead again, the small creature smashed.

Not making it up.

'Yes,' he said. 'Because as you very well know, this has been your doing.'

'No,' she said. 'No, Silas.'

'Yes,' he said again, 'it has. Because you are, behind it all, Abigail, behind all that soft vulnerable stuff, really quite a dangerous woman.'

*

119

'I want to go there,' she said, some time later.

She had left the living room, left Silas, gone upstairs to be alone, found herself unable to bear being by herself, to bear *being*; had begun to pace, first in the bedroom, then along the corridor up there, moving back and forth, back and forth, as if being constantly in motion could stop the thinking, the nightmare horror.

Nothing stopped it.

'I want to go to where you left him,' she said, back in the living room where Silas still sat in the same position, as if he had not moved a muscle. 'Maybe Charlie's not dead, maybe if we get to him quickly, he could be all right.'

'Don't be stupid,' Silas said. 'I told you, he's dead. Not dying, not injured. Dead. You know about death, Abigail, and so do I.'

'But we can't just leave him.' An image of Charlie in a dark alley, on the ground, all alone, filled her mind, and she put up her hands, jammed her knuckles in her eyes, trying to blot it out. 'He's my *friend*.'

'Was your friend.' Silas was very hard. 'Your former manager, who is now dead and gone and beyond your help or anyone else's. And if you go anywhere near him, you'll be dropping me – your *husband*, remember? – in deepest crap.' He fixed her with one of his flat, stony stares. 'Or is that what you'd like? To send me to prison? Get rid of me?'

Abigail stared back at him, not really seeing him, not knowing, at that moment, *what* she saw. Too many things, flashing with blinding painfulness past her mind's eye: Silas beating Charlie, Francesca in the ambulance, her father smashing against the wall, Eddie flying into the air . . .

She cried out, one long, terrible wail of anguish, and ran from the room again, but there was nowhere to go in the house, nowhere to escape to, so she went upstairs and pulled on jeans and a sweater and shoes and went back down to the front door. Her hands shook so hard that it was hard to turn the keys, take off the chain, but she managed it, he didn't come to stop her. And then she was outside in the cool night air, surrounded by the trees that separated the house from the hill, and for a moment or two being out brought a measure of relief, but then that too was gone.

Walk, she told herself. *Leave.*

She stood still, on the pathway, feeling paralysed.

One foot in front of the other, Abigail.

She began to walk.

Exhaustion brought her back, together with the knowledge that there was no escape from this anywhere, though she dreaded having to ring the bell and confront Silas again because she had not, before she'd left, possessed the sanity to remember her keys.

The door was already open, Silas standing waiting for her.

'I thought you'd gone,' he said, his voice soft and scared, like a boy's.

Abigail came closer, saw that his eyes were red, his cheeks wet, but felt not a shred of compassion for him.

'Nowhere to go,' she said.

She passed him swiftly, trying not to touch him. Silas followed, close, but not too close, like a wary dog.

'I didn't mean it,' he said, going after her into the kitchen.

'What didn't you mean?' Abigail asked. 'To kill a good, kind man for giving your wife a comfort hug?'

'You shouldn't have been with *him* for comfort.' Humble dog already in retreat, tears already dry. 'You should have been with me.'

'You should have stayed in church, for your godson's christening.' It seemed a lifetime ago, and trivial beyond belief by comparison, yet still the words fell from her mouth as if they had a will of their own. 'Though since you didn't stay, I don't suppose you are really his godfather now, and thank Christ for that, at least.'

She thought, as she had once before, after the recital, that he was going to hit her, and she knew now he was capable of that and much more.

'Your doing, Abigail.' Words instead of slaps.

She turned to the kettle, refuge of the desperate, to make tea, as her Auntie Betty would have, and Francesca before her, and . . .

'All of it,' Silas said. 'You drove me to it.'

She picked up the kettle, gripped the handle tightly.

'Your fault Charlie was invited,' Silas bludgeoned on. 'Jules might have done the actual asking, but she still did it for you.'

My fault.

She put the kettle down, trembling again, sagging inside.

My fault.

'Your fault for going with him to his flat,' he said. 'You have to admit that, surely?' He paused. 'Surely, Abigail?'

'Yes,' she said.

'You do see that then?' Silas persisted.

'Yes.' The dreadful weariness was returning. 'Yes, I suppose I do.'

'No suppose about it,' he said.

All my fault.

'Whatever you say, Silas.'

'So you'll help me, as I asked.'

She'd forgotten what it was he'd asked her to do.

'Burn my clothes,' he said, reading her mind.

She was the dog now, whipped, cornered.

No, she said in her mind.

'Yes,' she said out loud.

'Would you like the cash from Nagy's wallet?'

Silas asked Abigail that as they stood, side by side, a little way past the fishpond, right at the back of the garden, burning his cut-up suit and shirt and shoes in the old bin that the gardeners – always different, anonymous people these days, booked periodically through an agency in Fortis Green – sometimes used for burning leaves and twigs.

'You could use it for flowers,' Silas said.

Abigail's face pinched in disgust.

'Just a thought,' he said.

He added the ten and five pound notes to the fire, stopped them from being blown out again, poking them with a branch he'd picked up from beneath an apple tree – and watched, with equal and conflicting amounts of detachment and compassion, as his wife was sick for the second time that night.

'Poor Abigail,' he said.

'You know, don't you,' she said, when they were back in the kitchen and he had switched on the kettle to boil, 'that nothing happened between me and Charlie?'

'You chose him over me,' Silas said. 'At the christening.'

'I chose Jules and Ollie,' Abigail said. 'Your sister and nephew, remember them?'

'You went home with Nagy,' Silas said.

The kettle boiled, but neither moved to touch it.

'Where he cooked me pasta, which I couldn't eat, because I was so upset over you,' Abigail told him. 'And he opened a bottle of wine, which I drank too much of, because of *you*. And he called me a cab and walked me to it and gave me a *hug*.' She was shaking, feeling sick again. 'And because of those terrible crimes, you—'

'Lost my temper,' Silas interrupted, his tone bitter. 'Lost control.' He was trembling too. 'Like you, Abigail, on the motorbike.'

'I was a *girl*,' she said. 'A young girl.'

'You were you, Abigail.'

'And it was an accident,' she said. 'Don't twist it, Silas. You've never done that before.'

'Your mother twisted it in the ambulance, remember? Told you to lie.'

'I hate you,' Abigail said, and found, to her great dismay, it was true.

'How much?' Silas asked. 'Enough to hurt me? Kill me?'

'Don't be idiotic,' she said, violently.

'You don't hate me, Abigail,' he said. 'You love me.' His eyes filled, abruptly, with tears. 'That's why you'll keep my secret. Same reason as I've kept yours. Because we do still love each other.' He wiped his eyes. 'Need each other.'

Later, during the endless night, Abigail, alone in their bedroom but unable to rest, let alone sleep, went to the music room, found Silas there, sitting upright on her small, straight-backed chair rather than on the chaise longue where he usually sat.

'Oh.' She turned to leave.

'You left your cello at Jules's,' he said, distantly.

'Yes.' She steeled herself, turned back to face him. 'I don't think I can do what you want, Silas.'

'There's nothing more you'll need to do, if no one asks any questions.'

'You've just killed my friend.' The words still sounded and tasted unreal. She clenched her fists tightly, the tips of her fingernails marking tiny crescents in her palms. 'And now you want me to cover for you, and you call that *nothing*.'

'You're my wife. I'd do it for you – have done it for you, as I keep having to point out. I've told no one the truth about you, have I?'

'You told Jules,' she reminded him. 'Not that I mind.'

'Ah, Jules.' Silas stood up. 'You trust Jules, don't you, Abigail?'

'Of course I do.'

'You're very fond of her.' Growing sharper now, less remote.

'You know I am.' Abigail's fists unclenched, her palms stung. 'What in God's name does that have to do with anything?'

'Maybe a good deal—' Silas walked over to one of the biscuit-coloured, sound-insulated walls, fingered the covering '—if you need a better reason than our marriage to side with me now.'

Abigail felt suddenly drained again, went to her chair, sank down onto it.

'Would you say,' Silas asked, 'that keeping Jules safe is important to you?'

'Of course I would,' Abigail replied tiredly.

'Good,' Silas said. 'That's good.'

'I still don't see . . .' She was too weary to go on.

'You will,' he said, 'when I've told you.'

'Told me what?' Fresh dread pushed away some of the fatigue. 'Silas, what now, for God's sake?'

He regarded her soberly, then walked over to the chaise longue, sat down.

'Comfort needed,' he said. 'Quite a story to tell.'

*

He took her, when he had finished, back out into the garden, carrying a torch, and showed her.

'We buried him here.' He stood on the crazy paving, shone the beam of light onto the moss now bordering each slab of stone, then directed the torch to the bench seat. 'Almost exactly under that.'

'I don't believe you,' Abigail said.

'I was twenty,' Silas said. 'Jules was fifteen. Ask her, if you like.'

Abigail felt pressure building in her head.

Too much, she thought, and began to turn away.

'Tell anyone about Nagy—' Silas's voice halted her '—or even *think* about leaving me – and "anyone" includes Jules, by the way – and she'll be the one I drop right in it. And when they come and dig up our dad and start asking questions about how he died, I'll tell them it was Jules who was with him at the end.'

Nightmares piling on nightmares.

'I thought,' Abigail said, 'you said he died of natural causes.'

'He stopped breathing,' Silas said. 'I suppose that's natural enough.'

He went to bed and she returned to the music room, longing for her cello, desperate to transfer a portion of her despair into something musically wild and brutal. Charlie's mischievous, round face bobbed up and down in her mind like a drowning man's, alternated with Jules's and little Ollie's.

She found no comfort in the room – even the golden fox's eyes peering out of the painted forest on the wall seemed to mock her now – so she left again, roamed around the house, began to head out into the garden, but abruptly stopped, unable to imagine ever going out there again.

A man was buried out there, or so Silas claimed.

Maybe he *was* making it all up, after all. Maybe he was just taunting her. Maybe there was something deeply warped inside his brain – *warped brain, better than killer's brain* – and he was making up horror stories to scare her, punish her.

She went to the phone, tried Charlie's home number, heard it ringing and ringing, felt hope die completely, felt anger, *rage*, rise again, ran up the stairs and into their bedroom.

Silas was asleep, his face peaceful in the dim moonlight gleaming through a chink in the curtains. Abigail stared down at him for a moment, then stooped, took hold of his left arm, shook him awake.

'What?' He looked sleepy, confused. Innocent.

'You want me to tell anyone who asks that you were home, that I talked to you here, but I didn't. If they check, they'll know I didn't call you from Charlie's.'

124

Silas shrugged. 'So you won't tell them that – they won't ask anyway.'

'But when I got back and you weren't here, I phoned the studio and left a message.'

'I know. I deleted it.' Silas sat up.

'When? On your way home from murdering Charlie?' She shook her head. 'I don't believe you.'

'I checked the machine by remote,' he said. 'Deleted it by remote.'

'They'll be able to tell that I called the studio from here,' Abigail said.

'They won't know who made the call, will they?' He looked up at her. 'God, you really are quite stupid sometimes. I'll simply say I checked my machine. Not that anyone will check, because Nagy was mugged. Wandering around alone in the dark in Notting Hill, his wallet on him, what did he expect?'

She stared down at him, hating him.

'I do hate you, you know,' she said.

'How can you hate me,' Silas asked, 'for loving you so much?'

Chapter Twenty-Five

She felt, all through the next day, like a car out of petrol yet still rolling on, fuelled by unreality.

She waited for someone – Toby Fry, perhaps, at Nagy Artists – to phone about Charlie, but no one did, and of course, since she was just a client – not *even* that, really, after Silas's accusations about the charity thing – there was no reason why anyone should call her as any kind of priority.

Jules called quite early on, asked tentatively after Silas, though Abigail knew she was checking to make sure she was okay, not her brother, and she knew, too, that she ought to offer to go to the flat, help with the clearing up, but she could not face being with Jules today, and so she said only that Silas had gone to work and that she sent a kiss to Ollie and no more than that.

'Are you all right?' Jules asked. 'No problems after Charlie got you home?'

'None,' Abigail answered.

She realized, abruptly, that Jules didn't know she'd gone with Charlie to his flat after they'd left her place, thought for a second of saying nothing at all, but the trouble with lies was that they tangled you up in the end.

'Charlie didn't actually take me home,' she said. 'We had a couple of drinks together at his place, and then he called me a cab.'

'Oh,' Jules said. 'Okay. So long as you're all right.'

Abigail said again that she was, and then she said that she had to go, because her toast was burning, and she doubted whether Jules believed that. But then again, Jules was presumably supposing that if Abigail was *not* fine today, it was because she and Silas had probably had a row over his walking out of church yesterday, and if only that were all.

If only.

She went to the Broadway, bought all the papers she could carry, sat on the upper floor at Crocodile Antiques, checking through them all, letting her coffee go cold, found nothing; went home and sat through all the London and South-East news bulletins, watching erratically, like a child daring to look at something that might be gruesome, then quickly looking away again before they actually saw it.

Yet in Abigail's case, for now at least, there was nothing to see.

She spent most of her time thinking about Silas and why he had done – or even *claimed* to have done, since she still lived in the hope that he might have been lying – such terrible things. Perhaps, she wondered, attacking a pile of ironing in the kitchen, her back resolutely to the window so that she might not raise her eyes and see the pond, the tale about Paul Graves was the clue to it all? Had Silas's and Jules's father been a dreadful man, maybe an abusive father or husband? Something must have happened to make Silas – the best, most precious thing in her life – capable of such . . .

She pushed it away, pushed the iron back and forth across one shirt after another, creating new creases, oblivious, uncaring.

It came back again, forcibly enough to make her want to scream.

To run away, never come back.

Silas came and went, driving back and forth to the studio, speaking to her with a mixture of kindness and trepidation, and Abigail saw that despite all the ugly bravado that night, despite the overlying coldness and, for the most part, apparent absence of emotion, there was now a desperate fear in him.

Of what? she asked herself. Of her leaving him, or of her reporting him to the police? Was he really depending on her feelings for Jules, if not her love for him, to stop her informing on him?

She slept out of exhaustion on the second night, but dreamed that she was lying on the lawn in their garden wrapped from head to toe in cling-film. She could see through it, hear through it, but she couldn't breathe, and all the while, Silas was sitting on the stone bench by the fishpond watching her with the most loving of smiles, but she couldn't *breathe* and he made no move to help her.

She woke up gasping and sweating, found him beside her, watching her.

'Okay?' he asked.

'Nightmare,' she said, and got out of bed.

'Want me to make you a hot drink?' Silas asked.

'No, thank you,' she said.

They came next morning, fifteen minutes after Silas had gone to Crouch End.

Abigail had been up and dressed for more than an hour, had turned down his request that she go with him, was drinking a third cup of coffee in the kitchen, trying to summon the strength to go back out and buy the papers all over again.

No need now.

Two young men in dark suits, one with dark, wavy hair, the other shaven-headed, both holding warrant cards, expressions sober.

One made the introductions, asked if she was Abigail Allen, told her he was Detective Constable Lowe from Central London AMIT, and then he told Abigail his colleague's name, but by then she'd ceased hearing *what* he was saying, was having enough difficulty not crumbling because they were there, because they had come to see her, and what did she do now, what did she *do*?

'We need to speak to you—' the first man said '—about your associa-tion with Mr Charles Nagy.'

'What about him?' She heard her voice emerge, sounding normal.

First opportunity for truth already gone.

Pray for us sinners.

It had been years since she'd said a Hail Mary, alone or in a church. Even two nights ago, in the depths of the horror, the words had not come to her, but now, faced with these men, faced with the decision she was going to have to make in the next few moments – *seconds*, now that she had already missed her first chance – the prayer seemed suddenly to fill her mind, blocking out everything else.

Now and at the hour of our death.

Not her death, Charlie's.

Hail Mary, full of Grace.

'Ms Allen,' Detective Constable Lowe said.

Abigail stared at him and the other man, found that they were in the liv-ing room, and she had, she supposed, invited them in, but she couldn't recall doing so.

'I'm afraid I have some bad news for you,' he went on.

'Unless you've already heard,' the other man said.

She looked at them blankly, all her emotions, terror, anger, *shame*, con-cealing themselves – and oh, Christ, she'd been there before, hadn't she – *'Never say that, not to anyone'* – she was all-too practised at the arts of lying about death.

They suggested she sat down while they told her about Charlie, and there were no more prayers filling her mind, different words now, clam-ouring to be heard:

He did it. Silas did it. My husband did it.

'Oh, God,' she heard herself say. 'Oh, poor Charlie.'

'When did you last see Mr Nagy?' DC Lowe asked.

They knew that, she realized, that part of her brain quite clear. If they hadn't known that, they wouldn't have come.

'The day before yesterday,' Abigail replied. 'Sunday.'

'What time, Ms Allen?' the second man asked.

'A long time,' she said. 'We were at a christening first.' She shook her head, ran her right hand through her hair. 'Sorry, you mean the last time.' She shut her eyes, opened them again. 'I'm not sure. About ten-thirty, eleven. In the evening.' She shook her head again. 'I don't remember the exact time, I'm sorry.'

'That's all right,' DC Lowe reassured her. 'It's a dreadful shock. Please take your time.'

'Charlie made me some pasta, and then he ordered me a cab.' Her heart had begun to pound so violently, it was hard to believe the men couldn't hear it. 'He saw me out to the car when it came.' She closed her eyes again briefly. 'And that was it. When we drove away, Charlie was waving.'

'Yes,' DC Lowe said. 'That's what your cab driver told us.'

'Oh,' Abigail said.

'Did you notice anyone in the street when you and Mr Nagy came outside?' the second officer asked. 'Anyone hanging around or just walking along?'

Last chance.

She shook her head. 'No one,' she said.

It was, suddenly, just for a few moments, frighteningly easy for her to lie. She had left Charlie before it happened, she *had* seen no one, nothing suspicious.

She thought back to the scene.

Walking out of Charlie's front door, turning towards the cab, parked a little way along the road, close to Garden Walk, where Silas had told her . . .

She shuddered.

'All right?' DC Lowe said.

Abigail nodded, remembered that the cab driver had been reading, realized that he'd been unlikely to have noticed much, could not have been a reliable witness.

'There was a van,' she said.

'What kind of van?' the second man asked.

'I don't know,' Abigail said. 'It was white, I think.'

'Was there a driver?' he asked. 'A passenger?'

'No,' she answered. 'Not that I noticed. It was just there, parked across the road from where the cab was waiting for me.' She shook her head.

'There wasn't anything special about it – the van – but I'm trying to think what I saw.'

'Good,' DC Lowe said, encouragingly.

The men waited.

Abigail shook her head again. 'That's all,' she said. 'There was nothing.'

Except Silas, somewhere, watching, waiting.

'No one,' she said, and the moments of finding it a little easier were gone.

'When you were driving away, perhaps?' DC Lowe asked. 'Anyone parking a car, coming around the corner, maybe? Any other vehicles at all that you noticed, coming in the other direction, passing your cab?'

'Nothing,' Abigail said again. 'If there was anyone – I'm sure there must have been other cars – but I don't remember noticing anything.' She paused. 'I was very tired.'

And drunk.

She waited for them to tell her that the driver had seen something, someone, a man with golden hair in a suit, waited for them to say that they knew she was lying, that they knew she knew what had happened to Charlie and who had done it, and maybe they could hear the words going around her head again.

He did it. Silas did it.

DC Lowe was asking her something, and she realized she hadn't heard, forced herself to concentrate again.

Tea. That was all. He was suggesting tea.

She knew she ought to offer to make some for them, but all she wanted, now that she had told her lies, compounded her sins, was for them to leave as quickly as possible, and so she shook her head, told them she didn't want anything, offered them nothing, hoped that they would see it as shock rather than inhospitableness.

And then, abruptly, sickeningly, she heard herself asking them what exactly had happened to Charlie, and DC Lowe answering that it seemed to be a case of a particularly brutal mugging.

It looks exactly like a mugging, Abigail heard Silas saying.

Bragging.

Tell them.

'We'll need you to make a statement,' the second man said.

'If you're up to it,' DC Lowe said.

Abigail hadn't realized till then that there were tears in her eyes. Grief, the policemen probably thought, and that was true enough, except that the grief was not just for poor, lovely Charlie. She was grieving for other deaths too. Of her marriage. Of her belief in her husband.

Of the last remaining shreds of her own innocence.

'Of course I'll make a statement,' she said.

She showed Silas the card they'd left her, in case something came to her.

'How did they know you'd been there?' he asked.

'I don't know,' she said. 'I think the cab driver told them.'

'You did well,' he said, 'from the sound of it.'

'You think so?' she asked, ironically.

'I'm sorry you had to deal with it on your own,' he said.

'I got used to dealing with things on my own in the past,' Abigail said. 'I expect I'll get used to it again.'

'What do you mean?' Silas asked.

He looked afraid again.

Of her leaving him. That was all he had to be afraid of now, she realized, since she had done what he'd wanted.

'You're not alone, Abigail,' Silas said. 'That's the whole point, isn't it? Of what we have. So long as we have each other, we'll never be alone.'

'Funny,' she said, dully. 'I don't think I've ever felt this alone before.'

Jules phoned early that evening.

'Have you heard?' She sounded upset.

'Yes,' Abigail said.

'I just saw it in the *Standard*,' Jules said. 'I can't believe it.'

Abigail swallowed. Forced the words out.

'The police were here.'

'Oh, my God,' Jules said.

'I was one of the last people to see him,' Abigail said.

'I was trying to work it out.' Jules paused, horror still sinking in. 'It must have happened soon after you left. Oh, my God, suppose you'd been with him?'

'I wasn't,' Abigail said, almost harshly.

'Are you all right?' Jules asked. 'Is Silas there?'

'No. He's at the studio.'

He had gone, looking pained, almost bereft, shortly after their last exchange.

'Shall I come over?' Jules offered.

'I'm all right.' Abigail looked down at her left hand, saw that her nails were cutting into the palm again, made no effort to unclench her fist. 'You've got Ollie, and Silas will be home soon.'

'I could bring Ollie over,' Jules said, 'if you'd like.'

'No,' Abigail said. 'Thank you, but I'm fine, Jules.'

'I'm just so sorry.' She was very gentle. 'I didn't know him as well as you, obviously, but I really liked him.'

'Me, too.' Abigail was close to tears again, wanted desperately to put down the phone, put an end, at least for a little while, to the fabrication.

'Have you ever met Charlie's sister?' Jules asked.

'No.' Abigail remembered, vaguely, his mentioning her once or twice.

'He told me about her after the christening,' Jules said. 'I think he said she's called Maggie.' She thought back. 'Maggie Blume. She has an art gallery in Swiss Cottage. Charlie said he adored her.'

Abigail put down the phone, her hand shaking violently.

It rang again just seconds later. She thought, for a moment, that she might scream, but she did not scream and the phone kept on ringing.

'Darling, are you all right?' Jules was anxious.

'Yes,' Abigail said. 'Sorry.'

'Don't be daft,' Jules told her. 'You're very upset.'

'I'm okay,' Abigail said.

The urge to scream had gone, a great weariness in its place.

'If you don't want me to come over now,' Jules said, 'how about coming over tomorrow for lunch at the flat?'

'I don't know.'

'You could pick up your cello,' Jules said. 'Or I could drop it off.'

'I'll come,' Abigail said.

She hadn't known what else to say, could think of no good excuse, at that second, to refuse. Besides which, the prospect of seeing Jules and Ollie was as pleasant as any prospect could have been.

Except how was she going to spend any time with Jules, her friend, Silas's sister, and *not* tell her what had really happened to Charlie?

It was horribly easy to keep silent, as it happened, her ability to lie to Jules even more frightening to her than it had been with the police. And infinitely easier to pretend, for a while, that life was sane, than to talk about faked muggings or to ask questions about allegedly long-buried fathers:

'Jules, did you *really* help Silas bury your dad in the back garden?'

Let alone:

'Silas implied that you did something to your father to help him on his way?'

Abigail sat by the summer-bare fireplace in Jules's sitting room with Asali beside her, looking at Jules, breast-feeding Ollie in an armchair close to a photograph of Ralph. She felt sure, suddenly, that the tale about Paul Graves, at least the part about Jules's involvement, had been a lie, a piece of gratuitous, unspeakably sick nastiness.

Except that she knew now, didn't she, that Charlie's death had been no lie?

Unless maybe – one more meagre hope to cling to – Silas had just been outside Charlie's home obsessing about her being inside, waiting to see when or *if* she would leave. And maybe after she'd driven off in the cab, there really *had* been a mugger, and maybe Silas had simply been a witness, had decided to use the fact to punish her?

Cling to that, Abigail.

And to the abusive father notion, too, a peg to hang his wickedness on.

'So the police didn't really seem to have anything?' Jules broke into her thoughts, and moved her son, gently, from one breast to the other.

'Not that they shared with me,' Abigail said.

Jules fell silent again, waiting while Ollie settled, and then she said:

'I expect someone will call you, about the funeral.'

Abigail felt sick.

'I expect they will.'

She stroked the dachshund, managed not to shudder at the prospect of Charlie's funeral, knew that if she was invited, there would be no way she could bear to attend.

Chapter Twenty-Six

'You'll have to go,' Silas told her, twelve days later, after Toby Fry had telephoned, at last, to let Abigail know that the funeral was to take place that coming Sunday at a Jewish cemetery in Hertfordshire.

'I can't,' Abigail said.

'I'll come with you,' Silas said.

'You couldn't. It would be obscene.' She felt sick. 'How could you stand it?'

'I've stood worse,' Silas said.

Abigail said nothing, chose not to ask – not to *know* – what 'worse' might be.

She had gone through the last fortnight with the sense that she was living with a man she had thought she knew well, but who she now realized she did not really know at all. Her husband was a stranger, alien to her. A man who claimed to have killed because of her, which was, she supposed, one reason why she had lied to the police for him. Silas had told her he'd killed Charlie because of *her*.

Which was part, she supposed, too, of what was keeping her from leaving him.

Those three words, still repeating themselves in her head.

All my fault.

She saw no police at the funeral – neither DC Lowe nor his partner, nor anyone looking in any way out of keeping with the other mourners – yet all parts of the service were horrific to Abigail. First the gathering of mourners outside the chapel, then the prayers inside, some in English, some in Hebrew, and the eulogy, everyone clutching little black prayer books, saying Kaddish together, everyone seeming to know it but Abigail – though at least, for a while, in the chapel, she was separated from Silas, who stood on the opposite side of the hall with the men, and if anyone would have told her just a few weeks before that she might be grateful to be apart from him, she would not have believed them.

'All right?' he asked, outside, beginning the long walk to the grave.

She neither answered nor glanced at him, wondering how she could bear to stand beside him during the next part, while Charlie's coffin was lowered into the ground, and she had been right, it *was* an obscenity, and she was as guilty of it as Silas was.

Hail Mary, full of Grace, the Lord is with thee.

She shut her eyes as mourners took turns shovelling earth onto the coffin's lid, and her mind slid back to her parents' funeral.

No grace for me.

No forgiveness, for that or for this, then or now.

'Come on,' Silas said, softly against her ear.

Abigail opened her eyes, saw that they were all moving away, back towards the chapel for more prayers, and the women and men separated again, and she was no longer listening at all, vaguely heard the rabbi extending an invitation to go back to someone's house, telling them about yet more prayers that evening, and then it was, finally, over.

Silas found her in the crowd almost instantly.

'We have to file past the mourners,' he told her.

'No,' Abigail said. 'We can't.'

'We have to,' he said.

She saw that he was right, that a long queue was forming, that several people were now sitting with their backs to the wall, shaking hands or kissing and exchanging a few words with each person who passed them.

'I *can't*.' She felt panic rising. '*We* can't.'

'Of course we can.' Silas found her hand, pulled her into the line. 'It's nothing. Don't think about it, just do it.'

She took her hand out of his, looked at his face, saw that he was pale but composed, felt a fierce, bright flash of hatred for him and looked away again, straight ahead, through the people ahead of her, into space.

'Abigail.' Silas nudged her, pushed her.

She looked down, saw a woman of about seventy, red-eyed and exhausted looking, a younger man beside her, dark-haired, very strained and another woman of about forty, Abigail supposed, wearing a black suit and trim hat.

Maggie Blume, she guessed, quailing.

She did what the man directly before her did, shook hands with the older woman and then the man, and then –

'Abigail?'

The younger woman took her hand and did not release it.

'You're Abigail Allen, aren't you?' she said. 'I've seen your photograph in Charlie's office.' She paused. 'I'm Maggie, his sister.'

Abigail looked down at her, saw Charlie's warm eyes looking out of her face, and yearned for the floor beneath her feet to part, so that she might descend, as poor Charlie had, down into the earth, into oblivion.

'I'm so sorry,' Abigail said, through lips that felt numb.

'I'm Abigail's husband.' Silas moved beside her, extended his right hand. 'Silas Graves.'

'Yes.' The bereaved woman shook it cursorily.

'We're both extremely sorry about your loss,' Silas said.

'Thank you,' Maggie Blume said, noticeably cool, then looked back at Abigail. 'Will you be coming back to our house?'

Abigail shook her head. 'No, I don't—'

'I'm afraid we can't,' Silas said swiftly.

'I'm sorry.' Abigail felt faint.

'It's all right,' Maggie Blume said, looked at the still-long queue of people waiting, and beckoned Abigail closer. 'I just want to tell you—' she lowered her voice to a whisper '—in case it's been troubling you, that Charlie didn't blame you for a second for that nastiness with the charity.'

Abigail stared down at her, tried to find the right words, came up empty.

'And I want to make sure you know how he felt about you.' Maggie took her hand again, clasped it. 'I'm so glad he was with you that last evening.'

'How did you know?' Abigail asked, stupidly.

'I phoned him while he was making you supper.'

Behind her, people shifted, politely impatient.

'Better move on.' Silas took Abigail's arm. 'Come on, darling.'

Abigail looked down at Maggie again. 'Thank you.'

'Thank you for coming,' the other woman said.

'We're very sorry,' Silas said again.

Maggie Blume did not answer him.

'It must have been his sister who told the police I was there,' Abigail said when they were back in the car. 'Not the cab driver, after all.'

Silas started the engine.

'You never mentioned her phoning Charlie,' he said.

'I didn't know,' Abigail said. 'And even if I had, why should I have told you?'

'Common sense,' Silas said. 'In the circumstances.'

He reversed carefully out of the parking place, joined yet another queue, of cars making their way out onto the narrow road.

'Down to her then,' he said, looking in his rearview mirror. 'The police turning up like that, hassling you.'

Abigail turned, stared at him again.

'Don't you feel anything?'

He returned her gaze. 'What do you think?'

'I don't know,' Abigail said.

The car moved forward a few feet, then stopped again.

Silas took another look into his rearview mirror.

Saw Charlie's sister standing outside the chapel with a group of people.

Talking to them, but not looking at them.

She was looking, he was certain, at his car.

Not at Abigail, but at him.

She looked, he felt, even from that distance, puzzled.

Chapter Twenty-Seven

He had just gone out to the car next morning, and Abigail, who – needing to be occupied, finding idleness intolerable – had agreed to assist with a children's sitting at ten o'clock, had just returned to the kitchen to ensure that she really had turned off the gas hob, when the phone rang and she picked it up before the answering machine could take over.

'It's Maggie Blume.'

Abigail's legs went, and she sat quickly down.

'Abigail?'

'Yes.' She couldn't breathe. 'Sorry, we were just on the way out.'

'I won't keep you,' Charlie's sister said. 'It's just that I didn't get a chance yesterday to ask if the police have been in touch with you.'

Abigail felt blood drain from her face and hands.

'Yes,' she said. 'They came some time ago.'

'Oh,' Maggie Blume said. 'Then I take it you weren't able to help them?'

'No.' Abigail took a breath. 'I'd already left Charlie when it – happened.' She sounded almost normal, hated herself for it. 'So there wasn't anything I could really tell them.'

Her lips – her whole face – felt numb again.

'And when you left,' the other woman said, 'you didn't see anyone in the road? No one in a parked car, perhaps?'

'No one except my cab driver,' Abigail said. 'Though as I told the police, I was very tired after a long day.'

'Yes,' Maggie Blume said. 'Charlie told me.'

Getting into the VW beside Silas, Abigail told him about the call.

'Was she okay with what you said?' he asked.

'She seemed it,' Abigail said.

'No problem then,' Silas said.

*

At eight-fifteen on Thursday morning, while Silas was taking a shower and Abigail was putting coffee beans into the grinder, Maggie Blume telephoned again.

'I spoke to the police again yesterday,' she said. 'I thought you might be interested in an update.'

The numbness returned – the left half of Abigail's face this time, and her fingertips, and she wondered, dimly, if perhaps she was going to have a stroke.

Make it a large one, she thought, wryly, then instantly retracted, asked God to forgive her or, at least, to make her punishment less horrible than that.

Perhaps Silas is your punishment.

That thought shook her profoundly.

'Abigail?'

Maggie Blume's voice roused her.

'Yes,' Abigail said, and saw that she'd spilled coffee beans all over the worktop. 'Sorry. Something was about to boil over.'

'No update to speak of, really,' the other woman said.

Abigail didn't know what to say, said nothing.

'They're very kind and polite, but I get the feeling they don't hold out too much hope. Someone told me that random muggers are very hard to catch.'

'I suppose they must be,' Abigail said.

'That's the real reason I'm phoning you again,' Maggie Blume went on. 'For Charlie's sake, to ask you to please, please keep on thinking, trying to remember, and if even the tiniest thing comes back to you—'

'I'll tell you,' Abigail said swiftly. 'Or rather, the police.'

'I could give you a number.'

'No need,' Abigail said. 'They left me a card.'

She was still shaking when Silas came down in his white towelling robe, hair slicked down and darker-looking from the shower.

'She called again,' Abigail said.

'What now?' Silas saw the scattered coffee beans, shook his head, went to wipe them away.

Abigail reported the conversation she'd had with Maggie.

'Don't you think it's strange,' she asked, 'the way she keeps phoning me?'

'Not especially.' Silas put the lid on the grinder.

'You don't think she—' Abigail hesitated '—might suspect something?'

'Don't get paranoid,' Silas told her.

'Hardly paranoid,' she said hotly. 'Considering.'

'From what you've told me—' he remained calm '—I'd say this is simply a bereaved sister clutching at straws, and you just happen to have been the last person to have been with her brother.'

'Maybe you're right,' she said.

'Anything else,' Silas added, 'is just your guilty imagination.'

Abigail retreated up to the music room.

Played the cello for her mother until her arms ached.

Chapter Twenty-Eight

Maggie Blume, walking from her mansion flat in Randolph Avenue to Maida Vale tube station the following Tuesday afternoon in the first week of May, was just starting to cross Elgin Avenue when she spotted Silas Graves on the opposite side of the road.

Watching her, camera in hand.

Raising it.

Taking her photograph.

Silas, looking through the viewfinder, observed her distraction.

He lowered the Nikon, turned his head slightly, saw the van – yellow, with large black lettering blazoned on the side – coming, too fast, towards her; saw Maggie Blume realize, an instant too late. Saw her stumble and fall.

Saw the van hit her, toss her into the air and down again, hard, onto the road.

He waited, feeling sick, until the worst of his nausea was past, and a good cluster of people had gathered around her, and then he crossed the road and joined the small, horrified crowd.

'Poor, poor woman,' a man beside him said. 'Didn't stand a chance.'

'Dreadful,' Silas agreed. 'Has someone called an ambulance?'

The man nodded, seeming unable to tear his eyes away from the limp, bloodied rag-doll that was all now left of Maggie Blume.

'No go, though, is there?' he said. 'She's had it, poor thing, hasn't she?'

'Dreadful,' Silas said again.

And raised his camera to take another picture.

Before turning and walking away.

'Have you seen the *Ham & High*?'

Jules's voice, on the phone late on Friday morning, was terse.

'Not yet, no,' Abigail said, brushing her hair. 'What's up? I'll be with

143

you soon.' Drew was taking time off for a dentist's appointment that afternoon, and she'd promised to go to the shop at one-thirty, so that Jules could relieve Ollie's babysitter.

'More awful news, I'm afraid,' Jules said.

Abigail's stomach pitched. 'What's happened now?'

'Maggie Blume's had an accident,' Jules said. 'Knocked down in the street.'

Abigail dropped her hairbrush, opened her mouth to ask how Maggie was, but no words came out.

'It's just so unbelievably horrible,' Jules went on. 'Brother and sister both gone in such a short space of time.'

'Gone?' Abigail echoed.

'Instantly, apparently,' Jules said.

Operating on automatic pilot was becoming second nature to her, Abigail dismally observed as she worked through her shift at the bookshop. She had taken care to arrive with only a minute to spare, so there would be no time for conversation with Jules, and after that it grew a little easier, with just books for company and the occasional customer. And maybe her desperate need to occupy herself had improved her sales technique, because she sold more than one title to each person who came in, though the thought that Jules would be pleased by that shaved not even the smallest edge off her shame for keeping the truth from her.

Maybe not for much longer.

She had decided that much, at least; had told herself, *vowed* to herself as she went through the motions of bookselling, that if these new worst suspicions were realized, that if Silas *had* done this latest unspeakable thing, she would not only leave him, but she would also go first to Jules with it all – *all* – and then, unless Jules beseeched her not to (Abigail wasn't sure what she would do if that happened, would worry about that if it did), she would phone the number on that card, tell DC Lowe everything, and if they charged her with perjury, so be it.

And if Silas threatened her . . .

The truth.

All that mattered now.

Maggie Blume's art gallery in Swiss Cottage was easy to find; an oasis of calm in the midst of traffic-pounded Finchley Road between a Chinese restaurant and a dry cleaners.

A woman in a black suit with very short blond hair, sitting at a small polished rosewood desk halfway to the rear of the gallery smiled vaguely as Abigail approached, then, looking at her more closely, said:

144

'You were at Charlie's funeral, weren't you?'

'I was.' Abigail, already wishing she hadn't come, introduced herself.

'I'm Yolande Ross,' the other woman said. 'Maggie's partner.' She motioned to a chair on the other side of her desk. 'You look in need of a seat.'

Abigail sat down.

'I think we're all shell-shocked,' Yolande Ross said.

'I was just across the road—' Abigail had prepared her script on her journey from Crouch End '—and I noticed the gallery, so . . .'

'You've not been here before?'

Abigail shook her head.

'Maggie's pride and joy.' Yolande Ross's eyes filled. 'Sorry.'

'No, please.' Shame coursed through Abigail. 'It's a beautiful gallery.'

'Thank you.' Maggie Blume's partner paused. 'Can I get you something to drink? You do look very pale.'

'Nothing, thank you,' Abigail said. 'I'm fine.'

She realized that the other woman was waiting for her to go on.

'I didn't really know Maggie—' she faltered slightly '—at least, not till Charlie's funeral. It's just that, coming so close to his death . . .' She took a breath, forced herself to get to it. 'Do you know what happened, exactly?'

'Yes,' Yolande Ross said. 'Unfortunately I do.'

Abigail waited for the sword to fall.

'Two of the witnesses – there were several, I gather – told Simon – that's Maggie's ex-husband – that it was entirely her fault. That she'd stepped out into the road, hesitated, for some reason, then walked on, right into the van's path.'

Abigail saw she was close to tears. 'I'm so sorry. I didn't mean . . .'

'I'm all right,' the other woman said. 'It's just so unlike Maggie to be scatty, but they all said she seemed miles away.' She wiped her eyes with a tissue she'd been clutching in her left hand. 'Probably thinking about Charlie.'

'No one else to blame then,' Abigail said.

Yolande Ross shook her head. 'I'm not sure if that makes it better or worse.'

'I don't suppose,' Abigail said, 'it makes much difference.'

That's all right then, she told herself ironically, her cheeks burning with the ugly flippancy of her thoughts as she drove the Mini back to Muswell Hill.

No need to leave Silas now.

Even if poor Maggie Blume had been thinking about Charlie, Silas had only actually killed – *probably* killed – one sibling, after all.

So no need to mention it to Jules, let alone the police.

Only one death.

Unless you counted the father in the garden.

'Jules phoned me earlier,' Silas said, as Abigail was transferring their lamb chops from grill to plates to table. 'She told me about Maggie Blume.'

Abigail sat down. 'Did she?'

'I can't help wondering,' Silas said, 'why you didn't tell me.'

'I would have,' she said.

'I suppose, really,' he said, 'I do know why.'

Abigail said nothing.

'You think I might have done away with her.' He paused. 'Understandable, in the circumstances.'

Abigail looked down at the chops, thought she might be ill.

'It's all quite extraordinarily sad, of course,' Silas said. 'But you must admit, in a macabre sort of way, it is also rather convenient.'

She had wondered if there was anything left that he could do or say to shock her further. 'How can you possibly say something like that?'

'You were the one getting so freaked out by her calls,' he said. 'Just as well for your state of mind it was so plainly, undeniably an accident.'

Abigail thought about the sparse report in the paper.

It had given no real details.

'How can you be so sure about that?' she asked.

'I can,' Silas said, 'because I was there.'

Chapter Twenty-Nine

He had described it to her as the purest of coincidences – his happening to be on Elgin Avenue at that moment – but from then on, anything that had been left of Abigail's peace of mind had been blasted away.

'You're getting very thin,' he remarked two weeks after Maggie Blume's death. 'Almost as skinny as when I first saw you.'

She played the cello every spare moment now, could no longer bear to face Jules, had told her on several occasions that she was too busy practising and working with Silas to come to the shop.

'That's just business,' Jules had said in her easy way. 'Couldn't you at least come over to the flat? Spend a little time with Ollie and me? We miss you.'

'I will.' Abigail went on lying. 'As soon as I've mastered the new piece I'm working on.'

There was no piece. Just a jumble of notes now, sometimes raucous and aggressive, sometimes painfully beautiful and tender.

No piece or peace.

She went, frequently now, into the garden, gazed at the pond and the bench, at the place where Silas claimed he and Jules had buried their father.

When she managed to sleep at night, she dreamed either of being suffocated in clingfilm while Silas watched, or of the yard at Allen's Farm. Of Eddie and the Beastie and her family, dead and dying.

And finally, feeling that she might very soon explode with guilt and shame and unhappiness, no longer able to bear it entirely on her own, she went to church.

Abigail had no faith to speak of. Her Catholic mother, having married the vaguely Protestant but fundamentally irreligious Douglas Allen, had decided that if he was prepared to accompany her at least fairly regularly, she would try hard not to mind too much going to his 'kirk', so long as he raised no objections if she and Abigail went to Mass at *her* church when he was not of a mind to go.

'God is God,' Francesca had allowed.

Auntie Betty and Uncle Bill had been Church of Scotland, so their kirk, for the duration of her life in their home, had become Abigail's, after which, left to her own devices, she had almost wholly lapsed. She had prayed, off and on, through her life; usually, during her childhood, by rote, Hail Marys and Our Fathers; later, after innocence was gone, out of fear and her daunting isolation, just in case God really was there. Though that, too, had brought more fear, for if He was there, then He had been there in the yard that day, too, and more recently, through all the days and weeks of her terrible lies, and then . . .

Forgive me, forgive me, forgive me . . .

Never enough. Ever.

Now, after the shocks upon shocks of the last several weeks, Abigail had come to the realization that it was not so much God she needed to communicate with, but someone safely bound by their ministry. A person unable, so long as she made her approach in the prescribed manner, to betray her.

Or rather Jules.

Increasingly, it was Jules – sensitive, generous Jules – and, by extension, Ollie, who were on Abigail's mind and conscience.

'I don't matter,' she said, on her knees in the confessional at the end of the third week of May. 'Not any more.'

She had chosen Saint Peter the Apostle for no reasons other than because she had passed it regularly since coming to live in Muswell Hill, and because it had an old, comfortable looking graveyard and looked to her, in general, more welcoming than some churches.

'Bless me, Father, for I have sinned.'

The penitent's ritual beginning.

'It's been—'

Stumbling already, no recollection of when she had last made her confession.

The priest had been gentle with her, welcoming, and so she had gone on.

Her own sins only for now. Familiar, well-trodden ground, God knew.

Forgive me.

She left Silas's sins untouched. Waiting, perhaps, to see if this revisiting of her mother's beliefs might, after so long, bring the slightest easing of her beleaguered conscience. Knowing already that it would not, for it never had before, and besides, her own sins alone were not, this time, what had brought her here. Her conscience was not what mattered now.

The man on the other side of the grille sounded quite young, his voice softly Irish-accented, fleetingly reminding Abigail of a violinist she'd known at the Conservatoire who'd been raised in Dublin. The priest was matter-of-fact but kind, seeming to realize that she had not truly come for the sacrament of reconciliation, neither for an act of penance nor even absolution. That she was profoundly troubled, and, most of all, that she needed to talk.

'It's all right,' he told her once, when she paused. 'We have time.'

He gave her nothing new. She had expected nothing new. Regarding her parents and young boyfriend, he said it had been a tragic accident and she had been very young.

'What about letting the boy take the blame?' she said, harshly.

No names. She never used names, not even here in the confessional.

'Not too late—' still gentle '—if you wanted to put that right.'

Silas had said, more than once, that her lying had made no difference to Eddie or his parents, but Abigail had always known that, whatever the case with poor Eddie, the truth might have made a tremendous difference to his parents.

'It might help you,' the priest said.

'I don't matter,' she said.

'You couldn't be more wrong,' the priest told her. 'You matter very much.'

'My soul, you mean.' She sounded cynical, had not meant to, did not *feel* cynical. That was Silas's department, not hers; hers was guilt, which was still, when all was said and done, what had brought her here.

'Don't you believe in souls?' the priest asked.

Her mother and father and Eddie pounded through her mind again, followed sharply, even more violently, by Charlie and Maggie Blume.

'I don't know,' Abigail answered, though the truth was she had often hoped, even prayed, that there was no such thing as an immortal soul, or an all-seeing God, let alone eternal damnation – and all the Hail Marys in the world weren't going to help her now, and what was she *doing* here?

She got abruptly off her knees.

'I'm sorry, Father,' she said, and stumbled out of the confessional, hurrying out the way she had come through the cool of the church, moving even faster out through the doors into the brighter, noisy world of traffic and humans whose consciences were lighter and cleaner, people who had not killed or cast blame, who did not live with a murderer . . .

'Oh, *God*,' Abigail said.

She wiped her eyes, took a breath, and moved back amongst them.

*

She went back two days later, sat in a pew near the back of the church in a dark corner. Not praying or even really thinking, just sitting, feeling very tired.

Helpless.

And then the priest – who was, in the flesh, young, fair-haired and tall – came out from the vestry and glanced her way, and she stood up and left.

Not ready.

The next time, on her knees again just five days later, she told him everything.

Let it out in all its ugliness, thought she heard his intake of breath when she told him about Charlie – not that she used his or any other name, or made any reference to her relationship with anyone concerned, priestly rules or not. And then, after she told him about the father buried in the garden, about the woman run down in the street, about perjuring herself to the police, about not being able to even think of leaving Silas in case he carried out his threat to make trouble for Jules – and in any case, she said, it was all down to her, of course; everything, if one came to analyse it, was *her* fault . . .

After she had said all those things to the man on the other side of the confessional partition, she thought she detected something else, in his tone of voice.

He thought her mad.

Jules confronted her. Arrived one morning in the first week of June, unannounced, with Ollie in his buggy.

The baby was beaming. His mother was not.

'I'd like to know—'

'Why aren't you in the shop?' Abigail cut in, to divert her.

'Drew's minding the shop.' Jules pushed the buggy past Abigail, waited until the front door was closed, glanced around. 'He is out, isn't he?'

'You mean Silas?'

'Who else?' Jules was still grim-faced.

'He's in town, at a meeting at one of—'

'I don't really care where he is,' Jules interrupted again, 'so long as I get to find out what I've done to merit this treatment.'

'Jules, won't you—'

'And even if I have done something bad—' Jules forged on '—though I've absolutely no idea what that might be – then what on earth Ollie's done to deserve the same?'

'Nothing,' Abigail said. 'Oh, God, Jules, you've done *nothing*.'

'Then what the hell is going on with you?'

Abigail looked at her friend, her husband's sister, into her dark, challenging eyes, and knew that she wanted, more than anything, to share it all with her. Told herself that no matter what Silas had said about making trouble for Jules, surely he would never do such a terrible thing to his own sister?

A man who could kill another man for hugging his wife could do anything.

'I'll tell them it was Jules who was with him at the end.'

Abigail looked down at Ollie, sweet innocent baby.

Telling Jules might make her feel better. Telling the police the whole story and leaving Silas might make her feel even better than that.

Except, of course, that it was all her fault.

Not Paul Graves's death, she reminded herself.

But if she did tell, and if Silas did carry out his threat and destroy Jules's life, and Ollie's, then that *would* be her fault, too.

Abigail blinked, looked up at Jules still standing there.

'Come in,' she said, 'and have a coffee.'

Jules stayed where she was. 'Are you going to tell me what's going on?'

Abigail felt her soul sag.

'There's nothing to tell,' she said.

'In that case—' Jules turned Ollie's buggy around.

'Please, Jules, don't go.'

'I thought—' Jules opened the door '—you and I were friends.'

'We are,' Abigail said. 'Jules, of course we are.'

'Friends,' Jules said, coolly, 'share problems with each other.'

And she pushed the buggy out of the house.

Even in the loneliest times of her life before Silas, Abigail's isolation had never been quite as painful as it was now.

He had, since Maggie Blume's death, done everything possible to be a good, almost a perfect, husband. He was kind to Abigail but didn't crowd her, gave her time and space to herself. All through the rest of May and on through June, he insisted on taking her out, to restaurants and the cinema and, twice, to concerts; he bought her flowers and helped out more than usual with cooking and housework and shopping. When she came to work at Edison Road, he consulted her more than he had in the past, began inviting her along, even when no assistance was needed, on the more interesting of his shoots.

He even asked her if she wanted him to help her find a new manager.

'Why?' Abigail asked. 'So you can get jealous and arrange another mugging?'

'Don't be silly,' he said. 'If you don't want to play professionally any more, that's fine with me, though I think it's a pity.'

'Pity or not,' Abigail said, 'I don't want another manager.'

'You will still play for me, won't you?'

'If you insist,' she said.

'I don't insist.' Silas looked wounded. 'It just gives me pleasure.' He paused. 'I suppose I have that in common with your mother.'

Abigail went back to Saint Peter the Apostle. Not to Mass or to the confessional, for that had not helped her at all, but she found that she did seem to find a degree of comfort just sitting quietly inside the church or wandering among the old graves outside.

The priest joined her, one warm afternoon, moving over the grass so lightly and silently that she had no opportunity to flee.

'How are things?' he asked, with no pretence at not recognizing her.

Abigail looked at him, seeing him close up for the first time. He was, as she had thought, young and slim, with narrow features that reminded her, a little, of a greyhound's.

'All right,' she replied, then paused. 'All wrong.'

His blue eyes were keen. 'Feel like talking about it? Or would you rather be left alone?'

'I feel alone,' Abigail said, 'most of the time. Though, of course, I'm not really. Just in my head.'

'I'm Michael Moran, by the way,' he told her.

For just a moment, while they shook hands, Abigail became aware of his calmness as something almost palpable, transmitting itself to her. And then it was gone, and already she regretted its loss.

'Would you like to come into the presbytery?' the priest asked. 'I'm sure that Mrs Kenney, my housekeeper, would rustle us up some tea.'

Her hesitation was brief. 'Yes,' she said. 'I would like that very much.'

And went with him.

Silas watched from his car, parked between a Shogun and an old Metro on the single yellow line on the opposite side of the road.

Watched as they went inside together.

His head ached, and he rubbed the furrow between his eyebrows, looking down at his digital camera, at the last shot he'd taken of them in the churchyard.

The priest was young and attractive.

Silas scrolled back through the previous shots until he arrived at the one he wanted to see again.

Abigail, at the instant she had first looked up at the other man.

With her wide grey eyes.

His heart lurched with sorrow, remembering that other first time.

152

Their first time.

He couldn't remember if he'd ever seen her look at Nagy that way.

Couldn't *remember*, because whenever he thought about Nagy, blood clouded, blasted away the memories, and sounds, too, of groaning and dying.

So he couldn't remember how she had looked at Nagy.

But this was not a man, this was a priest – so it couldn't be, *couldn't* be. He would not let it be.

Chapter Thirty

'I've arranged something special,' Silas told Abigail in the third week of July. 'Something I hope will be good for you.'

'What is it?' she asked.

'A surprise.' He saw the alarm, the suspicion, in her expression, and smiled. 'Nothing like the recital,' he said. 'This is a trip.'

That startled Abigail, for they'd travelled nowhere together since Deauville.

'Where to?' she asked.

'Please,' Silas said. 'Allow me to surprise you.'

She heard his polite, gentle voice – he had many voices, she had come to realize – and felt too tired to argue. 'How will I know what to pack, if I don't know when or where we're going?'

'It's next weekend,' he told her. 'You won't need much.'

Abigail asked herself, several times as the week went on, if she really wanted to travel anywhere with a killer. Each time her answer was the same: she had already been living with a killer for weeks, eating, working, sleeping (not making love, not that, not since Charlie), so why should travel be different?

And in any case – whatever Father Michael Moran said – she was still a killer herself. And if it were not for her, Charlie would be alive, and probably Maggie too. And, by having chosen not to tell DC Lowe, by having stayed with Silas, she had become, had *made* herself, his accomplice. And whether she had done that for Jules's and Ollie's sake, or for Silas's, for love's sake, she had done it.

For better, for worse.

Worse.

No real doubt about that.

When she discovered, at Heathrow, that their destination was Edinburgh, she balked, but Silas dealt with the moment in his kindest fashion.

'If you truly don't want to go,' he said, quietly, at the check-in, 'I've no intention of trying to make you.'

'You couldn't,' Abigail told him.

'But I've had such hopes,' he said, quietly, 'of being able to do something just for you – truly just for you – for once.'

The woman holding their tickets smiled.

And Abigail, seeing the intensity in her husband's eyes, recognizing that it was, without a doubt, genuine, gave way.

He took her to the Caledonian Hotel – and she had been so desperately afraid that he would take her to The George, the hotel her daddy had been taking them to for her mother's birthday lunch that day, and the relief when it was the Caley instead was so great she could almost have danced.

If you can even think of dancing, Abigail, you're as wicked as he is.

Their room was wonderful, with high ceilings and a castle view – to the side, Silas pointed out, remembering the childhood fear she'd told him about that the castle might collapse onto Princes Street.

'See?' he said. 'Perfectly safe.'

Abigail remembered when he said that why she had loved him so much.

Blocked out the rest.

Got into the huge bed with him, and showed him.

When she saw, finally, the next day, a warm, humid summer's day, where they were going in their rental car, she became rigid with shock, her feet tramping hard on the floor mat in front of her seat, as if she were the driver, braking violently.

'How *could* you?' She stared at him. 'Silas, how could you do this?'

His jaw tightened, but he went on driving.

'You've never been back, have you?'

'You know I haven't,' Abigail said, her voice strangled.

'I thought – I still think – it could help you,' Silas told her.

The sign above the old gate was gone, no other replacing it.

'Please stop,' Abigail said, faintly.

He drove on. Through the gate.

Onto the long lane that led to the house.

Abigail shut her eyes, heard the roar of the Beastie, felt the wind in her hair.

'Open your eyes, darling,' Silas told her.

'No,' she said. 'I can't.'

But they were all there anyway, despite the cover of her eyelids. Dougie and Francesca, all done up for her birthday. And poor Eddie

Gibson, riding pillion, one arm around her waist, his hand on her shoulder, trying to warn her about the mud.

She thought her brain would burst.

'Get me out of here,' she told him.

Silas looked at her, at the eyes still clenched shut, at the tormented face.

'All right,' he said.

He took her, still in shock, to the churchyard where her parents were buried.

A sweet-smelling place, full of wild flowers, old and peaceful.

He held her hand, led her, and she didn't fight him, too numb for that.

'You can hate me if you have to,' he said, 'but I did this for you.'

He pointed to a handsome wooden bench on the path close to the grave.

Abigail looked, read the inscription carved across the top.

IN LOVING MEMORY OF FRANCESCA AND DOUGLAS ALLEN.

'I left out Eddie's name,' Silas said. 'It didn't seem right, since he's not buried here, and with people believing he was the one riding.'

'Oh, God,' Abigail said, quietly.

'Are you all right?' he asked, still holding her hand.

She didn't answer.

'Do you want some time alone?' he asked.

She nodded.

'Okay.'

She waited, heard his feet crunch away on the gravel path, and then – whether out of weakness or some primitive need – she dropped onto her knees in the grass.

Not to pray. Not even just to feel.

If I feel now, she realized, *it will overwhelm me.*

Their funeral came back to her again. Dark clothes, grim faces, eyes gazing at her, some in sympathy, some avidly curious. The coffins going down into the big grave. Her aunt and uncle on either side of her, Auntie Betty's hand gripping her arm. Not for comfort, Abigail remembered feeling. Out of duty.

More than she deserved. So much more.

Mea culpa.

She stood up quickly, jerkily, before she gave way to that.

Turned away from the grave, saw Silas standing about ten yards away on the path, watching her, felt hot rage balloon inside her – and then burst and melt away.

His eyes were pained.

For her.

She walked slowly back to him, through a cloud of midges.

Midges that day too.

'Okay?' he asked.

'I don't know,' she said. 'Perhaps.'

Silas looked towards the church. 'Want to go in?'

'Why not?' Abigail said.

It was dark and smelled of damp and held no solace or even memories, and they did not stay long, both wanting to be back in the light and air.

'Not a very comforting place,' Silas said as they emerged.

'No,' she agreed.

'I was thinking,' he said, casually, a few miles further along the road, 'about church.'

'What about it?' Abigail asked.

'Just that, perhaps,' he said, 'if you wanted, we could go together sometimes.'

'Why—' her surprise was genuine '—would we want to do that?'

'I just thought it might comfort you a little,' Silas said.

'No,' Abigail said. 'Not me.'

'Really?' he said.

She heard the altered, cooler tone, looked at him. 'You all right?'

'Why wouldn't I be?' Silas said.

Chapter Thirty-One

He watched her again, a fortnight later, in the second week of August, in conversation with the priest at Saint Peter the Apostle.

She looked animated.

He took a rapid series of photographs, zooming in, then examined them.

Saw that the priest admired Abigail.

That the feeling was mutual.

He drove away from the church too fast, continued speeding most of the way to Crouch End, was aware, when he saw a police car, that he'd been lucky not to get stopped, went on speeding anyway.

He didn't care about fines or safety.

Everywhere he looked, *everywhere*, he saw her eyes, gazing at the priest.

Perfidious Abeguile.

Chapter Thirty-Two

Jules came to lunch the next Sunday with Ollie, pleased to be invited, bearing no grudge for the unexplained period of apparent aloofness.

'You're looking better,' she said to Abigail, half way through their roast beef, the three of them sitting around the old kitchen table, with Ollie in his buggy between his mother and uncle, sucking on a Yorkshire pudding.

'Am I?' Abigail smiled at her, speared a roast potato, glanced at Silas.

'Abigail always looks lovely to me,' he said, rather stiffly.

'I'm not talking about beauty,' Jules told him, then turned back to Abigail. 'You look calmer than when I last saw you. Or at least spent any time with you.' She looked down at Ollie, reached down to stroke his cheek, received a gurgle in response, then added, without rancour: 'Though that was after Charlie.'

'I was shocked then,' Abigail said.

'Of course you were,' Jules said.

'But yes,' Abigail agreed, 'I think I am feeling rather better now than I have for some time.'

Silas stood up, left the table and the kitchen.

'Something I said?' Jules asked.

Abigail flushed, shook her head, put down her knife and fork. 'He's been a bit strained,' she said, 'since our weekend away.'

Jules looked at the closed door. 'I was a bit troubled,' she said quietly, 'when he told me about that—'

'You knew about it?' Abigail was surprised.

Jules nodded. 'He was very enthusiastic, planning it, concerned to get it just right for you.' She paused. 'I told him I was worried about the effect that going back to Scotland, being so much closer to the farm again, might have on you.'

Abigail was silent for a moment. 'He didn't tell you then.'

'Tell me what?'

'He didn't just take me *close* to Allen's Farm. He took me through the gate, up the lane, right to the house.' She saw Jules's dismay. 'It's all right,' she reassured her. 'I was dreadfully upset at first, obviously, thought he was being terribly cruel. But then I saw that he genuinely believed he was trying to help.'

'Help?' Jules looked dubious.

Abigail shrugged. 'You know what they say about closure.'

'Stupid word,' Jules said, with feeling. 'You've no idea how many people used that to me after Ralph.' She shook her head. 'Closure. No such thing.'

'He'd had a wooden bench made,' Abigail told her, 'for the churchyard where my parents are buried, had their names carved on it. "In loving memory of . . ."'

'That was nice of him, I suppose,' Jules allowed.

Abigail thought about the stone bench seat out in the garden.

Another grave, the part Silas claimed Jules had played in it.

Dragged herself swiftly back.

'Anyway,' she said, almost brightly, 'I am feeling better.'

'Are you?' Jules looked at her searchingly. 'Honestly?'

Abigail, having almost forgotten what it felt like to *be* honest, found it hard to meet her gaze. 'Not about that day, about what I did, to my parents and Eddie, of course not. Nothing's ever going to make me feel better about that.'

'If it's any consolation,' Jules said, slowly, thoughtfully, 'I truly can't imagine Silas ever wanting to be deliberately cruel to you.'

Abigail thought about Charlie, gritted her teeth.

'I know he can be impossible at times,' Jules went on, 'but—' She broke off, seeing Abigail's expression. 'What is it?'

Abigail shook her head, then, suddenly, abruptly, said: 'He's—'

Jules waited a second. 'He's what, darling?'

'Nothing.' Abigail shook her head again, rose from her chair.

'Abigail, what's wrong?'

'It's nothing, Jules,' Abigail said. 'Truly.' She thought the lie must show on her face, in her eyes. 'I'm just concerned about Silas.' She went to the door, seeking escape. 'I'd better see if he's okay.'

Jules sighed. 'Take your time,' she said.

Abigail found Silas lying down in their bedroom.

'Are you all right?'

'Headache,' he said. 'Sorry.'

'Have you taken something?'

'Just,' he answered. 'Tell Jules I'll be down after a nap.'

'Of course.' She saw how pale he was. 'Want anything else?'

'No,' he said. 'Thank you. Tell Jules I'm sorry.'

'No need to apologize for having a headache,' Abigail said.

It was confusing, she thought, closing the door quietly, that odd, cool, not *quite* chilly, politeness of his that had begun near the end of their Scottish trip, had been coming and going since then. Hard to understand . . .

Not so hard as living a constant lie, not as grotesque as continuing to sleep beside, sometimes – only very occasionally, but still sometimes – letting a murderous husband make love to her. Not as strange as asking him solicitous questions about his headache, as if she cared.

Yet she did, she still *did*, and that confused her more than anything.

She shoved the thoughts away again, as she always did.

Returned to the kitchen, found Jules washing up the main course.

'He's got a bad headache, says he's sorry.'

'Not coming back down?' Jules squeezed Fairy Liquid onto a sponge.

'Maybe in a while.' Abigail produced another smile. 'Leave that, Jules. We've got pudding to have first. And then I want a long cuddle with my godson.'

At least this time Jules stayed.

Chapter Thirty-Three

'You never ask,' Abigail said to Father Moran, 'about the things I told you in confession.'

They were sharing the afternoon tea that Mrs Kenney – a grey-haired woman who always greeted Abigail with friendliness, then vanished discreetly, coming and going with trays or messages like an unassuming ghost – had brought them in the sitting room of the presbytery adjoining Saint Peter the Apostle. It was a simply furnished room, but far from austere, filled with family photographs and a considerable, varied and colourful collection of cushions and rugs, all made, the priest had told her, by parishioners over the years.

· It was the last Thursday afternoon of August, and Abigail was very tense. It had taken several of these tea sessions – usually arranged when she knew Silas was shooting fashion models in town – for her to come to this, to find the inner strength to match her deep inner sickness.

'Is it because you're not allowed to ask?' she ventured. 'Or because you didn't believe me?'

Or – she thought but did not add – because he had guessed that she was talking about her husband.

'Why would I not believe you?' Father Moran asked.

'I wondered . . .' She hesitated, put down her cup.

'What did you wonder?'

'If perhaps—' it was hard to go on '—if you thought I might be mad, saying such terrible things.'

'I did not, and still do not, think you in the least mad.' Father Moran waited, watching her intently. 'What is it, Abigail? Do you want to talk to me some more? About those matters?'

The urge to unburden herself more completely was powerful.

Never say that, not to anyone. Francesca's dying command about that older tragedy, not these later horrors, and anyway, long since broken. Yet still, it seemed, with the power, even now, to choke off the words in her throat.

Abigail looked away from the priest, shook her head.

'I don't think I can.' Cowardice, she realized abjectly, nothing to do with her mother. 'I'm sorry.'

'It's all right,' Father Moran said gently. 'When you're ready.'

Sitting in the VW on the road beyond the church and presbytery, Silas looked at his watch and saw that his wife had been inside, with the handsome God-botherer, for the longest time yet.

He wondered what they were doing.

Remembered Charlie Nagy with his arms around her.

Sex didn't enter his mind, not with these two, at least not yet.

He supposed that what they were doing was talking.

About private, confidential, intimate matters.

Matters that were for himself and Abigail only.

True treachery.

Chapter Thirty-Four

Jules was unpacking wholesalers' boxes at the back of the shop on the first Monday morning of September when she heard the door open and her brother's voice calling her name, and hurried forward.

'The studio's been broken into,' Silas said, pulling out one of the chairs around the small reading table, sinking onto it.

'Are you all right?' Alarmed, Jules scanned him for injury, found him pale and agitated but otherwise apparently unscathed. 'Did you disturb them? Did they hurt you?'

He mustered a feeble smile. 'Didn't know you still cared, sis.'

'Don't be silly.' Jules looked him up and down again. 'Not hurt then.'

Silas shook his head.

'Coffee?' She paused. 'Did you see them?'

'Long gone when I got there.'

'Thank God for that.' Jules poured him a mugful. 'Have the police been?'

Silas nodded. 'The worst of it's the bloody mess.'

Jules put the mug down on the table, drew out a second chair, sat beside him. 'Did they take much?'

'Hard to tell, but I don't think so.' He picked up the mug, but his hand was unsteady and he set it down again. 'I think there's more damage than theft. That's why I had to get out, come here. It's the malice of it that's got to me.'

'At least neither you nor Abigail was there.'

'Thank Christ,' Silas agreed. 'But it's freaked me out, I can tell you.'

'What did the police say?'

'Not much.' He picked up the mug again, took a sip. 'They did their usual stuff, dusting for prints, but I don't suppose it'll lead anywhere.' He raked his hair with his free hand, in his habitual gesture. 'I'd better get back, start clearing up, get the door fixed.'

'You've left it open?'

'I stuck something over the glass, and the keys still work, though I'd better get the locks changed.'

'I'll shut up for a while, come back with you.' Jules got up. 'Is Abigail coming here or going straight to Edison Road?'

'I'm not telling her,' Silas said.

'Why ever not?'

'I don't want to burden her with it.'

'You can't not tell her.' Jules was incredulous.

'She isn't all that strong,' Silas said.

'I think she's immensely strong.'

'You think all women are as tough as you, Jules.' Silas put the mug down again, shook his head. 'But Abigail's still broken inside. Bits all glued together, but sometimes I can almost see them coming apart.' His eyes were sad. 'I worry for my wife.'

'Share things with her,' Jules told him. 'That's the way to make her stronger, Silas, darling. You, too.'

Telephoned in the end by Jules, told how shocked Silas was, Abigail came directly to Edison Road to meet them and to help with the clearing up of the mess.

'I can't tell you how grateful I am to you both,' Silas told them.

'No need,' Abigail said, and went on cleaning.

'A bit of gratitude never hurt,' Jules said.

'Not sure why I got so worked up about it,' Silas said.

'It's horrible being burgled,' Jules said. 'Isn't it, Abigail?'

'I don't know,' Abigail said. 'It's never happened to me.'

'Anyway,' Silas said, 'I'm better now, thanks to my women.'

'Not so much of the "your women",' Jules told him.

'Sorry,' he said.

That night, though, he jolted out of sleep in a cold sweat.

'Nightmare,' he told Abigail, and sank back against his pillow.

She raised herself up on one elbow, looked at him. 'What about?'

'Two men,' he said. 'Breaking in – here, not the studio.'

'What happened?' She could see from his eyes, even in the half-light, that it had been bad. 'Tell me, Silas.'

'Attacked us,' he said, and shuddered. 'You, too.'

'Just a dream,' she said. 'Go back to sleep.'

'He's sleeping very badly,' Abigail told Jules a fortnight later in the shop. She had begun working there again, regularly, just after the studio break-in, and Silas had raised no objection, which had, despite everything, pleased her.

168

'He was in a pretty bad way when I saw him the other day,' Jules said.

'Last night's dream was about you. Your flat being broken into.'

'Poor Silas,' Jules said.

She wondered, later, after Abigail had left, if it was she or Silas who was most fragile; thought about their respective childhoods and teenage years.

She and Silas came close, Jules decided. But Abigail still won.

Hands down.

Having finished a practice session in the music room one evening the following week, Abigail made a couple of cups of coffee and carried them into the living room.

Silas was snoozing, feet up on the sofa in front of *News at Ten*, so, moving quietly, she set down the drinks on the coffee table.

'Jesus, Abigail!'

His voice so startled her that one of the cups tipped, coffee cascading over the table and onto the carpet. She looked at Silas, saw that he was pale, breathing hard, sitting bolt upright.

'You scared the life out of me,' he said. 'Creeping round like that.'

'I wasn't creeping,' Abigail said. 'Just trying not to wake you.'

'You should know better,' Silas said. 'You know I'm wound up.'

'Take it easy.' She headed for the door, to get something to mop up with.

'That's what I was trying to do,' Silas said.

'I'm beginning to think he should see the doctor,' Abigail told Jules on the phone.

'What for?' Jules asked. 'Tranquillizers?'

'I don't know,' Abigail said. 'He certainly needs something to calm him. He's so jittery, I'm worried he'll have an accident.'

'He should try yoga.'

'Can you picture Silas in the lotus position?' Abigail was wry.

'Ralph and I tried it a few times—' There was a smile in Jules's voice. 'We were absolutely hopeless at it, but it made us laugh, relaxed us that way.'

Abigail was silent for a moment.

'I still can't picture Silas,' she said.

She went for tea again with Michael Moran a few days later, mentioned, casually, the strain Silas had been under since the break-in.

'He should contact the victim support people,' the priest suggested.

'He was offered something like that by the police,' Abigail said.

'Said he didn't need it?' Father Moran saw her nod. 'Many people – men especially – think it's admitting to weakness, when that's the last thing it would be.'

'At least,' Abigail said, 'he's talking to me about it.'

'He's a very lucky man,' the priest said, 'to have you.'

She wondered which Silas he was referring to.

Victim or killer.

Chapter Thirty-Five

'Meet me for lunch today?' Silas said at breakfast the following Monday, the last in September.

'I'm working at the shop. Drew's on holiday, remember?'

'I'll talk your boss into giving you a lunch break,' he said.

'If you have influence,' Abigail said. 'Better not go too far though.'

'How about Florians?' Silas suggested. 'Twelve-thirty?'

'Lovely,' Abigail said, pleased.

She waited for him in the restaurant, just a short walk from Jules's Books, sipping a glass of their Pinot Blanco, wondering, as she always did now when she was idle, what kind of woman could look forward with any degree of pleasure to seeing a man like Silas? A man who could do such terrible things?

As always, the answering thoughts came all too readily, bounced painfully back and forth.

A woman who had done worse.

Not worse.

Almost. As good as.

Bad as.

She waited 'til one-fifteen, then ordered a smoked chicken salad, ate it swiftly, went back to the shop to relieve Jules, and phoned the studio.

'Oh, God,' Silas said. 'I completely forgot.'

'Maybe it's time,' Abigail said, 'I got a mobile.'

'You'll have to let me make it up to you,' he said. 'On Saturday evening.'

Midway through Saturday afternoon, soon after she'd come home with several bags of food from Marks and Spencer, Silas phoned to confirm that he'd booked a table at Loch Fyne, opposite Florians, but that because he was engrossed in a complex developing job, he wondered if she would mind taking a cab and meeting him at the restaurant.

'I could come to the studio,' Abigail said.

'Go straight there,' he said. 'That way you can have a drink if I'm a couple of minutes late.'

'Would you rather cancel?' Abigail asked. 'I don't mind.'

'I would,' Silas said. 'I'm looking forward to it far too much.'

She took a cab from the house, arrived at the restaurant five minutes early, ordered a glass of white wine, then sat contentedly back.

Fifteen minutes passed. Then thirty.

Abigail found a phone, rang the studio, got the engaged tone – not the usual Call Waiting message – tried again, gave up, returned to the table, studied the menu for the third time, debated ordering a bowl of lobster bisque, then went back to the phone and tried again.

At least, she thought, walking briskly, irritatedly, the studio was only a few blocks away. Though all the more reason for Silas to have come to the restaurant, if the phone was out of order – no matter how 'complex' his job was – to explain himself.

She had already taken her keys from her bag, but the basement door, with its sleek sign – SILAS GRAVES – was unlocked.

Abigail pushed it open.

'Silas?' she called.

The outer office was empty, lit by a single lamp.

The door to the dark room was closed, the red light above the door on.

'Silas?' she called again. 'Are you in there?'

She waited several moments, growing alarmed. Ordinarily, she knew better than to enter when that light was glowing, but in the circumstances, he might be ill . . .

'I'm coming in,' she called.

And opened the door.

She heard his wordless shout at the same instant that the sweet-smelling liquid hit her eyes.

She screamed, her hands flying up, shielding them.

Too late.

Chapter Thirty-Six

All she remembered, later, of the first hours, was the agony and terror, and Silas's anguished voice wailing, repeatedly:

'Oh, my God, oh, God, what have I done?'

There had been other voices too, kind, more practical voices, and fingers prising her hands away from her face so that they could help her, checking that she was breathing properly, that whatever the terrible liquid had been that had so wounded her eyes hadn't burned her throat or windpipe – and oh, Christ, her eyes *hurt*, she'd never known anything to hurt so *much*. And they were washing them with something, and she was fighting them, she couldn't help it, but then they gave her something, she remembered a needle – before or after they took her out of the studio, up the steps, to the ambulance – shooting something into her system that had, mercifully, swiftly, taken away the worst of the pain, calmed her at least a little.

Your husband did the best thing in the circumstances,' someone's voice said in A&E at the Whittington, while they were still irrigating her eyes with sterile saline. 'Cold water right away,' the voice said. 'Not as good as this, but a start.'

'I told him to do that,' Abigail said, trying not to cry, not sure if she could cry.

She remembered, suddenly, that she had screamed it at him.

That Silas had just stood there, making helpless, agonized sounds.

'Cold water!' she had screamed. 'Now, for God's sake, before anything!'

'Then you did just the right thing, Abigail,' the voice told her now, gently.

Voices. Men and women, paramedics, doctors, nurses, porters, all muddled into one in the painful, terrifying semi-darkness, all giving her kindness and treatment and information, some of which, much of which, she scarcely understood at the time.

'You were very lucky,' someone said, told her again that the chemical might easily have damaged her oesophagus or trachea.

Lucky.

Abigail thought, for the first time, of her face.

'Is my face burned?' she asked.

'Just your lids,' they said, 'and around your eyes.'

The skin burns would be painful for a while, they said, but would almost certainly heal well without plastic surgery.

'Lucky there too.'

Lucky.

She did not ask the question uppermost in her mind, could not bring herself to ask, waited, in agony, all kinds of agony, physical and emotional, for someone to tell her how *lucky* she'd been about that too.

That she was not going to be blind.

But no one told her that.

The punishment then, at last.

The thought came to her while they were transferring her to Moorfields.

She remembered thinking once, after Charlie's death, during one of Maggie Blume's telephone calls, that maybe Silas was her punishment.

Wrong.

Blindness was to be her sentence.

Pray for us sinners.

Oh, dear Christ.

They admitted her, began treating her with drops every few hours, gave her tablets, explained at every stage what they were doing and why, which medications were to lessen inflammation, which were for healing, which for pain, which for lubrication, which were to prevent infection.

She could see light and shapes, but nothing more.

Light, at least, she told herself. *Better than dark.*

She lay in the hospital bed, heard strange sounds, tried not to weep.

The police came, asked Abigail if she wanted to press charges against Silas.

'Grievous bodily harm,' the policewoman's voice said.

Try murder, she thought, her mind fuzzy from the drugs.

Remembered Silas's anguished wailing after it had happened.

'Of course not,' she said. 'It was an accident.'

They told her they would come back later, went away, and some time after that a nurse came to say that Silas wanted to know if she would see him.

'Why wouldn't I?' Abigail said, wondered, briefly, stupidly, why he had asked such a thing – then realized exactly why.

The nurse went to get him.

'I thought,' he said, taking her hand tentatively, as if he thought she might snatch it away, his voice still afraid, 'you might never want to see me again.'

'Odd,' Abigail said, 'how often we use that word.'

'Which one?'

'See,' she said.

'Oh, God,' Silas said.

She lay very still, her fear rising. That kept on happening, she'd noticed since the accident; the fear rose to unbearable, screaming-pitch levels, like mercury shooting up in a thermometer in a cartoon, till the top bulged and exploded, and then it fell again, became something slightly more manageable, then soared again.

'I've spoken to the ophthalmologist,' Silas said.

She said nothing, the fear continuing its climb up the scale.

'She says there's every reason to hope that the drugs they're using will be enough to heal both eyes in time.' He paused. 'They're both pretty bad for now, but the left eye's a little worse, apparently.'

'What if they don't heal?' Abigail asked, very softly.

'Then they can operate,' Silas said.

'What kind of operation?' Her voice shook.

'I don't know exactly,' Silas said. 'It's not something they rush into, apparently. She said they like to wait, give the eyes time to settle.'

'How long?' Abigail asked.

She waited for his reply, then heard a curious new sound, and realized that he was crying.

'Don't,' she said. 'Please don't do that.'

'Sorry.' He blew his nose. 'Oh, God,' he said again. 'Oh, God, what have I done to you?'

'What I would like to know,' Abigail said, 'is *why* you did it.'

'I thought,' Silas said, 'you were another burglar.'

He explained, wretchedly, what he had already explained to the police. That while he had been at work in the dark room during the afternoon, the phone had rung several times, and that each time the caller had hung up.

'And the idea started nagging at me that it was something to do with the break-in, and maybe it was going to happen again.'

'Why didn't you tell me?' Abigail asked.

'I didn't want to worry you,' Silas said. 'You were getting ready for our evening, and I really felt you were actually looking forward to it, which made me so happy, and God knows I was looking forward to it too, and oh Christ, darling, you can't *begin* to imagine how terrible I feel about—'

'Please just go on,' she said. 'Tell me what happened.'

'That was it, really,' he said, helplessly. 'Because of the phone calls, I fell behind with the work, and that stressed me out too, and first I was worried about running late for our dinner, and then I suppose I got absorbed in the job again and lost track of time, forgot you'd already be at Loch Fyne waiting for me—'

'But I called out,' Abigail interrupted, 'twice, before I came in.'

'I didn't hear you,' Silas said. '*Obviously* I didn't hear you, or else—' He began weeping again.

'Oh, for God's sake,' Abigail said, 'do shut up.'

'I'm sorry,' Silas said again, composed himself, went on.

He had still been concentrating on the work when she'd opened the dark room door, and he hadn't heard her voice at all, had just felt the sudden rush of cool air, had taken intense fright, seen the door opening.

'It was all pure reflex. I just picked up the first thing to hand.'

'Developer,' Abigail said. 'They told me.'

She'd felt sick when she'd heard, still felt it now. Some developers, she knew, were alkaline based, and alkaline was worse than acid for eyes. She knew that, and Silas certainly knew that, and God knew he must have been half out of his mind to have picked that up, let alone thrown it.

'I know,' Silas said. 'Christ, I *know*. They seem to think, thank God, that my washing your eyes out with water helped a bit.'

'I told you to do that,' Abigail said.

'No,' Silas disagreed. 'You didn't. You were screaming.'

'I'm sure I was telling you to get water.'

'Definitely not,' he said. 'You're confused, darling. It's understandable.'

'Blindness,' Abigail said harshly, 'will do that every time.'

'Don't *say* that,' Silas said. 'You're not going to be blind.'

The police came again, and she told them how jumpy Silas had been since the break-in, that she was entirely certain – and there were few things in life nowadays that she felt certain about, but this, at least, *was* one of them – that if he'd had the remotest idea it had been her entering the dark room, he would never have thrown the developer.

'Throwing it at another person,' the policewoman pointed out, 'would still have been an offence.'

'But he thought he was in danger,' Abigail said. 'And anyway, it wasn't another person, was it? It was me, and I *know* it was an accident, and I certainly don't want to press charges.'

They went away again.

Left her wondering at her loyalty.

At her treachery against Charlie.

In her new, semi-dark world, the faces of Silas's dead and of her own seemed clearer than ever. More unbearable than ever.

Go away, she said silently to Charlie and his sister.

Please, she said to her mother and father and Eddie, *let me rest.*

'How the hell,' Jules asked Silas, walking out of the hospital with him after her first visit, 'could you have done such a bloody terrible, bloody *stupid* thing?'

'Don't you think—' he glanced, hot-cheeked with embarrassment, at a passing doctor '—I feel bad enough without you making it worse?'

'I don't give a stuff, just this minute, how you feel,' Jules told him. 'It's poor Abigail I'm concerned with, not knowing if she's going to be blind or not.'

'Please,' Silas said, 'don't say that, I can't bear it.'

Jules paused on the pavement outside in City Road and stared at him in disgust. 'You'd better bloody well bear it,' she said. 'She needs you.'

'I know she does,' Silas said. 'That's the only good thing about this – that I'm going to be able to take care of her for as long as she needs me.'

'Good thing?' Jules echoed, disbelieving. 'There's nothing remotely good about this. Abigail's in terrible pain, and she must be so *frightened*.'

'I know that, Jules,' Silas said, 'without you telling me.' His eyes went flatter, colder. 'No need to twist my words.'

'Then stop sounding so fucking selfish,' Jules said.

Though Abigail's left eye, her doctor, a kind, but practical woman, confirmed, had taken in more chemical than the right, both eyes had Grade Three corneal burns.

'Is that good or bad?' she asked.

'Better than Grade Four,' the doctor answered.

'But not as good as Grade Two.' Abigail said.

'Still good news though.'

The words the ophthalmologist used were, for the most part, familiar from other usages, yet at times Abigail felt she might have been learning a new language.

Corneal abrasion, epithelial loss, corneal scarring, perforation.

Limbal ischaemia.

The limbus, Abigail learned, was the border between the cornea and sclera.

'The sclera's the white part?' she checked.

'The sclera coats every part of the eye except the cornea,' the doctor said.

'And ischaemia's something to do with blood supply,' Abigail ventured.

'Exactly,' the other woman said.

'And the blood's not getting through?'

'To less than half the limbus in each eye,' the doctor said.

Abigail asked the question at last.

'What does that mean, to my vision?'

'There's likely to be significant haziness,' the doctor answered.

'But I'm not going to be blind.' Abigail felt her whole body tremble.

'Not blind.' The doctor took her hand. 'And not forever.'

Not forever.

More – yet again, the old, damning part of her mind told her – than she deserved.

'Long way to go,' the doctor added.

'Surgery?' she asked.

'Possibly,' the other woman said. 'Too early to say.'

They would wait, she explained, for several weeks, probably even months, before they made any decisions regarding stem cell transplantation or corneal grafting or keratoprosthesis, or . . . .

More words.

Not blind.

The only ones that mattered for now.

'How bad do I look?' She hadn't thought too much about that before.

'Bit battered,' the doctor told her. 'Nothing that shouldn't heal pretty well.'

'It still hurts,' Abigail said.

'You haven't been complaining.'

'I didn't like to.'

The doctor squeezed her hand again.

'You've every right, Abigail.'

They sent her home after five days – and another round of questions from the police – with Silas, a bag of medication, a sheaf of instructions for him, and the date of her first outpatient appointment.

'How do you feel?' he asked her in the car on the way.

'Good,' she said, her eyes masked by plastic shields, 'to be out.'

'Nervous, too, I expect,' Silas said.

178

'About how I'm going to manage?' Abigail said. 'Terrified.'

'No need,' he told her. 'And it's not *you*. It's we. *We're* going to manage this together. It's the least I can do.'

'Yes,' she said.

They had been counselled at length before her discharge about the house, about the kind of help she could rely on, suggesting she ask Silas to consider organizing a bed on the ground floor, giving him hints about the removal of obstacles so that Abigail might experience a degree of independence in safety.

'She won't need to,' he had told them. 'I'll be there all the time.'

They had pointed out that, however noble his intentions, this might not be possible. He told them that since it was he who had done this awful thing to Abigail, there was certainly no question of nobility, and that there was absolutely no doubting that he would be there for her at every minute of day and night.

'She can depend on me completely,' he had said.

No doubting how much she needed him now, he thought on her first night back at the house, watching her trying to find her way round their kitchen.

More than that, better than that, she knew it.

Not a permanent need, of course. One of these days, weeks, months, those lovely eyes would probably be fit again to look at her priest – at other men – but by then, perhaps, she might have come to realize that *he* was the only one she would always be able to depend on, no matter what.

The only one who would love her despite what she had done.

Maybe even *because* of what she'd done.

Two of a kind. Kindred spirits. Perfect match.

She had to learn not to let other people get in the way of that, of their perfect relationship. Other men, especially.

This time together, this needy period, would, he hoped, bring her that realization, the understanding that *he* was all she needed, would ever need.

He had known, when he'd planned it, that there was a risk that the injury to her eyes might be even greater than this, that she might have been permanently blinded or scarred, and those prospects had twisted his heart.

Always a price to pay.

And the doctors all seemed reasonably optimistic that, in time, her vision would be at least improved, and that the scarring would be minimal.

That Abigail would, ultimately, be perfectly beautiful again.

Would look at, and be looked at, by men.

Cross that bridge . . .

Chapter Thirty-Seven

'I wish,' Abigail said, 'I could go out.'

It was the beginning of November, she had been home for ten days and it was already driving her mad.

The first few days had been difficult, but living in fog as she was, there had been no question that she had needed all the help Silas could give her, and she had still, at that early stage, found his tender determination to be 'her eyes' – as he insisted on calling himself – quite moving. Only *quite*, given his responsibility for her situation, though at least his sense of guilt was something she found all too easy to relate to, so much so that on several occasions she had found herself the comforter, rather than the other way around, comfort twice leading to lovemaking, and then, too, Silas had been tender and caring and meticulously careful to avoid touching her eyes.

By day ten, though, feeling almost trapped by his determined devotion, she was beginning to feel distinctly stir crazy.

'Certainly we can go out,' Silas said. 'Where would you like to go?'

They were in the kitchen, where he had made her an omelette for lunch – discouraging her every time she made the slightest attempt to help – and then washed up and cleared away.

'I meant by myself,' Abigail said. 'For a walk.'

'You can't,' he said. 'Obviously.'

'I know that, Silas,' she said. 'I just said I wished it.'

He looked at her disconsolate expression and felt, first, compassion, then irritation because of her ingratitude.

'Don't you realize yet,' he asked, 'how sorry I am?'

'How could I not realize?' Abigail said. 'You've told me enough times.'

'I hope I've done more than tell you,' he said. 'I've done all I can to help you, given up a lot of potential business to look after you.'

'Jules would come to help,' Abigail said. 'You haven't let her.'

'She has the shop and Ollie *and* Ralph's smelly old dog,' Silas said. 'And I'm your husband, not Jules.'

'What on earth does that have to do with it?' Abigail said, crossly.

Silas bit his lip, then counted silently to five.

'If you were able,' he asked slowly, pleasantly, 'to go out on your own, where would you go?'

'I don't know,' Abigail said. 'Anywhere.'

Silas watched her face intently.

'To church, perhaps?' he asked.

She knew from that second on.

Thought she knew. It was hard to be sure, though perhaps, she suspected, she just didn't *want* to be sure. Did not want to know.

Did not want to believe him capable of such a thing.

Of hurting her – *her* – deliberately.

Why would he do such a thing? she asked herself repeatedly.

He would *not*, came the reply, which she fought desperately to believe.

Yet surely that question of his had been some sort of warning?

He had asked her something about church, she remembered, the day he'd taken her back to Allen's Farm, shortly after they'd left the graveyard where her parents were buried. He had said something about going together in the future, and she had asked him why they should want to do that, and he had said that it might comfort her, and she had told him no.

'No. Not me,' she recalled saying, swiftly, truthfully.

He had looked at her then, she remembered now, quite strangely.

And that was when that curious change in him had begun.

That night, after he had fallen asleep – easy to tell, from his breathing, that he was sleeping – she lay beside him, in her hateful new darker-than-dark privacy, and thought about his all-too-well-established jealousy and possessiveness.

Charlie's face presented itself again.

Go away, Charlie. She twisted the corner of the duvet in one hand, squeezed it hard, though not so violently that the movement should wake Silas. *Please, Charlie, just for a while.*

She still tried, regularly, to lie to herself about that horror. To pretend that what Silas had told her *was*, despite all the evidence to the contrary, a fabrication, that he had just been playing a cruel game with her, as he had about Maggie Blume. Told herself again that either he had seen the genuine mugging, or had found out about it, somehow, and pretended to her that he'd done it, pretended that his clothes had blood on them and had to be burned.

182

Just to hurt me.

Better than hurting Charlie.

Killing Charlie.

Silas had been jealous of Charlie.

And Charlie was dead.

Then Maggie Blume had begun asking questions.

And Maggie had been killed.

In an *accident.* Confirmed.

And Paul Graves was – might be – buried in the garden.

Abigail remembered what Silas had said about the manner of his father's death. After she'd said something to him about natural causes.

'He stopped breathing,' Silas had said. 'I suppose that's natural enough.'

Forget them, Abigail told herself now, lying in the dark room.

Forget Paul Graves and Charlie and Maggie.

Concentrate on yourself – on what happened to you.

And the thing that Silas had said today, after lunch.

About church.

He knows, she thought, *about Father Moran.*

Beside her in the bed, Silas stirred, gave a small moan, was still again.

If he knew about her visits to Saint Peter's, Abigail went on working it through, if he knew about her cups of tea in the presbytery, then that had to mean that he had been watching her.

Following her.

If he was following her, but had said nothing about it, that had to mean that, absurdly, impossibly – *not impossible, not with Silas* – he must be jealous.

Of a priest?

A good-looking, young priest.

That was when the answer came to her. To the question she had asked herself earlier:

Why would he do such a thing?

Because of his jealousy.

Because he had seen her with another attractive man.

Because a blind woman . . .

Stop it.

Because a blind woman could not see.

Could not see other men.

Abigail felt suddenly very ill. A flush of heat shot up through her neck, suffusing her face, sweat ran down her back and trickled down between her breasts, and she thought she might be sick.

Automatically she began to reach for the bedside lamp – then remembered there was no point turning on a light.

A sob rose in her throat, was barely suppressed.

Beside her, Silas stirred again.

Take deep breaths, Abigail.

She inhaled, slowly, exhaled, then did the same again.

The sweat, cold now on her face and body, dried, and the nausea faded away with the worst of the panic, as she reached a decision.

Tomorrow, somehow, she would telephone Father Moran.

Tell him what had happened, share her new fears with him.

Ask for his help.

Chapter Thirty-Eight

It was so hard getting even a minute to herself.

Silas was more than her helper, he had turned himself into her shadow – and the pity of it was that she did still need him so badly.

'See how you need me,' he had said several times.

Another motive, perhaps, Abigail thought now.

Making her dependent on him.

'It's all right,' she told him after another lunch, after he'd made her a sandwich, served it to her, cleared away, made her coffee, helped her to the sofa and set the radio beside her for the Afternoon Play. Abigail had always enjoyed listening to the radio, but never more than now, and that, plus the Walkman that Jules had brought her within days of the accident – *accident* – together with a pile of audio books, had been keeping her sane.

Maybe sane.

'It's all right,' she said now to Silas. 'You can go and do your own thing for at least a couple of hours.'

'The play's only on for forty-five minutes,' he said.

'I know,' Abigail said testily. 'I can still go on listening.'

'What if you need something?'

'I won't.' She paused. 'Why don't you go out, Silas? You really ought to spend some time at the studio, read your post, pay some bills.'

'What if—?'

'If the house starts burning down,' Abigail cut in, 'I promise to phone you.'

'I take it,' Silas said, 'you'd like to be alone?'

'My,' Abigail said, 'but you're perceptive today.'

She noticed, when he gone (and she was sure he really had left, because she'd heard his footsteps out on the front path receding, and then she'd heard the VW's door open and bang shut and the car drive away, and it was true what they said about other senses compensating for a lost sense, even as rapidly as this), that he hadn't brought her the telephone.

Not a mistake, she felt sure, even if it did go against the meticulous care he'd been taking of her.

She fetched it herself. Bumped into the edge of the coffee table and stubbed a toe on the way back, and she thanked God several times each day for the knowledge that if her vision did not improve in time despite the medication, surgery would almost certainly help her, that the vast majority of corneal grafts were successful, that even if a first transplant were to be rejected, there could be a second.

Corneas of the dead.

Thanking God for other people's death and bereavement.

More guilt.

Yet she did thank God for the reassurance, for the knowledge that she would not be blind forever, and it was hard to imagine how she might be feeling were it not so, had transplants not been invented and perfected.

Don't imagine, she told herself now, briskly, vowing to remember to donate to Moorfields and the RNIB.

The cordless phone, once she was safely back on the sofa, was quite easy to manage, so long as she took her time and remembered to navigate from the raised dot on the 5 key, and she didn't know the number of the church or presbytery, but she phoned directory enquiries and had them put her straight through.

They took so long to answer she was afraid there was no one there.

'Please,' she said, waiting. 'Please be there.'

'Saint Peter's.'

A woman, breathless. Not Mrs Kenney.

'Is Father Moran there, please?'

'Afraid not,' the woman said. 'Who's speaking, please?'

'When do you expect him back?' Abigail asked.

'Not for some time.'

Abigail's heart sank. 'I'll try later,' she said.

'He won't be back later,' the woman said. 'Who's speaking, please?'

'A parishioner,' Abigail said, unsure why she hadn't given her name.

'Father Moran's gone away,' the woman said.

Abigail was thrown. He hadn't mentioned any forthcoming travel plans, though there was, of course, no reason why he should have.

'Is he on holiday?' she asked.

'Would you like to leave your name?' the other woman persisted.

'Abigail Allen,' she said, and felt her cheeks flush.

'Father Moran,' the woman volunteered, as a reward, 'has gone on retreat.'

'Oh,' Abigail said, helplessly. 'Is that likely to be for a week or so?'

'Rather longer than that, I'm afraid.' The woman paused. 'Would you like the locum priest to contact you, Mrs Allen?'

'No, thank you,' Abigail said, quickly, and, fingers fumbling, ended the call.

Silas came back a few minutes later.

'You can't,' Abigail said, 'have been to the studio in that time.'

'I haven't,' he said. 'I just went for a bit of a drive.'

He sat down beside her. It was an effort not to stiffen.

'No radio?' he asked. 'Play no good?'

'I didn't bother with it,' Abigail said.

'Did someone call?' he asked.

'No,' she said.

She remembered that the phone was still beside her, realized that if he chose to, Silas could press the redial key and find out who she'd called.

'No,' she said again, and picked it up. 'I was just about to call Jules.'

And did so, immediately, before he could take the phone from her.

'Jules's Books.'

Abigail felt better just hearing Jules's voice, though it was – like all conversations she had these days, with Silas always close by, listening – essentially superficial. Ollie was gorgeous, Jules said, and longing – according to his mother – to visit his auntie, and the bookshop was quite buoyant for once.

'How are you coping?' Jules asked. 'Do you need anything at all?'

'I'm coping quite well,' Abigail answered. 'Thanks to Silas.'

'Still doing the "I can't bear it if you won't let me help" bit?'

'Very much so,' Abigail said.

'At least he is helping,' Jules said. 'Though so he bloody well should.'

Abigail longed, suddenly, desperately, to have a real, frank conversation with Jules, for if Father Moran was gone—

And wasn't *that* a bit of a coincidence, his going on retreat at this precise moment, and had he really *gone* on retreat, was he all right, was he *safe*?

But since he was, at least for the moment, gone, then the only person left who she could think of trusting fully was Jules.

Still Silas's sister, though.

Hard to be entirely certain where her ultimate loyalties might lie.

And even if they were to swing against Silas, there was still his threat to make trouble for Jules if Abigail did speak to her.

Silence still best for now then.

Silence, hand-in-hand with the new haze of her world, and her loneliness.

For she was alone now. Never *left* alone.

But lonelier than she had ever been.

Chapter Thirty-Nine

'You really should try playing,' Silas said, not for the first time.

'I don't want to play.'

She had told him so over and over again. Had, in fact, made a pact with herself *not* to play the cello until she could see again, be wholly herself again. But Silas-the-carer had also, she had noticed increasingly, been turning into Silas-the-tyrant who would not take no for an answer.

'You'll feel better if you play,' he said now.

It was morning, and they'd only just got up, but already Abigail felt weary.

'I won't feel better,' she said, quietly.

'But you never look at the cello that much when you play,' Silas reasoned. 'It's mostly instinctive now, surely?'

'I read music,' she said. 'And of course I look down, you just don't notice.'

'Surely it wouldn't matter, for now, if you played imperfectly,' he persisted. 'Better to play badly than not at all. And I'll bet there's plenty of music you know by heart – or you could just play scales.'

'For God's sake, Silas,' Abigail snapped, 'how many times do I have to say the same thing? I don't want to play.'

'You're a silly girl,' he chided.

'You sound,' she said, 'like my mother.'

'Better be careful then, hadn't I?' Silas said.

Living in the fog was making her paranoid. Turning every vague conjecture into full-blown suspicion.

She felt hemmed in and, despite – or perhaps because of – his endlessly tender care, afraid. Trapped by his love and devotion and by her own dependence.

At her next hospital appointment, nothing seemed significantly changed. She could still see light and some shape, but the mist was still there, shrouding everything.

Nothing, they assured her, that had not been anticipated at this early stage.

'Are you sure?' Abigail asked, though it was perfectly true that they had warned her it would be this way.

They said they were absolutely sure, gave her more drops and thick wrap-around dark glasses, warned her that if things improved, she might be photophobic, painfully dazzled by light.

'You look very glamorous and mysterious,' Silas said.

And took her home again.

He began to nag her almost ceaselessly about playing, guided her one afternoon into the music room.

'I wanted to go to the bedroom,' Abigail said.

She pulled away from him and turned around.

Silas shut the door.

Abigail compressed her lips, reached for the handle, began to open it.

'No,' he said.

'What do you mean, *no*?' Again, Abigail reached for the handle.

'I want you to spend some time in here,' Silas told her, and took her hand.

'I'm not having this conversation,' Abigail said. 'Let go.'

'Not till you give this a try.'

'Let go of my *hand*, Silas.'

'You're behaving like a child.' He kept a firm grip on her.

'Stop treating me like one.'

'I'm only trying to do what's best for you,' he said.

'Jesus.' Abigail felt herself beginning to quiver with anger. 'Jesus.'

'Not my department,' Silas said, coldly, and tugged her forward towards the middle of the room, where her cello waited, lying on the carpet beside her chair.

'I'm not going to play, Silas, so all you're doing is wasting your time.'

'For God's sake, Abigail.' He jostled her another foot further, pushed her down onto the chair, then swiftly picked up the cello and thrust it at her. 'All I'm asking is that you give it a try.'

Abigail folded her arms reflexively around the instrument. 'Why isn't it in its case?' she demanded.

'Because I came in earlier and took it out.' He bent down, picked up the bow, put that into her right hand.

'Get out,' she said.

'I want to hear you try to play,' he said.

'Get *out*,' she yelled.

190

Silas looked at her, shook his head.

'Suit yourself,' he said.

For the first five minutes after he left the music room, Abigail wept with anger and frustration, clinging to the cello.

Its familiarity, its feel, its smell, comforted her.

'Damn you, Silas,' she said, because she knew, already, that he was right.

It felt wonderful. It felt better than anything had in weeks.

She resisted the desire to remove the glasses and wipe her eyes, just mopped at her cheeks with the back of one hand. Then wiped both hands, one at a time, over her jeans.

Got into position, tightened the bow hair, took a deep, preparing breath.

And began to play.

Outside, in the corridor, Silas leaned against the wall, and smiled.

Tears in his eyes.

It was working. She was realizing, slowly and often painfully, but realizing it just the same.

That she did need him.

Could not do without him.

Chapter Forty

Jules arrived, unannounced, two mornings later, with Ollie.

Silas opened the door.

'What are you doing here?'

'We've come to relieve you,' Jules said. 'If you're going to let us in, that is.'

Silas stepped back, and Jules pushed the buggy over the threshold into the entrance hall.

'I don't need relieving,' he told her. 'Abigail and I are doing fine.'

'Abigail's told me,' Jules said, 'and I agree, that you need a break.'

Silas frowned. 'When did she tell you that?'

'Last night.' Jules saw his expression, smiled. 'She told me not to take no for an answer, said you'd argue about it.'

'Baba,' Ollie said.

'Yes, my love,' his mother said. 'Advanced child, your nephew, Uncle Silas.'

'I don't need a break, Jules,' Silas said.

'Then maybe Abigail does,' Jules said, gently.

'Did she say that?'

Ollie began wriggling in the buggy, wanting freedom.

'Soon, Ollie,' his mother told him, and looked back at her brother. 'Abigail didn't say that in so many words, darling, but that's only because she doesn't want to hurt your feelings.'

Silas stood still, said nothing.

Jules recognized that particular brand of silence, had lived with it for many years before Ralph had come into her life, taken her away.

'Don't, Silas,' she said. 'Please, for Abigail's sake.'

He eyed her with distaste. 'You'd better go and find her then,' he said. 'She's upstairs in the music room.'

'Would you like,' Jules asked, 'to have Ollie for a bit?'

'By all means,' Silas said coolly.

*

Now that she had begun playing again, Abigail found she could hardly bear to stop.

As at other bad times in her life, she surrounded herself with the music, let her fears, her heightened, painful emotions, become submerged in it.

She heard neither the knock, nor the door opening.

Her music filled her ears, her whole world.

Standing just inside the room, Jules waited another moment, then lifted her hand and rapped loudly on the inside of the door.

'It's Jules,' she said.

Abigail lowered her bow, her heartbeat rapid from exertion and emotion.

'Jules,' she said, breathlessly. 'Thank God.'

'I don't want to disturb you,' Jules said. 'Shall I wait till you're finished?'

'Making my awful noise, you mean?'

'It was a beautiful noise,' Jules told her.

'Whichever,' Abigail said. 'You're not disturbing me.' She still held the cello. 'Is Ollie here?' She tilted her face, listening.

'He's downstairs,' Jules said, 'with Silas.'

'Okay,' Abigail said.

'And I'm closing the door,' Jules told her, and did so. 'How are the eyes?'

'A wee bit more shape to things,' Abigail said. 'Still very foggy though.'

'And you?' Jules asked. 'How are you feeling?'

'I'm okay.' Abigail paused, listening. 'Have you got it?'

'In my bag,' Jules answered. 'Though I think we should hang on till I've actually persuaded Silas out of the house, don't you?'

'Yes,' Abigail agreed. 'If you think you can.'

'I'll manage it somehow.'

They went downstairs together, found him in the living room, with Ollie in the large playpen bought by Abigail some months back from Mothercare.

'We both think,' Jules said, right away, 'that you should go to the studio.'

'What for?' Silas asked.

'You need to go,' Jules said. 'You know you need to. You have to go through the post, check your e-mails.'

'I check e-mails from here,' Silas said.

'You must have clients,' Jules said, 'who'd like to find you actually there.'

'And bills?' Abigail asked. 'They must need paying.'

He shrugged. 'I'm not bothered at present.'

'Not the greatest idea, surely?' Jules said. 'Alienating clients and suppliers.'

'Gaga,' Ollie said. 'Baba.'

'Jules is right,' Abigail said. 'After all, you'll want business up and running when I'm better, won't you?'

'And won't you?' Silas queried.

'Of course,' Abigail said, calmly.

'*Gaga*,' Ollie said again, more forcefully.

'Clearly,' Silas said, getting up off the floor, 'I'm not wanted here.'

'Don't get huffy, darling,' Jules said.

'I'm not a bit huffy.' He dusted down his jeans. 'I'll leave you to your women's chat.' He looked at his sister. 'You'd better realize you need to be extra careful. Two handfuls to take care of.'

'Charming description,' Abigail said.

'You know what I mean, sweetheart.' Silas paused. 'Sure you can manage, sis?'

'Silas, for God's sake,' Jules said, 'just go.'

It took another ten minutes of fussing around and advising Jules of every conceivable pitfall Abigail might possibly encounter around the house, before Silas finally left.

'Right,' Jules said, from near the living room window. 'He's gone.'

'Sure?' Abigail sat on the couch, Ollie on her knee.

'Absolutely.' Jules came over. 'Let me take this chap.' She picked him up. 'Downstairs loo all right with you?'

'Fine.' Abigail stood up, took a second to position herself, then walked towards the door. 'All clear?' she asked.

'Perfectly,' Jules said.

At the door, Abigail paused. 'Thank you.'

'What for?'

'Letting me go by myself. For remembering I'm an adult.'

'I could see you were okay,' Jules said.

'I'd have been better with a stick to help me poke my way around, but Silas says I don't need one, because I have him.' Abigail paused. 'I'm afraid I do need you to organize me now.'

'All set,' Jules said. 'Very simple, as you know.'

She walked behind Abigail as far as the guest lavatory near the kitchen, Ollie squirming in her arms, protesting.

'I'm just going to put him down.' She did so. 'And here—' she took something from her pocket '—is what you need, ready for use.' She reached for Abigail's hand. 'This is the right end, okay?'

'Okay,' Abigail said, tensely.

Went into the room and closed the door.

'Tell me,' she said, afterwards.

Jules took the strip from her, looked at it.

'Positive,' she said, quietly.

'Oh,' Abigail said.

'Do you want to sit down?' Jules asked, tentatively.

'I think,' Abigail said, 'I want a drink.'

'Not the prescribed approach,' Jules said.

'No,' Abigail said.

She had taken her time in the loo, steeling herself. Had already concluded, over the past several days and nights, that if she was right – and she'd known there was a chance she was, because she'd stopped taking the Pill the night he'd thrown the developer in her eyes, though her missed period and nausea might easily have been down to stress – but still, if she was right, it would alter everything.

Babies always did, of course.

A little more so in her case, she realized, wryly. This had, necessarily, to change her outlook on everything. Silas included.

Silas, especially.

'Jules,' she said now. 'Can you please phone the studio?'

They were back in the living room, drinking tea while Ollie, back in the playpen, chewed at the left ear of a soft blue rabbit.

'Do you want to tell him?' Jules asked.

'No,' Abigail said sharply. 'I want to make sure he's still there.'

Jules sought no explanation, went straight to the phone.

'Just a reassurance call,' she told him. 'To say we're fine and to tell you there's no need to hurry back. I can make us some lunch, and then—'

'Whatever are you both up to?' Silas broke in, his tone light.

'Nothing much,' Jules said. 'Women's chat, as you put it.'

'Tell him—' Abigail pitched her voice so he could hear '—I want him to stop worrying about me and take his time.'

'Abigail says—'

'I heard,' Silas cut in. 'Don't you have to get back to the shop?'

'Not for a long while,' Jules said. 'So you just get down to some work and enjoy your time out.'

'I will,' Silas said. 'Thanks, sis. See you later.'

Jules ended the call. 'He was fine about it,' she said.

'Was he?' Abigail said, sceptically. 'Probably testing us.'

Jules frowned, glanced at Ollie, who'd dumped his bunny and was now playing with his fabric bricks, then looked back at Abigail. 'What do you mean?'

'Me,' Abigail said. 'He's testing me.'

'I don't understand,' Jules said.

'No,' Abigail said. 'You don't.'

Jules saw that though her eyes, behind the dark wraparound glasses, were almost invisible, her face was quite shockingly pale. 'Darling, what is it?'

Abigail took a shaky breath, let it out.

'Tell me.' Jules went to the sofa, sat down beside her. 'Please.'

'I'm pregnant, right?'

'So it seems,' Jules said.

'I told myself,' Abigail went on, 'that if I was, if it was true, then that meant—'

Jules waited a second or two. 'What?'

'That I no longer have any choice but to tell you.'

Jules said nothing.

She had a bad, unspeakably bad, feeling.

She looked at her brother's wife, and waited.

Chapter Forty-One

She began with what was, suddenly, the most important thing of all.

Her baby.

'If Silas finds out I'm pregnant, I think he may want me to terminate it.'

'No.' Jules's reply was swift and instinctive. She paused, forced herself to think about it, became more certain. 'No, Abigail, he wouldn't.'

'You're the one,' Abigail reminded her, 'who once told me you thought he might be possessive enough not to want to share me with a child.'

They were still sitting side by side on the sofa, and she could hear Ollie happily playing in the playpen in the corner. She felt sickened by what she'd just said, by all that she still had to tell Jules – not least by the insensitive speed with which she was going to have to deliver all her blows. But the clock was ticking, and there was no knowing how long Silas, temporarily deprived of his role of caregiver-guardian, might be prepared to permit them alone.

'I said that quite a long while ago,' Jules said, distressed.

'Just after you'd told us you were expecting Ollie,' Abigail said.

'But even if it might, possibly, still be true,' Jules went on, 'I don't think for a moment that he'd want you to have an abortion.'

Abigail recognized the pain and revulsion in her sister-in-law's voice. 'I'm afraid I'm not so sure.'

'I see.' Jules took a moment. 'If you're right,' she said slowly, 'then surely the only answer has to be to talk to him.'

'No.' Abigail said the word starkly, forcefully.

Jules looked at her.

'There's more, isn't there?' she asked, already filled with dread.

'Yes,' Abigail said. 'I'm afraid there is.'

She told Jules about Charlie and Maggie.

She heard her soft, disbelieving gasps, thought, but was not certain, that Jules was weeping; heard and felt her stand up and move away from the sofa – probably, Abigail felt, simply to be away from *her*, the woman destroying her world with her secrets – perhaps, from her point-of-view, her lies.

'I understand,' Abigail said, painfully, 'if you don't believe me.'

Jules, over by the playpen, staring down at her child, still didn't speak.

'I've tried so very hard,' Abigail went on, 'not to believe it myself. To tell myself that Silas was lying, making things up to torment me.'

'Why,' Jules said, quietly, 'should he do that?'

'I don't know,' Abigail said. 'I realize now that I don't understand him at all.'

She reached up and, fingers shaking, pulled off the wraparound glasses, unable, suddenly, to bear their protective oppression, and it was a little better without them, the gloom lightened a little more, shapes a little more distinct than they had been, her sister-in-law faintly discernible.

'I want,' Jules said, abruptly, 'to take Ollie upstairs.'

'Yes,' Abigail said. 'Of course.'

'I don't want him to hear any more,' Jules said.

'It's just that we may not have much time before Silas comes back.' Abigail winced at her own callousness, felt guilt kick her again, violent as a steel-capped boot. 'I'm sorry.'

'It's all right.' Jules bent over, stroked her son's soft hair, pulled herself together and straightened up. 'He won't have understood any of it.'

'Even so,' Abigail said, 'I shouldn't have said it in front of him.'

'Too late,' Jules said.

Faintly, Abigail saw and heard her sister-in-law come a little closer and sit down again, not beside her on the sofa, but in one of the armchairs.

'I do, by the way, believe you,' Jules said tightly. 'God help me.'

Relief and sorrow shook Abigail. 'I'm so sorry,' she said again. 'I've wanted so badly to tell you.'

'Why didn't you?' Jules asked.

'I couldn't,' Abigail said.

'You could have,' Jules said. 'You should have.'

'No.' Stark again. 'I couldn't. Because of your father.'

For another moment, Jules was silent, and then she asked, in a voice strained to the limit: 'What about my father?'

Abigail took a deep breath and repeated to her what Silas had told her about Paul Graves's death and burial, and about Jules's alleged part in those things.

'He said—' she came, at last, to his threat '—that if I told anyone – including you – about what he'd done to Charlie, he would tell people that you were the one who was with your father at the end.'

'Meaning what?' Jules was confused. 'Tell which people?'

'I presumed,' Abigail said, 'he meant the police.'

'And what did you think he meant about my being with our father?'

'I'm almost certain—' Abigail's heart beat rapidly '—he was implying that you might have done something to him.'

'God,' Jules said.

Now Abigail was silent.

'If anyone,' Jules continued, 'did anything to our father—'

'It was Silas,' Abigail finished for her.

'God,' Jules said again. 'Dear God.' She stood up, went back to the playpen, bent down and scooped up her son, hugged him close. 'Oh, God, Ollie, your uncle is a terrible man.'

'Jules, I'm so sorry to spring all this on you, but I didn't know what else to do, and he hasn't let me alone since he threw that stuff in my eyes, and I suddenly realized this might be my last chance—' Abigail snatched another tremulous breath '—and I haven't told you yet about Father Moran.'

Jules, still clutching Ollie, was staring at her.

'Jules?' Abigail grew agitated. 'Are you there?'

'You're not telling me—' Jules's voice was quite faint with horror '—*please* say you're not telling me that Silas throwing the developer at you wasn't an accident.'

'I'm not sure,' Abigail said, frankly. 'I think there's a very good chance, though, that it might not have been. I think it's possible that he might have done it – set up the whole thing, right back as far as the break-in – because he was jealous again, because he'd found out I'd been going to see a priest and not telling him.'

'Surely even Silas couldn't be jealous of a priest?'

'Father Moran is a man,' Abigail said, quietly. 'A young, good-looking man.' She thought about the priest's supposedly coincidental absence, but said no more, knew she'd burdened Jules with more than enough already.

Jules was silent again, too bewildered, too shocked, to speak.

'I am so sorry to say these things,' Abigail said again, 'so terribly sorry, because he's your brother and you love him. And I still love him too, in a way, in spite of everything, and God knows I've done unspeakable things myself—'

'You,' Jules said, as she had many times before, 'didn't mean to do them.'

'I still did them,' Abigail said, 'though that's not the point now, is it?'

'No,' Jules said. 'I suppose not.'

She sat down on the sofa again, put Ollie between her and his aunt, kept one arm gently around him, needing to feel his warmth, his solidness, against herself.

'I really have begun to think,' Abigail went on, 'that Silas may be more than a little mad.'

The two women sat quietly for a while.

'First things first,' Jules said, at last, her voice a little stronger. 'We have to get you out of this house.'

'You mean, for the baby,' Abigail said.

'For you,' Jules said, 'as well as the baby.'

'I'm not important,' Abigail said. 'I don't count.'

They both heard the key in the front door lock.

'Oh, God,' Abigail said, panicking. 'I didn't hear his car.'

'It's okay,' Jules said, reaching past Ollie, touching her arm. 'Leave him to me.'

'Don't—'

'Don't what?' Silas said, from the doorway.

Jules stood up, and Abigail, instinctively, moved closer to the baby, put her arm protectively around him.

'I was going to make us some coffee,' Jules lied swiftly, 'but Abigail said she wanted to try making it herself.'

'That's ridiculous,' Silas said. 'Dangerous.'

'I'll have to learn to do far more than make coffee,' Abigail said, 'if it turns out I'm going to be permanently blind.'

'But you're not going to be,' Silas said, 'thank God.'

He regarded his nephew on the sofa beside his wife.

'Sure he's safe like that, sis?' he asked Jules.

Jules gave him a withering look. 'As houses.'

Silas gave a small shrug. 'I'll make the coffee then.' He paused. 'Have you had lunch yet?'

'Not yet,' Abigail said.

'We've been talking,' Jules said, quickly, 'and we both agree it's high time Abigail had a change of venue, so she's coming to the shop with me this afternoon.'

'Not your best idea,' Silas said.

'It's a very good idea,' Jules told him. 'The bookshop's perfectly safe.'

'Nowhere's perfectly safe,' Silas said. 'What are you planning to have her do? Stocktaking? Or cleaning, perhaps?'

'For starters—' Jules ignored his sarcasm '—Abigail's going to keep me company, since Ollie's going to his playgroup for two hours, and Drew's off.'

'I'd love to go,' Abigail said.

'And what about me?' Silas asked.

'You,' Jules said, 'can take it easy for a change. Put your feet up.'

'Time off,' Abigail added, 'from looking after me.'

'I'm your husband,' Silas said. 'That's what I'm here for.'

He insisted on helping her upstairs so that she could change her clothes.

'She doesn't need to change,' Jules had said moments before.

'Abigail takes a pride in her appearance,' Silas had told her. 'Her hair's a mess, and those jeans have got stains on them. Ollie's handiwork, I think.'

Both women had known there was no point arguing.

'I suppose,' he said now, as they reached the bedroom, 'you're going to tell me you can get ready without me.'

'You know I can,' Abigail said. 'You sorted the wardrobes so cleverly, and anyway, shapes really do seem to be getting a wee bit clearer.'

'That's good,' Silas said.

And left her.

Went downstairs.

Back into the living room, where Jules was sitting on the carpet with Ollie.

'You may as well leave,' Silas said.

'I'm sorry?' Jules said.

'I said you may as well leave,' Silas repeated, 'since Abigail won't be going anywhere with you today.'

Jules knew, at that instant, that the gloves were off. How, exactly, she had no idea, but Silas knew that Abigail had been telling her about him and Charlie and Maggie Blume and their father, and perhaps even that she suspected her blinding might have been deliberate. Abigail had said, earlier, that she believed Silas had left them alone as a kind of test, and suddenly Jules realized that she had been right.

Stay calm, she told herself.

'Abigail,' she said, 'wants to come with me.'

'Abigail,' Silas said, very coolly, 'does not want to come with you to the bookshop for the afternoon.' He paused. 'Abigail *does*, I suspect, want to get out of this house with you, and to *stay* with you. To leave me.'

'Don't be so ridiculous.' Jules tried to smile. 'Of course she doesn't.'

She looked down at Ollie, absorbed again with his rabbit – and he was such a good, sweet, easygoing child, and so much of that came from Ralph.

Supposing he'd inherited his uncle's traits?

Never.

'Come on, my love,' she told Ollie, and picked him up, with the toy.

'I'm not a complete fucking moron, Jules,' Silas said, suddenly, harshly.

'No,' she said, quietly. 'I know you're not.'

'Nor am I given to idle threats,' he said.

Jules held tightly to her son, looked into her brother's face.

'So you'll believe me,' Silas said, 'when I tell you that if you do any-thing – *anything* at all – to assist Abigail in leaving me, I will—'

'Silas, I haven't a clue what—'

'I can promise you, Jules—' he drove on over her words ' – that it would be the very last thing on earth I wanted to do. But if you do help Abigail, if you do leave me no choice, I *will* do it.'

'What will you do?' Jules sounded hoarse, her throat felt constricted.

'Kill you,' Silas said. 'And Ollie.'

Upstairs, in their bedroom, Abigail had put her jeans into the laundry bag and pulled on what she hoped was a clean pair, and now she was fastening the button at the waist, and her hands were shaking again, so it was taking longer.

She wondered – finding a sweater, one of those with wider necks that Silas had piled up for her; no roll-necks for the time being, in case they rubbed her eyes – how Jules was managing downstairs.

Thought she'd been right to involve her at last.

Prayed she had been.

The urge to throw herself at Silas after he made his threat against Ollie, the urge to rip at his cold, flat green eyes, was more overpoweringly intense than any physical pain Jules had ever experienced. But her child was in her arms and so, instead, she stood frozen, clasping Ollie even closer, trying to shut herself off from this man who looked like her brother, but who was, in truth, some kind of *monster*.

Scenes from their past flickered through her mind like old movie clips. His cold-heartedness after their mother and stepfather had died, his refusal to allow them to be buried together. His rage when the terms of Patricia's will had given this house to her instead of him; the way he had emotionally blackmailed, *manipulated* her into signing it over to him.

Their father's curious death and grotesque burial.

She felt suddenly, violently sick.

'Once too often,' Silas said.

'What?' Jules was too confused, too appalled to take in any more.

'One betrayal too often.' He shook his head. 'You coming here today with that *thing* my wife asked you for – and you weren't even going to *tell* me, were you, that it was positive?'

'No,' Jules said, reeling. 'I was not.'

'Lucky for me then that I already knew.' He watched his sister's face. 'Don't you want to ask me how I knew?'

Ollie, who'd been unusually silent since she'd picked him up, gave a long, breathy sigh and shifted in her arms, reminded Jules that Silas, his own uncle, had just threatened to kill him.

Get him out.

That was the most important thing in the world right now, that she take him away from this house, get him to safety.

Abigail, too.

'I'm going upstairs,' Jules said.

'I've been taping her calls,' Silas said. 'Not legal, of course, but not hard. And even if I hadn't, I'm not remotely as stupid as the pair of you seem to believe. I've been taking care of most of Abigail's needs, after all, since she came home from hospital, so I know she's not on the Pill any more and that she missed her last period.'

For the first time, looking at him standing between her and the doorway, Jules felt actually afraid of him.

'Let me pass, Silas,' she said.

'I'm guessing that Abigail's a bit apprehensive about being pregnant just at the moment,' he went on. 'But I think in time she'll be happy about it.'

'She thinks,' Jules said, 'you might want her to terminate it.'

The pupils in Silas's eyes dilated, spread black anger over the green.

'I would sooner,' he said, 'terminate Abigail than my baby.'

Jules felt suddenly dizzy, clung tighter to Ollie, afraid of dropping him.

'I thought,' she said, 'you didn't want a child.'

'In the past, perhaps not.' He paused. 'Before Abigail betrayed me, too.'

In her arms, Ollie shifted again.

'Baba,' he said.

'It's all right, my love,' Jules murmured, and rocked him.

'Getting heavy, isn't he?' Silas said.

Jules didn't answer.

'Want me to take him?' Silas asked.

Over my dead body.

Abigail had said she thought he might be more than a little mad, and suddenly Jules hoped with all her might that he was entirely, *hopelessly*, mad. Because otherwise it could only be that he was entirely wicked.

She did not want her brother to be wicked.

'Maybe, finally,' he said, 'if we have our child, there may be one person in this world who'll love me forever—'

'Silas,' Jules said.

'One person,' he went on, 'who won't let me down.'

'I'm going to go now,' she tried again. 'I'll just go up and see what—'

'You will not go up and see *anything*,' Silas snapped violently. 'Get out, by all means, Jules, and take Ollie with you, but you're not taking my wife or child.'

'I only want to—'

'Forget it,' he cut her off again. 'Take your son, if you want, but that's all you're taking, is that clear enough?'

Jules stared at him.

At her stranger-brother.

Knew she had no choice.

'Very clear,' she said.

And went.

Abigail was sitting on the edge of the bed, running her fingertips over the loafers she'd just put on, trying to make certain they were a matching pair, when she heard the front door close and, a second or two later, Silas's tread on the staircase.

She stood up, paced her way over to the door, opened it.

'Was that Jules?' she called.

'Leaving.' Silas came into the room. 'She's taken Ollie to his play-group.'

'But I was going with her,' Abigail said.

'You're not going anywhere.'

'Why not?'

'You're not to be trusted,' Silas said. 'Any more than Jules is, or our mother was.' He took her hand. 'Come on.'

'Where?' Abigail felt fear and anger mounting.

'The music room.' He began to draw her out of the bedroom.

'Silas, stop it.' She pulled away, groped for the wall, laid a hand flat against it to balance herself. 'What the hell is going on?'

'Best thing for you—' he gripped her arm this time, tightly, propelled her with him along the corridor '—is going to be your cello.'

He opened the door to the music room.

'Music,' he said, 'is supposed to be good for unborn babies.'

Abigail wanted to scream. She was as certain as she could be that Jules would not have told him, at least not voluntarily, but he *knew*, and that was all that counted now, and she was going to have to be extra careful, for her child's sake.

My child. Even in the midst of this new bizarreness, the thought thrilled her, pierced her with a wild, frantic kind of joy.

'Can't have you getting in a state.' Silas manoeuvred her into the room, closed the door behind them. 'Risking my baby's health.'

'I'm not going to play,' Abigail said.

Don't show him you're scared, she told herself, even as fear clutched at her.

'I think you should,' Silas said, sounding reasonable.

'I'm going to the shop with Jules.' She tried to concentrate on exactly where she was in relation to the door. 'As we arranged.'

'You're not going anywhere,' he said again. 'Not for a very long time. Not, that is, unless I go with you.'

'Don't be ridiculous,' she said.

'Jules called me ridiculous, too,' Silas said.

'She was right.'

'Right or not,' he said, 'you'd better listen to what I'm telling you.'

'You can't possibly think,' Abigail said, 'I'm going to let you stop me going anywhere I choose to.'

He pushed her, quite hard, then caught at her left arm to stop her falling.

'Sit down,' he told her.

'I will not—'

'Sit *down*.'

He manhandled her onto her chair, picked up the cello from where she had left it after Jules's arrival with the pregnancy testing kit, thrust it into her arms.

'Play or don't play,' he said. 'I don't care any more.'

'Just as well.' Anger lent her bravado.

'But you will not be going anywhere without me, Abigail,' he assured her, 'until after my child is born.'

'*Your* child.' The word was scornful, outraged.

'You'll be with me, or you'll be locked in.'

'You wouldn't dare do—'

'The bedroom door and windows will be locked at night, and the phone—'

'I'll smash the windows,' Abigail said. 'Scream my head off.'

'Don't push me too far,' Silas said.

She heard the strange, dangerous note in his voice, and bravado left her.

'You're mad,' she said, quietly.

'Takes one to know one,' Silas said.

She fought down panic, struggled to regroup.

'I've outpatients appointments at the hospital,' she said. 'And if I'm having a baby, there'll be antenatal visits too.'

'I'll be with you for all those,' Silas said. 'Obviously.'

'Not every minute,' Abigail said.

'I'll make sure everyone knows about your tragic past,' he said. 'Your fragile mental state.'

'They won't believe you. Certainly not the people who already know me.'

He shrugged. 'Beside the point, since you won't be telling them anything, because you know who'll suffer if you do.'

'Jules already knows about everything.' Abigail gathered strength again. 'You can't threaten me with hurting her any more.'

'Not Jules,' Silas said. 'Ollie.'

Dread gripped her, gnawed at her heart.

'You wouldn't,' she said.

'Jules believed me when I told her the same thing.'

Abigail said nothing, felt him move, detected his shape in the fog drawing away from her back towards the door.

'Why else do you suppose she's abandoned you?' Silas asked.

And left the room, locking the door behind him.

Chapter Forty-Two

'Priorities,' Jules said to herself and the dachshund back in her Highgate living room, surrounded by normality.

Nothing looked normal, nothing *felt* normal.

Late November outside. Colder and much bleaker inside, in her heart.

'Priorities,' she said again, sank into an armchair, then swiftly sat upright, shifted to the edge, knowing there was no time for comfort.

First priority. Get Ollie to safety. Somewhere safer than here or his playgroup.

She looked down at him, still strapped into his buggy, sound asleep.

Not safe here. Not any more.

Then, next, *somehow*, find a way to help Abigail.

Another woman, with a different, normal family history behind her, might, she supposed, be on her brother's side at this moment, rather than on her sister-in-law's. Would be outraged by Abigail's allegations, think *her* mad. But Jules had spent too many years, put too much effort into trying to forget her own dark times with Silas.

Her mind lurched back again now to their father's death.

To Silas's refusal to inform anyone.

To the appallingly grisly burial, which she had countenanced.

Only fifteen, Jules.

A strange, bizarrely sheltered fifteen at that, sheltered by her brother.

Till Ralph.

Silas had been so cold when she'd fallen in love.

Jules recalled, suddenly, the conversation not long before Ralph's death in which she'd told Silas that she'd shared their secret about the garden grave with her husband. Silas had been icy for a few moments, hadn't he, but then he'd surprised her, said his own marriage had helped him understand her need to confide in Ralph.

That he didn't mind, so long as Ralph didn't tell anyone.

She remembered talking to Silas about Ralph's trip to South Africa.

And then, soon after that, he'd gone to Deauville with Abigail, and had been called back for some glitzy magazine commission – for *Sleek*, she seemed to remember – and he'd phoned her, asked her to take his place, keep Abigail company.

Which was why when Ralph had come home, Jules had still been in France, and Silas back in London taking photographs.

Her spine prickled.

When Ralph had died, Silas had been in London.

No one had ever, from Jules's point-of-view, come up with a truly satisfactory explanation for Ralph's having bought the lethal dinner that had caused his fatal anaphylactic shock.

Fatigue after the long journey.

The pathologist and Coroner might have accepted that, but Jules, knowing Ralph so much better than anyone, never really had.

Silas had not wanted Ralph knowing about their father's grave.

Then, when it was too late, after Jules had told him, Silas had not wanted Ralph telling anyone about it.

Had been in London, taking photographs.

Though if she thought about that last-minute commission, she didn't recall ever seeing any of his work in *Sleek* magazine.

You weren't reading magazines, you were grieving for Ralph.

Who had died because he'd eaten a little of a dinner that he would have *known* was dangerous to him. Who would never have bought it in the first place, never have put himself in the position of touching a dish containing ingredients he wasn't certain of. Unless someone else had bought the dinner.

Brought it to the flat. To Ralph.

Someone familiar, perhaps, who told him it was safe.

And Ralph, who *had* been weary, might have been hungry, too, might have believed that person.

And Silas had been in London.

'Dear God,' Jules said now, and stood up.

A man who could threaten his own baby nephew was capable of anything.

Anything.

Jules, feeling light-headed and nauseous, shook her head.

Running out of time.

'One person who'll love me forever,' Silas had said about their baby-to-be.

Which meant that, perhaps, for as long as she was pregnant, Abigail might be safe – so long as she behaved as Silas wanted her to. But though Jules realized now that her sister-in-law's massive guilt complex had, till now, made her far too acquiescent with Silas, even Abigail, with all her suspicions and fears – and for now at least so much more helpless and vulnerable than before – would not be able to tolerate much more, and *then* what?

And what might happen once the child was born?

One person who'll love me forever.

Jules looked down again at Ollie, then found the phone and dialled the shop.

'Jules's Books.'

She heard, with gratitude, the familiar Yorkshire-accented voice.

'I need a favour, Drew,' she said, straightaway. 'A big one.'

'Anything,' he said, without hesitation.

Jules told him that she needed him to shut the shop and go home, that she would, if he agreed, be bringing Ollie over to his place, that she might, very probably, have to leave him for the rest of the day and perhaps overnight because what she needed was a really safe person to leave him with.

'What's happened?' Drew asked anxiously. 'Are you all right?'

'I'm fine,' Jules lied.

'Something must have happened,' Drew persisted.

'Nothing I can tell you about, Drew.'

'Fair enough,' he said.

'Is it all right then?' Jules asked.

'Actually,' he said, 'could you give me a couple of hours?' He paused. 'Only there's some shopping I promised I'd try and get in for an elderly neighbour who's just had her hip done, and she can't get about on her own yet, and if I could just shut up shop and get that in for her . . .'

Jules thought about it.

She wasn't ready to make a move yet, needed time to plan.

'Do your neighbour's shopping, Drew,' she said.

Chapter Forty-Three

At the house, Silas finished making a sandwich for Abigail, poured orange juice into a glass and carried a tray, complete with her array of eye drops, upstairs to the music room.

She was sitting on the chaise longue.

'Late lunch,' he told her, 'even if you haven't been playing. All healthy ingredients. Wholemeal bread, chicken breast, salad.'

'I'm not hungry,' Abigail said.

'You should eat,' Silas said. 'For two, as they say.'

'Where did you go?' she asked. 'I heard you go out.'

'I had some errands to run,' he said. 'I knew you'd be safe in here.'

'Safe?' She was incredulous. 'Locked into a room.'

'I'll wait with you, if you like,' Silas said, companionably, 'while you eat your sandwich. And then I can help you with your drops.'

'I'll do my own drops,' Abigail said.

He had put the tray down on one of the small tables, then pulled it closer to the chaise longue, made sure she knew where it was, but she made no move to touch it.

'I do hope you're not going to be childish, for the baby's sake.'

'I told you, I'll do the drops.'

'You need to be careful,' he said, 'not to muddle them up.'

'I'll manage.'

'Don't let your anger with me harm your eyes,' Silas said.

'Jesus,' Abigail said softly.

'Please eat,' he said.

'Are you going to let me out?' she asked.

'I can't,' he said, 'for the present.'

'Then I shan't be eating,' Abigail said, 'for the present.'

'We'll have to see about that,' Silas said.

He left the room and locked her in.

Ten minutes later, as he was leaving the house again, he heard the cello.

Chapter Forty-Four

At his flat in Wood Green just after five-thirty, Drew Martin – having bought and delivered his neighbour's shopping – was now listening to Jules's instructions for Ollie's feeds.

'I don't know why you're fussing so much,' he told her finally. 'It's not as if I've never sat for Ollie before, and I've even got the travel cot, and have you forgotten I have two little nieces and I'm a godfather *and* this young chap quite likes me?'

'Ollie loves you,' Jules said.

Tears sprang unexpectedly to her eyes and she blinked them quickly away, made a foolish gesture of rubbing her nose as if she'd been about to sneeze, knew she hadn't fooled Drew for a second.

'I'm getting very worried about you,' he said.

'I'm fine,' Jules said, brightly. 'But I don't know when I'll be back.'

'I know,' Drew said. 'You've told me, and you've told me I'm not to tell anyone else I've got him, including your brother, though I can't begin to think why not, but that's okay, and I won't tell him or anyone else, cross my heart and hope to die.' He bent to ruffle Ollie's hair. 'So you go and get up to whatever it is you're getting up to.' He paused, still troubled. 'So long as you really are all right, and there's nothing else – nothing more – I can do for you.'

'You're already doing the most important thing,' Jules told him.

And then she kissed her son, tried not to burst into tears, and left.

Chapter Forty-Five

Silas had come to release Abigail from the music room shortly after six, offering no explanation as to where he had been.

Not that she had asked him.

On strike.

If she refused to comply with anything and everything he demanded of her, she had rationalized some time ago, then, given her pregnancy, surely he was bound to see that he had no choice but to back down himself.

Wrong to use her baby as a bargaining tool, she knew that, hated herself for it.

Needs must.

And hating herself was no novelty.

'Since you won't eat or speak to me or play for me,' he told her in the bedroom just before nine o'clock, 'you might as well go to bed.'

'I'll go to bed,' Abigail said, 'when I feel like it.'

She waited for him to lock her in, leave her, but he didn't budge, sat on the bedspread on his side of the bed, reading a book. She could hear the familiar swish of pages being turned at intervals, knew from the sound that it was a paperback, wondered, idly – bored, by now, as well as furious and frustrated – which book he was reading, if it was still the Ian Rankin . . .

Silas had, during the period of his greatest contrition, read to her for hours at a time, and she had found considerable comfort in escaping into fiction.

If he tried reading to her now, she thought with a sudden, almost overwhelming surge of rage, she would seize the book, somehow, and *slug* him with it.

He did not try. Did not speak to her again.

Just went on silently reading until she could bear it no longer.

'I'm going to bed,' she said, abruptly.

She heard him close the book.

'Would you like me to help you undress?' he asked.

'What I would like,' she said tightly, 'is for you to leave me alone.'

'Not till I know you're safely tucked up,' Silas said. 'I don't want you falling and hurting my baby.'

'*Our* baby, for God's sake, Silas.'

'But you, apparently, don't want me any more,' he said.

'What I don't want,' she said, 'is to be your prisoner.'

'So I've decided to settle—' he ignored her '—for having, and keeping, my child.'

Chapter Forty-Six

Jules was back home in her flat again, Asali beside her, walked and fed and feeling her mistress's tension.

Jules stared at the television in her living room, seeing nothing.

Waiting.

Dressed in dark clothes, like a burglar. Black roll-neck sweater and the old olive-green combat-style trousers she used for serious cleaning work at home and at the shop because of their comfort and wealth of zipped and velcro-fastened pockets.

Everything she might need – so far as she'd managed to calculate – was by the front door. A torch, and the biggest screwdriver she'd been able to find – in lieu of a crowbar – which she hoped, fervently, she wouldn't need to use, since she still possessed a set of keys to her brother's house.

The keys lay beside the screwdriver.

Not much use if Silas had bolted all the doors.

Or changed the locks.

Even if he had, though, there was a ground floor side window that opened onto what he called the utility room, but which had, in their early childhood, been called the laundry room. The window was a push-up, sash affair that had never, at least in the past, either locked properly or opened fully. Jules remembered using it once, as a child, to squeeze through after she'd accidentally got herself locked out, and she had no recollection of either her mother or, later, Graham getting it repaired, and until today, she'd forgotten all about it, so maybe . . .

She had been smaller then, of course, could not be sure that even if it did still open she'd be able to get through the gap, hence the substitute crowbar with which she planned, if absolutely necessary, to force either that window or the side door.

She had considered her other main option, had worked through the logistics of reporting Silas's crimes to the police and letting them deal with getting Abigail out; but the more she'd gone over it all, the more insane her collection of accusations had sounded even to herself.

One murder disguised as a mugging. A witness-supported road accident that Silas had just happened to see. A grievous assault on his own wife who had repeatedly insisted, both to the police and hospital personnel, that it had been purely accidental. A body buried in the garden of her former home. A wholly unsubstantiated threat against herself and her baby.

And Ralph.

They'd probably think her barking mad. And even if she did manage to persuade them to send a couple of officers round to the house, if Silas had by then, made sufficient threats against his wife and their unborn child there was every chance Abigail might feel compelled to tell them nothing was wrong.

'So,' Jules said to the dachshund, 'all down to me.'

Chapter Forty-Seven

Abigail was undressed, in bed.

All alone in the dark.

Silas had waited till she was ready, had, true to his word, locked the bedroom and en-suite bathroom windows, unplugged the telephone and taken it out of the room before locking her in.

She wasn't certain which was more appalling. The fact that she was trapped, virtually blind and alone, with no immediate prospect of rescue, or the knowledge that Silas might, at any moment of his choosing during the rest of the evening or night, unlock the door and come in, perhaps even come to bed.

You've been sleeping with him for months.

With a murderer, God help her.

All changed now. All different now.

She laid her right hand on her flat stomach.

Because of you.

The baby had changed everything.

That and, of course, Silas's threat to hurt Ollie.

She'd put the radio on a while back, had hoped it might calm her a little, at least distract her from her predicament, allow her to pretend again, for an hour or so, that she was a normal woman lying in bed trying to get to sleep.

Book at Bedtime had not worked, and anyway, she wanted to be alert to any sounds, to feel just the slightest bit more prepared, less vulnerable, when Silas did decide to make his next appearance.

So she sat, propped up by pillows, determined to stay awake.

Don't sleep.

A lullaby sprang into her mind, something sweet and gentle that Dougie Allen, her poor lovely father, had sung softly to her when she was very small. She hardly remembered any of the words. *Rest your head . . .*

'Not now, Daddy,' Abigail said into the darkness.
Rest your head.
'Please,' she said.

Chapter Forty-Eight

Drew adored babies, especially Ollie, who he had, through circumstances, come to spend much more time with and know far more thoroughly than either of his sister's children or even young Harry, his godson, whose family did at least live in reasonable reach, unlike his nieces up in Harrogate.

Content, for the most part, as he was with his life (and working for, or rather *with* Jules, as she always emphasized, was a big part of his contentment), one of the things he did find himself fretting about now and again was the great likelihood that he might never have children of his own. Nick, his treacherous lover, had talked at one time about their adopting or even looking into surrogacy, but then again, as Drew had, alas, come to learn, Nick had talked a lot of codswallop.

Drew had fed Ollie and changed his nappy, and now the little lad was sleeping again in the travel cot beside him on his couch, the telly turned lower than usual so as not to disturb him.

Drew sighed, one of his broody sighs, and gazed down at the sleeping boy.

Jules had looked very ... *peaky* was the word his mum would have used.

And frightened, he thought.

'Never mind, Ollie,' he said softly, soothingly. 'Mummy will be back for you soon.' He hesitated, being a great believer in honesty, even, daft as it might be, with sleeping babies. 'Soon as she can, sweetheart, all right?'

The front door bell rang.

'Goodness.' Drew smiled. 'That was quick, wasn't it?'

Chapter Forty-Nine

Jules had been watching the house through the trees for several minutes from her car, parked a little way down the hill.

Time to go.

She got out, closed the door as noiselessly as she could manage, stuck the keys in the top left hand pocket of her trousers, closed it securely and made her way, silently, courtesy of her battered trainers, towards the house.

Not the front door.

Absurd. Her brother's house. Her family home, bequeathed to her, *her*, by their mother.

She paused, brought her thoughts firmly to the present.

The house was in absolute darkness, at least so far as she could tell, and she had seen no activity since her arrival. Nor was there any sign of Silas's VW, but then again the garage door was shut, so it might be – probably was – in there.

Better skulk a little more.

Not so absurd at all, not after his threats.

And her new suspicions about Ralph.

Rage surged, shaking her, physically and emotionally.

Not now, she told herself. *Later, but not now.*

She made her way around the house to the right-hand side, watching her step, managing without the torch, afraid of alerting the Brooks or perhaps some passer-by, to the possibility that she might be a burglar.

There was the window, just past the side door, in its still promisingly not-quite-straight old timber frame.

Jules stopped.

Door or window?

The door – leading to the little anteroom beside the kitchen – was preferable, obviously, except that meant taking out her old bunch of house keys – four Chubbs and five Yales, several more keys than doors, no identifying tags on any of them – which were bound to jangle as she tried them out. And even if she did find the right one and the lock had not been changed, there was still the matter of the inside bolts at top and bottom of all the external doors, and even if they hadn't been used and if she did get the door open, it might creak or groan . . .

Not as loudly as a stiff, warped window.

With one gloved hand, Jules unzipped a pocket, pulled out the house keys carefully, gripped them tightly, holding them against her pullover to muffle any sounds, then withdrew the torch from her velcroed right thigh pocket (the left-hand one held the screwdriver), shone the beam onto the Chubb lock and tried the first key.

No go.

This was mad.

Go to the front door.

That was what she ought to do before things got completely out of control. Go to the front of the house like any normal, respectable family member, try her keys there and, if that failed, ring the bell and knock, loudly, until Silas had virtually no choice but to answer. And if he didn't want to let her in, if he left her no choice, then she could go next door and rouse the neighbours, and that, at least, was bound to get her across the threshold.

Except that Max and Tina Brook probably wouldn't want to get involved in any unpleasantness, wouldn't want to come inside with her, and even if she told them just a *tiny* morsel of the truth, even if they believed her – *especially* if they believed her – they would very likely bolt back to the safety of their own house, lock the doors and call the police.

Which might be best all round.

Truth and justice, and safety for Ollie and Abigail and her baby.

And prison for Silas.

Her big brother, whom she had loved so deeply. Still loved.

But how *could* she still love someone who had done such terrible things, who had, at the very least, pretended to his wife that he'd killed a man? Who she had now even begun to suspect of killing her husband?

Who had threatened to kill Ollie.

She made up her mind. No more procrastinating. She was here, now, at this side door, with at least a chance of entering the house without Silas realizing. Better just to go with her first instincts, get inside and take it from there.

She tried a second key, slid it into the lock, met no resistance.

Turned it.

Stood quite still, listening.

Open it.

She gripped the old door knob, and turned it slowly.
The door opened.
Creaked.
Jules switched off the torch, hardly daring to breathe.
It was pitch dark inside. No sounds except the wheeze of the boiler.
Go. For God's sake, just go.
She stepped into the dark.

Chapter Fifty

Abigail was sleeping.

In her dream, she was a child again in the kitchen at Allen's Farm.

Three tiny kittens, black as coal, lay in a basket on the stone floor near the stove, while Nell, one of the border collies, snoozed close by.

The aroma of baking bread hung in the air.

Abigail's mother was sitting in a rocking chair, knitting something pink.

Her stomach was swollen with pregnancy.

In the dream, Abigail knew that *she* was the unborn child.

Safe in the dark.

She heard a sound.

A man's footsteps, coming towards the house across the yard.

Abigail smiled into the dark.

She knew it was her daddy coming.

Already, she felt a rush of love, could see him even before he came into the house, a newborn lamb tucked beneath his jacket, one of the needy wee ones that her ma would bottle feed and keep warm till it was stronger . . .

She felt so safe.

But the man came in and it wasn't Abigail's father, but Silas, his gorgeous hay-coloured hair flopping over his forehead, his eyes softer, a more luminous green than she had ever seen them.

Yet what he brought with him, *within* him, was neither soft nor beautiful, and suddenly she felt a dark clamminess in the air, and Silas was looking at her, looking right at her – and that wasn't possible, Abigail knew, because she hadn't yet been born, was still safe inside her mother, so there was no need to feel so afraid . . .

But she was, desperately so.

He turned away from her, from her mother, and scooped two of the black kittens out of their basket.

'No!' Abigail screamed. '*No!*'

But being not yet born, she was not heard, and though the kitten that was left in the basket mewed plaintively, Silas gave it not so much as a glance as he lifted his two captives by the scruffs of their necks – and then, twisting his body around, like an athlete preparing to throw discus, he whipped back and hurled them both against the wall.

Abigail screamed again.

While her mother went on knitting, and blood ran down the wall in rivulets.

And suddenly Abigail was outside the house, born and full-grown now, standing in the yard, staring at the stream of blood flowing out through the front door of the farmhouse onto the cobblestones and mixing with Francesca's and Dougie's and Eddie's . . .

Abigail woke up.

Still in the dark.

Chapter Fifty-One

Jules had decided, earlier, in the semi-sanity of her flat, on two alternative approaches. Her preferred option would be to locate Abigail and bundle her immediately, if necessary with no more possessions than the clothes on her back, out of the house, into her car and over to Drew's.

The second option – much more probable, unfortunately – was that if she encountered Silas, she would bluff it out, tell him that Ollie was safely out of his reach and that she had left a message with one of her neighbours stating that if neither she nor Abigail got in touch next morning, they should call the police, make them send an officer to the house.

And if Silas called her bluff?

Call the cops, scream for the neighbours, kick him where it hurt.

Whatever it took.

Even after she'd moved away from the sounds of the boiler and the fridge's startlingly loud rumbles, the voice of the old house still intermittently broke into the night silence of the deserted ground floor. Knocking pipes and creaking boards, the mantel clock, ticking away, then, startlingly – on the dot of one o'clock – chiming.

Even Jules's own breathing sounded raucous in her ears.

No other sign of life down here.

She turned the torch back on, as sure now as she could be that they were both upstairs in bed, which was just what she had been fearing most.

Full-on confrontation with Silas, with Abigail still half-blind.

Jules steeled herself, then began to make her way up the staircase.

If Silas was asleep, that might render him at least a little vulnerable, too.

She reached the upper floor, lit her way to the bedroom door, then switched the torch off again, ran over her plan such as it was: she would open the door sharply, switch the overhead light on, hoping, with a bit of luck, to dazzle Silas and thereby briefly get the upper hand.

She reached the door, put out her shaky, still gloved hand.

Think of Ralph.

Think of Ollie.

She turned the handle.

Nothing happened.

Jules fumbled for the sliding switch on the torch, trained the beam on the lock, saw the key.

She turned it, opened the door and turned on the light.

Silas was not in the bed, or in the room.

Abigail was half sitting up, startled out of sleep.

'We don't have any kittens,' she said, confusedly.

'It's only me,' Jules said, softly. 'Where's Silas?'

'I don't know.' Abigail shook her head, fully awake now. 'He locked me in a long time ago. I didn't mean to fall asleep.'

Jules crossed to the bathroom, found it empty. 'I don't think he's in the house.' Abigail was already out of bed, feeling for her dressing gown.

'Don't bother with that, darling,' Jules told her. 'We're getting you dressed and out.' She pulled off her gloves, stuck them in one of her pockets, went to the wardrobe, dug out jeans, sweater and loafers. 'Here.' She put them all into Abigail's arms. 'Put these on while I listen at the door.'

'Don't go looking for him, Jules,' Abigail said. 'He's gone quite mad, talking about keeping me locked up till the baby's born.'

'Did you hear him go out?' Jules watched her pull on the jeans, zip them up.

Abigail shook her head. 'But he's been coming and going since you left.' She pulled the sweater carefully over her head, mindful of her eyes, then put on one shoe, fished around for the second, found it, tilted her face up anxiously. 'Jules?'

'I'm here. It's okay.' Jules noticed Abigail's dark glasses on the bedside table, went to pick them up. 'Here.' She handed them to her. 'Your glasses.'

Abigail put them on. 'Where's Ollie?'

'Safe with Drew,' Jules said. 'Ready?'

'My bag,' Abigail said.

Jules looked round, saw it on the dressing table chair, went to pick it up, handed it to Abigail. 'Let's get out of here.'

They were downstairs, halfway to the front door when Jules hesitated.

'I ought to call Drew, warn him.'

'You don't think Silas might—?' Abigail stopped, appalled.

'Stay here, don't move. I'll be right back.'

She ran into the kitchen, returned a long minute later.

'No reply.'

'Maybe he's—'

'We have to get there.' Jules gripped her arm. 'Let's go.'

They both heard the key in the lock.

Jules saw the front door open.

Silas stood in the doorway, Ollie asleep in his arms.

'Going somewhere?' he asked.

Abigail gave a small moan of fear.

'He's got Ollie,' Jules reported and, swiftly, firmly, propelled her back to the foot of the staircase. 'Abigail, go back up to the bedroom and lock yourself in.'

'I'm not leaving you,' Abigail said.

'I'll be fine,' Jules said sharply. 'Go *on*.'

'Yes, go on, Abigail,' Silas said, and closed the door behind him.

'What are you doing with Ollie?' Abigail said.

'Abigail, please, do as I say,' Jules told her. 'It'll be okay.'

Abigail fumbled for the handrail, sucked in a desperate breath, and went.

Jules waited for her to disappear from sight, then turned to Silas.

'Please give Ollie to me,' she said, quietly.

'He's fine with his uncle,' Silas said.

Everything Jules had planned to say on confrontation flew out of her mind.

'You must know,' she said, 'there's no point to this nonsense about trying to keep Abigail locked up. It's mad to even imagine you could do such a thing.'

'Then that must make me mad,' Silas said. 'Because one way or another, I'm not planning on letting Abigail leave me so long as she's pregnant with my child.'

In his arms, Ollie stirred, whimpered.

Jules held out her arms. 'Please give him to me.'

Silas looked down. 'Still hard to see his father in him, don't you think?'

'I see Ralph in him all the time.'

Just speaking his name brought the rage back to the surface.

'You killed him too, didn't you?' she said. 'You came to see Ralph that last night, brought him that food.' She watched his face, knew already, without doubt, that she was right. 'You told him it was fine, and he believed you.'

'You shouldn't have told him about our father,' Silas said, calmly. 'Your fault, really, Jules.'

*

233

Listening at the top of the stairs, Abigail felt such a violent attack of nausea that she thought she might pass out. Her hands moved to her stomach, then down to her womb.

She had to protect it now.

Not *it*. Him or her.

She reached for the wall to help guide herself, more frustrated than ever about her lack of vision, about having to move so *slowly* when every instinct cried out for her to run back downstairs and help Jules and Ollie. Yet common sense told her that if she fell, and if Silas heard her, that would help no one at all.

Especially not my baby.

She reached the bedroom, hesitated, changed her mind and went on, to the music room. Took the key from the outside of the door, went in, closed the door and locked herself in.

Now she couldn't *hear*.

She began to pace, knew the dimensions of the room well enough, despite the fog, to walk back and forth without bumping into walls.

Thinking about what she had just heard.

For all that Silas had told her about Charlie, for all her other suspicions – more than just suspicion now, of course, God help them all – it had never, *never*, for one single instant occurred to her that he might have done that hideous, abominable thing to his own sister's husband.

She stopped pacing, remembering again how Jules had loved Ralph. Remembered Silas – her beloved Phoenix – and dear Christ, even that made her feel violently sick now, her blind, *truly* blind, adoration of him – remembered him going ahead of Jules to open their kitchen door, being the one to find Ralph's body.

Remembered Jules cradling him on the floor.

Remembered Ralph's poor contorted face.

Remembered Silas pointing to the phone on the floor near the body, saying that Ralph must have dropped it while trying to call for help.

When all the while, it had been *him* . . .

Abigail moved into the middle of the room, found her cello and bow, groped for her chair, sat down and began to play.

Blotting it out again.

Still downstairs in the entrance hall, Silas and Jules both heard the cello.

Its raucous pain.

'Right.' Still holding Ollie, the baby awake now, Silas pushed past Jules to the staircase.

'Give him to me,' she said, desperately, following him up. '*Please* Silas.'

He ignored her, turned towards the music room, tried the door.

'Abigail,' he called, loudly. 'Let me in.'

The sounds from inside stopped.

'Give me my son,' Jules said, behind Silas.

He rapped on the door.

'Abigail,' he shouted. 'Open this door.'

'You stay put, Abigail,' Jules called, her voice even louder.

Silas whipped around. 'Be quiet.'

Ollie began to cry, his cheeks looking hot.

'It's all right, my love,' Jules told him, trying not to cry herself, trying to calm at least her tone for her child's sake. 'Silas, please, just give him to me.'

Silas's eyes were flat and colder, deader than pebbles now.

'My God.' Jules couldn't help herself. 'I never realized how right our mother was, wanting to leave this house to me.'

'Shut up,' Silas said.

Ollie's crying grew louder, and he thrust out one free, pudgy arm towards his helpless mother.

'She must have seen it in you,' Jules went on, driven now by pure rage. 'The rottenness, even back then.'

'Shut the fuck *up*,' Silas said.

'She couldn't have known the extent of it, though,' Jules pushed on. 'How could she? How could anyone have begun to guess what a wicked, sick—'

Silas's slap was hard enough to propel her backwards.

Jules's head struck the wall with a sickening crack.

'Oh,' she said, and slumped to the floor.

Inside the music room, on the other side of the door, Abigail heard the cracking sound, and then the silence – and then Ollie's wail, growing louder, more hysterical.

'Abigail, open this door!' Silas bellowed from the corridor.

For an instant she covered her ears, then outstretched her arms again to help herself back towards the chair.

She sat, dragged up the cello and bow again.

Began to play again, playing, *playing*, trying to hide inside the music. Failing.

'Right,' Silas told his nephew.

He carried Ollie, still howling and struggling now for freedom, along the corridor to the bedroom, where he stepped inside and dumped the child down on the floor.

'Scream all you want in here,' he said, shut the door, locked it, stuck the key in his trouser pocket and returned to the music room, stepping past Jules.

'I'm going to kick this in now, Abigail,' he yelled.

The music stopped again.

Silas stepped back, kicked hard at the door, his boot splintering wood. Behind him, on the floor, Jules moaned.

Silas kicked the splintered panel again, hard enough to smash it, bent to thrust his arm through, located the key on the inside, extricated it, used it to unlock the door.

'Ready or not,' he said and stepped through.

From her hiding place behind the door, seeing his blurred shape entering, feeling his anger almost as palpably as heat, Abigail took a deep, shuddering breath, lifted the cello high over her head and then brought it down against his shoulders, sending him to his knees.

Outside in the corridor, Jules gave another moan.

'Jules?' Still clutching the cello, Abigail groped her way out of the room. 'Jules, where *are* you?'

'Here. I can't seem to stand yet – whacked my head.'

Abigail made out her shape, crouched down, keeping her left arm around the neck of the instrument as she sought to try to help the other woman.

'Jules, grab hold of my—'

'Ollie,' Jules broke in urgently. 'Get Ollie out and call the police.'

'Not leaving you,' Abigail said.

'You have to get Ollie out,' Jules said. '*Please.*'

'All right.' Abigail got to her feet. 'I'll get him.'

Gripping the cello differently now – a weapon for now, not a musical instrument, and she thought she could almost picture her mother encouraging her – she groped her way to the bedroom door, felt for the key.

'Oh, God, Jules, he's taken it, he's got the *key.*'

Inside the room, Ollie's crying was a little less shrill.

'Break it down,' Jules called to her.

'All right, Ollie.' Abigail raised her voice encouragingly. 'I'm coming.'

She heaved the cello up under her arm, used both hands to swing it back, heard Jules's warning cry too late.

'I don't think so,' Silas said, behind her.

He made a grab for the instrument, but Abigail held onto it.

'You open the door then,' she said. 'For Ollie's sake.'

'Can't do that,' Silas said.

He took hold of her right arm.

'He's just a *baby*,' Abigail beseeched him.

'Even so,' Silas said. 'I can't let you take him out of here now.'

'You *bastard*.' Abigail tried to wrench her arm away, but he was too strong.

'Don't make me hurt you, Abigail.' He began to wrest the cello from her. 'Not while you're carrying my baby.'

They both heard movement behind them.

'Leave her *alone*!' Jules grabbed Silas's right arm, kicked at his legs. 'Abigail, get away, get out of here!'

Silas let go of Abigail, turned and punched his sister in the face.

Abigail heard Jules's shout of pain, saw her sister-in-law's shape sink to the floor, saw Silas looming at her again, gave a cry of terror and hit out with the cello, heard a crunch, knew she'd struck him hard.

'Bitch,' he gasped. 'You absolute *bitch*!'

Hanging onto the instrument with her left arm, holding it tight against her body, Abigail turned towards the staircase, put out her right hand to the wall for balance, feeling her way.

Silas's fingers grasped her right ankle.

'No!' She stumbled, steadied herself, but his other hand grabbed at her knees. '*No!*' she screamed.

Panic filled her, *overwhelmed* her, and rage, too, and searing, agonizing memories of all the terrible things he'd already done, to the others and to her. And Ollie's cries were magnifying, piercing her ears, echoing in her mind, and Abigail knew she had to stop Silas before he did worse.

His hands were dragging at her legs.

'*No!*' she screamed again. 'I won't *let* you!'

She raised the cello high again, higher than before, and with every remaining ounce of strength, brought it down again.

Silas screamed.

She knew, right away.

Knew what had happened.

What she had done.

As the cello, its sharp metal spike impaled in Silas's body, swayed, vibrating with his final scream of agony.

And became still.

Chapter Fifty-Two

Observing Abigail's state-of-mind, and swiftly realizing the strong likelihood of her giving a self-destructive first, and crucial, interview to the police, Philip Quinlan – the lawyer recommended to Jules by Stephen Wetherall, her mother's old solicitor – suggested to his client that she might find it easier to let him read a brief, prepared statement rather than face questioning.

'What would I say, in this statement?' Abigail asked.

They had arrested her back at the house, cautioned her, then taken her to the police station, booked her in at the custody suite, and now she felt adrift in the fog. All things familiar gone. This kindly stranger, Philip Quinlan, her lifeline, her only hope of survival.

She was no longer sure she wanted to survive.

'The truth,' Quinlan replied to her question. 'That you don't deny killing your husband, but that it was in self-defence.'

'I don't know that I was defending myself,' Abigail said. 'I know I was afraid for Ollie and Jules.'

'And for yourself,' Quinlan said.

'I don't know,' Abigail said.

'I think you do know,' the solicitor pressed on, gently but firmly. 'You and Jules have already told me that your husband had threatened to kill her and Ollie, that he was out of control when—'

'I'd already hit him,' Abigail interrupted, 'before the last time.'

It came back to her, the sound of the spike entering his body. She felt sick, her left hand flew to cover her mouth.

'Are you all right, Abigail?'

She took a deep breath, laid her hand, shakily, back in her lap.

'Yes,' she said.

'You hit your husband,' Quinlan reminded her, 'because he had just slapped and knocked down his sister, and because he'd just kicked in the door to get to you.'

'Yes,' Abigail whispered.

'Then that's what you'll write in your statement.' He paused. 'I know it feels impossibly hard right now, Abigail, but I want you to believe that we really do have a strong case of self-defence, so long as—'

'I can't write at the moment,' she said, abruptly.

'No,' Quinlan said, still gentle. 'Because your husband threw a chemical substance in your eyes in September.'

She nodded.

'I can write everything down for you, Abigail,' he said.

'Thank you,' she said. 'But I think maybe I'd rather just speak to them, answer their questions. Tell the truth.'

'Are you sure?' Quinlan asked.

Abigail nodded again.

'I'll be with you, sitting beside you,' he said.

'Good,' she said. 'Thank you.'

A doctor – the Forensic Medical Examiner – came to check that she was in a fit condition to be questioned, and the sense of drifting, of floating in the fog, stayed with her through that and on through the interview itself, conducted by a male detective inspector named Fletcher and a female constable whose name Abigail forgot the instant she'd heard it.

'Did your husband try to kill you?' DI Fletcher asked.

'No,' Abigail said. 'But he had already hit Jules, and he was trying to stop me from getting Ollie out of the bedroom.'

'And you had already hit him with your cello,' Fletcher said, referring to notes made earlier, at the house, 'knocked him down, you think, before he tried to restrain you.'

'Yes.'

She told them that Silas had been keeping her a prisoner.

'But at that precise time,' Fletcher said, 'you had locked yourself into the music room, hadn't you?'

'Yes,' Abigail said again.

It went on and on for what seemed a long time. The fog was like a shroud now. She felt cold and alone, despite Philip Quinlan, and very, very tired.

They began to ask her about the cello.

About the spike.

'Isn't there usually a rubber tip on the end of these extendable spikes?' The woman DC asked that question.

'There used to be one,' Abigail said. 'It came off a long time ago.'

'And you never bothered to replace it?' the DC asked.

Abigail shook her head.

'For the tape—' the DC said '—Mrs Graves just shook her head.'

'So you knew,' Fletcher took over again, 'when you rammed the cello down onto your husband, how sharp the spike was?'

Abigail felt very sick again.

'I didn't have time to think about it,' she said, quietly. 'Not till after.'

On and on.

They finished the interview and took her back to the custody suite, where the Custody Sergeant took over the proceedings.

'Are you Abigail Graves?' he asked her.

'I am,' she said.

'You are charged . . . '

The sergeant's voice was a monotone as he stated the date, and Philip Quinlan gripped Abigail's left arm, and he seemed proficient at guiding, she had thought as they'd left the interview room, and the police all seemed unfazed by her blindness, too, and she supposed they were used to arresting all sorts for all kinds of crimes.

'. . . you did murder Silas Graves,' the sergeant told her, 'which is contrary to common law. You do not have to . . . '

Murder.

Mother, father, boyfriend, husband.

'Abigail.' Philip Quinlan's voice drew her back.

On and on, in the fog.

They were speaking to each other now, not to her, discussing bail. Quinlan was saying that she had a fixed address and no previous convictions, and DI Fletcher was saying something about failure to surrender, and Quinlan said something about her sight and her pregnancy and her admission that she had killed Silas.

On and on.

'It'll just be overnight,' Quinlan told her, 'and they'll look after you.'

He was waiting, Abigail felt, for her to panic, perhaps to cry or plead, because the FME had declared her fit to be locked in a cell at the station till morning when they would take her to Haringey Magistrates' Court for her first appearance.

'It's all right,' she told him.

'Try and get some rest,' he said, 'if you can. I'll be organizing bail, so you don't need to worry about that, and I'll be telephoning, too, to make sure you're okay.'

'Are you really sure Jules is all right?' Abigail asked.

Quinlan had already told her that Jules had been seen by a doctor, had gone to A&E for an X-ray, had been pronounced fine and sent home.

'Quite sure,' he said now. 'And Ollie, too. No need to fret about them.'

She felt his discomfort, felt, abruptly, as if he was the one in need of soothing.

'I'll be fine,' she said, found his hand, gripped it.

'Brave girl,' he said.

She had wanted it – she realized much later, when a degree of rationalization had been restored to her – to be bad.

And it had been.

The stench and the sounds, of human distress and anger and sickness. The disorientation, worse for her because of the fog – though maybe it was less so for her than for most at lights out, no great drama for her, just grey to black.

It was not just Quinlan's two telephone calls that had saved her, but also, she thought afterwards, oddly, the poor, anguished man in the cell next to hers. His swearing, his raging, his throwing of things, the hideous, repetitive, sickening sound of what she thought might have been his head banging against the wall, a sound so disturbing that it had made her huddle on her own hard bunk and jam her hands over her ears to try to blot it out.

But it *had* saved her, for at least a part of the night, until they had calmed him, from something much worse. Her own thoughts.

About what she had done.

Killed him.

The *way* she had done it.

Killed her husband.

The father of her child.

Killed Phoenix.

Chapter Fifty-Three

'I'm worried about her,' Jules told Philip Quinlan in his document-cluttered Chancery Lane office on the twentieth of December.

Nineteen days had passed since Silas's death.

Eighteen since Abigail had appeared at Haringey Magistrates' Court and been sent to a bail hostel because the house had, to begin with, been the crime scene, and afterwards Abigail had not been able to contemplate returning there, and Jules, as a key witness to the crime, had not been permitted to offer her flat, and there had been no one else.

Eleven days since the judge at the Old Bailey had granted Abigail bail.

All the conditions worked out in advance this time. Jules standing surety in the sum of ten thousand pounds. Abigail's agreement – though it had been a little like getting an agreement out of a sleepwalker – that she would report each day to Hornsey Police Station. The condition of residence no longer a stumbling block, because Father Moran had returned to Saint Peter the Apostle earlier than expected from retreat (and at least his temporary disappearance had not, after all, been connected with Silas), had learned of the tragedy, and suggested she come and stay with him and Mrs Kenney in the presbytery.

'She thinks she should be in prison,' Jules told the young, bespectacled, composed but unmistakably deeply motivated, lawyer now.

Abigail had consented to their meeting without her, had said she had no objections to their talking about any aspect of the case, or about her psychological state. She knew how concerned they both were for her, was grateful to Jules for her love and to Quinlan for his kindness, had no secrets now from either of them, yet she felt, deep down, beyond their help.

'I know,' the solicitor said. 'Own worst enemy at present.'

'I suppose we should be grateful,' Jules said, 'she's agreed to plead not guilty.' She bit her lip. 'I keep worrying she's going to change her mind.'

'My worry is that I'm not quite sure how much I'm getting through to her,' Quinlan said. 'I've explained to her that self-defence is the only possible *full* defence against a murder charge, though when it comes to it, I'll be listing all possible defences: self-defence and provocation and diminished responsibility.'

'Abigail was totally responsible,' Jules argued. 'She was saving our lives.'

'Nevertheless,' Quinlan went on steadily, 'if this weren't so clearly self-defence, diminished responsibility could be very useful. Battered Woman's Syndrome comes to mind.'

'Yes,' Jules gave way. 'All right.'

'I am concerned, though, that our case could suffer down the line if Abigail isn't wholehearted about testifying in her own best interests.'

'I know what you mean,' Jules said. 'And about not getting through.' She shook her head. 'All I want is to help her any way I can, but I think Abigail believes that deep down I must be blaming her, even hating her, for killing Silas. I've told her I might just as well blame myself for being such a fool as to try and rescue her in the middle of the night, but it makes no real difference.'

'Are you,' Quinlan asked gently, 'blaming yourself?'

'In some ways, yes, of course I am,' Jules admitted. 'But that doesn't mean I don't know – really *know*, I mean – that it was all Silas's fault.'

'But still,' Quinlan said gently, 'you've lost your brother.'

He waited while Jules fought for a moment against tears. He had met her several times since her brother's death, had liked her immediately, felt glad that the feeling appeared mutual. The police having swiftly interviewed her with the intention of making her a prosecution witness, had dropped Jules like a hot brick when she had not only backed up Abigail's story, but also dramatically strengthened it. Quinlan had briefly feared that they might raise the suggestion that Jules – having told the police, among other things, that she believed Silas had murdered Ralph Weston, her husband – might have conspired with Abigail to kill him. They had *not* suggested any such thing, and the lawyer had felt relief for her.

Nevertheless, even if Jules was trying to face up to the terrible things Silas Graves had done, Quinlan knew better than to overlook the fact that she had plainly loved her brother deeply. And grief, as he had observed over the years, could be a complicated and unpredictable creature.

'Sorry,' Jules said, composing herself again.

'You're allowed to grieve,' Quinlan said.

Jules nodded, then dredged up a smile. 'So what can we do for Abigail?'

'You go on doing what you have been,' he said. 'Being Abigail's very good friend, letting her spend time with your little boy – I know she's very fond of Ollie.'

'That's not nearly enough.' Frustrated, Jules ran a hand through her hair. 'She's a mess, Philip. I mentioned corneal grafting to her the other day – something they've said they may want to do ultimately, if her sight doesn't improve sufficiently – but Abigail wouldn't even talk to me about it, and I'm sure it's because she's decided she's not deserving enough.' She took a breath. 'Then there's the pregnancy.'

Quinlan frowned. 'Not taking care of herself?'

'Michael Moran says she's started eating, which is something, and Abigail *says* that taking care of the baby's the only thing that matters, but I'm not convinced she accepts that means really, truly taking care of herself too.'

'Package deal,' Quinlan said succinctly, 'but she currently hates the wrapping.'

'That's about it,' Jules said.

'What else does Father Moran think?'

'That she's a mess, that she needs professional help.'

'Already organized,' the solicitor said. 'Psychiatrist and psychologist.'

'But they're just to help with the case, aren't they?' Jules said. 'We think – Michael and I – that Abigail's going to need long-term help, if she's ever going to start really healing.'

'I entirely agree,' Quinlan said.

'But surely she shouldn't have to go to too many different people,' Jules pressed on. 'Maybe you could have a word with one of your experts, see what they can suggest?' She paused. 'I'll gladly pay.'

Philip Quinlan smiled at her. 'I'll have a word,' he said.

It had been clear to him, from the outset, that Abigail's state of mind was likely to be the prosecution's greatest ally.

'There's really very little doubt in my mind,' he had told her, 'that we have a very good chance of convincing a jury that this was self-defence.'

'How can you really prove that?' Abigail had asked.

'By producing as much evidence as possible,' Quinlan said. 'Though it isn't as much a question of our having to be the ones to *prove* it, as of the prosecution having to *dis*prove it.' He had paused. 'Same with provocation, if we were to choose to raise that as a defence – the burden's on them to disprove.'

Abigail had sighed. 'At least you're not trying to pretend I'm completely innocent, the way Jules is. Because I'm not, obviously. I did kill Silas, after all.'

'I really would much rather,' Quinlan had told her mildly, 'you didn't keep saying that, Abigail.'

The old memory, of Francesca dying in the ambulance, had come to her again.

You mustn't say that.

Enough lies.

'But it's the truth,' she said. 'I am a murderer.'

'And your plea, when the time comes, will be not guilty by reason of self-defence.' Quinlan had remained steady. 'That you only used such force to defend yourself as was reasonable.'

'But my force killed him,' Abigail had said.

'In self-defence,' he'd insisted doggedly. 'I cannot stress this often enough, Abigail. There is not the slightest question that you killed your husband in self-defence.' He'd waited for a response. 'You do still accept that?'

Abigail had remembered Jules's cry of pain and Ollie's screams and her own sheer, undiluted terror.

'I do,' she had agreed, quietly. 'Yes.'

'Then, please, just try to remember that,' Quinlan had said.

The police, Quinlan knew, had felt, during their early encounters with Abigail and Jules, that they might be dealing with a case of at least one, if not two, seriously disturbed minds.

'Talk about bizarre,' DI Ken Fletcher had commented.

A man gruesomely dead, pierced by the extended spike of a cello which had previously been used to batter him. A half-blind, pregnant woman (who claimed now, but had denied at the time, that her husband had deliberately thrown a chemical in her eyes, because of his alleged jealousy of her friendship with a priest) freely admitting that she had killed her husband in a moment of terror, believing he might be going to kill her, his own sister and baby nephew. And she and Julia Weston, the other woman, both rambling on about past crimes, including a murder disguised as a mugging and a poisoning by peanuts . . .

Neither Fletcher nor Philip Quinlan – no one now except Jules, Abigail and Father Michael Moran – knew about the body in the back garden of the house on Muswell Hill.

It had been Jules, visiting Abigail one afternoon at the presbytery, who had suggested telling the police about the fishpond and the stone bench and what lay beneath.

'What for?' Abigail had asked.

'It might help your case,' Jules had said.

'I can't see how,' Abigail said. 'They've already heard worse about Silas.'

'Then it might help me,' Jules had said.

'How could risking getting yourself accused of God knows what help you?'

'At least I could stop lying,' Jules said.

'But it's not just you to consider, is it?' Abigail pointed out.

'Ollie, you mean.'

'Of course, Ollie,' Abigail had said. 'Not now, perhaps, but later.'

'And what happens when we sell the house?' Jules had asked, quietly, aware that the priest or his housekeeper, having left them alone to chat, might return at any time. 'Do we just *leave* him?'

'Unless you decide not to sell,' Abigail had said.

'Neither of us is ever going to want to live there again,' Jules had said.

'Well, then,' Abigail had said. 'I don't see what else you can do.'

She supposed she was guilty of double standards.

Had not yet told Jules that she had confessed to Philip Quinlan that it had been she, not Eddie Gibson, who had ridden the motorbike when he and her parents had been killed.

'What do you want me to do with this?' the lawyer had asked.

'I don't know,' she had said. 'Except that I think I'd like his parents to know.'

Quinlan had thought for a while.

'May I be frank?' he'd asked, finally.

'Frank as you like,' Abigail had said.

'It's waited nearly fifteen years,' he said, 'and I doubt if raising it now would do your case any significant harm, but neither would it help you.'

'You want me to wait till it's over before telling them?'

Quinlan had watched her face, her eyes still hidden by her dark glasses.

Fifteen years.

'If you think you can cope with that,' he said.

'Why not?' she said, wearily.

Chapter Fifty-Four

Drew Martin, who had, to all intents and purposes, vanished off the face of the earth after the night of Silas's death, reappeared on Boxing Day morning at Jules's front door.

Ollie's first Christmas had come and gone.

Their first after Silas.

They had gone to Midnight Mass at Saint Peter's out of gratitude, more than anything, to Michael. Jules had sung carols, weeping some of the time.

Abigail had stayed silent. The fog before her eyes still inside her too.

They were all trying, gently but constantly, to persuade her to believe in the future, but Abigail found it impossible to do so.

She believed in the child she was carrying.

Kept, all through Midnight Mass, her hands clasped over her womb.

Speaking to it.

I'm sorry, my love.

She told it, her daughter or son, all the time, *all* the time, that she was sorry, begged her child to be strong and healthy and safe.

All the rest – her eyes, her trial – was nothing.

You are everything, she told her child.

'Lord hear our prayer,' the congregation said in unison.

Please, God, bless and protect my baby.

Her only prayer now, over and over again, wherever she was.

All that mattered.

'I'm so ashamed,' Drew Martin said now, put down the gift-wrapped parcels he'd been holding, and burst into tears.

'For God's sake, Drew,' Jules said, 'where have you been? Your neighbour said she'd seen you leave, so I knew you were safe, but—'

'I was in Harrogate,' he said. 'Hiding at my sister's.'

'But I rang Pauline,' Jules said. 'She said she hadn't seen you.'

'She never told me you'd phoned till Christmas Eve,' Drew said. 'She didn't want me getting involved, said there wasn't anything I could do, and I got so angry with her that I walked out, came straight back down to London, and I wanted to come yesterday, but I didn't think it was right, not on Christmas Day, and I know Pauline was only trying to protect me, but still.'

'It's all right,' Jules said.

'No, it's not,' Drew said. 'And it's not Pauline's fault, it's all mine, because I knew, really, that you'd be trying to find me, but I was scared to talk to you, and I don't know how I can be such a snivelling little coward.'

'It's all right,' Jules said again, and put her arms around him. 'You're here now, sweetheart. Better late than never.'

He had been so afraid that evening because Silas had made such awful threats against him, he explained while Jules made a pot of tea and proved to him that Ollie really was perfectly unscathed.

'He said if I didn't let him take Ollie, he'd send some men round to break my arms and legs, *and* he said he knew where my sister lived, and I needn't think that her family would be any safer.'

'Oh, God, Drew—' Jules was freshly appalled '—I'm so sorry.'

'Why should *you* be sorry?' Drew blew his nose. 'I'm the one who let him take your baby, and I'm just so *ashamed*.'

'It's my fault,' Jules said. 'I should never have put you in that position.'

'And then I heard he was dead, and I didn't know what to think.' He was speaking at breakneck speed, purging himself. 'Part of me wanted to race back to be here for you, but then another part of me thought – God help me – that you were better off without him, and Pauline kept telling me to wait till things settled down, and I know it was wrong, and if you never want to see me or speak to me again, Jules, I'll understand.'

'You're here now.' Jules poured him a second cup of tea, spooned sugar into it, stirred it for him. 'Stop torturing yourself, Drew.'

'I haven't slept, and I've hardly eaten, and I know I'm weak, and I *know* you must hate me, whatever you say, and I don't blame you.'

'I don't hate you at all,' Jules said.

'You're just being kind,' Drew said. 'And if you want to fire me—'

'That's the last thing I want to do,' Jules broke in. 'Especially now, when I need more time off from the shop to be with Ollie and help support Abigail.'

'But—' He stopped and his cheeks coloured.

'But what?' Jules asked.

'Abigail did it,' Drew said. 'She killed your brother.'

'Because she had no choice,' Jules said, steadily. 'And what she could use now, what we could *all* use, sweetheart – if you could stand it – is for you to tell the police that Silas threatened you.'

'I couldn't,' he said, newly horrified.

'It might really help Abigail's defence,' Jules said.

'But are you sure you want me to?' Drew asked.

'Because he was my brother, you mean?' She was gentle.

'And you loved him,' Drew said. 'Didn't you?'

'Very much,' Jules agreed.

'Then how can you . . .?' He trailed off again.

'I think you'd better wait,' Jules told him, 'until you've heard it all.' She blinked away her own sudden tears. 'Then I think you'll understand a little more.'

Chapter Fifty-Five

It was Michael Moran's idea to look for the photographs.

'I don't know why I didn't think of it before.'

It was the twenty-eighth of December, two days after Drew's return, and Moran had come, without warning, to the bookshop to suggest they went together to Edison Road.

'Busy time for you, surely,' Jules said.

'Busy or not,' he said, 'some things have to be dealt with.'

In all the painfulness, he told her, he had forgotten that the last time Abigail had come to see her before he'd gone on retreat, he had noticed a man with a camera standing in the road beyond the church. He had seemed – though Moran had not been certain – to be taking photographs of himself and Abigail, and he had wondered at the time if it might perhaps have been Silas.

'Only you've never said anything about such photos being found.'

'I don't know,' Jules said, 'if anyone's searched the studio.'

She had been there a handful of times to see correspondence and to hand over the books and papers to the accountant and solicitors dealing with Silas's estate, had found the place almost unbearably hard to be in.

'The last thing I want,' the priest went on, 'is to increase your pain or Abigail's, but it occurs to me that they might possibly help just a little to illustrate your brother's state of mind.'

The studio gave up more than they had anticipated.

More than Jules could bear.

A series of photographs first, in one of Silas's locked desk drawers, of Abigail embracing Charlie Nagy beside a car.

'Mr Nagy's road, do we presume?' Moran said to Jules.

'Possibly,' she said. 'Probably.'

She turned to the next photograph, felt sick.

A man lying face down on a pavement.

253

'Oh, dear God,' Jules said. 'Charlie.'

Father Moran looked at it, then at her face.

'Want to sit down?'

Jules shook her head, still staring at the picture, wondering why on earth Silas had kept such things, when clearly they might, were he still alive, have been used against him. Had he been proud of his achievements? Or had he wanted, perhaps, to be found out?

Please God, the second.

'I'm so sorry, Jules,' the priest said. 'This isn't fair on you.'

'None of this is fair on anyone, Michael.'

He was looking at one of the other photographs they'd found in the drawer.

'Do you know who that is?' he asked.

'Yes,' Jules said, faintly.

It was Maggie Blume, standing in a familiar looking road.

Elgin Avenue, she was almost sure, where Maggie had been knocked down.

Another shot left her in no doubt.

Maggie lying in the road, a small crowd around her.

'Dear God,' Jules murmured.

'Mr Nagy's sister?' Moran checked.

Jules nodded.

'I really am very sorry,' he said.

'Me, too,' she said.

They were both silent for a few minutes.

There was a plastic wallet at the back of the drawer, more photographs in it.

Jules put out her right hand to pick them up, saw it was shaking.

'Want me to?' Father Moran asked.

She nodded, watched his face as he scanned the rest of the pictures, not looking at them herself, not daring to.

'Oh, my,' he said, softly.

A shudder went through Jules.

You have to look.

The priest handed them to her swiftly, averted his eyes.

They were not what she had feared.

Not of Ralph.

All of Abigail, playing the cello. All at different stages of their life together. Some nude and laughing. Some of her playing with great intensity, hair sweeping over her face, eyes closed. Some of her staring at the photographer, her expression frustrated, even angry.

Some of her playing, wearing her dark, wraparound glasses.

254

Jules put them down on Silas's desk.

'Better get these others to Philip,' Moran said, gently. 'Don't you think?'

Jules nodded, not yet able to speak, not really wanting to think, still wondering what else might be hidden in this room or in the studio or dark room.

'Jules?'

'Yes,' she said.

'Do you want to go on looking?' he asked, gently.

'No,' she said. 'Not really. We've enough to prove that Silas was at least there when Charlie—' She stopped, the bleakness of it all choking off the words.

'I know,' Moran said.

'I'm not even sure,' Jules went on, 'how much it's going to help Abigail. She didn't see the photos, after all.'

'I think they might help,' the priest said. 'Add another layer to the evidence.'

'Maybe.' Jules sighed. 'It certainly won't make any difference to Silas.'

Justice for Ralph and Charlie and his sister already handed down, after all.

By Abigail.

She looked at the desk, then around the office.

Remembered her brother at work in here, and in the studio itself, surrounded by lights and umbrellas and all his photographic paraphernalia.

Closed her eyes, hoping to store up the normality in her mind.

Saw, instead, Silas lying on the floor with the spike in his chest.

The only time she had envied Abigail her blindness.

Chapter Fifty-Six

Abigail waited until after the New Year to break the news to Jules that she had decided against having the first corneal graft until after the birth of her child.

'It would mean a general anaesthetic,'she said, 'and there might be all kinds of drugs, and there's no real proof that they're safe, and then, after the surgery, they tell you not to do strenuous exercise for quite a long while, so they'd probably want me to have a caesarian, and I don't *want* that, I want a natural birth.'

'But if they said it was safe,' Jules said, 'then you'd be able to see your baby.'

'Not necessarily,' Abigail said. 'Even if things go well, they say you can be very blurry for quite a while, even distorted, and you have to keep going as an out-patient for ages, which would be difficult with a wee baby.' She took a breath. 'And if you ask me, Jules, which is more important, my vision or a healthy child. . .'

'No contest,' Jules said, 'of course. Though if—'

'There's nothing you can say I haven't thought of.'

'What if waiting longer lessens the chances of success?'

'Waiting won't make any difference,' Abigail said. 'They've told me that. The damage won't get worse, and sometimes the longer they wait, the better.' She paused. 'But even if it weren't, as you said, no contest.'

'All right,' Jules said.

The Pleas and Directions Hearing in Abigail's case took place at the Central Criminal Court two days after Ollie's first birthday in the first week of February.

Right up until the last instant, when Abigail, in the dock, was told to stand up and asked for her plea to the charge of murder, Jules, sitting in the public gallery, heart pounding, palms damp, was terrified of what she might say.

257

'Not guilty,' Abigail said.

Jules sat back, shut her eyes, gave thanks.

The image of her brother on the floor, dying, then dead, sprang back into her mind, more bloodily clear than ever.

She opened her eyes again, looked down at Abigail, asked herself, as she had many times before, if, grief and sorrow and profound confusion notwithstanding, there was after all any part of her that did blame her.

Knew that there was not.

The closer Abigail came to the birth, the less interested she became in her case.

'I need to spend time with you,' Philip Quinlan told her on the phone in April.

'The trial's not till late November,' she said.

'The better prepared we are, the greater our chances of acquittal.'

'I'll do,' Abigail said, 'whatever you tell me.'

'I need you to meet your barrister,' Quinlan said.

'And I need to go to natural childbirth classes with Jules,' she said.

'You'll have to do both, Abigail,' the solicitor said, with rare exasperation.

'If I have to, I will,' she said.

There was, for the moment, a semblance of serenity within her, and a vast longing to meet her child for the first time, to touch her or him – and she had asked, before her first scan, not to be told which it was, and Mary Hine, her sensible and very kindly psychologist, had tried but failed to persuade her to discuss, among many other things, her reasons for that decision.

'That doesn't matter,' Abigail had told her. 'All I'm focusing on is making sure my baby's safe and healthy.'

'And the other things you need to think about?'

'I'm choosing to blot those out,' Abigail said.

'Choosing,' Mary Hine repeated.

'Yes,' Abigail said. 'This is deliberate. I'm choosing to channel all my strength into my child.'

'Yours and Silas's,' Mary Hine said.

'Of course,' Abigail had answered.

And Silas's.

It came to her regularly, the concept of Silas-as-father. Not in the comforting way that it must have come to Jules, thinking of Ollie as Ralph's child. This was haunting rather than consoling, dragging with it undeniable fear because of what Silas had become, of what he might perhaps always have been, deep within himself. Often, when those thoughts came

258

she pushed them forcibly away, but in weaker, less guarded moments, Abigail still felt overwhelmed by the old, now infinitely sad, rush of love for Silas, as if all the dreadful things had not happened – and after that, inevitably, came the guilt, worse, stronger than ever, because she had killed the object of that love, the father of her child, and this new guilt was agonizing enough for her to long to be flayed alive.

No one really understood. They tried hard, her gentle, valiant circle of friends, but none of them could comprehend what it was to be Abigail Allen Graves just then, cocooned and marooned and isolated all at once.

Waiting.

Chapter Fifty-Seven

She did not admit to herself until it was over how much she had been hoping, with something close to desperation, for a daughter. Though it was only during one of the times of her terrible bleakness months later that she realized how illogical it had been for her to fear that a boy might be like Silas, when it was patently just as terrible to imagine a girl taking after her.

Killer-mother. Mother-killer.

Mary Hine and Michael Moran and Jules all wanted her to talk about it. 'I'm all right,' Abigail told them all.

She bore a son, on the fifteenth of July, and she was far from all right.

Not because her child was a boy, not just because he was Silas's son, but because he was *her* son, the son of the woman who had killed his father. And because as long as he had been within her, the rest of her life had been kept at bay, and now that was over. Now her son was out of her body, in the world, the terrible, beautiful, terrifying world. And she could no longer pretend to herself that the time was not coming when she would have to make the decision that might shape not only her own life, but his.

That was coming now, it was all coming, at breakneck speed.

His birth, she supposed later, when she could think again, had felt like a great tearing apart of her mind as well as her body. The pains had ripped through her and she had welcomed them, opened herself to them, felt temporarily liberated by them.

Gloria, she sang in her head, rejoicing even as she screamed into the fog, because this agony was, at last, what she deserved for destroying her child's father, Jules's brother, Ollie's uncle – *and Ma and Daddy and Eddie, don't forget them* – and they offered her drugs, which she refused, and Jules, by her side, tried to help her with her breathing, tried to make it easier for her, believed her wretched and helpless and thinking only of the child and its struggle. . .

Gloria! she screamed in her mind.

And then he was born, her new beloved, and she knew that the suffering had been fraudulent, no punishment at all, because it had brought him to her.

Phoenix's and Abeguile's son.

Her new, and best, beloved.

She could see no more of him than his shape, wanted no one to describe him to her – would *allow* no one to describe him. But she could feel him, run her fingers over every millimetre of him, hold him to her cheek, her lips, her breast; she could feed him, change his nappy, bathe him, breathe him in, taste him, whisper to him of her love.

But all the while, even then, she knew *it* was coming.

Chapter Fifty-Eight

She had the first corneal graft at the end of August. Ten days after her mother's birth-and-death-day.

Left eye first, the more damaged. The right, they had told her, would not be operated on for at least six months or even a year.

Now that her child was safely born, Abigail was more than ready for the transplant, prepared to push aside all her earlier thoughts of unworthiness; selfish again now, too hungry to see *him*.

Thomas Graves.

She had chosen the name because Silas had once told her that he liked it, would rather have been called Thomas than Silas.

'What about middle names?' Jules had asked.

'None,' Abigail had replied.

Names she had almost chosen roamed around her head: Douglas, Charles, Edward, Paul – each of them right and proper for their dead relatives and friends, but each one dead because of Thomas's parents.

And not Silas. She could not do that, could not take away the father and then bestow his name as a kind of consolation prize.

So no middle names for their boy.

'Just Thomas,' she said.

Lord, it was miraculous, this extraordinary gift of sight from a stranger, and Abigail had made herself think about the family of this normal, guilt-less person, about what they must have gone through to make this possible – and she *was* unworthy, infinitely so, but again she had succeeded in setting those thoughts aside and had gone ahead.

Just a few days back at Moorfields, the temporary change of bail conditions cleared with the court and police by Philip Quinlan, as it had been when she'd gone into the Whittington to give birth.

Easy – for her, at least – so *easy*. Going to sleep and waking up with it done, and just a little pain – nothing, *nothing*, considering the miracle –

263

and they were all so kind, and she felt such gratitude and humility, but none of that mattered as much as it might have, all that mattered now was getting to see Thomas.

Not yet, don't expect anything yet.

She knew, had been told, more than once, that it would take a long time, that at best her vision would be blurry for months, that it would probably fluctuate, that it would be a year until the stitches were removed, and fifteen or eighteen months till she could be fitted with a contact lens, and she would need to use drops, against rejection and infection, and there *was* a possibility, though not a great one, that the graft might be rejected, though then they could start again . . .

'All I want,' Abigail said, 'is to see my son.'

Before.

She saw him, blurrily, fuzzily, but she *saw* him.

'He's so *beautiful*,' she said.

Father Moran had come to collect her, take her back to the presbytery, where Jules and Ollie were waiting, with Thomas.

She was still wearing dark glasses, partly for protection, partly against her increased photophobia, and she would wear a protective plastic shield at night, and the eye was uncomfortable and watering, and it was still a maddening blur, but the fog had gone.

Enough for her to see him.

Gloria, she said inside her head.

Singing again now, not screaming.

'Isn't he wonderful?' Jules said, softly.

Abigail was sitting on the sofa, the baby in her arms.

Now, slowly, cautiously, she raised him a little higher, closer to her face.

Looking at his eyes.

The midwife had told her one day after his birth that they were a lovely blue, though of course that might yet change.

Since then Abigail had asked no one, nor had anyone told her.

Now she peered through the new window of her own left eye.

Steeling herself.

'Green,' she said, quietly.

'Beautiful,' Michael said, warmly.

'Like his father's,' Abigail said.

She let no expression pass her face.

'Are they,' she said to Jules, 'like his?'

'Yes,' Jules said.

'Sea-green,' Abigail said.
'Yes,' Jules said again.
Understanding.

Chapter Fifty-Nine

'Now,' Philip Quinlan said to Abigail on the telephone in the first week of October, two days after Thomas's baptism at Saint Paul the Apostle. 'I need you to start working with me right now.'

Abigail, sitting in her bedroom at the presbytery, in an old rocking chair that Mrs Kenney and Father Moran had retrieved for her from the basement, gazed down at the still blurry sight of her son, lying contentedly in her arms.

'Abigail,' Quinlan's voice nudged her. 'Are you listening to me?'

'Of course,' Abigail said. 'What do you need me to do?'

'To concentrate,' the solicitor told her. 'On preparations.'

Here it is.

She felt the calm inside her disappearing, as if all the warm blood in her veins and arteries was being sucked out, being replaced by ice.

'For my trial, you mean,' she said.

'For your defence,' Quinlan said.

Coming now.

'Only seven weeks now,' he added. 'And a great deal to do.'

Tell him, Abigail.

'No,' she said.

'I'm afraid there is,' the solicitor corrected her. 'I know it's very hard, with Thomas and your eyes, but that's all the more—'

'I mean, no, there isn't going to be a trial,' Abigail said.

'I'm sorry?' Quinlan sounded momentarily confused.

'I'm going to change my plea,' she told him. 'To guilty.'

She tried to imagine his expression, felt suddenly deeply sorry for him, and ashamed, as if he had been taking great pains to prepare a feast for her, and she was telling him she'd just begun a diet and couldn't eat it.

'I'm not saying I don't want to offer any defence,' she said, quickly. 'I'm not quite mad, I don't want a life sentence – I have a son to think of now. You can tell them provocation or diminished responsibility or whatever you like, I don't mind, but I'm definitely pleading guilty to manslaughter.'

'Why?' Quinlan asked.

'Because of Thomas. Because I don't want to gamble between walking free and risking life.' Abigail paused. 'And because I am guilty, and because I want to tell the judge that I do feel remorse, and I want to tell Eddie's parents, at long last, that I'm so sorry for what I did to him and to them, and—'

'Abigail,' Quinlan cut in. 'We have to talk about this.'

'I've made up my mind.'

'Even so.'

In her arms, Thomas gave a small whimper.

'I really have done all the thinking, Philip,' Abigail told him gently.

She stroked her son's hair. White-gold for now, too early to tell if it would be the same colour as her own hair, or turn into soft golden hay, like his father's.

'I want you to come in to the office,' Quinlan said. 'Please.'

'All right,' Abigail said.

'Tomorrow,' he said.

'So long as you don't try to change my mind.'

'We'll discuss the options,' the solicitor said.

Abigail heard the forcefulness of his tone and her heart sank at the prospect of the meeting, for there was no point to talking now, not when she'd made up her mind.

'Ten o'clock,' Quinlan said. 'And allow plenty of time.'

Chapter Sixty

'She won't budge,' Quinlan told Jules and Father Moran four days later at his office. 'She said we're welcome to talk about her behind her back all we like, so long as we don't kid ourselves we can change her mind.'

'But if we let her do this,' Jules said, 'she'll go to prison.'

'It isn't as simple as "letting her do" anything,' Quinlan said, 'unless she were to wish to plead guilty to murder and go to prison for life, which mercifully she does not. If we're going to try to prove diminished responsibility – possibly using Battered Woman's Syndrome – we're going to be in the hands of the psychiatrists and psychologists. I've already had reports, of course, but bearing in mind Abigail's shift in attitude, I've written further letters of instructions asking for an addendum to those reports.'

'Then what?' Jules asked.

'Depends on the reports,' the lawyer replied. 'If I feel convinced that were a jury to read them, they'd believe that there was an abnormality of mind at the time of the killing, *and* if I'm satisfied that there's no risk of over-egging the omelette, because the very last thing we want is a Hospital Order—'

'You mean they could commit her?' Michael Moran looked horrified.

'Conceivably, but hopefully not in this case,' Quinlan said. 'The psychiatrist and psychologist have to state that they feel her mental responsibility was substantially impaired at that *moment*, and that her actions were not in any way premeditated.'

'Sounds like a balancing act,' Moran said.

'After that,' Quinlan went on, 'if I *am* satisfied with the reports, I'll pass them to Trevor Butler – Abigail's QC-in-waiting – and if he feels similarly, he'll contact the prosecution's barrister and the court, and the other side will appoint their own experts who'll meet Abigail several times and then make their own reports.' He took a breath. 'Then, if – as we hope – those experts agree that there was an abnormality of mind, then however much the prosecution may hate the idea, they'll have no choice but to accept diminished responsibility.'

'Which would mean what?' Jules was struggling to follow.

'Things would move pretty rapidly from there,' Quinlan said. 'We'd get a hearing almost immediately to enter the new plea and apply for bail, while we put all our most helpful character references and reports together for the judge.'

'How long?' Moran asked.

'Probably four weeks.'

'Then what?' Jules asked.

'Then it's sentencing,' Quinlan said.

They all sat in silence for several moments.

'You still believe you could get her off, don't you?' Jules asked.

'On self-defence, yes,' Quinlan said. 'But I couldn't guarantee it.'

'And then she could get life,' Jules said.

'Don't forget,' the solicitor said, 'that if our own expert reports aren't satisfactory, no one else will ever get to see them, and the case will go to trial, and then we can still run all three defences, self-defence, provocation *and* diminished responsibility.' He paused. 'Much the same if the prosecution's shrink disagrees.'

'If they do both agree on diminished responsibility,' Moran asked, 'might Abigail get a suspended sentence or probation?'

'Possible,' Quinlan said.

'But not probable,' Jules said.

Quinlan's smile was grim. 'Up to the judge.'

'Has Abigail told you,' Jules asked, 'she wants me to have Thomas if she gets a custodial sentence?'

'She has.' Quinlan smiled. 'One of her better ideas.'

'But she's his mother,' Jules said. 'She should be with him.'

'Of course she should,' the lawyer agreed. 'And she knows that there are mother and baby units available, in some cases.'

'I'm not talking about being with him in *prison*.' Jules was horrified.

'No,' Quinlan said. 'I know you're not.'

Chapter Sixty-One

On the twenty-third of December, just under five weeks after the experts instructed by Philip Quinlan had reported that, in their opinion, at the time of Silas's killing Abigail had been 'suffering from such abnormality of mind as had substantially impaired her mental responsibility', the prosecution's psychiatrist and psychologists arrived at the same conclusion.

'Just too late to make it before Christmas,' Quinlan told Abigail on the phone. 'More waiting for you. I'm sorry.'

'I don't mind,' she said. 'At least Thomas and I can have his first Christmas together. He may be too young to appreciate it, but I'm not.'

Jules arrived at the presbytery ten minutes later, found Abigail up in her bedroom changing the baby's nappy.

'We've got a buyer for the house,' she said. 'Chain-free and in a hurry.'

Abigail told her that was good news, then reported her own.

'Oh, Lord,' Jules said. 'How do you feel?'

'Let's not talk about that,' Abigail said. 'Tell me about the buyer.'

'A family called Salter. Very nice couple, according to the estate agent, supposedly madly in love with the house and garden, not wanting to change much.'

'Children?' Abigail asked, thinking, as she knew Jules had to be, of the pond.

'Young teens.' Jules remembered Silas's prophesy that the house would go, one day, to a family with older children. 'So what do you think?'

'It's your decision,' Abigail said.

It had been a long time selling. Plenty of people had come to look in the early days, most of them intrigued, Jules had realized, by the prospect of seeing a recent murder scene at close quarters, but genuine buyers had balked when it had come to actually contemplating paying to live there.

And none of them, of course, had known about the grave.

'They do sound perfect,' Jules said, 'all things considered.'

'But?'

'Isn't it all a bit much? Everything coming at once?'

'For the best, perhaps,' Abigail said. 'Getting everything sorted.'

The last word – *sorted* – hung in the air as she finished fastening the clean nappy, picked up the baby and kissed the top of his head.

'I can't help worrying,' Jules said, 'about the pond.'

'Of course you can't,' Abigail said.

'Not so much about these people finding out, because with a bit of luck they never will, especially if they really do like it all the way it is.' Jules paused. 'And if and when they sell up some time in the future, and if their buyer does decide to get rid of the pond, even if they dig up the whole area—'

'Don't think about that.'

'I was going to say that even if the worst does come to the worst some day, at least Ollie and Thomas will be older.'

'True.' Abigail sat down with her son in the rocking chair. 'How do you really feel about selling?'

'We've been through all that,' Jules said. 'We've agreed neither of us—'

'This isn't a case of "us",' Abigail said. 'It's the house your mother left you.'

'Which I moved out of a long time ago,' Jules said.

Abigail shifted the baby to her left arm, so that she could see him more clearly.

'And how do you really feel,' she asked, 'about leaving your father's grave?'

'That it's terribly wrong,' Jules said. 'But then everything about it, whatever really happened to him, what Silas and I did—'

'What he made you do.'

'I still helped,' Jules said, 'and anyway, there's no undoing any of it.' She took a breath. 'There's something else.'

'You want to move away,' Abigail said.

Jules's cheeks flushed. 'How do you know?'

'Because it's obviously the right thing for you to do,' Abigail said. 'If I go to prison, and you have Ollie and Thomas, and the house is sold, and maybe the flat too, you'll certainly have plenty of money to buy something beautiful well away from here.'

'Not too far,' Jules said. 'You don't have to worry about that, if—'

'I won't worry,' Abigail said. 'Even if you can't visit, at least I'll be able to picture the three of you somewhere lovely and new and different.'

'And when you come out,' Jules said, with an effort, 'it'll be the four of us.'

'That really would be lovely,' Abigail said.

272

'*Will* be,' Jules said.

Abigail nodded, though she could not, for now, imagine that at all, because all her imaginings were of prison, of being shut away.

The right thing. The only thing.

'And there's still a good chance,' Jules said, 'that you might not go to prison.'

'Don't harbour false hopes, Jules.'

'They might not be false.'

'They are,' Abigail said. 'I'd bet on that.'

Chapter Sixty-Two

On the second of February, after four final weeks on bail during which Philip Quinlan and Trevor Butler had prepared for the sentencing hearing, Abigail sat in the dock in the Central Criminal Court listening as first Sara Gallman, QC, stood for almost an hour outlining the case for the prosecution, then, for almost as long again, as Butler spoke in mitigation for the defence.

Through it all, every last painful second of it, Abigail was aware of Eddie Gibson's mother and father up in the public gallery. Felt their eyes on her, raking over her, hating her as much, she guessed, for their son's posthumous loss of good name as for his death.

Looking forward, she had no doubt, to the sentencing.

Three years.

'I don't understand how he could *do* that,' Jules said afterwards as she and Quinlan and Michael Moran adjourned to a pub for stiff whiskies. 'After all she's been through in the past year alone.'

'It's conceivable,' Quinlan said, 'that having held onto her liberty long enough to give birth and spend some time with Thomas, and have the graft, might have had a negative influence.'

'The grand luxury of eye surgery out on bail, you mean,' Moran said ironically.

'Jesus.' Jules downed a large gulp of whisky and winced.

'It could have been worse,' Quinlan said.

'Please don't start talking about maximum sentences, Philip,' Jules snapped. 'It could – should – have been nothing at all.'

They all took large swallows of their drinks, all trying to blot out the memory of how Abigail had looked being taken down from the dock.

'All things being equal,' Quinlan said, 'and with tagging, she should be out in, say, fifteen months.'

'What happens to her second operation?' Moran asked. 'I believe they were wanting to do that in the summer or autumn.'

'That'll have to wait,' Quinlan said.

'Didn't you know?' Jules was sarcastic. 'Abigail's partially sighted now, and this kind of surgery is "elective".'

'Lord save us,' Moran said, and finished his drink.

'Another?' Quinlan asked.

'She's going to miss the rest of Thomas's babyhood.' Jules was close to tears.

'At least—' Moran patted her hand '—she'll know he's with you and Ollie.'

Quinlan stood up. 'And God willing, she'll be back with Thomas again before his second birthday.'

'I didn't know you were a believer, Philip,' the priest said.

'Every now and then,' Quinlan said.

Chapter Sixty-Three

It began in Holloway.

Abigail told Jules on the telephone – using her first, already disproportionately precious, phone card – that she was all right, that they had kept her in the hospital wing until they could be reasonably certain she wasn't going to crack, and she and Jules both knew that it had been suicide watch, but neither used the words, both fighting to keep the short conversation as upbeat as they could.

Abigail asked Jules to pass on her special love to Ollie, whose second birthday it was, and Jules told her that she would give Thomas a big cuddle from his mummy.

'No need,' Abigail said. 'I told him on our last night that I was giving him every ounce of my love, asked him to hold it inside himself till the next time we can be together. Daft, of course, but it made me feel a wee bit better.'

'Not daft at all,' Jules said, 'but I'll still give him that extra cuddle.'

'Philip's already been to see me,' Abigail said, after a moment. 'He was very comforting.'

She had found, as the long limbo months of bail had passed, her liking for Quinlan growing ever stronger, had even begun to foster some romantic hope that the bachelor solicitor and Jules might realize how suited they were, and *she* had certainly noticed that, even in her depths, though it was something of a surprise to Abigail that she was still capable of being romantic.

Only for Jules, not you, not ever again.

'Anyway, I'm all right,' she said now. 'So you and Michael don't need to worry about me.'

A lie on that day.

Still a lie a month later.

She had not understood quite how it would be. Not just the imprisonment itself, nor even Holloway, with its five bleak floors, six women to a cell, its grinding grimness and a misery so deeply entrenched that Abigail sometimes felt, or imagined, that even with her one still blurry, but functioning eye, she could see it ingrained in the walls and floors, descending from the ceilings like a kind of fallout.

It wasn't that that she minded so much. That was what she deserved.

Killer-mother, mother-killer.

It was being without Thomas, now that she had been with him, seen him, knew the feel of him, the sounds of him, the sheer beauty of having her child. Now that she had been, *was*, a mother. Now that she had lost him.

She was still certain, most of the time – *not so certain at night, the lowest, sleepless time* – that she had done the right thing in admitting her guilt and letting Thomas have his safe, happy start with Jules and Ollie.

'But are you *sure*?' her friends had all asked her, over and over again, until she had thought she might explode with the agony.

So long as he was safe and happy, that was all that counted.

She did not count.

Having to give him up, even to Jules, the best person in her life, had almost felled her. The pain of handing him over that last time, of turning her back and walking away, had been so intense, so all-consuming, that she had actually believed, for several moments, that she might die of it.

She had not, of course, and now here she was, a number now, convicted at last, with all the others, locked away from society paying the price for what they had or, in some cases, she supposed, had not done. And in many ways, she felt, this new life was not so terrible, and the women she lived with were all right to her, interesting women, many with kind hearts, less rough than they might have been with her partly because of her eyes, partly because they understood what it was like to miss children, and partly, too, Abigail was well aware, because of the nature of the crime she had committed. And even those comparatively few women who were abusive to her, or even violent, had their stories, she imagined, their reasons for becoming that way, and she was afraid of them sometimes, but that was just a part of it, she told herself, part of her sentence; and it was called punishment, yet the prison officers she encountered were decent enough to her, and it had been agreed that when her next Moorfields check was due she would be escorted there and back; and they gave her food to eat and a roof over her head and work to occupy her, and they let her *live*, so it was not, in truth, nearly bad enough, was it? Not for her.

Mother-killer, killer-mother.

Except for being without Thomas.

That was real punishment.

For the first time.

Jules came to visit, according to regulations, once a fortnight, while Abigail was waiting to learn if she was to be moved on. And no one could say yet where that might be, how far away, and though her need for checks on her corneal graft might affect the decision – expensive enough to arrange for the two officers to take her from and back to Holloway – her being the mother of a small baby would have no great impact since she had made it clear that she had no intention of letting Thomas come to see her. Not here nor in any other prison, because it would only, she said, be for her own selfish sake, would do nothing for him at all, and so it would make no real difference where they sent her.

Jules, hoping she would change her mind, sent her regular updates and photographs on both boys.

Ollie looked wonderful, boisterous and happy.

Thomas looked . . .

Abigail stared at the pictures of her baby son for so long that her vision grew even hazier and her eye hurt.

He looked like a normal, healthy baby, but now that she could no longer see him in the flesh or feel or hear him, he seemed unreal to her, like a mystery.

It was not detachment, nothing as unfeeling as that, just that appalling, acutely painful, *unreality* of looking at his photographs. And the worst of it to her was that if she could no longer feel him, then neither could he feel her.

'Please let me bring him next time,' Jules said on her second visit in April. 'I could bring both the boys, and Michael could come, too, if you wanted.'

'No,' Abigail said.

'Just Thomas then?' Jules said.

'No.' Abigail's eyes were hidden, as usual, behind her dark glasses.

'Why *not*?' Jules knew the answer to her question, yet it still frustrated her, being so patently wrong. 'It wouldn't hurt him at all – this isn't a terrible place, not for the ones who come and go, certainly not for a young baby.'

'They search you,' Abigail said.

'They're not rough,' Jules said. 'They certainly wouldn't be rough with Thomas, I promise you.'

'No,' Abigail said. 'Please stop asking me.'

'But all you're doing is adding to your torture, darling.'

'Not as much as seeing you carrying him out again.'

Jules knew that was still only part of it.

'Don't you think, even now, that you're being punished enough?'

Abigail was silent for a moment.

'If they move me a long way away,' she said, 'I shan't want you to come. I don't want you driving long distances on motorways.'

'It's up to me whether I come or not.'

'Not if I don't send you visiting orders.'

'Don't even joke,' Jules said.

'Sorry,' Abigail said. 'But you've got enough on your plate with Ollie and Thomas and the shop – you can't keep loading yourself with me too.'

'You're not a load.' Jules was almost angry.

'Sorry,' Abigail said again.

Chapter Sixty-Four

'Wow,' Jules said, on her first visit in June.

'What do you think?' Abigail asked.

Her hair had been cut short, almost savagely, Jules thought, and while it reasonably suited her sister-in-law's good bone structure, it also emphasized her gauntness.

'I like it,' she said.

'Liar.' Abigail smiled. 'It's easier to manage.'

'I'm sure,' Jules said. 'And I'm not lying. It's just that your hair was so beautiful.'

'Silas would be upset,' Abigail said.

'Is that why you did it?'

'Not really.' She shrugged. 'Maybe a touch of out with the old.'

Jules nodded, shifted in her chair, glanced briefly at the next table, then swiftly averted her eyes, and that was an unwritten rule she had quickly picked up on: *keep your nose out* – all anyone could do to protect the meagre-enough privacy they had with their loved ones.

'What's up, Jules?' Abigail asked.

Jules took a breath. 'I've found a house,' she said. 'A cottage.'

'Okay,' Abigail said. 'Tell me about it.'

'It's in Suffolk, just outside a village called Foldingham.'

'I've never been to Suffolk,' Abigail said.

'Very pretty, lots of old villages. Bit flat for some tastes, but great for cycling, lots of winding lanes.' Jules smiled. 'When you get out, after you've had the second op, we could buy some bikes, get fit together, really get to know the place.' She paused. 'That's only if you approve of the cottage. I'll send pics with my next letter, but I wanted to tell you about it face-to-face first.'

'You don't need my approval,' Abigail said.

'I most definitely do,' Jules said, 'since it's going to be our house.'

'Not legally,' Abigail said. 'Not in any way, for a long time.'

'Not all that long,' Jules said, 'the way time flies.'

'Not in here,' Abigail said.

'No,' Jules said. 'Of course not. Sorry.'

'No need,' Abigail said.

'You have to like it as much as Ollie and I do.'

Abigail smiled. 'Does Ollie like it then?'

'Certainly seemed to when I took him.'

'Then who am I to disagree?' Abigail said.

The cottage was white stone with a thatched roof and a pretty garden with trellises, apple trees and a stone table and bench seat.

Jules had hesitated when she'd first seen the seat.

So similar to the one Silas had concreted by the pond over their father's grave.

Ollie's and Thomas's grandfather's grave.

Just a bench, Jules.

No real similarity at all, she had told herself firmly, and moved on.

It was perfect, substantial enough for two adults, two children and an old, rheumatic dachshund, and it needed a new heating system, and Jules planned to put in a new bathroom, but the kitchen was charming, and the living room faced south.

And it held no memories and had the added blessing of anonymity.

Perfect.

'It sounds gorgeous,' Abigail said.

'It is,' Jules agreed. 'It really is.'

'What about Jules's Books?'

'I'm going to sell it as a going concern,' Jules said. 'Only real stipulation that they keep Drew on, if he wants to stay.' She paused. 'No book shop in Foldingham, so I might think about that.'

'Won't you miss London?' Abigail asked, after a moment.

'Don't think so,' Jules said. 'I can always visit.'

'What about Philip?'

'What about him?' Jules's gaze was calm.

'I thought you'd been seeing him.'

'One drink, one dinner,' Jules said. 'Hardly *seeing* him.'

'He's been to see me again,' Abigail said.

'I know.'

'He's a lovely man,' Abigail said.

'I know that, too,' Jules said.

282

'Do they have a law practice in Foldingham?' Abigail asked.
'Stop trying to matchmake,' Jules said. 'It'll never work.'
'Pity,' Abigail said. 'It gives me something nice to think about.'
'Afraid I can't oblige,' Jules said, 'not even for that.'

Chapter Sixty-Five

On the first Saturday of July, eleven days before Thomas's first birthday, three days before they were due to vacate the flat and move to Suffolk, Jules dropped Ollie at the presbytery for a visit with Michael, and went to Muswell Hill.

She told herself it was on impulse, though it had, in truth, been lurking in her mind for weeks.

Perhaps, she thought, *they won't be in.*

If they were not at home, she vowed, that would be it. She would take it as a sign and accept it and go away without a backward glance.

A Lexus was parked in the drive.

Jules rang the bell.

Nina Salter, a pretty woman in a white shirt and jeans, recognized her instantly.

'Hello,' she said, warmly. 'Forgotten something?'

'I hope you don't mind,' Jules said. 'I know I should have called first.'

'Not at all.' The other woman opened the front door wider, stepped back. 'Please do come in.'

Jules stayed where she was.

'It's just,' she said, 'that I'm moving away in a couple of days, leaving London, and I thought, maybe—'

'You'd have a last look round,' Nina Salter finished for her.

The memories were in the air, ghosts dancing around her head. Perhaps, Jules thought, if the other Salters had been there, defining it more clearly as their home, she might have felt more removed, but as it was, with only this friendly woman present, offering her tea, then tactfully keeping her distance, the house, for all its new furniture and clutter of strangers, felt as familiar as ever.

She had hoped, unrealistically, to bypass the first floor, her need, above all, to go into the garden to say a final farewell to Paul Graves, but without risking drawing special attention to the pond, there was, of course, no way of avoiding a swift tour of the whole house. And there it all was again, so starkly, blood-chillingly clear: the room in which she'd found her dead father, from which she and Silas had carried his body bag down to the garden; the master bedroom in which first her parents had slept, then her mother with Silas, then her mother with Graham, then herself with . . .

Oh, Christ.

The music room.

'I adore that room.'

Nina Salter's voice broke into the memories.

'That lovely wall,' she said, 'was one of our main reasons for wanting the house so badly.' She stood back as Jules came out. 'And the garden, of course.'

Jules had managed not to look down at the floor near the staircase as they had come up, had steeled herself, kept her chin up, stepped over the place.

Not this time.

She paused, made herself look down.

Remembered the astonishment and agony in Silas's face.

'Are you all right?' Nina Salter asked, quietly.

'Yes,' Jules said. 'I'm fine.'

The other woman turned, started back down the stairs.

'How about some fresh air?' she suggested.

'Please,' Jules said.

The only thing that had changed in the garden was the amount of care now being lavished upon it. Lawn recently mown, borders neat, roses pruned, paths weeded.

Jules walked slowly towards the pond.

It was the one place she had fervently hoped to be alone, but perhaps because of that moment of concern up in the corridor, Nina Salter was now sticking close.

They stepped onto the crazy paving.

The bench was as it had been.

'Max Brook told us you and your brother did all this yourselves.'

Jules looked at her. 'We did.'

'Marvellous,' Nina Salter said. 'We absolutely love it.'

'Would you mind very much,' Jules asked, 'if I sat down for just a moment?'

'Not in the least,' the other woman said.

Jules went to the bench and sat, and now Nina Salter withdrew a little way, wandering over to the pond.

I'm sorry, Jules said, in her head, to her father. *Really so very sorry.*

For his death.

For leaving him.

'Oh.'

She looked up, saw that Nina Salter was frowning into the pond.

'What is it?' Jules asked, and stood up.

'Look,' the other woman said, and pointed into the water.

Jules looked.

Saw a large goldfish lying on the surface near the grey carved stone Cupid.

She felt as if insects were crawling on her skin, all over her body.

'That's the second one in two days,' Nina Salter said.

Jules couldn't speak.

'Did it happen that way to you?' the other woman asked.

Not at all accusing, just enquiring.

'Once or twice,' Jules said.

'Oh, well,' Nina Salter said.

Jules dreamed that night that three dead goldfish were lying on the carpet in the corridor near the top of the staircase, exactly where Silas had died, and the following night she dreamed of more dead fish lying on a bed, and Abigail was standing over them saying that it was all her fault that they had died.

In daylight hours, and during the evenings, while she was finishing the packing or feeding Thomas or trying to convince Ollie that boxing up his own toys was not the most helpful idea in the world, she wondered how many more fish would have to die before the Salters decided there was something wrong with the pond. Before they decided cleaning might not be enough, before they brought in an expert who would take away a sample of water for testing, and come back with the police because the type of pollutant they'd found could only come from human remains, and then . . .

Enough.

She and the children would be in Foldingham by then, but the police would come to find her there, and by the time she was sent to Holloway, Abigail would probably have been moved on, so she would be on her own, and the children would be taken into care, and -

More than enough.

287

Chapter Sixty-Six

They moved to Suffolk.

To their untainted white cottage close to the pretty village where no one knew them or anything about them. Where Ollie and Thomas both thrived.

Where Jules met with new neighbours and familiarized herself with the local shops and nurseries and schools, and began decorating.

And sent change of address cards to a very few people, and a stream of photographs of the cottage and the children to Abigail, promising her that as soon as her local support network was a little more established, she would come to visit her.

Michael Moran came to see them, stayed for a weekend in the spare room.

'It's not decorated yet,' Jules had told him.

'Do you imagine,' the priest said, 'that would matter to me?'

He told her that he had been to see Abigail the previous week, had found her looking a little better, a little more at peace, he thought.

'Did you know that Philip's been a few times?' he asked. 'And not on legal visits, just to see her?'

Jules said that she did know.

'What a lovely man he is,' Moran said, 'for a lawyer.'

Jules said that he was.

'I hope he'll be coming this way soon,' he went on.

'You never know,' Jules said. 'He's a very busy man.'

'I hope you've told him he's welcome,' Moran said.

'He knows where we are,' Jules said.

'I think,' the priest said, 'maybe he'd like to know that he would be welcome.'

Jules shook her head.

'Not you too,' she said.

*

289

She found an empty shop in Foldingham three doors from Valerie's, which sold home-made chutneys and served fresh-ground coffee and sandwiches.

'Looks like there's going to be a second Jules's Books,' she wrote to Abigail in August, telling her, in the same letter, that even if she wouldn't be able to see her on the day itself, she would be thinking of her on the fifteenth.

Francesca Allen's birth-and-death-day.

Formerly the worst day in Abigail's calendar.

Another day now, of course, the thirtieth of November – the day Silas had died – to rival it.

No one got in touch about dead goldfish or human remains.

Nothing from the Salters.

Nothing from the police.

Philip Quinlan came to visit, though not to stay, and good as it was to see him, Jules knew, with a touch of regret, that the romantic thoughts both Abigail and Michael Moran had harboured for them were wishful, nothing more.

She settled into her new life, found a nursery and crèche she trusted, to make it possible for her to organize the shop and visit Abigail periodically.

Still in Holloway, where the authorities had decided to wait for the stitches to be removed from her left eye before transferring her to another prison – probably Styal in Cheshire, Abigail reported stoically, which was bad news from the visiting point-of-view, but not the very worst otherwise, she said, since some prisoners were allowed to work on farms and gardens.

Humanity all around, Jules thought darkly.

Abigail hadn't mentioned the suicides that had been written about in the press, at Styal and in Holloway, seldom talked about the darker side, the rule of drugs and tyranny or about the fear of those things or of the madness, perhaps above all, the fear of *going* mad. But despite one assault on her that Jules knew of, a scare that had resulted in an unscheduled visit to Moorfields – no further damage to either eye, mercifully – Abigail had survived, was still surviving, and maybe it was because she'd been lucky in finding decent allies inside, or maybe it was because she had, from the outset, been so hellbent on finally doing the time she'd always felt she deserved.

Or maybe it was just because Thomas was waiting for her.

Chapter Sixty-Seven

When Abigail – in and out of Styal after a happily brief time, now in the open prison at Askham Grange near York – became eligible for her first weekend out of prison, she refused to come to the new cottage, her reasons wholly unrelated to the distance between Yorkshire and Suffolk. For one thing, she tried to explain to Jules during one of their all-too-brief phone calls, she hated the idea of ruining what would, after all, be the introduction to her future home.

'And it *would* be ruined for all of us,' she said, 'knowing I'd have to leave again as soon as I'd begun to take it in. When the time does come, really come, I want to know that's it, home.'

'But mightn't it give you hope?' Jules asked. 'Something real and solid and lovely to look forward to? And it is lovely, darling.'

'It might,' Abigail replied, honestly. 'If what I'd said was the only reason.'

Not even the main reason, not by a long chalk.

Thomas was the main, the *only* real reason. Not seeing the cottage, seeing *him*, actually being with him again, and then having to surrender him up at the end of the weekend, would, she knew, without doubt, be simply unbearable.

'And I'm so afraid,' she told Jules now, 'I won't be able to hide my feelings, that he'll pick them up and get upset, and he's much too young for me to put him through that.'

Jules was silent.

'And if he doesn't get at all upset when I leave him again,' Abigail went on quickly, afraid of disintegrating into tears, 'because he doesn't have the slightest sense that I'm his mother – and how could he? – then to be honest, Jules, I'm not sure what that might do to me.' She took a breath, gritted her teeth. 'Which is why I've asked if I can stay at the presbytery again, and please don't suggest bringing Thomas to see me there, because it won't be any easier.'

*

It was Michael Moran, finally, who came up with a way for Abigail to at least see how beautifully Thomas was progressing without any risk of emotional upheaval for the child himself.

Jules would come to London with the children and stay at Drew's flat, and on the Saturday afternoon in question would take Thomas out for a gentle stroll at some pre-arranged spot.

'What if it rains?' Abigail asked.

'I daresay Jules will cope with that,' Moran told her. 'And if it thunders, or if Thomas has the sniffles, or we're all kidnapped by aliens, we'll postpone for another time. Don't look for problems, Abigail.'

No rain, colds or alien abductions. Just sunshine and a gentle breeze as Michael Moran sat beside Abigail on a bench near the duck pond at Golders Hill Park, holding her hand tightly as Jules, close enough to Abigail's left side, to her good eye – and it *was* so much better now that the stitches were gone – picked Thomas up out of his buggy and lifted him high in the air.

Abigail heard his throaty, baby-chuckle.

Saw his sweet mouth open with delight.

Saw Moran put him down on the ground, saw her little boy standing on his own two sturdy legs. Wanted to get up and seize him, to cover him with kisses and inhale his scent. To run away with him, anywhere, *anywhere*.

She sat quite still on the bench, let her mind fly into the fantasy, embrace it, then crash back down to earth.

'Not yet, Abigail,' Moran said gently. 'But one day.'

She could not speak.

Waited until after aunt and baby were gone, then turned towards her other utterly dependable, true friend, and let him hold her while she sobbed her heart out.

'He is a most beautiful child, don't you think?' Moran asked her later.

They were back in the sitting room at the presbytery, drinking the whisky-laced tea he had made for her himself (better, he'd told her, than the endless cups of black coffee she was these days in the habit of drinking).

'And very happy, thank God,' he added.

'Thank Jules,' Abigail said.

'Thank God and Jules,' he said, easily.

She drank some of the hot tea.

'Do you think,' she asked after a while, 'maybe it might be better for Thomas if I never go to Suffolk?' She felt as if her mind was burning with the agony of her thoughts. 'If I stay out of his life altogether?'

'No,' Moran answered. 'I do not think that at all.'

'But you said yourself that he's happy.'

'With his auntie caring for him, and his cousin for company, yes, of course, and that's good, very good,' the priest said, energetically. 'But only because his greatest blessing is yet to come.'

'Me, you mean.' Abigail was cynical.

'Yes, indeed,' Moran said. 'His reunion with his mother.'

'I'm not so sure,' Abigail said, slowly. 'I've been wondering, for a while now, if perhaps I shouldn't ask Jules to adopt him.'

The priest's mouth compressed tightly for a moment.

'That is the first time,' he said, 'that I've heard absolute and complete shite come from your lips, Abigail.'

She looked at him in surprise.

'I use the word advisedly,' Moran said.

Chapter Sixty-Eight

'We need to talk some more,' Abigail told Jules on the phone three weeks before her scheduled release date, 'about my tag.'

'What more is there to talk about?' Jules said.

'Are you sure you're not going to mind it? Having people coming into the cottage and connecting the thing to your phone?'

'Our phone,' Jules said. 'And frankly, I wouldn't much care if a platoon of prison officers moved into the cottage with you, so long as you're coming home.'

Abigail paused.

She seldom did that with the phone card ticking down.

'I was wondering,' she said, 'if maybe I shouldn't go to Michael's till after they take the tag off.'

'Then stop wondering,' Jules told her.

'But what if something goes wrong? What if I miss my curfew one evening, or commit some small, stupid crime and they make me go back?'

'You won't do either of those things,' Jules said.

'But what if—'

'You're coming home, Abigail.'

Chapter Sixty-Nine

On the first Thursday morning of May, with the Yorkshire air smelling fresh after a heavy shower and the sun sliding out from behind dark clouds, Michael Moran met Abigail outside Askham Grange.

'Hallelujah seems about right to me,' he said and embraced her.

Abigail hugged him back briefly, tentatively, then pulled away.

'I can't believe you've come such a long way for me.'

'And why wouldn't I?'

Moran tried to take the plastic HM Prison bags of accumulated possessions from her, but Abigail held onto them tightly and he didn't press her, just turned and began to lead the way back to his car.

'Jules wanted so badly to be here,' Moran said, 'but with having to stay overnight and the little ones to think of, it wasn't possible.'

'How are they?' Abigail's tone was almost neutral.

'They're all wonderful.' Moran smiled. 'And your son is spectacular, as you'll see for yourself in just a few hours.'

'I could have made my own way, Michael.'

'No one was going to let you do that,' he told her. 'It's been no hardship, I can assure you. I stayed the night at a charming B&B.' He paused. 'Are you hungry, by the way, Abigail?'

She shook her head, saw they were nearing his car, saw it was the same old blue Ford Granada he'd always driven, felt oddly comforted by that, then remembered that her first duty as a semi-free person was to see her probation officer.

'You know I have to go to Ipswich first,' she said.

'I do,' Moran said.

He waited as she put her bags into the back, then got into the passenger seat.

'All right?' he asked.

'Fine,' she said, and fastened her seatbelt.

Two of Moran's words were going around and around in her head.

Your son.

A stranger.

She, more to the point, a stranger to him.

They took a break after two hours at a pub just off the A1, Moran devouring toad in the hole, Abigail hardly touching a cheese sandwich.

'Still living on that muck?' The priest looked disapprovingly at her black coffee. 'Would you not fancy something a little stronger?'

'No, thank you.' Abigail smiled. 'Later, maybe.'

'I'm sure your probation officer would understand it was me who'd led you astray.' Moran grinned. 'Maybe you're right.'

He tried and failed several times on the rest of the journey to engage her in conversation, to ease her tension, but she would not be drawn, felt sufficiently tightly strung to snap in two, thought, as they approached Ipswich, that if Michael were to stop the car for long enough again now, she might consider fleeing. Curiously – or maybe not so curiously – she found herself suddenly, intensely, missing her friends at the prison, and some of them *had* become good friends, and they'd looked out for each other, all in the same sinking, stinking ship, some denying, month after month, others holding their hands up and getting on with it; a few more like her, welcoming it, letting it roll over them, willing it, at times, to drown them.

And now here she was, sitting in this familiar car beside this familiar man who was behaving as if nothing so uncivilized as murder and imprisonment had separated them, had ever happened, come to that, and for the first time Abigail almost resented Moran, felt isolated from him, trapped by him.

'Would you like to stop a while?' he asked her suddenly, gently, as if reading her thoughts. 'Take another wee break before we get into town?'

'Yes.' She paused. 'No.'

He glanced sideways at her, found it hard, as always, to penetrate the dark glasses she still wore. 'Which is it?'

'It's no,' she said. 'I'm all right.'

'Get it out of the way then, yes?'

'Please,' she said.

It wasn't, in any case, the meeting she was nervous about. That was nothing by comparison to many of her daily encounters over the past fifteen months.

It was what was to come later.

In the cottage just outside Foldingham.

Chapter Seventy

It was just as Jules had described.

Almost, but not quite, chocolate-box, the clean white stone, the thatch, the attractive little front garden. No actual roses around the door, thank God – though why shouldn't there have been, she wondered, angry with herself – what was *wrong* with fucking roses round the door?

What was wrong, she answered herself, was that they were like ads for happy-ever-after.

No such thing.

'What do you think?' Michael Moran broke into her thoughts.

'It's pretty,' Abigail said.

He pulled off the narrow, peaceful road into the little driveway.

Abigail stared at the front door, braced herself.

Moran turned off the engine, remained still in his seat.

'I don't know,' Abigail said tightly, 'if I can do this.'

'You'll be all right,' he told her, gently.

The front door opened, and there she was.

Jules, in jeans and a T-shirt, smiling and alone.

'We thought,' Moran said quickly, 'you'd prefer no fuss.'

Abigail opened her door, fingers numb.

'Yes,' she said, and got out.

'Welcome home,' Jules said, and hugged her.

'Thank you.' Abigail's mouth felt bone dry.

The hallway was narrow, with a small oval mirror on one wall beside four brass coat hooks – one occupied by a waxed jacket, one by a raincoat – and an umbrella stand in the corner near the door.

Three pairs of wellington boots were lined up along the floor. One adult size in green, one bright yellow in what she supposed was Ollie's size.

The third pair was very small.

Abigail's heart began to pound.

'Here's Asali,' Jules said, softly.

Ralph's old dachshund came out from the back of the house, very grey now, stomach bowing like an old, overloaded bookshelf. She wagged her tail, but Abigail ignored her, hardly saw her, could hardly breathe.

From the other side of a door came the sound of a child's laughter.

'Ollie's minding Thomas,' Jules said. 'They're meant to be crayoning.'

Moran came from behind Abigail, noted her pallor.

'Need another minute?' he asked.

'Abigail?' Jules looked at her.

'Why don't you both go ahead?' Her lips felt like cardboard. 'I'll follow.'

'No problem.' Jules threw Moran a swift glance, and opened the door.

'Mummy, Thomas drew on his tummy!'

'Did he, darling?' Jules said.

The chintz-covered sofa and armchairs and small oak coffee table had been pushed out of the way to create a larger play space for the children, who were sitting on the floor with large pads of paper and two open boxes of wax crayons.

'Look.' Ollie got up, went over to his cousin, tugged up his smudgy T-shirt and pointed at the red and yellow smears.

'Wow,' Jules said.

'Thomas, how very clever of you,' Moran said from behind Jules.

'Tummy,' Thomas said, looked up at his aunt and giggled.

And then he stopped giggling, looking past her and Father Moran.

At someone else, just entering the room, taking off a pair of very dark glasses; a woman with short, slightly spiky hair almost exactly the same colour as his own.

'Is that—?' Ollie broke off, stilled by his mother's hand on his head.

Thomas was gazing with open curiosity.

'Lady,' he said.

'Hello, Thomas,' Abigail said.

And looked down at her son.

Into his beautiful sea green eyes.

Steady, she told herself.

She drew a deep, steadying breath. Knelt slowly down on the rug.

Held out her hand.

'Hello, my darling,' she said.

Jules let out a small sigh.

'I think—' Moran cleared his throat '—I think I'll go and make som tea.'

'Is it her?' Ollie hissed at his mother.

Jules nodded, whispered back: 'Yes, it is.'

'Oh,' Ollie said, more loudly, and then, moving forward quickly, he tapped his little cousin on the shoulder. 'Thomas, this is your mummy.'

Thomas said nothing, just went on staring up at Abigail.

'Why is she crying?' Ollie asked.

Chapter Seventy-One

It was, as Michael Moran had told Abigail it would be, all right.

The cottage, a homely place, settled around her comfortably enough. She often felt, during the first weeks and months, as if her son was a human puzzle she needed to solve, trying to slide into place, as he grew and flourished, all the snippets of information with which Jules had kept her supplied at every stage of Thomas's development up until her release.

He was a beautiful little boy, physically startlingly like his father at that age, but more at ease with other people, Jules said – recalling tales their mother had related – than Silas had been.

Less easy, it seemed to Abigail, with her.

'My fault,' she said to Jules. 'I'm too tense around him.'

'It'll pass,' Jules said. 'You'll start to relax, and then he will too.'

Ollie, Abigail found, helped her more than anyone. A warm, natural person, like his mother, he seemed to comprehend his aunt's great need to draw closer to Thomas, and he became her ally, involving Abigail in games he played with his cousin, whispering to her about things that Thomas found particularly enjoyable and, more important, those he either disliked or feared.

Their anonymity in Foldingham had stuck fast, for which both Abigail and Jules were profoundly grateful. With Jules's Books doing nicely, its proprietor and Abigail alternated between childcare and bookselling and fitting into village life, and if any of their neighbours were especially curious about the two women living with their children, they were too well-mannered to show it.

'Don't you think it's time you began playing again?' Jules asked Abigail, six months after she had returned to Moorfields for her second corneal graft.

Once the cello had ceased to be evidence for the prosecution, Jules had sent it to Foote's in Golden Square to be repaired, after which she had taken it to the cottage and placed it in the attic, waiting for its owner to ask for it, but still it stood in its case in that dark corner, unclaimed.

'I can't,' Abigail said. 'It would bring it all back.'

'But don't you need to play to be properly *you* again?'

'I'm afraid to play.' Abigail paused. 'I'm afraid to touch it.'

'I know.' Jules persevered gently. 'You could try. You could always put it away again, after all.'

Abigail did not put it away again.

It was, when she took it from its case, just an instrument after all, bringing her peace, as it so often had.

Ollie did not like the sound.

'Maybe I should stop,' Abigail said to Jules. 'Maybe he remembers that night.'

'He'll get over it,' Jules told her firmly. 'Besides, Thomas loves it.'

Which was true, making Abigail quite absurdly happy. Maybe this, she thought, was how Francesca must have felt when she was little. And for once, at least for a short time, her pleasure was not instantly blown away by guilt, because she realized, too, that her mother would have loved the idea of Abigail finding a path to her son – Francesca's grandson – through her beloved music.

Via her old cello.

The cello that killed his father.

There it was again, bales of sackcloth being heaved back onto her shoulders.

Done your time, she told herself. *Stop now.*

Easier said than done.

The secretary of the Foldingham Musical Society – a woman named Felicity Barr – having been alerted by neighbours who had heard the sound of Abigail's cello through the cottage's open windows, approached her one day in Shad & Sons, the butcher's.

'They've had a string trio, apparently, for a good few years,' Abigail told Jules later. 'According to Mrs Barr, they'd like to make it a quartet.'

'With you?' Jules asked. 'How wonderful.'

'I told her it was out of the question.'

'Why should it be?'

'Because I'm only playing for myself now.'

'And the rest of us, I hope.' Jules grinned. 'Ollie excepted.' She paused. 'You used to play in a quartet in Glasgow, didn't you?'

'Long time ago,' Abigail said.

Lifetime ago.

*

She went on refusing for another three weeks, but then, as Mrs Barr's persistence and the friendliness of the other society's musicians won her over, she gave in. The music was gentle stuff of a middling standard, played with great verve and warmth, and Abigail found it exactly what she needed.

'You're looking wonderful, I must say,' Philip Quinlan said when he came to visit. 'Very fit and happy.'

'I feel it,' she said.

Surprised, because it was true.

Chapter Seventy-Two

When Thomas was six years old, he came into his mother's bed one night – as he loved to do when he wanted to chatter or just to cuddle – and told her that one of his friends at school had a new little brother, and that he thought he should let her know that he didn't much like the sound of that.

'You don't need to worry,' Abigail told him. 'If I ever do have another child, my darling, it won't be for a very long time.'

'But you might, one day?'

'It's not very likely,' his mother said. 'But it might be lovely for you to have a wee brother or sister someday, don't you think?'

'No,' Thomas said. 'It wouldn't be lovely.'

'But think of Ollie,' Abigail said. 'You love him, and he's mad about you.'

'Ollie's different,' Thomas said. 'He's my cousin, not my brother, and anyway, he was here before me, wasn't he.' He paused. 'If you had another baby, I would hate it.'

'Of course you wouldn't.' Abigail put one arm around him. 'You're just being a bit silly, aren't you, sweetheart?'

Thomas snuggled very close to her, the way he often did, the way he knew she loved more than anything, and after a minute she put both her arms around him, and he knew she was waiting for him to go to sleep.

'That's right,' she said, softly. 'Go to sleep.'

She felt his warmth, the beautiful, precious solidness of him, and remembered, suddenly, his father telling her, a long time ago, in their Phoenix-Abeguile days, that the first time he had seen her, when she had been carrying her cello out of the Wigmore Hall, it had made him think of how she would look carrying a child.

Thinking about the cello and about Silas made her tense up.

Thomas snuggled even closer, laid his cheek against her breast.

Looked up at her sideways.

'If you ever have another child,' he said, 'I might have to kill it.'

'Thomas,' Abigail said, quite sharply. 'You mustn't say things like that.'

'Why not?' Thomas asked. 'Ollie says you killed my father.'

Abigail felt her heart turn over and her stomach shrivel.

She looked down at her son's face. His cheek was still resting on her breast, only one eye fully visible.

Cold, suddenly, and as hard as a green pebble.

She felt very nauseous.

'Is it true,' he asked, in that same, normal tone, 'that you killed your mother and father, too?'

Abigail pushed him away, scrambled out of bed, ran into the bathroom and was violently and repeatedly sick.

After it had finished, as she sat back, still on the floor, leaning against the wall for support, pressing a wet towel to her face, she realized that Thomas was standing in the doorway, in his favourite red dinosaur pyjamas, watching her.

'It's all right,' he said, softly, uncertain now. 'I don't really mind.'

Abigail opened her mouth, tried to speak, but no words came.

'It's okay, Mummy,' Thomas said. 'About my father.'

The hand holding the wet towel trembled, suddenly, violently.

'It's all *right*,' Thomas said again. 'Someone told Ollie at school, but Auntie Jules told him it was an accident.'

He looked, Abigail saw, scared, frightened, perhaps, of the effect his words had had upon her.

Still shaky, she put out a hand to him.

Thomas remained in the doorway.

'I'm sorry, Mummy.' His voice wobbled.

'Nothing for you to be sorry about, my love,' Abigail said, weakly.

He stepped into the bathroom, stopped again.

'I wouldn't really kill a baby,' he said.

'I know you wouldn't,' Abigail said, her voice choked.

He came running then, flung his arms around her, so fiercely that the back of her head struck the wall. *Good pain,* she thought. *Passion pain.*

'Oh, God,' she said, putting her own arms around him.

He leaned back, resting all his weight against her forearms, and swiftly Abigail linked her hands together behind him to make him safe.

He was looking intently into her face.

'Have you any idea,' Abigail asked, 'how much I love you, Thomas Graves?'

'More than anything?' he asked back.

308

'More than anything or anyone—' she answered as most mothers reply to that same question '—in the whole wide world.'

His eyes were wet now, softest green again.

Phoenix's eyes.

'That's all right then, Mummy,' Thomas said.

Blood Knot

Denise Ryan

Frankie's life has just got a lot more complicated. Her marriage is collapsing and she's just discovered her husband owes a huge amount of money to some serious villains. And they've made it clear that if they don't get it back, it'll be Frankie who pays the price.

A mystery person offers to wipe out Frankie's debt in return for a favour. But whatever they want, it's got to be worth £100,000.

Praise for Denise Ryan:

'Lynda la Plante did indeed lead the way but consider also Denise Ryan's *Dead Keen* and *The Hit* in which danger and violence are never far away.' *Daily Mail*

Temporary Sanity

Rose Connors

When devoted father Buck Hammond's seven-year-old son is abducted and murdered by Hector Monteros, Buck takes justice into his own hands. Unfortunately, the TV cameras were rolling as Buck aimed his hunting rifle at Monteros's head.

The only viable defence is insanity, but the grieving father refuses to say he was crazy when he pulled the trigger. Attorney Marty Nickerson, until recently a Massachusetts prosecutor, has a tough role acting as his defence attorney. How can the jury acquit Buck when the shooting is right there on the screen for all to see?

Marty and her partner, Harry Madigan are already stretched thin when, on the very eve of the trial, a battered and bleeding woman staggers into their office. She's in deep trouble - her attacker's body has just been found, viciously stabbed, and he's an officer of the court. Now Marty has two seemingly impossible battles to win against her former colleagues.

But losing a verdict may be the least of Marty's worries, as her efforts soon lead to shocking revelations that bring fear to the Cape and devastating changes to Buck's trial.

Praise for Rose Connors:

'A gripping combination of crime novel, courtroom drama, and psychological suspense.' Linda Fairstein

'An engrossing tale of one woman's struggle with the elusive nature of truth and the random nature of evil.' Perri O'Shaughnessy

'For fans of legal intrigue...it doesn't get any better than this' *Publishers Weekly*

A SELECTION OF NOVELS AVAILABLE FROM PIATKUS BOOKS

0 7499 3434 4	No Escape	Hilary Norman	£6.99
0 7499 3323 2	Twisted Minds	Hilary Norman	£6.99
0 7499 3462 X	Blood Knot	Denise Ryan	£6.99
0 7499 3498 0	Temporary Sanity	Rose Connors	£6.99
0 7499 3461 1	The Plague Maiden	Kate Ellis	£6.99
0 7499 3529 4	To Die For	Linda Howard	£6.99

ALL PIATKUS TITLES ARE AVAILABLE FROM:

PIATKUS BOOKS C/O BOOKPOST
PO Box 29, Douglas, Isle Of Man, IM99 1BQ
Telephone (+44) 01624 677237
Fax (+44) 01624 670923
Email; bookshop@enterprise.net

Free Postage and Packing in the United Kingdom.
Credit Cards accepted. All Cheques payable to Bookpost.
(Prices and availability subject to change without prior notice. Allow 14 days for delivery. When placing orders please state if you do not wish to receive any additional information.)

OR ORDER ONLINE FROM:

www.piatkus.co.uk
Free postage and packing in the UK (on orders of two books or more)